Always

True

to You

in My

Fashion

wm

William Morrow

AN IMPRINT OF HARPERCOLLINSPUBLISHERS

Always

True

to You

in My

Fashion

Valerie

Wilson

Wesley

Designed by Gretchen Achilles

ISBN 0-06-018883-9

For Richard

Acknowledgments

I'd like to thank my good friends who also happen to be very fine artists—Janet Taylor Pickett, roycrosse, and Ben Jones—as well as curator/dealers—Sharon Gill, Camille Russell Love, and Tarin Fuller, Iandor Gallery—and collectors—Lewis Tanner Moore and Judy Heggestad—who shared some of what they know. My thanks also to Judy Miller, who offered salavation when I needed it. And to Karla Spurlock-Evans, Regina Joseph, Dee Watts, Larry and Betty Knapp, Benilde Little, Iqua Colson, Rosemarie Robotham, Stephanie Stokes Oliver, and Joy Cain, who are always generous with advice and kind words. My sincere thanks to my thoughtful, supportive editor, Carrie Feron, and my wise, understanding agent, Faith Hampton Childs. And, of course to my daughters, Nandi and Thembi, and my husband, Richard, who are always in my corner.

A Good

Man Is

Hard to

Find

You Always

Get Another

Kind

Chapter One

Randall Hollis was a strikingly good-looking man, and most folks swore it was his downfall. His skin was a rich coffee-brown, and he had a squarish chin edged by high cheekbones, a gift from his Ethiopian grandmother. His lips were full, sensual, and curled as easily with arrogance as pleasure, depending on to whom he was talking. He was built like a quarterback, with broad shoulders, and a tight belly that tensed or softened depending on where it was touched. His hair had been through various styles in the last few years: a fluffy Afro and wild dreadlocks in the eighties, a bad-boy baldy in the nineties, but had recently settled into a close-cropped, conservative cut that suited him well. He had a Duke Ellington elegance brushed with a rakish charm, and Medora Jackson knew she would be in love with him until the day she died.

It was the morning of her thirty-fifth birthday, and they had just made love for the second time that day. She gazed at him for what she promised herself would be the last time, and whispered, "It's time for us to let this thing go."

Time for me *to let it go. Me! Me! Me!* she said to herself. She kicked off the forest-green sheets wondering if the color was at fault (strong colors affected her physically) or if she was having a premature hot flash.

"Well?" She scowled at him.

"Well, what?" His face was blank.

"We've been doing this since we were in our twenties, and it's time to stop."

"Teens," Randall corrected her as he reached for the pitcher of mimosas standing on the night table that he'd mixed earlier that morning, poured some into a flute, and gulped it down, while keeping his eyes on Medora. "You were eighteen. I was nineteen. How could you forget something like that?"

"Nineteen, twenty—however long, it's too goddamn long. For both of us," she added, although she was talking about herself. "I'm thirty-five years old, Randall. Thirty-five!" Her voice rose dangerously close to a wail.

"And more beautiful with each year," Randall said in a fawning voice that made Medora roll her eyes and pretend to gag, but then she turned serious again.

"You'd keep this going on forever, wouldn't you? Coming up here, sleeping in my bed, eating my food—"

"Eating your food? What about Jezebel's last night?"

"You know what I'm talking about. There's nothing between us, except sex and *my* work. Nothing. And not even sex half the time." She stood up as if preparing to leave, then slumped back down on the edge of the bed. "We're not going anywhere with this."

"We're always going to be a part of each other's life. Why don't you just accept it for what it is?" Randall's expression was solemn.

"And what the hell *is* it?"

"It *is* what the hell it is!" He smiled, not so differently, Medora realized, from that first time he'd charmed her, at her cousin's graduation party, kissing her with an awkward passion that still made her stomach quiver when she thought about it. But that was a long time ago, and she was thirty-five now and sick of the way her life was going. The Randall Hollis era was over.

"So you're kicking me out?" His smile broke into a grin that was at the same time mischievous and seductive.

If I were my aunt Tillie, Medora thought, *I would smack that grin right off this man's face.* But she wasn't her tough aunt Tillie. She was her dear, dead mama, who had put up with mess from her charming, philandering husband until she died at fifty of a broken heart.

"Yes," Medora said, as the image of her weeping mother crossed her mind. "Yes, Randall. I'm kicking you out!" She narrowed her eyes to show she meant business.

"You need some more champagne. It's a shame to mix Dom with orange juice, so let's drink it straight. I'll make us an omelette as soon as—"

"Out!" Medora stood up and slipped on her green cotton robe.

Randall shook his head in mock seriousness. "Seduced and abandoned! You've got what you want from me and now you're kicking me to the curb. A used man, even my dignity gone!" He put his hands over his face and pretended to weep.

"Oh, stop acting like a fool!" Medora walked to the other side of the small bedroom and settled down in the rickety bentwood rocking chair across from him. "Look at you! Look at us! Most people our age have roots, kids, mortgages, and we're still fucking around."

Randall sat up in the bed, and the deep-green sheets draped themselves over the lower half of his nude body. Medora, who never failed to notice the beauty of colors played against each other, studiously looked away, gazing instead at the mahogany bureau on the opposite side of the room, the antique mirror hanging above it and finally at the red chenille rug on which she stood. She picked up a pillow that had fallen to the floor and tossed it into the bentwood rocker near the door. Randall sighed, his voice was serious when he spoke.

"I'm not acting like a fool, Medora. Well, maybe I am, but you're the only person in the world I can act like a fool around. Doesn't that say something?"

"Not very much, and frankly that surprises me. With all your women." The corner of Randall's lip twitched slightly, which made her smile. The women who floated in, out, and through his life were one of the unmentionables. Like his hairstyles of the past few decades, his women fell into categories: models and boho culture-freaks in the eighties, investment bankers in the nineties. Because he routinely confided everything about them to Medora—usually after the relationship had soured—she'd always considered herself above the fray. Until now.

He squirmed. She smirked. "I thought we got over that a long time ago.

You know how I feel about you, and, well . . . uh . . . you know, Medora, we have a special—"

"Oh, shut up!" Medora said, and he did with a sigh. She stole a look to see if the sigh was real; it seemed authentic.

"But you've always known that our . . . relationship . . . was special." He sounded sad.

"Well, those are two euphemisms if I've ever heard them: 'our relationship' and 'special.' Let's face it, Randall. I see you three, maybe four times a month, we talk about my work, old times, then we make love and go our separate ways. I want something more from a man I have a *relationship* with." She emphasized each syllable of the word, but also thought: *As if eligible men wanting a relationship with a thirty-five-year-old mostly broke artist were making beelines to my door.*

"We have more than just that." He looked genuinely hurt.

"Like what? Our annual birthday?" She waved her hand dramatically towards the bed where they had just made love. "I'd rather just go to the Diva Lounge and pick up some truck driver." To avoid looking at him, she poured herself what was left of the mimosas and without a glance in his direction began to rock in the bentwood rocking chair, and the squeaking of the chair was the only sound in the room until Randall broke the silence.

"Have I ever stopped you from getting involved with somebody else? I've even gone out and looked for you. Remember Joe Lucas? Handpicked! What about Wally Jackson? What was wrong with him? These were two good brothers. Your problem is you're too damn picky."

"My problem is *you*, and we both know it." Randall looked surprised and hurt, but Medora continued. "You're too damn selfish and greedy to really get out of my life, so I have to do it for you. Have you ever really loved anybody except yourself?"

"I thought we had an understanding."

"Understanding?"

He looked genuinely confused.

Medora sighed and let her tender side show. "I'm not really blaming you, Randall. I love you. Unfortunately, I will always love you, which has ended up being my problem, not yours. But this is the last time, the very last time, that we will be together like this."

"You really mean it this time, don't you?"

"Yep."

He gulped down the last of his mimosa, put the glass back on the night table, and gave a sigh. Another authentic one.

"What about the other stuff?" he mumbled.

"I don't know yet about the other stuff," she mumbled back.

The "other stuff" they were referring to was her work. Randall Hollis was the best independent art dealer in the city, and in the casually racist world of contemporary American art, it was nearly impossible for a black artist to find a dealer committed and powerful enough to promote and protect her work. He had sold Medora's work successfully ever since she started to sell, building his reputation along with hers.

Medora gathered up the empty pitcher and glasses and took them into the kitchen. Then she went into the bathroom, brushed her teeth, washed her face, and tried not to think about what she was feeling. A sense of desperation swept her.

Was she doing the right thing? Why stop things now?

"Because I am too good for this," she said to herself in the mirror. "I am too good to love a man as much as I love this one and get so little back. Because I am deluding myself, and I won't do it anymore!"

She smiled at her attempt to muster up strength, and as she rubbed moisturizer on her face she thought about her mother, another woman who had handed a man her heart and pulled back a stump.

People told her she looked like her mother, whose beauty those who knew her talked about still. Sometimes she could see her mother's face when she looked at her own: The perfectly oval face and almond-shaped eyes. The full lips that broke easily into a delightful smile or stubborn pout. The hair, with a mind of its own, that grew to her chin and framed her face in wild abundance. As far as Medora was concerned, her mother's looks hadn't brought much except a man who didn't stay home and an early death, so she gave them short shrift. She'd gotten her father's talent, which was worth much more. But her skin was definitely her mother's, she decided, as she spread the lotion on her face. It was as clear and smooth as a child's and the color of raw, dark honey. Wildflower honey, according to Randall. Despite her determination to cut him out of her thoughts, thinking about Randall and honey at the same moment made her remember Valentine's Day last month, when things had started out innocently enough over Red Zinger tea.

I t was snowing, and Randall came in from the cold with snowflakes stuck to his black cashmere coat and the flowers he held in his arms. He'd spilled them—dozens of roses, calla lilies, and lilacs—into her lap in a tumble of red, white, and purple, and Medora, whooping like a kid, smothered her face in their fragrance.

"Happy Valentine's Day! I never forget it!" he said.

Despite herself, Medora grinned even though she hadn't heard from him in three weeks, and when he'd finally called, she had slammed down the phone in disgust. Recalling that anger now, she pulled her face out of the flowers and glared at him. How dare he think she would be sitting here alone on Valentine's Day? The gall of this man who assumed she'd be waiting for him and not on some hot, heavy date doing hot, heavy things. Yet she'd known he would come as surely as he knew she would be here. Such was the unspoken bond between them.

A half smile poked its way onto her lips. Truth was, she couldn't stay mad at him long. A word, gesture, look always brought delight or forgiveness. And he was right. Valentine's Day along with Christmas and her birthday always delivered him to her. He hadn't missed one, not since their first youthful days together. How odd that such conventional holidays could mark so unconventional a relationship.

"So how many other bouquets did you drop off today?" Medora couldn't resist asking.

Randall looked pained. "You always assume the worst about me, Medora."

"Not always."

"Most of the time."

Medora smiled reluctantly and forgave him. "Thank you. I love these colors."

"I know you better than you think."

She got a vase, filled it with water, and brought it to the table. As she passed by him, he reached toward her to embrace her. She pulled away.

"I've decided we need some distance between us."

"Maybe you're right."

"We're friends, nothing more."

"I agree."

They sat down on the couch. On opposite ends.

"How's the work going?" he asked. That was one subject they both knew they could discuss without rancor.

She pulled out some sketches to show him, and he studied them with his usual enthusiastic interest. She brought in a pot of Red Zinger tea, two cups, and a jar of wildflower honey and placed it on the wooden cube that served as a coffee table.

Watching Randall view her sketches made her think of her mother, who would study her father's work with the same intense concentration. As she dripped honey from the red honey dipper into her tea, she thought of her mother again and how, like a mama bird feeding her young, her mother would drip honey into her open mouth when she'd been a kid. Smiling at the memory, Medora threw back her head and dribbled the honey into her mouth in a thick golden stream. Amused, Randall watched her for a few moments, then snatched the dipper, dunked it back into the jar and proceeded to drizzle it down her lip, chin, and throat. And then, with a sudden maniacal grin, he'd unbuttoned her blouse and pants, grabbed the whole jar and poured what was left over her breasts, down her back, and between her toes, and as she laughed hysterically, greedily licked it off.

"You know, I do love you," he'd uttered during their honeyed lovemaking, and she knew that in his fashion he did. He'd been nineteen the first time he told her that, and now he was saying those words again. But Medora wasn't the same woman she had been at eighteen, when they had vowed to love each other for the rest of their lives. Did he really mean it now?

And after that Valentine's Day, she didn't see him again, didn't hear from him. Not for weeks. Last night, on her birthday, was the first time they'd been together in a month. And here she'd actually hoped that those four magic words uttered in honey-kissed passion might actually change things between them. What a fool she was!

No more!" she said.

Still annoyed, she went into her kitchen, brewed a pot of coffee, and sat down at the end of the long pine work and dining table. She listened to Randall as he walked from the bedroom into the bathroom and as he turned on the shower. She poured some cream into her coffee, stirred it with a sterling spoon that had belonged to her mother, and took a swallow that burned her tongue. She heard him whistle a Miles Davis riff as he dressed and walked out of the bathroom and stop behind her. She could feel his eyes on the back of her head. She stared at her cup. He cleared his throat. She gazed out the long, narrow window facing her. He walked to the far end of the loft into her work space. She knew he was looking at the work on her easel that she hadn't planned to show him until it was finished. Much of Medora's work was abstract; she seldom drew figures and rarely worked in charcoal. But after attending an Alvin Ailey recital she couldn't forget the grace and strength of the dancers, so she decided to do a series of drawings on their movements. Charcoal, with its blunt edges so easily blurred, seemed the best way to interpret what she could remember. It was always like that with her work. Something would fascinate her, and she'd have to paint or sketch it until it was out of her mind. Like falling in love, her father once told her, falling in love with color, motion, and shape.

"It's the first of a series," she said.

"This one is really good," he said. He walked back across the room and sat across from her. His dark eyes, their lashes as long and thick as a child's, were serious behind the rimless glasses he wore when appraising art.

"Thanks. Your opinion means a lot to me." She owed him that much anyway.

"Do you think the series will be ready in September in time for the show or . . . ?" He didn't say the words but she knew what they were—or had that changed, too?

"That's six months from now. I don't know."

"Don't rush it."

"Don't worry, I won't."

"Do you still want me to represent you?"

She looked him straight in the eye. "I don't know about that either."

He paused for a moment. "I have a collector, a new one, who loves your work. She's got an amazing eye," he said after a moment.

"Good for you! Good for her!" Medora said, noticing the way his eyes shifted to the table. *He's fucking her*, she thought.

"What do you think you want to do?" He changed the subject back to the show.

"Don't rush me."

"You know how much you mean to me."

"Go to hell!" Medora said.

"Oh, God, don't take it there."

They sat across from each other in tense silence for a while, neither of them speaking.

"I guess I better go," Randall said.

"Good idea," Medora replied.

He glanced at his watch, stooped as if to kiss her, then stood back up, changing his mind. She sat stiffly in the chair, cup in hand like a scepter. She didn't look in his direction until she heard him close the door, and then she stared at it, trying not to cry. Finally she made herself get up, go into the kitchen, and dump out her coffee, which was now lukewarm. She looked in the refrigerator, sniffed a container of sweet 'n' sour shrimp she'd ordered two days ago, threw it away, then heated up a can of navy bean soup. She finished half the bowl and threw that away, too. Her stomach felt queasy, too much champagne on an empty stomach, too much anxiety about letting Randall go.

We have what we have.

She showered, dressed, and went back into her studio. She glared at the drawing Randall had admired, roughly snatched it off the easel, and pushed it behind several unfinished canvases stacked against a wall. Then she propped up a canvas she'd primed the week before and began a new painting, working steadily until her legs ached. She went into the kitchen, made herself a cup of peppermint tea, and settled down in front of her work to think about what had happened.

Randall had been her first lover, and she had been his, a little aside that he had only recently admitted. It was so typical of him, not to tell a woman something like that. Nineteen seemed old for a man to lose his virginity, she told him when he confessed, and added, only half joking, that he seemed determined now to make up for lost time. What took you so long, she'd asked, and he answered, dead serious, that it was his mother's influence. Lydia Hollis and Thetas Wright Jackson. That was a pair for the textbooks. Two impossible parents. One thing she and Randall had in common.

If there was just sex between them she might be able to accept the limits of their relationship. She had certainly had her share of purely sexual relationships in the past few years. There was a simplicity about them that she had grown to appreciate. Go for drinks. Go to dinner. Go to bed. Go home. Her detachment gave her a certain independence. But Randall was always there, hovering in the recesses of her mind, even while she was lying beside another man. She could never really let anybody else in.

And there was her work. He was the first one to really see her as an artist, the first to see her potential and encourage her to fulfill it. Even at eighteen he had believed in her. He'd changed his major from business to art history in college because he said that he had learned to love and appreciate art through her eyes. Their professional lives had been interwoven ever since.

Medora was humble enough to know that much of the success she had begun to enjoy as an artist was more than simply luck. Nobody would deny she had talent, but talent guaranteed nothing. There were dozens of artists far more talented than she who would never receive the reviews, grants, or solo shows she had. Luck was important, but two factors had ensured her success: Thetas Wright Jackson and Randall Hollis.

Thetas Wright Jackson—or T. W. Jackson, as he was popularly known and signed his work—was only a couple of years younger than the great ones—Romare Bearden, Jacob Lawrence, Norman Lewis. He had broken into the world of contemporary American art at a time when nobody else of color was getting through. By the time he was fifty-five, his work was finally beginning to receive the attention it deserved. But three years later when Medora was twenty-eight his eyes betrayed him.

Medora suspected that her paintings received the acclaim they did partially because she was T.W.'s daughter and the powers that be felt sorry for him and ashamed of the way they shunned and undervalued his work for so many years. She was reaping the rewards that should have belonged to a previous generation of black artists, and that knowledge brought its own particular pressure. Although T. W. Jackson had gotten her into the room, her own talent and determination had gotten her a seat. Her father's contacts in the art world and the money he now received for his work made it possible for her to live off her work. And when she turned thirty he gave her his loft.

It had once been a floor in a sewing factory. Medora swore she could still hear the hum of the machines pedaled by young immigrant women running seams down dresses and trimming sturdy collars with cheap lace. The factory was in an ethnic corner of a New Jersey city, about fifteen miles from New York City, that maintained its exotic flavor and style, but the women who once climbed the twelve flights of stairs to their shop would hardly recognize it now.

The windows were long and narrow and reached from the ceiling to the floor; sunlight poured in from all sides. Medora had furnished it minimally: a high-backed mission rocker, its seat covered in muted kente cloth, where she now sat sipping her tea; a narrow bench of the same style from the same period that was pushed under the pine table; a long multi-pillowed green couch across from the rocker; an oddly shaped oriental rug spread on a wide-planked floor that a recent sale of lithographs had enabled her to have scraped and stained. The walls were either eggshell white or pale yellow, depending on how the sun hit them. Various knick-knacks filled the floor-to-ceiling bookshelves: a tattered rag doll that once belonged to her grandmother, mysteries and romances from her aunt Tillie, cobalt glass and green china, sandalwood candles and myrrh incense.

Some of the paintings on the walls were her own, but most were by her father or his friends who had traded their work for his. In today's art market, some could bring enough money to carry Medora through five years of expenses, and her father dutifully paid the insurance on them (another "gift" to make up for lost time). But Medora never thought of this work as investments. She held too many sweet memories of those who had drawn or painted them. The fascinating chaos of their lives, loves, and studios had drawn her into the world of art as much as her own need to draw. His friends had been her baby-sitters, role models, and mentors, and had shown her the possibility of living her life as an artist. Randall routinely reminded her how much some of their work was worth, offering the names of collectors who would eagerly pay that and more, but Medora always turned him down. They were her legacy from her father, and she'd finally forgiven him enough to accept it.

For most of her life, Medora had been angry at her father—for his absences, his infidelities, and the thoughtless cruelty that had marked his relationship with her mother, who had been too fragile to fight back. Yet Medora knew she was lucky to have had a T. W. Jackson in her life. As lucky as she was to have had a Randall Hollis.

Randall knew how to make money for the artists he represented because he knew every aspect of the art world. He knew who the players were and how to flatter and cajole them. He knew which nonprofit boards to join and who to suck up to at cocktail parties and openings. He didn't mind bowing, scraping, and kissing a rich man's ass so the artists he worked for wouldn't have to. When she was broke, he loaned her money so she wouldn't have to ask her father and helped her apply for grants. When things got tight, he reduced his commission to a pittance of the hefty 35 to 50 percent dealers routinely received. What would she do if she let him go?

She went into the kitchen to get some honey for her tea and the memory of last month's honey-sweet sex came back in a rush. Their connection would not be an easy one to break. The mere memory of how she felt when he made love to her brought on a shiver. She couldn't look at one of her paintings without remembering what he had said about it. She trusted his instincts more than she trusted her own, and that was no damn good.

The phone rang, and she picked it up. Some part of her hoped it was Randall. It was her father.

"Happy birthday, baby! So, which one is it now? Thirty-four?"

"Thirty-five," Medora snapped. Even now, T.W. still had the power to hurt her.

"I was just kidding with you, baby. I know how old you are."

She smiled at his feeble attempt to make things right. "How are you feeling, T.?" That was what she often called him now instead of Daddy, which was still loaded with too many disappointments and unmet expectations to be said easily.

"I'm standing. Guess that's saying something. Still can't see, though," he added as if it were a joke.

T.W. had developed macular degeneration, first in his right eye and then in his left, when he turned fifty-eight. Now at sixty-five, he could see only glimpses of things from the sides and objects that lay straight ahead. He could see well enough to get around, to make it into his building with the help of his doorman, care for himself, take care of basic needs, but he couldn't make out faces or lines, and boundaries were blurry. He couldn't see the details, and details were the only thing that counted.

"So how is this *thirty-fifth* birthday going for my baby?"

"Great!" She forced her voice to be cheerful, but his hearing was as sharp as a cat's, and he picked up the hesitation in her voice.

"So, what happened?"

"I told Randall I didn't want to see him anymore."

"I didn't know you two were seeing each other."

"We weren't."

He didn't say anything for a moment, trying to figure out the contradiction, and then got down to what was important. "Who you going to get to handle your work? There ain't nobody in this town who you can trust as much as that boy. Never let pleasure interfere with business, baby."

"You sure didn't, did you?" she snapped at him again, amazed how fresh the anger still was. *I am thirty-five years old and still mad at my father; what the hell is wrong with me?* she thought.

"I'm just telling you that somebody who knows and respects your work, who won't try to rip you off, is hard to find. Don't be throwing the baby out with the bathwater."

"So you think I should keep sleeping with him so he will keep selling my work?"

"Now, that's your business, and you know I don't want to know nothing about that," he said demurely.

"Then what are you saying?"

"Well . . ." T.W. paused, trying to figure out exactly what he was saying. "I just know how hard it is to get a good dealer, and I know how foolish you women can be about, well, this kind of thing."

This kind of thing! No matter how hard he tried, her father could never seem to get it right. She changed the subject. "What time you want to go over Aunt Tillie's?"

"Whenever the lady wants us to come," T.W. grumbled.

Ever since her mother's death ten years ago, Medora had gone to her aunt's home for dinner on her birthday. Five years ago, her father had begun to join them. From the first, Aunt Tillie blamed T.W. for her sister's death, and old anger died hard. His condition, however, had brought out some late-blooming sympathy; she could finally be in the same room without cussing him out.

"Is seven okay?"

"Six is better. I get tired early these days. So what are you going to do for the rest of the day?"

Medora knew his question was a veiled request for her company, but a second painful encounter with another troublesome male was more than she could take on one birthday.

"I need to work. I started a new piece this morning," she said, which was a surefire way to get out of any engagement with her father, who respected above anything else her right and need to paint.

"Tell me about it," he said quietly.

"I'm not sure where it came from."

"Something just came over you and you went in a different direction," he said, immediately understanding. "Tell me how it looks."

He was probably the only person in the world who truly understood how important her work was to her, and as she explained she imagined his face: the keen-angled features, full lips, dark brown eyes, which once flashed as quickly with anger as laughter, and were now so distorted behind the thick lenses of his glasses.

"I was in the park the other day, right after that storm. And this tree, it must have been there for a hundred years, had been struck by lighting, right down the middle, and you could see its insides, almost like the lighting had cut into its heart. I could almost hear it weeping.

"I don't know what it is or why it made me feel the way it did, but it just touched me." It was always hard to put her feelings into words; it was easier to draw or paint them. "And I'm painting that, the way it looked when I saw it, and how it made me feel. I'm into green these days. Maybe it's the serenity of blue and the passion of yellow mixed together in so many variables, but I've fallen in love with green—of all the colors in the world to fall in love with," she added with a self-conscious laugh as if talking about a person.

Her father didn't say anything for a long time, and Medora wasn't sure he was still on the line until he cleared his throat. She knew he must be remembering what it had been like for him, to be enchanted by some figure, shape, or color and to be consumed by the need to capture it.

"I'll be there at six, okay?" she said.

"Yeah. That's fine. I just hope that woman doesn't start her mess with me again." He was bringing it back to the present, away from what he'd lost, but the sorrow was still in his voice.

"It's my birthday; the truce is always in place on my birthday."

"Tillie should remember that the past is always the past. It's dead, and it should stay that way."

"Like my mother?" She said it without thinking, then immediately regretted it. "I'm sorry, Daddy." She offered the word as an olive branch.

"Never be sorry, baby. Not for anything. Never. You hear me?"

"Yeah."

Another pause. "See you at six?"

"Six it is," he said and hung up.

She put the phone down and returned to her work only to be interrupted by another caller bearing birthday greetings.

"Hey, Birthday Girl! Congratulations on your thirty-fifth!"

"Hi, Eliza!" Medora said as the image of Eliza Johnson, who had skin the color of cocoa and large expressive eyes, came into her mind. Eliza was a potter whose unique, irregularly shaped pots had caught on in some of the hipper department stores, and she was finally on the verge of being able to support herself through her art. When they met, however, Eliza had been down on her luck and working in a health-food store while raising her young son by herself. Over the last few years, their casual acquaintanceship had grown into a solid friendship, and Medora now considered her one of her closest friends. There was always a smile in Eliza's voice, which was usually accompanied by the one on her dimpled face, and the sound of that voice, crackling with good cheer, never failed to lift Medora's spirits. "Thanks for calling. I just got off the phone with T.W."

"You don't sound too happy. What happened?"

"Nothing with T.W. It was Randall. I threw him out of my apartment—and my life—this morning. A birthday gift to myself. To tell the truth, I feel kind of down about it."

Eliza hesitated for a moment before responding and then said, "Maybe you can still be friends."

Medora gave a snort of disgust. "You know better than that. It's impossible to turn a relationship as carnal as ours into a platonic friendship."

"But you were platonic friends once."

"Yeah, before we *both* lost our virginity."

"I keep forgetting he was your first love."

Medora snorted again, bitterly. "Yeah, first love and a subway token will get you to the Studio Museum."

They both chuckled at that, and Eliza said, "Try not to be too hard on yourself about still caring. You've loved this man for as long as I've known you. He's been part of your life ever since you were, what—twenty?"

"Eighteen." Medora smiled thinking of how Randall had reminded her of that fact earlier that morning. "I was eighteen, he was nineteen. We met our first year in college." Despite herself, Medora sighed. "I guess there'll always be a place in my heart for him."

"And I'm sure there'll always be one for you in his."

"Yeah, along with the dozen or so other women who have claims on that particular piece of his anatomy."

"And the piece about two feet to the south," Eliza added, which made Medora laugh. "How about some champagne later on? I can get a sitter for Eli and pop by with some goodies."

"No, I'm champagned out. I'm going over to my aunt Tillie's with T.W. tonight."

"Well, have fun. And don't worry about this thing with Randall. It will work itself out."

"It already has, as far as I'm concerned. Talk to you later," Medora said, and hung up. She put on a stack of the CDs she always played when love got her to feeling down—blues and ballads by Bessie, Dinah, Billie, and Sarah—and started to paint.

Chapter Two

The collector whom Randall described as having an "amazing eye" was Anastasia Reese-Mitchell, and contrary to what Medora assumed, they were *not* sleeping together—at least not yet. On a Friday night, the week after Medora threw Randall out, Anastasia, or Ana as she preferred to be called, was dreaming about her late husband Jerrod. In her dream, he was screaming at her the way he had nearly every day of their six-year marriage.

"You're dead, you son of a bitch! Go back to hell!" Ana yelled and woke up trembling. She took a few deep breaths, glanced at the clock, which read 4:02 A.M., and went back to sleep. At midmorning, the phone rang. Assuming it was her son, Danny, she picked it up on the second ring. It was Randall Hollis calling from his car asking if they were still on for today. It took her a moment to recognize his voice. Embarrassed to still be in bed at ten, she forced herself awake.

"Sure, yeah, of course," she said wondering what they were on for.

"I'm going to be in Jersey. My mother is ill, and I need to spend time with her. I was thinking that I could pick you up and we could ride back to the city together." She remembered then; they were catching a "last chance" show at the Studio Museum in Harlem. "I thought maybe we could have an early dinner, around five or six. I'll bring you back, of course," he added as if she might have some doubt.

"But isn't that a lot of trouble?" she asked.

"No. Actually, I'd like to have dinner with you."

"I'd like that, too,"she said, then immediately wished she hadn't. Up until now, her relationship with Randall Hollis had been a professional one. She had met him some time ago at a program sponsored by her woman's group on collecting African-American art. He was the guest speaker, and she was impressed by the breadth of his knowledge. They had exchanged cards and met informally at his loft, and she had taken his suggestion on the purchase of several pieces of art and been pleased with his recommendations. Good sense told her to keep this relationship on a collector-to-art-dealer basis; this sounded like a date. After he hung up, she thought about calling him back and telling him she'd changed her mind. But that might sound as if she deemed it more important than it was. It was just dinner, after all. No big thing. Eager art dealer trying to impress wealthy collector. She was making too much of it.

She laid in bed a while longer considering what to wear, then got up and went through her morning ritual—fifteen minutes of meditation, during which she focused on *not* focusing; a few yoga stretches, thirty stomach crunches, on which she cheated. Finally, she sat down at her vanity table for her *true* meditation, a silent greeting to the three photographs of her "angels" who were no longer with her in the silver filigreed frames that were arranged on top.

The largest one was of her mother, which had been taken the last year of her life. She was sitting in a rocking chair next to Danny, who had just turned six. It was Christmas and they both grinned for the camera as they strung popcorn to be hung on the tree standing behind them. Ana could recall everything about that day: the aroma of the popcorn mingled with the piney fragrance of the tree; Mahalia Jackson belting out "O Holy Night," which had been her mother's favorite; her mother's eyes as she smiled through her pain to please her grandson.

"Good morning, Ma," Ana whispered as she did nearly every morning.

She then turned to the photograph of her father. He was a handsome man, ebony-skinned, with a strong, square chin. A brown fedora was rakishly slanted over one eye, and he wore a brown sweater that age and wear had turned nearly the same shade as his hat. He stood beside a boat, the *Anastasia*, which he'd named for his daughter, and held a string of fish somebody else had caught. They had always laughed about that photo: Walt Thomas posing for posterity with somebody else's catch. He was dead of lung cancer ten years after the photograph had been taken, cigarettes and factory fumes having choked the life out of him.

The third photograph was of her best friend, Mali, whose dreadlocks fell fetchingly over her big eyes and whose wide grin lit her round face in gaiety. Mali had been struck by a car and instantly killed last March on her way home from her nightly jog. The only salvation Ana had was that they had spent her last day together viewing art in a museum in New York. Tomorrow would be the anniversary of her death.

When Jerrod was alive, he made no secret of his contempt for her "shrine" to her parents, which he considered sentimental and foolish.

"Why the hell don't you join the world of the living?" he'd say, playfully at first and then cruelly. He prided himself on living in the here and now; once you were dead, you were gone. Grief, in particular, made him uncomfortable. He was dead himself by the time Mali was killed, so Ana didn't have to listen to his mouth about the latest addition to her shrine. People assumed that losing her husband and best friend within a year of each other would devastate her, but it was the loss of Mali that nearly destroyed her. Mali and the laughter she brought into Ana's life had made her marriage to Jerrod bearable. If he had outlived Mali instead of the other way around, Ana was sure she would have gone insane. Mali lived almost a year after his heart attack, just long enough to have had the last laugh (and a wild uproarious howl it would have been) if she'd chosen to laugh it. Ana's eyes watered at the thought of her.

"Not now!" she said aloud, burying her feelings and making herself think about her "date," or whatever it was, as she showered and tried to force out the loneliness that so often engulfed her. Tomorrow and her memories of her friend would be bad enough. Maybe this "date" would be a good thing.

Without a doubt, Randall Hollis was the most interesting man she'd met in the two years since her husband's death. He was handsome—definitely fine, Mali would have put it—and loved art as much as she did. But she was a "wealthy widow," as her lawyer constantly reminded her, and should be wary of handsome young men eager to help her spend her late husband's fortune. Art dealers were notorious when it came to spending other people's money.

If she had it to do over again, Ana knew she would have majored in art history and worked in a museum or gallery. Works of art exhilarated her, touched her in a way she found hard to put into words. When she gazed at a new piece, she could feel its energy, as if it spoke directly to her, and she was changed by each encounter. She could easily spend hours in a museum, and she often did, walking through the galleries until her feet hurt and her neck ached from gazing. She felt at peace when she was in the presence of great work, as if she had stumbled onto sacred ground.

Now that she had the means to do it, she was eager to build a collection. She felt comfortable working with Randall Hollis both because he was one of the few black art dealers around and because he knew the market and his way around a world she found both unfriendly and confusing. The work of African-American artists, always undersold and undervalued, was her passion, and Randall Hollis knew what to buy and where to buy it. Yet the few times they were together she felt strangely vulnerable. He was a very attractive, seductive man. If he had been older, she might have been interested in him, but he was at least ten years younger and that made her uncomfortable.

For what it was worth, however, she knew that if she chose to do so, her dating a young man probably wouldn't bother her son, Danny.

"Men do it all the time, Ma." Danny had commented recently, as he weighed in on what he termed her "boring" lifestyle. Danny, who lived in his own duplex apartment in a town nearby, had spent the night, and they were sitting on stools in her kitchen eating breakfast. She knew that for years, Danny had secretly hoped that she and his father, her ex-husband Daniel, would get back together. Now at twenty-five, he had finally accepted reality. "You're too hip for some of these old dudes who be calling here sometimes. You're only forty-seven, that's not old."

"That's old enough." Ana had put on her reading glasses to make her point. "And I'd like to know what old dudes you're talking about." With the exception of Nate Jones, an old acquaintance who had once been Mali's lover, no man worth noting had called within the last six months.

"Well, guys your age take out women ten, twenty, thirty years younger and nobody says squat," Danny had continued. "Age is no big thing anymore, believe me. Take me: I wouldn't mind dating an older woman, say some honey in her early thirties. Someone with some *serious* life experience." Ana chuckled. Her son's observations about life, love, and lust never failed to delight her. "I got to get away from these young women. You know what I mean?" Sorrow flickered in his eyes, and the smile on Ana's face faded. She knew that Taylor Benedict had just crossed her son's mind.

"Maybe you've got a point, son." She watched him closely.

"I saw her yesterday at the mall." His mood darkened, and with it Ana's. She knew without explanation who the "she" was.

"It's time for you to let her go, Danny," she said.

When Ana had married Jerrod, she and then sixteen-year-old Danny were swept into his social circle, and the Benedicts were one of the first families they met. Danny was taken with Taylor the moment he laid eyes on her. Ana had watched helplessly when seven years later, Taylor broke her son's heart with as much feeling as she'd show a roach trapped under her Prada heels. They'd be hawking snowshoes in hell before Ana forgave her.

"I think I must still be in with love her."

"What you are is infatuated with her, Danny, and there's a big difference."

"Whatever it is, it still hurts."

"She didn't feel the same about you, Danny. I'm not sure at this point in her life if Taylor is capable of feeling anything for anybody besides herself. You are twenty-five years old. Someday you'll find a woman who will value who you are and what you have to give. Taylor has some growing up to do," she said, making a stab at diplomacy and adjusting her voice to make it sound light. "Maybe you do need somebody a little older. Maybe I should start asking for volunteers among the 'honeys' who play golf at the club."

Danny's half smile rewarded her effort.

"So, exactly *who* do you have in mind for me?" she asked, as if she were actually interested.

"Rahim's older brother; you know the dude."

"Rahim's older brother!"

"He's thirty-three, and Money is always asking about you. How's your mama doin', Danny? She seeing anybody? If the dude weren't so doofus, I'd jack him up for checking you out, but, hey, you never know!"

"*I* know." Ana said, shuddering. "Thanks for caring, son, but I'm happy by myself, with myself. At least for the time being."

She smiled now, as she recalled the conversation. Truth was, Randall Hollis probably wasn't all that much older than Rahim's older brother. She'd never asked his age, but he'd mentioned at least one political event recalled through the prism of childhood that she remembered as a young adult. As far as she knew, they shared no common historical references, and, with the exception of art, no common interest. Different eras. Different tastes. Different styles. There was no way anything could develop.

Yet Mali would have had no problem with such a relationship. A man's age had never been a problem for her. She had once been gleefully involved with both a twenty-nine-year-old social worker and a sixty-seven-year-old banker during the same ten months. "I highly recommend it," she'd say with a playfully salacious wink, her voice hinting at carnal pleasures that Ana, after four years of stilted sex with Jerrod, could only imagine.

"Run!" Mali muttered the first time she met Jerrod. The meeting had been over a dinner thick with forced goodwill in an overpriced Manhattan restaurant. Jerrod had insisted upon ordering, for both of them, the "perfect" dessert—a frothy concoction of ice cream, almonds, and crème de cacao that Ana belted down to please him, even though it turned her stomach.

"I should have run!" Ana said to the mirror as she patted astringent on her face and recalled that dinner. "If I weren't such a damn coward I would have run like hell."

Examining herself in the glass, she felt her old insecurities creeping back; they always accompanied the memory of Jerrod. She shook them off quickly, as she had learned to do throughout her life during what Mali called her periods of reclaiming yourself. It had taken her decades to claim and cherish who she was—years of "black is beautiful," "lovely black queens," and "the blacker the berry"—to rid herself of the particular brand of self-hatred black and white America inflict upon dark-skinned black women. It was finally the undeniable handsomeness of her son that made her realize her own beauty.

It was also Daniel, her first husband. Their son and her love of self were the gifts he left her with, gifts that Jerrod had tried to steal. Daniel had never stopped telling her how lovely she was and promising her that someday she would grow into her beauty. If only he had been able to grow into his.

I am trapped in the past, she said reproachfully to herself as she patted on moisturizer. It was a disturbing thought that she pushed out of her mind as she pulled on jeans and a T-shirt and headed across the hall into her kitchen.

When Ana bought the house the year after Jerrod died, it had been described as a "charming cottage with a big heart," realtor-speak for a small two-story house in a section of town known for its ostentatious mansions. On the first floor was the master bedroom with its marble en suite bathroom, replete with standing ten-nozzle shower, oversize whirlpool bathtub, bidet, and double sinks that initially struck her as shamelessly extravagant, but which she quickly got used to. A screened porch off her bedroom led to a large backyard flanked by a small kidney-shaped pool on one side and a garden where she loved to sit and read on the other. The kitchen, where she prepared her breakfast, faced a combined living and dining area backed by a wall of windows that faced the garden and a field-stone fireplace that ran the length of both rooms. Throughout the house hung her growing collection of art. It was an airy, whimsical house, designed by an architect who obviously loved beauty, sunshine, and space. She was glad that Jerrod had never lived here with her and knew she would be happy in this house for the rest of her life.

It was a chilly morning, the beginning of a March day that could swing as easily back to winter as to spring. Ana considered lighting a fire but changed her mind; she'd build one tonight if it was still cold. She poured Grape-Nuts into a blue china bowl, sliced a banana on top, and sprinkled it lightly with brown sugar. She juiced three oranges into a glass, gulped the juice down with six vitamin pills, and then went to the front porch and picked up the *Times*, which she opened to the business section. She stopped suddenly in the middle of surveying her stocks. Old habits, particularly those learned from Jerrod, died hard. *Why start out the morning as he had taught you to do?* she asked herself as she folded the newspaper in half and placed it beside her plate. Gazing out the window at nothing in particular she munched her cereal.

But Jerrod Mitchell was still there. He always was.

She had met him at a fundraiser, one of the first she organized after leaving her job. He donated twice as much money as anybody else, and his generosity impressed her. Fundraising was her second career. Twenty years before, she'd started out in the special events department of a midsize New Jersey marketing firm, and slowly worked her way up to vice president. She held a lofty title but little else, so when the inevitable tightening of belt came, she was the first to be squeezed out. Mali was sure it was because her white male subordinates were uncomfortable taking orders from a black woman. Ana suspected as much, but her severance package was generous and she was sick of the office politics, so she left without a grumble.

Jerrod Mitchell overwhelmed her with his money and power, and it felt good in the beginning to be dominated by a rich, powerful man. When he asked her to marry him six months after they met, she took a deep breath, closed her eyes, and quickly said yes. Danny was sixteen by then, and she felt he needed a strong male role model; she was tired of the buck always stopping with her. Her severance pay was running out much faster than she thought it would, and at forty, she knew she'd never be able to find a job that would pay the kind of money she and Danny were accustomed to living on. Danny would be headed for college in two years, and she hadn't managed to save half of what would be needed. Her heart had its doubts, but her head told her that Jerrod Mitchell was the best thing that could happen to her.

The honeymoon, which lasted two weeks, was followed by six years of pure hell. He never hit her, but used his voice like a weapon, pounding her down with his will. The first time he screamed at her, his harsh voice slapping her like a hand, she couldn't believe he was speaking to her. Her life had always been filled with gentle men. In forty years, no man had ever raised his voice or insulted her, certainly not her father, who spoke in a gentle whisper, and never Daniel, who often wasn't aggressive enough. Jerrod was a domineering, abusive bully with a temper who scorned and tormented her son and threatened her safety. When he dropped dead in the arms of one of his pretty young secretaries, she didn't grieve a day. Maybe that was why he haunted her.

She had always been careful with money, so her considerable wealth changed very little about the way she lived. She kept a watchful eye on her accountants and investments and provided generously for her son. Although money never meant that much to her, it did make things easier, but she had paid dearly for that luxury. She was thinking about that high price when the telephone rang and she answered it.

"Hey, Dutch." The name startled her. It was short for "Duchess," which was short for Anastasia, the ill-fated Grande Duchess of Imperial Russia, for whom her mother, who loved history, had named her. Dutch was Nate Jones's nickname for her; he was the only one who used it.

"Nate?" she asked, even though she knew.

"Who else? How you been?"

"I've been fine."

"How's the boy?"

"He's fine, too. . . . Is Daniel okay?" She had taken a deep breath before she asked it, expecting the worst, almost hearing it. Except for her, Nate Jones was the only person in the world who cared whether Daniel Reese, her ex-husband, lived or died.

There was a pause. "Same as always, Dutch. Same as always. I saw him over on Route 280 as I was coming off the Parkway. He had a dirty rag doing people's windshields. He didn't see me at first, but then he recognized me and asked if we could talk. So he got in the car, and I drove him around the block a couple of times. Didn't say too much, but he wanted to know about you and the kid, how you were, what you were doing, that kind of thing. He wanted to know if I could arrange for him to see the two of you. I told him the kid was a man, and you had a new life, but I promised I'd give you the message and do what I can. That was about it."

Ana closed her eyes trying to match the image Nate described with that of the man she had once loved.

"Drugs and booze got the boy so much out of his mind," Nate continued, "I don't think he'll even remember that he asked me, but I told him I'd tell you so I did."

Daniel and Ana. Mali and Nate. The sound of Nate's voice brought it all back. They were tied forever in time. Nate and Mali and Daniel and Ana. It had been the four of them in high school and those first few years of college. And once it had been Nate and Ana, before she broke up with him to go with his best friend. Then it had been Nate and Mali and they had outlasted Ana and Daniel by a lifetime.

"Ana?" Nate asked, puzzled by her silence.

"Yes, I'm still here."

"Do you want to see him? I can arrange it if you want me to. You and Danny can come by the club, I can find him, bring him here so he can say what he has to say, then the two of you can split. It might do the boy some good. A man has to come to terms with his daddy before he can come to terms with himself."

"Let me think about it," she said, but she had already made up her mind. She had decided long ago that Daniel Reese wouldn't cloud Danny's life with his own.

"How are you doing, Nate?" It was a stab at polite conversation more than anything else because she didn't want to think about Daniel or the past. His answer surprised her.

"I still miss her," he said. "You know it will be a year tomorrow. Just a year." Mali had loved Nate on and off for most of her life. But Nate had a wife, Essie, and she and their sons were the reason he said he could never do right by Mali. Ana resented him for that, and she resented him bringing Mali into the conversation now. He was the only man who had ever gotten the best of her friend, the one who had torn out her heart.

But who the hell was she to pass judgment on somebody staying in a bad marriage?

"How is Essie? The boys?" The moment after she said it, she realized that she shouldn't have asked about his family so soon after he'd mentioned Mali. On second thought, maybe that was where it belonged.

"The boys are grown men now and out of the house. Essie, well, she's still Essie. We've kind of gone our separate ways."

Gone our separate ways. What would Mali have made of that? Ana wondered.

"I just wanted to tell you about Daniel, and see how you all are doing." His voice was rushed now as if he was eager to get off the phone. It made Ana wonder if he had called as much about Daniel as Mali, if he simply needed to talk to a person who remembered and missed her as much as he did. There had been unfinished business between Mali and Nate, just as there was between her and Daniel. "Let me know what you want to do. But don't wait too long."

"I won't." She was lying and she knew it. She didn't want to think about Daniel Reese or see him again, and she didn't want her son to see him.

By the time Randall Hollis drove into her driveway, Ana had managed to put Nate Jones and why he had called out of her mind. She was wondering again if she'd made a mistake in agreeing to go to dinner with him and was running through excuses she could use to get home early. But it was obviously too late. He was driving a new E-class Mercedes, sleek and midnight blue, with shiny new rims and the sheen of a recent car wash. Ana prided herself on not caring about the traditional pretensions of the recently rich—the expensive furs, luxury cars, vacation homes in Sag Harbor or Martha's Vineyard. Ostentatious spending had been suspect in her straitlaced family. Her father was fond of mentioning the difficulties rich men had in getting into heaven. Even though Ana's mother would always claim with a chuckle that that particular biblical reference had resonance for him because he knew he would always be poor. But Ana suspected that her father would have been impressed by this car, perhaps as much as she was by the man who climbed out of it.

She watched him from the kitchen window as he came up the walk. She liked his self-confident stride, just a beat off cocky, that hinted he was a good dancer. He was dressed casually in a charcoal-gray sweater, cashmere she assumed, well-tailored slacks, and expensive loafers. She found handsome men intimidating, always assuming that they would give her—or any woman considered less beautiful than they—short shrift. But Randall seemed unaware of how good-looking he was, as if he didn't notice that every woman within half a block did a double take whenever he walked down the street. He was a man you could get used to looking at, she decided. She liked his voice, too, with its husky, sensual undertone.

"Beautiful place," he said, glancing around after they had exchanged the conventional greetings. He was quickly drawn to the groupings of paintings and drawings that hung on her walls. "You're really on your way to developing a strong collection."

"Thanks."

"When did you get this?"

He asked about a pastel and charcoal drawing by Charles Alston.

"It was on loan to a museum. I just got it back. I've just gotten another request for it. So I'm enjoying it while I can."

"It's generous of you to lend things out. Some collectors don't realize that you can never really own a piece; it's just yours to take care of for a while. So, how long have you lived here?"

"I moved in after my husband died," she said without thinking much about how it sounded. She wished she'd thought of a more graceful way to put it.

He changed the subject. "Sorry I was late. My mother was having some problems, as I said, and . . ." He broke off without finishing the sentence.

"No, you're fine," she said, filling in the space.

"Ready to go?"

"Sure."

She wondered aloud whether it was cool enough for a sweater. Ana's choice of clothing was always understated, and she wore a simple navy dress, which could slide easily from afternoon into evening. He suggested a shawl, and she choose one woven with cashmere and silk that Mali had brought back for her from New Zealand. Just wearing it made her feel Mali's presence as she wrapped herself in its softness and warmth when she stepped outside. There was an awkward lull in the conversation as they walked down the path to the car. Ana tried desperately to think of some light, easy patter to exchange, but she'd never been good at small talk, and apparently neither was he. They drove the first five miles in silence.

"Beautiful car," she finally said, echoing his words about her house.

"Thanks. I got it a few months ago, and I love it," he said with such unabashed pride it made her think about her father's adoration for his old truck. She'd learned how to drive on that thing, shifting the ancient gears from first to second, barely able to reach the clutch with her foot. It was nothing like the smooth motion of this one. He gave her a sideways glance, and a thrill, immediate and intense, went through her, which surprised her. She thought again about Mali. Such a reaction wouldn't have surprised her at all. Mali's spirit seemed perched on her shoulder today. The image of her best friend, smile beaming, dreadlocks flapping, passed through her mind and she chuckled. Randall glanced at her curiously.

"I just thought about something funny," she said, slightly embarrassed.

"Feel like sharing it?"

"No," she said, then added, when she saw how puzzled he looked, "kind of a private joke. My son claims I spend too much time by myself. Maybe he's right," she added for further explanation and then realized it probably wasn't the smartest thing to say. But she was too old to play games, even on a casual date.

"Well, I'm relieved to know you talk to yourself," he said. "I was in the supermarket the other day arguing with myself over whether I should buy asparagus or carrots. Talking to yourself means you enjoy your own company."

Ana doubted he was telling the truth but appreciated the attempt at gallantry. "Sometimes you can enjoy it too much."

"I really don't think you can. Believe me, I'm tired of running into women—and men—who don't enjoy their own company. That's always a bad sign."

"And do you run into a lot of women—and men—who don't?" she

asked coyly, passing her question off lightly, although she was really curious about the women rather than the men.

"Every now and then," he said with an impish grin that told her he knew what she was up to.

"You mentioned on the phone that your mother is ill. Is she feeling better?"

Randall's jaw tightened. "My mother, Lydia, has lung cancer, and it's killing her," he said. "My first memory of her is with a cigarette dangling out of her mouth. I hate the damn things for what they've done to her. What she's let them do to her. She still tries to smoke; do you believe that?"

"I'm sorry."

"No." He glanced at her with a slight but reassuring smile. "It's okay. She's dying and I have to get used to it, but it's very hard. It breaks my heart every time I see her."

Surprised by his words, Ana waited a moment before responding. "My father died of lung cancer. It was a long time ago, but I still remember how horrible it was for him, for all of us."

He nodded in agreement, and then added, "The real problem is that Lydia and I also have . . . I guess I should say a difficult relationship. We've had our moments, and, well, you know. I have to deal with all of that now, too."

Ana, touched by his candor, said, "Most mothers and sons do have their moments. Believe me, I know about that."

"Not like the ones we have."

"At least the two of you are comfortable enough for you to call her by her first name," Ana said diplomatically, even though it had struck her as odd that he would do so. Never in his life had Danny dared call her by her first name, even in jest.

"I've always called my mother Lydia. Ever since I was a kid. Lydia felt that the word 'mother' was too confining. Too predictable. And she doesn't like to be confined or predictable," he added in a tone that Ana found puzzling.

"Sounds like an interesting woman," she said more to herself than to him. The expression on his face told her to leave it alone.

"And your father. Is he still living?"

"No," he said with a finality that cut off further inquiry.

But talk between them did come easier after the exchange.

Mostly they discussed the show they were about to see and the work of some of the artists in it. Randall said he had grown up within walking distance of the Studio Museum, sharing some highlights from his early childhood before his mother moved to Newark, and that led Ana to recollections about her childhood in Washington, D.C., and the first time her father had taken her to see the Phillips Collection. It had been years since she had even thought about it.

"It was a Saturday morning, and he had just gotten off from work," she recalled. "He worked the night shift, so he was exhausted, but he put on his Sunday clothes, which weren't good enough, of course, for the people who worked there. But we walked into that beautiful old mansion like it belonged to us.

"And the funny thing was, once I was inside, the paintings *did* belong to me; they were mine, and the nasty attitude of the woman who took our money didn't even matter."

"Unfortunately that kind of elitist attitude still lingers in the world of art," Randall said with disgust. "They try to hide it now because they know that kind of exclusivity will get their government funding cut, but money and connections still dictate whose work gets shown and whose work gets bought. There are about fifteen walls in Manhattan that can make or break an artist, and none of them belongs to people who look like us." There was an angry edge in his voice that Ana hadn't heard before.

"It doesn't matter. They can't take away what is beautiful."

"But it takes money to keep the people who create that beauty alive," he said, but his voice had softened.

"I remember I felt like I was in church," Ana continued. "I felt like I was walking on hallowed ground that was there just for me to discover."

Randall smiled as if he understood. "Lydia is an artist," he said after a few moments.

"Your mother?" Ana asked, and thought with alarm, *Do I remind him of his mother?* "Is she a painter?"

His sigh was heavy. "She could have been, a very good one. She dreamed of it more than anything else. She never really had the chance to fulfill her talent, but she obviously had it."

"What a shame."

"Yeah. It really was."

"Is she still painting?"

He hesitated a moment. "No. I think she just got discouraged and gave it up. Almost out of spite."

"Do you think you got your love of art from her?"

"Yeah. I definitely did. It was one of the things in life she loved. The other being me," he said with a slight smile.

The awkwardness between them was back; she didn't know why it had come.

"Things are getting better, though, for black female artists who want to pursue their art, mostly because of people like you," she said, an obvious attempt at flattery that she didn't do gracefully.

"Nothing has really changed. Not enough to make a difference," he said.

"But some artists are beginning to get more opportunities," she added, trying to add a positive note to what was becoming a depressing conversation. "Like that young woman whose work I bought, I've forgotten her name."

Randall swerved as if trying to avoid hitting something in the road but recovered quickly. "Medora Jackson. Didn't mean to scare you." He threw her an embarrassed sidelong glance.

"I've driven with far worse drivers than you. My son, Danny, comes to mind," Ana said with a chuckle.

"I didn't know you had a son. What grade is he in?"

"Please don't try to flatter me," she said with a touch of annoyance.

"Well, how old is he?"

About ten years younger than you, she thought, but said, "He'll be twenty-five next month. I guess that really dates me, doesn't it?" *Why the hell did I add that?* she asked herself.

"So, what does he do for a living?" Randall said, not missing a beat.

"He doesn't do anything. He's still trying to decide." She tried to say it casually and then wished immediately that she hadn't elaborated. She didn't want to think about Danny or about her anger at his inability to hold down a job or do anything that remotely smacked of adulthood.

"Late bloomer, eh?"

"It's very sensitive subject," she said testily.

He glanced at her as if trying to gauge her reaction. "I'm sorry, but why?"

"You spoke earlier about issues with your mother. I'm terribly angry at my son for not trying to make more of himself. It's really the only thing we fight about," she said, wondering as she spoke why she was being so candid.

"Well, you shouldn't worry about it. It's probably a good thing. Most of the twenty-five-year-olds I know are so driven they make me feel lazy."

How many twenty-five-year-olds does he know? Ana thought.

"Don't put any pressure on him. He'll get where he's going sooner or later. That's very young, twenty-five."

"Not that young. I was twenty-three when I had him. I'll be forty-eight in November," she added, as if he couldn't do the math.

"Oh, really." A mischievous look crossed his face, and he said too quickly, "I'll be thirty-eight in September. Thought I'd throw it in, since we're talking age. Don't hold it against me, okay?"

"Your age or the fact that you mentioned it?"

"Both."

"If you don't hold forty-eight against me."

"If there is one good thing I have to give my mama, she didn't raise a fool," he said with a disarming smile, but it left Ana wondering why that was the *one* good thing she gave him.

After the museum, they decided on Greek food and ended up in a cozy, elegant place on the Upper East Side. It was Mali's kind of place,

Ana thought when they walked in. Sophisticated but not pretentious. The waiters knew Randall by name, and the owner stopped by to chat with a familiarity that told her this was a place he frequented. He seemed pleased that she liked it, which made her wonder how many other women he'd brought here, and if they had enjoyed it, too. Conversation came easily over dinner and grew more familiar with each glass of wine.

He didn't mention Jerrod Mitchell until they were headed back to Jersey.

"I really admired your late husband," he said as they turned onto the Garden State Parkway.

"Really?" The mere thought of Jerrod made Ana's body tighten.

"Yeah, I really did. He was the keynote speaker at my college graduation. He seemed to be one of those brothers who fought the good fight, no matter how long it took. All I could think of when I heard him speak was how I hoped I could be as successful and powerful as he was one day."

"Jerrod was certainly that, successful and powerful."

"I can't imagine how devastating it must have been to lose a man like that. You're so strong, Ana. I have such admiration for you. Some women never recover from that kind of loss. They would just give up on life, crawl into a shell, and live off the memory of their husband."

"A woman is more than her husband!" His naïveté irritated her.

"I guess what I'm trying to say is that my father was like that in a way, too: strong and powerful. Not successful like your husband, but he had a lot going for him, and sometimes I don't think I'll ever recover from losing him. Even though I was a kid when he died, his loss took its toll on who I am. But for you, to be married to a giant of a man like that."

"You were a kid, and losing your father was a harsher loss," she said.

"I guess I'm kind of in awe of you."

Ana studied Randall, trying to gauge his sincerity. It would certainly be easier to let things lie, let him, like everybody else, assume that the loss of Jerrod Mitchell had been the loss of her life. But she was an honest woman, sometimes to a fault. They had had a nice evening, and despite her reservations, she sensed there was something about this man, a capacity for intimacy and kindness, that called for the truth. So she focused on the road in front of her and told it.

"There was no love in our marriage, Randall," she began. "If I ever did love him, he killed it early on. He never beat me with his fists, but not a day went by where he didn't do it with his voice, where he didn't insult, humiliate, or make me feel like a fool.

"He was a cruel man, and he could be vicious to those who were close to him. I don't think he knew how to love, not anyone, not himself, and certainly not the pretty young woman in whose arms he dropped dead." The embarrassment on Randall's face made her add with a sympathetic smile, "Sorry to destroy your hero, but most heroes have feet of clay if you poke them, and my late husband's feet crumbled very easily."

"I'm sorry. I had no idea."

"How could you?"

He took his eyes from the road just long enough to gaze into hers, and she was struck by the understanding she saw in them. "I can tell, even from the little time we've spent together, that you deserve the best a man can give. He must have been a pretty sorry bastard not to know that."

"That he was, and I'll carry the the scars in my heart for the rest of my life."

They drove in silence after that. Ana wondered if had been wise to be so frank so early in the relationship, but then decided she didn't have a choice. She couldn't play games anymore with men, or with anybody else, for that matter. She didn't have the energy. This business with Jerrod and what he had done to her was part of who she was now, like her love for Danny and for his father and for Mali, and she wasn't going to hide it. But she did say after a moment, "Sorry I laid it on you like that."

"I'm happy you did. I like knowing about you. I'd like to know more."

She smiled politely, and admitted to herself that she was curious about him, too.

What inspired and touched him? she wondered. How had life changed him? She could barely remember herself at thirty-eight, except she knew that she had been overwhelmed by her life and loneliness, and worried about her son, who at fourteen seemed aimless and prone to depression. Randall seemed so confident and sure of himself. Had life ever thrown him its hardballs?

Randall turned the radio to a jazz station, and Ana recognized the solemn, elegiac tones of "Fontessa," a piece by the Modern Jazz Quartet that she hadn't heard in years and that had been one of her and Daniel's favorites. The first time they had made love it was playing, and for years afterward those elegant notes would bring him and that night back to her. Daniel had touched her that night with such adoration and reverence, and she had loved him more than she thought she could ever love anyone. How old had they been? Twenty-one, twenty-two? She could barely remember, it had been so long ago. Funny that she was hearing that song now, after all these years.

But there couldn't be more of a difference between the man who sat next to her tonight and Daniel Reese. Daniel was strung out at thirty-eight. Cheap wine at first, and then cocaine, and finally crack, its cheaper, harsher cousin. Liquor and drugs deadened him to everyone he knew and didn't want to remember: his friends, his family, and finally, herself and their son.

What could Daniel possibly have to say to her now?

The last time she had seen him had been fifteen years ago on Danny's tenth birthday. He'd pulled himself together enough to stop by to bring his son a toy that was far too young for him. He'd barely glanced at her. She'd tried not to notice the state of his clothes and how violently his hands shook when he ate a slice of cake. He left soon after coming. She didn't breathe well until the door closed behind him.

A man has to come to terms with his daddy before he can come to terms with himself.

Maybe it had been a mistake to keep Danny away from his father as long as she had, but Danny was grown now. He had never seemed to need him. He'd never asked to meet him. Yet there had been an urgency in Nate Jones's voice when he brought the whole thing up. Was there something he hadn't told her?

Ana didn't notice the flashing lights on the police car that followed them. Her thoughts were on "Fontessa" and the man she had once loved.

She didn't pay attention to the car behind them until Randall cursed softly and pulled to the side of the road. He glanced at the speedometer.

"I know I wasn't speeding," he said more to himself than to her. Ana felt the creeping sense of dread she always felt whenever cops came into view. It was a leftover from her childhood, she realized, the fear that would squeeze her stomach whenever the police stopped her father. Maybe she sensed her father's fear, his vulnerability. She felt it now. *It's just a cop doing his job, that's all*, she reminded herself. *Just a cop doing his job.*

But a black man had to be careful around the police, and she had taught her son to be cautious, never to talk back to them, to do whatever they said. Never give them an excuse to rough him up, or worse. She glanced at Randall. His fingers thumped an angry rhythm on the steering wheel. She hoped somebody had taught him the same rules.

"License and registration," the police officer said. His eyes were impossible to see behind his metallic sunglasses. His voice was robotic, contemptuous, and contrasted with his face, which was plump and nondescript, like that of a grocery clerk or gas station attendant. A white-bread face.

Ana knew there would be trouble. She could smell it. She wanted to warn Randall not to challenge him, to say nothing. She hoped he was old enough to know that much about white men in uniform: that they needed to see that you knew they had the power to kill you.

"What did I do, Officer?" His voice offered a challenge with a touch of snottiness that said, *Don't you think I know why you pulled me over, you dumb son of a bitch?* It made the hair stand up on the back of her neck. She could tell by the jerk of his lower lip that the cop heard it, too. She stared at her hands, not wanting him to see the fear that she knew was in her eyes, to see that she was afraid for Randall, or he would find a way to use it against him, against both of them.

"License and registration." His mechanized voice had no shading.

Give it to him! Give him whatever he wants! Ana tried to communicate her feelings to Randall without looking at him, without moving her lips. But she was also angry at herself for being scared of the cop.

"I'd like to know why I'm being stopped." It was a reasonable question, reasonably asked, but this was not a reasonable situation. As he spoke, Randall complied with the request, reaching into his pants for his wallet, which was black and elegant, and probably cost more than the cop made in a week. Another strike against him.

The cop examined his papers. "Get the fuck out of the car," he said.

Ana's breath caught in her throat.

"Get the fuck out of the car!" There was no change in his voice, no change in his manner, just an order, a command he that expected to be followed. Randall unbuckled his seat belt, glanced briefly at Ana and then away, his face taut with rage.

"Be careful," she tried to mouth, but her mouth didn't move.

"Did you hear me, get the fuck out of the car!" *Nigger! Get the fuck out of the car, nigger!* He hadn't said the word but Ana felt it, and she knew that Randall did, too. Randall climbed out quickly, his hands to his side.

"Hands up. Against the car. Now!" Jersey backwoods, that was what it was, Ana realized. As identifiably racist as Arkansas backwoods, as Kentucky, as Mississippi.

Without a word, staring straight ahead, Randall did what he was told, his hands held up as directed, his mouth tense, fury blazing in his eyes. He put his hands on top of the car, spread his legs. Ana stared at the dashboard because she couldn't watch his humiliation. She wondered what she could do to help, but instinct told her that it would make things worse if she got involved.

"Can you tell me what I did wrong, Officer?" His voice was dignified. He wasn't afraid. Ana respected him for that.

"Shut the fuck up, and stay where you are."

His eyes still on Randall, the cop walked back to his squad car and made a call on his radio. Randall stood, his hands on the hood of his car, his legs apart, and Ana sat, her hands tight in her lap. Ten minutes passed. It seemed forever. The cop came back. Ana watched him walking toward them, a sneer on his face.

"This your car?"

"Yes it is." He didn't add "sir," which Ana knew she would have at this point. Maybe that was the difference ten years made. She would have added "sir" without hesitation.

"This car isn't properly registered. Look at this." The policeman waved the registration in his face. "It's run out. It's expired. That's why I pulled you over, Randall. There's been reports of thefts of cars like this, and I called it in and they told me this one has expired, but I do see, Randall, that it is registered to you."

The use of his first name was meant to reduce him to a boy, and Ana knew that her presence as witness contributed to his shame. Randall looked straight ahead. Not dropping his head, not bowing.

"So, I guess if you're going to be driving a fancy, *leased* car like this, you better make sure your leasing company renews the registration, or take yourself over there to Motor Vehicles in East Orange and get it properly registered, isn't that right, Randall?"

He didn't move or answer. "Here you go." The officer handed him back his license and registration. Then he wrote him a ticket. "Okay?"

Randall stood up straight, looked the man in his eyes, and without saying anything else put his license and registration back into his wallet, got into the car, and pulled away, his eyes on the rearview mirror, still watching the cop.

They drove in silence. He held the steering wheel so tightly Ana could see that the blood had drained from his knuckles and his fingers. When they pulled into her driveway, he took a deep breath and blew it out slowly.

"Come in for a drink," Ana said.

She opened a bottle of good red wine, changed her mind, and poured a generous amount of Cognac into two snifters instead, then joined him on the couch.

"I don't know what to say." His voice broke.

"Don't say anything."

"The funny thing is that I should be used to it by how. Every black man in American should be used to it by now, especially if he has a nice-looking car, but it still cuts you to your core every time it happens, cuts you up inside, especially when . . ." He dropped his eyes, avoiding hers.

"There was nothing you could do."

"Except be white," he said, and they both laughed a little at that. But then he turned serious again, his voice bitter.

"The worst thing is that you feel so powerless. Especially with . . . well, with you being there, seeing it all and everything. It's bad enough for them to put you through that kind of crap when you're by yourself, but when you're with a woman . . ." The bitterness in his eyes was replaced by shame. "Especially one you're trying to impress. There's no coming back from that."

"And that was his point, Randall. That was why he did it like that, because I *was* there," she said gently. "And I'm still impressed. They can't take that away from you. Or from me."

They sipped the Cognac in silence, but there no awkwardness, just an easy comfort that Ana hadn't felt with a man in a very long time. A misty rain that had begun to fall had put a chill in the room. Ana lit the fire she'd promised herself earlier that day and then put on some of her favorite CDs—Bessie Smith, Dinah Washington, Miles Davis, John Coltrane.

His first touch was tentative, unsure of what she wanted or if she wanted him at all. The tenderness when he kissed her was something she wasn't used to. He eased back, as if fearful that he had assumed too much too quickly, and she kissed him back to reassure him.

Ana hadn't made love to a man since Jerrod, if she could even call what they had done making love. She had managed to forget about sex, to tuck it so deep that she never thought about or felt its absence. She hardly even had an urge anymore, which was so different from when she'd been young. When she was a girl, sex was always on her mind. She'd run her fingers up and down her young body, stroking herself and imagining how a man's touch would feel. What lunacy, she wondered then, would drive a woman to celibacy? But now it had become difficult to imagine her life any other way. When Randall gently pulled her to him, his fingers traveling the back of her neck, kissing her, then caressing her again, and what had been long gone came back.

Daniel awakened her sexually, and she had married him, the first man to whom she made love. There had been only two lovers between him and Jerrod, and the relationships had ended badly. She had never been able to give herself easily to a man, to casually allow his fingers to touch the intimate spaces of her body, to allow him to ease his body into hers. But when Randall kissed her, his tongue delicately tasting her lips and mouth, grazing her ears and neck, he chased away the lingering memory of Jerrod and the violence with which he always took her.

"Yes," she said, with no clear idea what she was answering to except the word came to her mind and she spoke it. *Yes.* To the first time to make love to a man in her own bed in her own bedroom in her own house. To *this* man she now wanted to feel inside her. And when they made love, she wept silently when she reached a climax because she had been able to give herself to him so easily, with no fear or regret, and because she knew this would not be the last time.

Chapter Three

When her phone rang, Taylor Benedict, the love of young Danny Mitchell's life, was playing a fierce game of strip poker with James Lawson, her best friend and former lover. They were sitting on a very worn kilim rug on the living room floor of Taylor's tiny one-bedroom Brooklyn apartment. Posters of paintings by well-known artists covered the walls, and the smell of scented candles floated through the air.

Taylor was not a classically pretty girl, but men found her angular face, quick smile, and undeniable sensuality irresistible. She was dressed in a red sweat suit and tangerine socks, quite different from her partner, who had stripped down to his ragged cotton briefs. She glanced at the caller ID, turned off the phone, examined her hand, and grinned. "Take 'em off!" she said.

"You're bluffing, right?"

She pulled the cards close to her chest. "Try me!"

"April fools, right?"

"I'll tell you what I'm going to do," she said, her face dead serious as she placed her hand facedown on the table. "I'm going to let you keep your drawers if you swear out loud that Taylor A. Benedict is the best poker player you have ever played with in all of your twenty-six years and you will do her bidding for the next six months."

James narrowed his eyes as he examined his cards. "Forget it. You got nothing!"

"You said it, not me."

He paused, giving his hand a last hard look. "I don't want to be sitting up here butt-naked when you haven't taken off even one of those tacky-ass socks. You can't have *that* many good hands," he added, trying to convince himself.

"Maybe not," she said with a crafty smile.

"Okay. I'm going to call you. Lay 'em down. Show me what you're working with!"

Taylor smiled victoriously as she spread out a straight. "Gotcha!"

"Oh, God." James sunk into himself. "I fucking quit!"

"You can't quit. It's too late. Take them off! I win!"

"I'm quitting, Taylor. I'm not going to lose my dignity *and* my drawers."

"Okay, Jamie, since we've been friends for so long—"

"Friends? What's this *friends* business?"

"*Friends* for so long, James. I'm going to give you a break this time. Especially since I've seen it all before."

"And enjoyed seeing it?"

"No comment."

"Oh, come on!" James said. "We *both* know better than that!" He had a teenager's wide, goofy grin, which beamed as he stood to his full height.

"Okay, I'll give you that." Taylor returned his smile.

"Who taught you how to play poker so good, kid?" he said, pulling on his T-shirt.

"You, fool! Don't you remember?"

James poured what was left from the bottle of wine into their wine-glasses and took a sip. "You've learned a lot since freshman year."

"You just got worse. You're the only person I ever play with," she added with a coy toss of her head.

"*Play with* are the operative words here."

"God, I hate writers."

"So do I," he said with a scowl, then chuckled. "So what are you up to tonight, Ms. Kick-My-Ass-at-Cards-Whenever-She-Feels-Like-It Benedict?"

Taylor gave a studied shrug. "I don't know. Whatever comes to mind, I guess."

"No hot April's Fools' Day date?"

"April Fools' Day is not exactly a big date night, James."

"Unless you're a fool."

"You are nobody's fool. You know that as well as I do."

"*Da-da-da-da-da-dum.* I'm just a fool in love!. . . ." James sang, ignoring her and making up a melody.

Taylor reached into the black Coach bag that sat on the table and pulled out a cigarette. "Sorry," she said as she lit it, "I couldn't wait."

"Why are you taking that shit into your pretty brown lungs?"

"Lungs are pink, not brown. You sound like my damn brother." She blew smoke out of her nose. James shook his head. "I'll stop when I'm thirty."

"So, how is the good doctor doing?" He playfully whisked the smoke away from his face.

"Alan, Jr.? Fighting disease and despair in West Africa. Curing the world of the world's ills, while his no-account sister sits on her ass smoking cigarettes and playing strip poker with an old beau." Her voice was lighthearted, but the sigh that followed wasn't.

"Get over it, Taylor."

"Get over what?" Taylor's wide-eyed glance was innocent.

"Stop comparing yourself to Alan."

Taylor responded with a laugh that wasn't one and snubbed out her cigarette.

"Don't let it get you down."

"I'm not letting it get me down," she said, telling the truth. The problem wasn't Alan, whom she sincerely loved and admired. It was the other one, whom she never mentioned but always lingered somewhere in the back of her mind.

James pulled on his jeans and, throwing her a mock-seductive look, said half jokingly before zipping them up, "I know something that will make you feel better."

Taylor scowled but then, caught in the spirit of the moment, said doubtfully, "You *really* think so?"

"Come on, Benedict, show some grace. A little sex in the afternoon is a great consolation prize."

Taylor grabbed a pillow off the couch and hurled it at him. "Why are you so disgustingly horny? And since when could sex with me be a consolation prize!"

"You're such a tease, Taylor."

"Go fuck *yourself*, James!"

"I'm not talking about sex," he said quickly, his voice serious. "I'm talking about not really saying what's on your mind, playing around. I've known you almost all my adult life, and something is bothering you."

Taylor studied him as if deciding whether or not to tell him the truth.

"Come on, I'm a writer. Writers are like shrinks. We figure out what motivates people. I want to know what motivates you." He looked at her expectantly. "So?"

Taylor sighed, and her face softened, which made her look younger than her twenty-five years. "Sometimes I feel like such a loser," she said.

James stared at her incredulously. "Why? You've had 'winner' written all over you ever since we were in high school."

"High school! James, do you know how long ago that was?"

"Well, some people never get over it!" he said with a self-deprecating grin.

"Who's the one who's not being serious now?" Taylor asked, but suddenly her eyes filled with tears. "Nothing I do ever turns out right."

"Taylor, you are like my parents' concept of 'perfect offspring.' Look at all the stuff you've accomplished! You came out of Spelman cum laude."

"Alan came out of Howard *summa* cum laude and then turned around and became a Rhodes scholar—"

"You're getting a master's degree at Seton Hall in art history. Do you know how often my parents batter me about grad school? It's all I hear! 'Why don't you stop this freelance journalist crap and get an MBA?'"

"—and graduates from Harvard Med, top of his class," Taylor continued as if she hadn't heard him.

"You're going to own your own art gallery someday! You'll get rich off of other people's talent and sweat! The American dream!"

"Like money means anything when your brother is out fighting AIDS, dysentery, or whatever the hell else he's fighting in the motherland."

James sat down beside her and took her hand. "Stop putting yourself down."

"I think I'm PMS-ing."

"Well, look on the bright side. At least you're PMS-ing. Did you hear about Lilac Jones? She'd probably give anything for a little PMS," he added, attempting to change the subject.

"Who?"

"Lilac Jones. The chick I took to the Links debutante ball. She's pregnant! And get this: Her daddy's law partner is the baby's father. According to my mother, who knows everything about everybody, his wife threw him out of the house because of her!"

Taylor's smile soured. "So, Lilac pulled a Pamela, huh?" James looked puzzled, and she clarified it. "Pamela? You know, as in the *new* Mrs. Alan Benedict. Pamela. My father's slut-girlfriend. The one he married a year and a half ago."

"*Oooh*, that Pamela." James cringed, but the reporter in him wouldn't let it go. "So, your father's new wife is pregnant?"

"Yeah. You mean you didn't hear? You've been following around too many dumb-ass rappers! They had the baby last year. I thought everybody knew about it by now. My mother's shrink had to put her on Prozac. Pamela sent out these tacky little announcements after the baby was born. Isn't that the most fucked-up thing you ever heard of? Hey, Pamela, dumb-ass whore, don't send birth announcements to your new husband's old married friends!"

"How is your mother doing now?"

"Better."

James gulped his wine and tried to think of something else to say. The reporter got the better of him again. "So, what did she have?"

"A girl."

"Sometimes a little sister can be a lot of fun," James said after a moment. "Like Sheila, my kid sister. Sometimes she's a pain in the ass, but basically I don't know what I would do without her."

"I had a sister once."

"Come on, Taylor, you never told me that. What happened?"

"She was my twin. She died the year after we were born. I lived. I never knew her. No big thing," she said with a shrug, and James regarded her skeptically because he knew Taylor's shrugs always meant something else.

"How come you never told me?"

"Nothing to tell," Taylor said, lighting another cigarette. "We were born. She died. That was it."

"Wow," James said, not being able to think of anything else to say and regarding Taylor with interest. "That's kind of a big deal. Did you ever read that stuff about how twins haunt each other from the grave? When I was a kid, I read this book about how one twin died and inhabited the body of the other and turned him evil. That was some wild shit! Did that ever happen—"

"Don't be stupid!" Taylor snapped, appalled at his insensitivity. But it was closer to the truth than she wanted to admit.

"What was her name?"

"Helena," Taylor said. "After my mother."

The fact that she had been born a twin and that her sister had died was a secret that Taylor kept to herself. She had learned about it inadvertently when she was four, eavesdropping on her mother who was talking to a friend.

"I had a sister?" Taylor screamed from her hiding place, and her mother had scolded her severely for listening to things she had no business knowing and quickly dropped the subject. But even at four Taylor was a bright child and bothered her mother until she told her the truth.

"And she died?"

Speechless, her mother nodded that it was true.

"What was her name?" Taylor asked.

"Helena," her mother answered.

"Like you?"

"Yes."

"Do you miss her?" Taylor asked, and her mother began to cry. "Do you want her instead of me?" Her mother, deep in her tears, had been unable to answer, and Taylor assumed that what she didn't hear was the truth.

Even at that age, she had sensed that part of her was missing. But it was unmentionable. She didn't want to make her mother cry, so she said nothing, and her dead twin sister, Helena, the one she knew her mother must have preferred because she had named her after herself, began to haunt her. Helena became her secret playmate. By the time she was eight, she would whisper the name to herself sometimes; it made her feel better just to say it. At eleven, she had seriously begun to ask herself why she had lived instead of her twin. Had she killed her sister in some way? There must be some reason why her death was never mentioned. Why God made her His choice. At twelve, Taylor became fascinated with death and the afterlife and she began to pray, kneeling at her bedside for hours, being the first to arrive at and the last to leave church on Sunday, muttering prayers under her breath whenever she thought she was alone.

She had always been, as her mother observed, a "passionate child," but her parents, alarmed by her fascination with mortality and the length and fervor of her prayers, took her to a therapist when she turned thirteen. It was to her therapist, whom she still spoke to every now and then, that she finally spoke her sister's name aloud and confronted her true feelings and fears.

By the time she was fifteen she had come to terms with Helena, and to her parents' relief, had become a predictably typical teenager. She was a highly motivated student in high school with good grades and a strong sense of self, and the ups and downs of her emotional life were not that much different from her friends'. She had also decided to become an artist and was encouraged by her parents to pursue her interest. In time, however, she realized she didn't have any real talent or passion for drawing, and that was the beginning of her goal to become an art historian. She was a junior docent in the local museum and a junior trustee for a small gallery. She loved learning about the lives of artists and was particularly drawn to stories about the ones with troubled pasts—Van Gogh, William H. Johnson, Jackson Pollock.

And sometimes, Helena, or the idea of Helena, still haunted her, and when she was depressed she asked herself some of those same tortured questions she had asked herself as a child. Those private thoughts gave a frightening edge to her depressions when they came, and she was haunted by the specter of her twin.

"Do you ever think about her?" James said, with no idea that he had stumbled upon a hidden demon.

"I think I am *definitely* PMS-ing," Taylor said, ignoring the question.

"Maybe if you tried to reach out to your dad and Pamela, you might be able to connect with her," James said. "I mean, your dad left your mom, not you."

"That's what he said, but I don't believe him." Taylor's voice was sulky.

"I mean maybe the new baby could be like the spirit of—" The look on Taylor's face made him stop mid-sentence; he knew he had made a terrible mistake.

"Leave it alone, James," she said, with no emotion in her voice.

"Well . . ." He tried to think of some kind of an apology, but couldn't come up with anything.

"Leave it alone!" Taylor lit another cigarette and inhaled deeply.

James sighed and left it alone and after a moment tried desperately again to change the subject. "So, what you got on for tonight?"

"Not much."

"Want to hang out? Vibe's throwing a big-deal party at Limelight. Ever since I did that piece on Kay-Joe, that rapper who drove his truck through the crowd at the Source Awards, I've been on their A-list."

"I don't know. I might have something else on."

"With Mr. Big?"

Taylor smiled, and James did, too, delighted to see her change of mood. "So, you're going out with him?"

"None of your business!"

"And where do I stand in all of this?"

"Where do you want to stand?"

James dropped down on one knee and sang a few verses of a popular song about getting married in a high falsetto voice.

Taylor interrupted his performance with a burst of laughter. "What the hell kind of marriage proposal is that? No, thank you. Find somebody else! If I'm going to get married, I want a real proposal."

"Like the kind you would get from Mr. Big?"

"Well, at least he wouldn't ask me like that."

"Money would probably have a big ol' ring from Tiffany's or some-where. Pull up in his long black Jag—"

"Mercedes!"

"In his long black Mercedes with his big-ass ring and make you his lit-tle wifey for the rest of your life! Real men leave that kind of macho shit behind in college, as far as I'm concerned. How old is he, anyway?"

"Thirty-six."

"Old-ass dude! He just wants some young fly chick to buy expensive toys for and show off. Don't you want more from a man than that?"

"Sounds pretty good to me."

"Careful! You're turning into Pamela! . . . I'm sorry," James added quickly, seeing the hurt in her eyes. "But think about it. What kind of relationship do you really have with this fool?"

"I don't know!"

"You left me for him, and you don't know?"

"I was never *with* you," Taylor corrected him. Still angry and begin-ning to get depressed, she went into the bathroom off the living room and slammed the door. Baffled, James sat for a moment and then knocked on the door.

"Taylor? Taylor Benedict? I'm sorry whatever I said to hurt your feel-ings. Come out and play, please. I miss you."

"No!"

"What's wrong?"

"I'm coming apart!" Taylor came back into the room and settled down in the chair across from him. James cocked his head with an expression somewhere between amusement and disbelief.

"You've got everything going for you, Taylor. You are a serious Black American Princess. Ms. B.A.P." he said. She avoided his eyes, and after a while he stood up. "Listen, I got a deadline to meet. I'd better split." He bent down and kissed her on the cheek. "Call me if you want to talk some more or check out the Vibe thing, but we'll have to take the subway. My ride is in the shop."

Taylor rolled her eyes, "Again? Trifling!" she muttered, but there was a smile on her face when she said it. It disappeared when James closed the door. She lit a cigarette, smoked it down to the filter, then lit another one.

She knew that most of what James had said was true. She knew she was smart, reasonably pretty, and her life was easy. Her father was putting her through grad school with a stipend to boot. She was privileged. A Black American Princess. Just like James said. But it was a sham.

No matter what she did or how much she accomplished, she always felt unworthy. As though she were taking something that really belonged to somebody else. Her therapist had told her once that she was experiencing a form of survivor's guilt for the loss of her sister, and Taylor knew that could be it. But knowing something in your head and feeling it in your heart were two different things.

Besides that, the whole mess between her father and mother had sent her into a tailspin. For one thing, she had reached the conclusion that her father really didn't care—probably never had cared—about what happened to her. He was a selfish, cruel man, she decided, and she made herself cut him out of her thoughts and mind. How could he leave them like he had? she asked herself. Deserting her, Alan, and her mother, Helena.

Taylor had always been in awe of her mother. Nothing ever seemed to shake her. As far as Taylor could see, Helena Benedict, always so stylishly thin and impeccably dressed, was a woman of steel, the unbendable Helena who spent her life doing and knowing the "right thing" to do in every situation. The right fork, the right spoon, the right friends, the right club, the right way to conduct one's life in the midst of chaos.

Taylor had always suspected that she was her mother's least favorite child. Helena, her namesake, would have been her favorite if she had lived. *She* was the one who would truly fit, and Taylor blamed herself for being the wrong kid in the right family. Her mother seemed to prefer her brother, and, early on, had taken over the raising of him. Alan always did what his mother said, followed her council, and his life—with its stellar achievements—reflected her effort. He was admired and successful, and her mother never missed a chance to mention his accomplishments to anyone who gave her half an ear.

On the other hand, Taylor had often heard her mother refer to her as a "contrary child," one who wore red to Sunday school and black to first grade; scorned Jack and Jill; refused to come out as a debutante the year she, Helena, chaired the event. If she was anyone's child, Taylor was her father's, who seemed amused by her rebellious nature. For one thing, she looked just like him—the same angular face, compact body, sardonic smile. He had named his son after himself, his wife had deemed it the "right" thing to do, but he'd fought her on the daughter who lived, and named her after his beloved father, who had died of a stroke the year he, Alan, finished law school. Taylor took after his side of the family, inheriting her father's spirit and stubbornness, along with his intelligence and ambition. She hated and loved the same foods, drank the same liquor, enjoyed going to the same places. Taylor was her father's daughter, and she was content to let her sister belong to Helena.

From the time she could understand what it meant, Taylor was aware that her father "fooled around," although nobody ever said it straight out. She knew him as well as she knew herself, and had decided long ago that if *she* were married to her mother—a woman so rigid, conventional, and unfailingly dedicated to the right and proper thing to do—she herself would have had no choice but to search elsewhere for the companionship and appreciation that Taylor was certain her mother was incapable of offering.

So, on that Sunday morning when Alan Benedict, always discreet until the end, blurted out that he had fallen in love with another woman and was leaving with her that afternoon, Taylor's world blew apart. She went into the bathroom and threw up for the next twenty minutes, then laid on her bed screaming and cursing her father with every dirty word she knew. And later, mouth sour from vomit, eyes swollen from crying, she had gone to her mother and hugged her with every bit of strength she had left. For the first time in her life, she and Helena were united. She hated her father and his soon-to-be bride with everything that was in her. He had betrayed her, tossing her loyalty back in her face and leaving her at the mercy of the woman she had deserted for him many years before. She swore on her sister's grave that she would never speak to him again. And she hadn't.

And Helena Benedict, the stalwart and strong with the backbone of steel, crumbled before her daughter's eyes, weeping, wailing, whispering confidences that Taylor listened to with the vengeance of a woman scorned. Their mutual hatred of Pamela, her father's beloved, bonded them as nothing else ever had.

Taylor became the dutiful daughter, available to her mother in a way that she had never been before, at her beck and call whenever she needed her. Yet she had been stunned by her mother's devastation. Within a week of her father's leaving, Helena Benedict lost all control. Her occasional glasses of wine became nightly guzzles of vodka, her mornings in bed stretched into afternoons. She cut out her weekly club meetings, avoided old friends and acquaintances, resigned from community boards to which she had just been invited, canceled lunches with women she'd known all her life. She was brought low by her husband's betrayal. But even as Taylor witnessed her mother crumble, she was amazed to find how much stronger she herself became.

Within two months of their quick divorce, Taylor learned to fill in the gaps. She called the plumber when the toilet was clogged, the electrician when the deck lights didn't work, the carpenter when the backyard fence came down. When money was short, she called her mother's lawyers, demanding that they force her father to pay the generous alimony that had been promised. As it had helped Taylor, therapy helped Helena Benedict, and she and her daughter began to talk. About why she had never confronted her husband about his infidelities. About what a fool she had been. But they spoke only about her mother's feelings. Never about Taylor's, or about what she felt. Taylor became the healing parent to her mother's injured child.

Why don't you go out, Mom? You can't just crawl into a hole and die. Don't let that bastard do this to you. It will do you some good to go out and prove to everybody that it didn't destroy you, Mom. Maybe you'll feel better if you get a facial, a massage, a pedicure. Don't let this get you down. Try not to get depressed. Did you tell your therapist about it? What did she say you should do? Don't let this get you down. You shouldn't let anybody make you feel this bad.

But sometimes Taylor was the one who needed healing. Some days she felt a raw, burning panic in the bottom of her belly, that made her shake so hard she didn't think she'd be able to stop. Sometimes she just wanted to crawl under the covers in the center of her bed and wait until daylight until her daddy came home. And she would torture herself with those old thoughts about her sister, whose life she feared she had taken. Then she would smoke a cigarette, like she did now, inhaling deeply, blowing it out, letting it go. Or smoke a joint. Open a bottle of wine and drink it until she got sick. And the fear and sorrow would stop. She would feel whole again and the dead sister that popped up whenever she felt weak and scared would go back into her grave.

When her phone rang again, Taylor glanced at the caller ID and prepared herself to give her mother another dose of support, but she was surprised and pleased by the strength she heard in her mother's voice.

"Hello, my dear. How are you doing, today?"

Taylor listened closely but there was no telltale slurring of words that meant she'd started the day with a Bloody Mary. She sounded almost like her old self. "You okay?"

"Fine, honey. I'm fine."

Taylor grinned, better now herself. "You sound great, Mom."

"I took that walk in the park like you said I should. It feels like spring, Taylor. I missed spring last year."

"We all did."

"What are you doing?"

"James just left."

"So, James Lawson is the man of the hour these days?"

"No."

"When are you going to introduce me to—"

"I'm not, Mom," Taylor said with slight irritation. That was one thing that hadn't changed; she still didn't want her mother in her business.

"I'm sorry," Helen said quickly.

There was an awkward pause, then Helen said, "I ran into Ana Reese-Mitchell the other day. She is such a lovely woman. I really enjoy talking to her. Have you spoken to her—"

"Another off-limit subject, Mom," Taylor said quickly. "Danny

Mitchell is a nice guy, but believe me, he's not for me. Try again." Although her words sounded cross, they were not meant to be. They could laugh at themselves and each other now, and it felt good to them both.

"How about dinner tonight, then? Is that a safe subject?" Helen asked.

Taylor thought for a moment, then said, "Not tonight, Mom. I might have something else going on."

"Your mystery man again?"

"You never give up, do you?"

Helena Benedict's deep-throated chuckle made her daughter smile. "Call me tomorrow?"

"Okay, Mom. I love you."

"I love you, too, baby."

Taylor hung up and dialed another number.

"I wondered when you were going to get around to calling me back," said Randall Hollis. "I called to ask you to dinner. Do I have to stand in line?"

"Depends on where you're taking me."

"How about Le Cirque?"

"April Fools, right? Nobody gets a reservation the night of."

"The maître d' owes me a favor."

"You just jumped to the front."

"Around eight o'clock?"

"Eight-thirty." Taylor settled back on the couch, a self-satisfied smile on her lips.

Chapter Four

It wasn't just that his penis had decided to play its own corny little April Fool joke on him. God knew it had happened to him before, so it wasn't about to freak him out. Hell, there wasn't a man alive who hadn't been able to get it up at one time or another. Even his uncle Reynard, the self-described player of all players, admitted to that. It was the one part of a man's body that wouldn't lie for him. His lips could grin when he hated somebody's guts; his hands could give a brother a high-five and still be plotting to cut his throat. But a cock always told the truth; if he wasn't feeling it, it wasn't about to cover his ass.

So, Randall blamed it on the wine they had for dinner and the stress of putting together the September show. He was tired, dead-dog tired, he said, and even though looking at her—thinking about her—usually got him hard as wood, it just wasn't happening tonight. Truth was he felt nothing. Nothing at all. No stirring anywhere within him.

Too many women. Too many damn women!

That was what Reynard would say. Uncle Reynard. His dead daddy's brother who tried to take over the male-bonding raising of him before he could pee straight. Reynard and his half-assed take on life, love, and the ladies was probably the reason he was in the shape he was in when it came to women.

It's a poor goddamn rat only got one hole!

Yeah, right, Reynard.

Lydia should share the blame, too. But mostly he blamed himself, because he couldn't seem to stay with one woman long enough to make anything work—including his penis, in this case.

Goddamn this shit!

He rolled over in bed, careful not to wake Taylor.

She'd been embarrassed for him, which made the whole thing worse. She wasn't old enough yet to understand the reality of men and their sex organs and that pity was the last thing a man wanted to see in a woman's eyes.

"What happened?" she said, not bothering to conceal her surprise when he went limp midstroke.

Wasn't it obvious? "Too much wine. It happens to the best of us," he said casually as he rolled off of her and kissed her throat.

"I thought wine made it better," she said in the jaded, whiskey-deep voice he'd found so enchanting the first time he heard it. She sat up and reached for a cigarette, which he hated because it reminded him of his mother but he didn't say anything, and that was another thing. Why was he making love to a woman he couldn't tell not to smoke in his own goddamn house?

He glanced at the clock. Four-thirty A.M. He must have drifted off to sleep at some point, but he was fully awake now. He considered getting up, reading the paper, which must be here by now, or *ARTNews*, which he'd left on his desk. He thought about working out in his exercise room, maybe doing a couple of miles on the treadmill, lifting some weights until he was tired enough to go back to sleep or awake enough to start the day.

Taylor stirred, and he studied her face in the darkness. She was a pretty little thing. Captivating face. Too damn young. Bare of makeup and expression, her face was as smooth and fresh as a kid's. He liked her body, though, which was athletic and angular, quite different from the soft, voluptuous ones he was usually drawn to. She looked almost boyish, hardly any breasts, which usually turned him off, but didn't in this case because she had a black woman's classic ass, big and round. He liked the women he slept with to look and feel like women, but Taylor was tough in an almost masculine world-weary way that said she could always give as good as she got. She seemed invulnerable, and he liked that. She was self-possessed in a way that only a naïve or very sophisticated woman would be. Ana Reese-Mitchell was sure of herself, too, but she'd won her self-confidence the hard, old-fashioned way. Taylor was different; hers came from a sense of entitlement, of always getting whatever she wanted whenever she wanted it without a fight. He hadn't seen it much in black women, and he found it fascinating.

She looked good, too, with a style that was casual but obviously expensive—Helmut Lang jeans, Prada tops, Gucci loafers. Her style called attention to her and whoever's arm she was on, which was his lately, and he was vain enough to enjoy it. He liked going places with her, liked the way other men stared at her. He liked the feel of her firm young body with nothing dependent about it. She was smart, too, which he valued in women; from the first he'd been drawn to that.

He'd been invited to lecture at the graduate school she attended, by Josh Littleman, an old friend who had given up trying to make a living in the world of art for a steady, dependable life in academia. He smiled when he thought about his old friend. Joshua's life seemed settled now in every way. Married five years. Three-year-old son. Baby on the way. Nice suburban house in a nice suburban neighborhood. Who would have thought that could happen to wild-ass Josh Littleman. Wilder even than he. What had tamed him? They joked about the "new Josh Littleman" over lunch before his lecture, and he'd been surprised how much calmer Josh seemed. But was he happier? It was hard for Randall to tell, and Josh would never admit it if he wasn't.

After lunch, Randall had given his usual spiel on the business of art to Joshua's class of earnest twenty-somethings eager to become curators, museum directors, consultants, and dealers. He noticed Taylor Benedict immediately, one of four black students in a class of forty. She sat in the front row, her gaze so intense it made him uncomfortable. But her questions were astute and sophisticated. She knew what she was talking about, and he liked that. After his talk, she told him she'd met him several months before at a lecture he'd given at her mother's club. He smiled politely, but he had no memory at all of meeting her before.

Oddly enough, at first his attraction to her hadn't been physical.

Their first "date," if you could call it that, had been a professional one. She and three fellow students came to his loft on a Sunday afternoon to view his collection. He had taken them out for drinks afterward, and that had been the end of it. Except he found himself thinking about her later; he was curious about her. So, when she called him to ask if she could interview him during semester break for her master's thesis, he'd said yes without hesitation. She came to his loft, tape recorder, pad, pen in hand, and fifteen minutes later they were in bed. That had been in December, four months ago. He'd seen her at least once a week since then.

Their relationship was loose and uncomplicated. He had no idea if he was the only man she was seeing, and he couldn't say that he cared, which spoke to the depth of their connection. She never asked him about the other women in his life, which was a relief since he didn't feel like explaining himself or lying about them. Things were simple. They met for dinner or drinks, usually at some costly restaurant or trendy bar, talked for a while about art or current events, then went back to his place—rarely to hers—and made love. Always more successfully than tonight.

But he had no idea what she thought about him. He didn't know if she enjoyed being with him or really even liked him. He suspected that he was just a means to some end, and he occasionally wondered what that end was and why that didn't disturb him.

She stirred again, as if she were having a bad dream. He gently touched her face. He knew nothing about her, not if her father was alive or if she had any siblings or what made her cry. She kept her distance. Like a man does with a woman he doesn't trust. Like he had always done.

Another trophy, Randall?

He could almost hear the amused contempt in Medora's voice. He stared at the ceiling, his thoughts now on Medora. She was always somewhere in his mind, he realized, hovering around the edges of everything he did, and she had been for as long as he'd known her. There were so many things he loved about Medora: the way she tipped her head to the side when she worked; the tilt of her nose; the hint of laughter that was always in her voice. Why couldn't she simply accept the fact that commitment to *anyone* was a leap of faith he wasn't yet able to make? Didn't she know that much about him? T.W., her own father, was like that, too. But maybe that was part of the problem.

He saw bits of Medora in every woman he knew. Even this one, Taylor Benedict, reminded him of Medora. Her spirit was the same, that fierce streak of independence and stubbornness. But she was secretive and controlling in a way that Medora could never be.

So what was he doing lying here beside Taylor? Why the hell wasn't Medora enough?

My problem is you, and *we both know it.*

Medora had called that one right. He felt a stab of self-disgust. He was greedy and selfish and everything else she'd said, but what the hell was he supposed to do about it at this point in his life?

Have you ever really loved anybody except yourself?

He wasn't even sure about himself.

It ain't nothing but a party, boy. Ain't nothing but a party!

He thought of his uncle again and was surprised by the rush of tenderness he felt. Reynard had always been proud of him, especially when he'd finished school and tried to make something of himself, like his daddy never did. But anything he did would be better than his daddy was, according to Lydia. Not even Reynard could fall that low in her eyes.

Why the hell had he told Ana those lies about his old man?

Lying to women came easily to him, sometimes too easily. Though it was better than a truth that half the time he didn't fully understand himself. But there was no excuse for him lying to Ana like he had, bragging about his father. Son of a bitch didn't even bother to marry Lydia when all was said and done. Probably had ten kids spread around the city. He should ask Reynard about that sometimes. The best thing his daddy ever did for him was die.

According to Lydia.

Why had he lied to Ana? Even about his age. That was a new one, adding two years instead of taking them off.

She could be good for him, there was no doubt about that, better than he was for her, better than he was for any of the women he was involved with. Or loved.

Just like his damned father. Shot in the head by some woman's jealous husband two months after he was born.

Sometimes I don't think I'll ever recover from losing him.

That was the truth, though. Maybe that was the goddamn truth.

He thought about the lie again and felt ashamed. He thought about the cop, too, the smirk on his face, his swagger, the contempt in his voice. There wasn't another woman he knew who could have handled that like Ana had, not even Medora, who would have cussed the bastard out, and they both would have ended up in jail. Ana, so embarrassed to be the "older woman." But age didn't have a damn thing to do with anything. He sure as hell didn't care. She was a beautiful woman, with a spirit that touched him. Some of the oldest, hardest women he knew were under thirty.

Like this one, maybe. Like this young Taylor Benedict.

Or maybe she wasn't. Maybe he had her completely wrong. He didn't know one way or the other. Maybe his dick did, though, in its own particular form of rebellion. Maybe that was the truth of tonight.

What did she see in him? he wondered again. A mentor, maybe. Why be kind to himself? What did he really have to teach somebody, even about his profession, which was mostly luck and grinning in somebody's face when you wanted to slap it. It was an ugly, racist business filled with ugly, petty people, and sometimes he felt like a high-class pimp, making his living off somebody else's sweat. And sometimes he felt like a high-class whore. Like the time with Alexandra Brookings.

God, he hadn't thought about her in a while.

He'd been new to the business, and one of his older, more cynical colleagues had hinted that one way a few of the male dealers got rich female collectors to buy was to offer a little something on the side. Like what? he asked, genuinely puzzled. What do you think? his friend said with a smirk that hinted that a young, good-looking black man like himself had that exotic "something" that some lonely, rich white woman just might want to sample. I know more than one lonely woman whose husband has emotionally abandoned her for somebody half her dress size and age. They'll beg you for it, why not give the client what she wants? his friend had advised. And so he had when Alexandra came along, who was as vulnerable and generous as anybody he had ever met in his life.

She wasn't a pretty woman, but she was kind, and when she laughed he could see how a man could fall in love with her. How he could fall in love with her. She genuinely enjoyed sex, which a surprising number of women whom he'd been meeting at that point in his life didn't. He liked to think that at least she'd gotten that much out of their relationship. That and the art, which for the most part had ended up being far more valuable than when she bought it. He'd sold her as much art as her rich husband would pay for, and a bit of himself along with it, and he had cared about her in his own way; he couldn't have made love to her if he hadn't. He wasn't that much of a whore. Not yet, anyway. But he knew it was mainly her money, even though occasionally he tried to convince himself it wasn't.

But this little Taylor didn't know that side of the business. She just saw the glamour of it—the openings, the money, the high culture and style. She just saw the beauty and purity of artists and what they did. She didn't know yet what he knew, that more than one up-and-coming artist had slept her way into some rich man's collection or some high-profile dealer's stable. She didn't know yet that sex could be as much a part of the equation as power and betrayal. She probably thought he could take her where she wanted to go. And maybe he could, an old dude with bucks and a lot of rich friends. Somebody like her daddy or her daddy's friends.

Or maybe she was just what she seemed—a young woman who liked him for who he was, except she had no idea who that was. Medora was the only woman who knew every wrinkle and wart. And she had thrown his sorry ass out.

He touched the curve of Taylor's cheek as gently as a father might, then got out of bed, careful not to wake her. He searched under the covers for his briefs, pulled them on and went into the living room. Closing the door behind him, he sat down on the couch to watch daybreak. It had been a long time since he'd done that, just sit and watch the sun rise or set. He closed his eyes and listened. Somebody took the elevator to the loft downstairs; a siren sounded outside his window; kids, probably not that much younger than Taylor, laughed and talked on their way back home. They sounded high on something, ecstasy more than likely. It had been acid when he was a kid. Weed. Peyote. Mostly weed, usually smoked with Medora.

Daylight filtered into the skylights and long, narrow windows and reflected off the stark white walls. His loft was austere, the furniture mostly black and subdued shades of gray and blue. There was little color except that which came from the paintings highlighted by subtly placed spotlights. Against a far wall were oak flat files, where he kept works on paper. Larger paintings were stored in an area adjacent to his loft. All of the art on his wall was by artists he represented, much of it Medora's. There were several large, bold oils, two or three pastels, and a delicate watercolor, a medium she rarely worked in.

In a narrow ebony bookcase in a far corner of the large room was a delicate pen-and-ink drawing she'd done of him several years ago. She'd sketched it quickly, but it was carefully rendered, capturing not so much his likeness but the hidden parts of him, his sensitivity and wariness. He picked up the drawing and studied it for a few moments.

My problem is you and we both know it.

He remembered the last time they'd been together and thought for a moment he would weep. He stopped himself. The truth was he loved Medora Jackson as much as he was capable of loving any woman, he was sure of that.

As much as he was capable.

He thought again about Ana, her yielding softness, the feel of her body against his, and the memory of it swept him in a rush of excitement. He chuckled at how quickly he had become aroused. Maybe he should have thought of Ana when he made love to Taylor. Maybe that was the secret to never going limp when you were with a woman: always think of the one you made love to the week before. What was that old saying about a hard dick having no guilt? That one was from Reynard, too, no doubt.

But where did it end?

Most people our age have roots, kids, mortgages, and we're still fucking around.

"The hell with you, Medora. Do whatever the hell you want to do," he said, startled by the sound of his voice in the empty room.

He went back into his bedroom, glanced at Taylor, who had spread out across the whole bed, slipped on some sweatpants and a T-shirt, and went into the small room off the living room, which he used as an exercise room. He ran four miles on his treadmill without breaking a sweat, bench-pressed more weight than he was used to doing, then laid out on a mat on the floor, with his eyes closed, trying to catch his breath. He showered quickly, slipped on clean underwear and a black terry cloth robe, and went into his galley kitchen to make some breakfast. The phone rang as he was squeezing orange juice. He glanced at the clock, which read 6:29 A.M., and then at the caller ID. *Shit,* he said to himself as he picked up the phone.

"What are you doing up this early?" He forced his voice to sound cheerful, but the tension in his hands put a lie to his voice.

"Can't a mother call her son just to say hello?" Without realizing he had done it, he drew in a breath. She called him son only when she wanted something she knew he didn't want to give her.

"How are you feeling this morning, Lydia?"

"Are you there by yourself?"

"No, Lydia. I'm not."

"Who is it this time? That sloppy bitch who thinks she can paint? She wouldn't be anything without you, Randy, nothing without you. You know that, don't you?"

"Stop it, Lydia!" He screamed into the phone, losing control. He tried to regain it, his fingers tightened. "Why do you hate Medora so much?" He knew the answer. It was because she knew how deep his feelings ran for Medora, and she was jealous. It was because Medora was more talented than she and lived the life that she once dreamed of living. She had hated Medora from the moment she laid eyes on her.

At the time, he'd had no sense of how possessive his mother was. Medora was the first girl he had brought to meet her, and he was certain that Lydia would like her as much as he did. Medora was shy, like her. She wrote poetry, listened to jazz, and read serious novels. And she loved art as much as he did. As much as Lydia did.

They met in a restaurant. Some sixth sense had urged him to take Medora there instead of to their apartment. He knew that Lydia could be overbearing, and he'd hoped that this neutral place would put them on equal footing. But the moment Lydia walked into the restaurant—dressed to kill in a chic black suit, her long hair hanging down her back like a girl's— he knew that "equal footing" was out of the question. She was dressed like a rival, and Medora, in worn jeans and an old sweater, was defenseless.

When she spoke to Medora, he could hear the bite of sarcasm in her voice, and he could see the cold disapproval in her eyes as she took Medora's measure. He had never seen his mother so haughty or cruel, and later at home, she had picked Medora apart with a venom that left him doubting his own feelings toward her. Such had been Lydia's power.

"So it is her, isn't it?" Lydia asked him now; her voice was flirtatious, almost seductive.

"No, it's not. But why don't you mind your own damn business, Mother."

"So, is it mother, now that I'm sick and dying, that I can't fight back! You are such a fuckup, Randy. You are such a fuckup!"

"Jesus Christ!" He whispered the curse to himself and then pulled in his breath, only to let it go again as he tried to get hold of his thoughts, his feelings. "Why have you called me at six o'clock in the morning? What is wrong?" Frustration mixed with both exasperation and concern was in his voice. Lydia began to cry.

"Why can't we be like we were, Randy? Why can't you treat me like you did when you were a boy? My boy?" There was a pause and then she started again, her voice angrier now. "You are acting just like him, you lousy son of a bitch. Just like him."

Is she fucking crazy? he asked himself as he always did whenever she lit into him like this. After all these years, why was she still harping on that sorry-ass dead loser? He had heard it so many times he didn't even flinch. He closed his eyes, defending himself against her anger, making himself smile as he continued to squeeze the oranges that were lined up on the counter in front of him.

"Have you taken your pain pills this morning, Lydia? Or were you too drunk to find them?" His voice was needling and unkind, and he wished too late that he hadn't said it.

"What do you care?"

"Lydia . . ." He was about to plead with her like he would plead with a recalcitrant, angry child. "If you don't take the pills, the pain builds up, and then you can't do anything about it. You have to take them every four hours like the doctor told you to, you have to—"

"I've been up all night, Randy. I'm scared, Randy. I'm so scared."

He put the knife down and sat down on the stool nearest the table. She began to cry in gasps that came from so deep inside her he could feel them within his own body. He thought about Ana for some reason and her son and the way he knew that she loved him. He wondered what she would make of his mother, what she would think of a woman like Lydia.

"Lydia, please stop crying," He closed his eyes and tried to will her to stop, remembering the times he used to do that when he was a kid. But it hadn't worked then and it didn't work now. "Please, Lydia. Please."

"Will you come to see me? You never come to see me. You never do, Randy. Never. Never."

"I was there yesterday, Lydia. Don't you remember?"

"I don't remember."

"Yes, you do."

"It's not enough."

Nothing is enough, he thought. "I talked to Mrs. Washington yesterday. You remember, the nice lady who lives next door? She's a nurse's aide over at Central, and she said she can look in on you. Maybe I can hire her to—"

"No! She talks too goddamn much."

"At least give her a chance."

"I said no!"

"I'll come today," he said. "I'll be over some time this afternoon."

"You promise? You promise?" She sounded like a little girl, a little girl pleading with her daddy.

"Yeah." He measured coffee into the glass container. Rinsed off the French press. Put the kettle to boil. He rinsed and dried two cups and placed them across from each other on the bar.

"When? When, Randy?"

"As soon as I can, Lydia." His breath left his body, caught somewhere in the top of his chest, and for a moment he couldn't breathe.

"When?"

"Lydia, when I can get there." He cracked six eggs into a bowl and whisked them for a moment and then put them aside. "I've got to go," he said.

"No!"

"I'll see you later, I promise." He hung up before she could say anything else, then he collapsed on the kitchen stool, dropping his head into his hands.

When he was a kid, he had envied those friends who had fathers in their lives, strong men who, he assumed, taught them what men needed to know to survive in this world—how to deal with white folks, how to face down a man without threatening him, how to leave a woman without breaking her heart. He envied that bonding that took place over baseball, beer, and bawdy jokes, and he was certain that it had given his friends an advantage in life that he could never have.

He knew differently now. He had the advantage. He had grown up with no myth about male superiority; he knew the truth. Women were the stronger sex, the ones with the power to create or destroy with a lifted eyebrow, titter, or sneer. Lydia had taught him that. And she was teaching him still.

"Randall? Are you all right?" Taylor touched his shoulder and he jumped. He had forgotten she was here.

"Yeah, I'm fine." He got it together quickly, grinned. "Feel like some breakfast?"

"I never have more than coffee and a cigarette," she said, but then glanced at the juice, and the eggs that sat in the bowl by the stove. "Wow! A real breakfast with eggs and everything? For me? Sure, okay." She tipped her head coyly to the side, giving a charming grin, and without thinking much about it, he kissed her on the side of her lips where the grin stopped, then led her into the bedroom to make love to her.

But she was the farthest thing from his mind.

I've

Got You

Under

My Skin

Chapter Five

Medora was good at denying things, and this was one thing she didn't want to face. The very thought of it made her nauseated, which on a bad day convinced her that her worst fear had come to pass, and on a good one made her blame the Chinese, Mexican, or Indian food she'd eaten the night before. It was easy to dismiss the signs. Spring, a promise in early March, was a reality by late April, and it thrilled her simply to step outside and sniff the air, which was another thing: Her sense of smell, like that of taste, was amazingly keen. By the end of the month, there was no denying the obvious; it had even become evident to others. The elderly woman downstairs, for instance, who still remembered the building when it had been a sewing factory took one look at Medora on her way to Easter Mass and uttered a hearty congratulations.

"For what?" Medora asked, pulling in her stomach and straightening her back. The woman tossing her a conspiratorial wink and hurried on her way. Medora managed to forget the woman's comment the way she did the period that didn't come. Her menses had always been erratic, she reminded herself. Her periods came and went, sparse or heavy, with a will of their own. Even birth control pills failed to control them. Hadn't they fooled her more than once with their willfulness? And, anyway, she was on the pill, which was supposed to be infallible. Ninety-nine percent sure. How could she possibly be that 1 percent? Her luck couldn't be that bad! But by the end of the month, when there wasn't the slightest trace of red, Medora had to face the truth.

"My body is paying me back!" she screamed that Saturday afternoon after she had checked the panty liner for the fourth time in an hour and found nothing. She went to her bedroom, fell down on her bed, and muttered to herself, "It is paying me back for the times I made love to that man, knowing how I felt about him, and convinced myself it meant less than it did. For being thirty-five years old and not having found some solid, sensible man to live a solid, sensible life with. For drinking wine, smoking grass, and acting like a heathen!"

"Heathen" was the word Aunt Tillie used to describe T.W., and Medora, staring at her bedroom ceiling, spat it out with the same vengeance her aunt did.

Yet how could she *not* have conceived? she wondered. They had made love that Valentine's Day with so much sweetness. How could it *not* have resulted in something sacred? That last kiss should have told her.

She went to her easel to try to paint, which she always did when she was upset. For as long as she could remember, sketching or painting had put her at ease, connected her to her center. She began to work on the painting she now thought of as *Lightning Tree*, the one she had described to T.W. on her birthday, and she was pulled into her work. Medora was never sure where a piece would take her. She'd start at one point, usually with a vague sense of its meaning, and end up going in a different direction, and such was the case with this one. When she did her first sketch, she thought it would be a study of a tree killed by a natural occurrence, but as she worked, the shape and colors—the ochre, brown, and green—brought out hidden feelings and new associations. When she'd visited the tree again, she'd noticed that tiny sprouts had taken root within the dead limb, which had particular resonance. There was new life hidden in the heart of the tree; the lightning had simply brought it forth.

After a while, she stopped painting. There were too many feelings brewing inside her. So, she made herself a cup of Red Zinger tea with wildflower honey (how the whole thing began, she ruefully reminded herself), sat down in her rocker, and rocked. The hibiscus in the tea had a particularly pungent bite. The honey, too, was especially good; the sweetness so intense she imagined she could taste the nectar that drew the bees into the flowers. But her new sensitivity to taste and smell just depressed her.

If I were to allow this condition to continue, she said to herself, this will be my life for the next seven months: herbal tea and honey; skim milk and vegetables; whole wheat bread and brown rice; nuts and fruits. No more espresso, wine, or the occasional joint. No more wild late nights, brandy after dinner, pigging out on chocolates. So much for forbidden pleasures except the one she had decided she needed least—Randall Hollis. They would be tied together for eternity. Her carefully made decision washed down the drain.

"Fuck!" she screamed in frustration.

If you'd done less of that, you wouldn't be in this predicament, she could hear Aunt Tillie—eyebrows furrowed, lips in a scolding line—utter in disgust.

She went to her bedroom, stripped off her clothes, and examined herself full-face and in profile in her mirror. Her breasts were different. She held each one separately. They were heavier. How could she not have noticed that before? The circles around the nipples were darker, more pronounced.

"I'm pregnant!" she said, repeating the words until they sank in. She sat back down in her rocking chair and cried.

Over the next few days, Medora was swept with a mixture of emotions. The strongest by far was panic, which traveled from the tips of her bright red toenails to her wild hair, which she didn't bother to comb. Next in line was fear. And then came self-disgust.

"How could I have let this happen?" she moaned repeatedly. "How could I have been so sloppy?"

And it wasn't the first time, she reminded herself, which made her feel worse. Although many years had passed between this unplanned pregnancy and the last, and she could dismiss that first time as a youthful misstep, she remembered the details vividly.

She was twenty-three, and the father had been the first man she'd made love to, besides Randall. That situation had been quickly remedied. She was far more concerned with her own life, which she was determined to live with as few encumbrances as possible, to mull over the taking of an unborn one. The pregnancy had been a mistake, pure and simple, not quite a one-night stand but close, and she couldn't think of anything more humiliating than going to a near stranger and dramatically announcing that she was carrying his child. So she had an abortion and never saw the man again. It was an occasional source of shame to her now to think that she hadn't bothered to tell him, that when she'd put her personal integrity on a scale with personal embarrassment, the balance had tipped in favor of her saving face. But regardless of what he had felt, she knew she would have done what she had to do, and had not been haunted by it. And she would do what she had to do this time as well, and not be haunted by this one either, despite the difference in circumstances. So, three days after she admitted the truth to herself, she bought a pregnancy test, which confirmed what she already knew. The next day she called her gynecologist for the name of an abortion clinic.

But random and sundry things kept getting in her way.

First it was the weather. She was on her way to her appointment at the clinic and was waylaid in the park. The lilacs that grew there reminded her of the White Shoulders perfume Aunt Tillie wore, and the scent of them that spring day sent her into reverie. So she sat on a bench lost in her thoughts as the sun warmed her face and made her too lazy to move.

The next day it rained, which inspired her to make a pot of lentil soup, her favorite since childhood. Its smoky comfort reminded her of her mother, who would make it for her when she was sick. After all these years, the smell of it still brought her mother back. She would serve it garnished with bits of crisp bacon in a bright blue bowl edged by triangles of thickly buttered wheat toast. Medora, feeling cherished, would sip tea sweetened with honey and weakened with milk in a green china cup while her mother sat in a nearby chair gazing at her lovingly, her hands loosely clasped in her lap.

Fresh thyme replaced the bacon in Medora's soup this rainy afternoon, and as she gulped it down she contemplated her situation. Counting from Valentine's Day, she knew she must be almost three months pregnant. Time was running out. But when she thought about the month of conception she invariably thought about the month of birth, which would be late October or November, the month her mother was born, and that thought made her cry. But everything seemed to make her cry these days. Even writing her own name, "Medora," which her mother would always remind her meant *mother's gift*, which she said she was, would bring tears to Medora's eyes. "I won't miss this crying part of it," she thought one night as she sniffled over the death of a polar bear cub on the Discovery Channel.

Yet still she waited, making and breaking appointments until two weeks had passed and the receptionist at the clinic, whose voice she now recognized, said, "I think you better think this thing over, honey."

"But I've made up my mind," Medora explained.

"I'm not supposed to be talking to a client like this," the woman continued, lowering her voice to a confidential whisper. "But how old are you, anyway?"

"I'm thirty-five. Old enough to make a decision." Medora tried to sound like a mature responsible adult.

"Thirty-five!" The woman sounded surprised. "I guess you should know what you're doing, but it don't sound to me like you've made up your mind."

Medora sucked her teeth at the woman's assessment but knew she was right. So she mulled it over yet one more time, trying to figure all the angles. She would have to make a decision, one way or the other, within a week at the very latest, and yet she still wasn't sure. The wise thing to do, she decided, was to seek advice. So, she turned to her three close friends Eliza, Devlin, and Trudy, who had been in similar situations and had come out on the other side.

Medora started with Eliza, the closest of the three. Eliza's live-in boyfriend had deserted her the month their four-year-old son, Eli, was born. Medora hadn't spoken to Eliza at length since the call on her birthday last month. Sipping coffee and munching an almond biscotti, she listened patiently as Eliza filled her in on the various details of her life. During a break in the conversation, she asked as casually as she could, "Is raising Eli by yourself as hard as it looks?" Eliza frowned before answering,

and Medora noticed for the first time the specks of gray that were generously spread throughout her friend's short natural hair.

"It's harder than it looks," Eliza said, pulling her son on her lap and
kissing his head, implying by the gesture that he was worth every effort. Eli,
who had his mother's color and eyes, shoved a broken cookie from a soiled
paper bag in Medora's direction. Medora pretended to take a bite and dis-
creetly placed it underneath her napkin. "Remember the day Lucifer fired
me?" "Lucifer" was the nickname the friends had given the mean-spirited
owner of the health food store where Eliza worked. "That was the worst day
of my life. Eli had an ear infection, which had been bothering him all night
and was why I'd been late for work in the first place.

"I came home, begged the baby-sitter to wait until the end of the week
when, lying like a thief, I promised I'd pay her. Then I just sat and stared
like a fool at my screaming baby. I had no money. No health insurance. No
mama. No daddy. No man. And now, thanks to my big mouth and Lucifer's
nastiness, no job! All I had was a sick baby who was the be-all and end-all of
my existence. I understood for the first time the meaning of desperation."

"What did you do?"

"You mean, what stopped me from taking my kid and jumping out the
window? Eli's eyes, that's what! I looked at this child, whose eyes were the
saddest things I'd ever seen in my life, and realized it was up to me to make
them smile again. So, I took my last thirty bucks, the brooch my mama
gave me before she died, and that worthless engagement ring from his
daddy and took a cab to the emergency room. Apparently it was a light
day in the pediatrics department because the head doctor, this fine-
looking brother, was on the floor.

"Anyway, I guess he could tell how desperate and broke I was because
he arranged it so I wouldn't have to pay for anything and gave me free
medicine for my baby's ear. On the way back home, I took the brooch and
ring and pawned them. Then I went to the market, bought enough kidney
beans, lentils, and black-eyed peas for a month, and enough flour and
yeast for four loaves of bread. The next morning, with recovering baby
and freshly baked peace offerings in hand, I went to see Lucifer and begged
him to give me back my job."

"You know all the regulars who came in that day gave him hell because he fired you. That man didn't know goldenseal from ginseng," Medora said.

"I figured as much. He even gave me a raise, such as it was." Both women laughed at the memory of that day. Eliza, sipping her coffee, carefully studied her friend's face. "So, why all these questions?"

"I just need to know."

"Why?"

"Let's just leave it—"

"Did you stick to your decision about Randall?" Eliza interrupted her, cutting to the chase, as she usually did.

"I told you I was going to put him out of my life, and I did."

"For real?"

"Yeah. Our relationship—and I use that word loosely—was going nowhere."

"I think in his fashion he loves you."

"'In his fashion' doesn't matter anymore. I'm sick of it."

"Do you still love him?"

"Well . . ." Medora dropped her eyes.

Eliza, studying her friend's face, said, "That 'well' was followed by what my writer friends would call a pregnant pause."

"Can you tell?" Medora straightened up and pulled in her stomach without realizing she'd done it.

"Are you?" Eliza's eyes grew big with surprise. Medora sighed. "Should I offer congratulation or sympathy?"

"I don't know yet."

"How pregnant are you?"

Medora sighed again. "In February. Valentine's Day, to be exact. Do you believe that?"

Eliza stifled a giggle, and Medora, caught up in her friend's reaction, chuckled, too. "Well, it's better than Halloween," Eliza added after a moment. "Then you were pregnant and didn't know it when we spoke on your birthday."

"Right."

"Have you told him yet?"

"The father?"

"Randall, I assume."

"No, I haven't told him yet."

"Medora! You're telling me before him? I know we're friends, girl, but—"

"Whatever I decide, it will have nothing to do with Randall Hollis," Medora said with a bitterness that made her friend cock her head to the side with concern in her eyes.

"But Randall is the father. The baby is half his, too. You owe him that."

"I don't owe that trifling Negro nothing!" Medora said, bristling with anger.

"I'm going to leave that one alone," Eliza said, taking a sip of coffee.

Two days later, Medora sat cross-legged on a giant pillow in the Manhattan loft of her friend Devlin Townsend, who had lost his partner, Delta, to AIDS two years before. Their adopted five-year-old daughter, Jasmine, who was small for her age but smart as the dickens, sat nearby studiously working on a puzzle.

"Be careful what you say, baby, she may look like she's busy, but she doesn't miss a trick." Devlin leaned toward Medora, emphasizing his words with a wink. Devlin had grown up in Maine, and Medora was always struck at how very "white" he looked. He was a tall, handsome man who wore his ash-blond hair in a traditional prep cut. He leaned toward L. L. Bean shirts, tailored slacks, and blue cardigan sweaters that matched his cornflower blue eyes. Years of living with Delta Tourney, however, had changed his Maine accent into a rumbling Georgia twang.

"What's the most difficult time you've had as a single parent?" Medora asked during a lull in their conversation.

"Losing Delta," Devlin said without a moment's hesitation, and Medora sighed as the image of her old friend came into her mind. Delta Tourney was a charming, loudmouthed, decidedly "black" sculptor who

Medora had known since college. She could remember vividly the day Delta and Devlin had brought Jasmine home. She was a biracial child with special needs whose hearing aid covered most of her tiny beige ears, and whose glasses were nearly as thick as those worn by T.W. She walked with a slight limp and you occasionally had trouble understanding her, but she was one of the most loving children Medora had ever met.

Devlin poured more wine for himself and glanced at Medora's still-full glass with a raised eyebrow. "Not a sip, Medora? You're the one who turned us on to rioja."

"Not tonight." She spread some Cheddar cheese on a cracker and took a bite.

Devlin turned to his daughter. "Grown-up time, Jas. Didn't Miss Williams give you some homework this afternoon?"

"Can I do it later?"

"Now!" Devlin said firmly, pointing toward her bedroom, and after a mild protest, Jasmine obediently headed to her bedroom, leaving the door cracked.

"Shut it, sugar," Devlin said without missing a beat, and Medora chuckled as the door closed. "Sometimes I think that hearing aid makes her hear twice as well as the rest of us," he whispered to Medora. "I'll be in to look it over, that work you're doing," he said to Jasmine, then turned his attention back to Medora. "You know that Delta was the one who really wanted to adopt. I was completely against it. Pissed off about it, as a matter of fact. Not me. I wanted him to myself; I didn't want to share him. I didn't think a child could add anything to our lives but chaos. Particularly a child who needed so much help."

"But you know as well as I do that there was nobody in this world who could refuse that man anything he wanted, and Delta Tourney sure wanted that little girl. So there we were, two aging queens pushing a stroller down the middle of Broadway. And I loved every minute of it. Those years before Delta got sick were some of the best we ever had, and even afterward, dealing with his illness, Jasmine was a comfort to me, to both of us. She still is. I don't think I could have made it without her. Of that I'm sure."

Medora dropped her eyes to her untouched wine before she glanced back at her friend's face, which she knew was filled with the anguish that had been there in the last days of his partner's life.

"Delta used to say that he had come to terms with his own father through raising Jasmine. Jackson Tourney was a brutal old bastard, but my daddy was brutal, too, in his own way, with his indifference and hostility. Raising Jasmine brought out in both of us what neither of us had gotten from our fathers. Delta, with his gentleness, and me . . ." He chuckled self-consciously. "I listen to every word that girl says and answer her before it gets out her mouth good. Nothing she says is insignificant to me. Delta's mama, bless her soul, used to say you come to terms with your parents through your kids, for better or worse, and I guess there's some truth in it. Children give you back tenfold what you expect; they fill in those gaps in your life you had no idea you had."

He studied Medora's face as he sipped his wine, trying to read what she didn't want him to see. "So, why don't you tell me what madness *really* made you brave the crowds on the subway to settle on my SoHo couch this Tuesday afternoon?" Medora cut off a piece of cheese and after a nibble or two shared why she had come.

"What have the two of you decided to do?" Devlin nodded his head in a vague way toward the window. Devlin's loft was a stone's throw from that of Randall Hollis, and his casual gesture told Medora he had quickly guessed the identity of the father.

"He is irrelevant to my plans."

"If you decide to have the baby, he'll become very relevant very quickly, believe me."

Without replying and defying the warnings about early pregnancy and alcohol, Medora drained her wineglass and gave Devlin a defiant look. Devlin shook his head sorrowfully.

So, are you going to have it?" asked Trudy Douglass the next day. Trudy had been a friend since high school. She was a willowy woman with an extraordinarily pretty face. Her skin was what they used to call café au lait—a pretty brown with a splash of cream, and her dark auburn hair floated around her head in an unruly halo. Medora, settling comfortably on the low-slung couch nestled against the wall, didn't reply. She picked up the copy of *ARTNews* on the coffee table and leafed through to a folded page, which featured a two-page spread on Trudy and her work.

"Nice," she said with admiration edged with envy as she skimmed the article. "Why didn't you tell anybody you were going to be in it? If they were doing a piece on me, I would have been e-mailing all over town."

Trudy shrugged as if it didn't matter one way or the other. "If she were still around, my mother would be proud," she said as she took the magazine from Medora and studied her image. "They should have used another shot. This one makes me look fat." She put the magazine down and turned back to Medora. "If you're going to get rid of it, don't wait too long, like I did."

"I don't know what to do. I've been going around trying to get some insight, like Diogenes walking through Athens with his lamp looking for an honest man." Medora gave a halfhearted smile.

Trudy smirked. "You probably had about as much luck as he did, too, or you wouldn't be here. By the way, why *are* you here?" There was a touch of hostility in Trudy's voice, and Medora wondered for a moment if asking her opinion was a wise thing to do. "You have to look into your heart, have the courage to make your decision, and then live with what you decide."

"Why did you do what you did?"

Trudy looked startled, and then said, "Joyce is better off where she is, with the family who adopted her. I knew after the first few weeks of mothering that I wasn't cut out for it. I couldn't deal with a baby and do my work, too. That was my choice: my baby or my art, and I chose my work."

She lit a thin cigar and continued, "I didn't really have a relationship with the father, anyway. I thought I did, but I didn't. I'm warning you, Medora, men don't change. What you see is what you get. Don't be caught in the same fantasy about Randall Hollis that I had about Gregory Davis. He didn't give a shit. The whole thing was an accident. I just didn't have enough good sense to get an abortion while there was time." She took a drag off the cigar, then snubbed it out hard, as if emphasizing her point. Medora wondered if she was making the same mistake.

"You do have fantasies about Randall, don't you?"

"If I did, I'm over them now."

"I'm glad to hear that, because Randall Hollis is one of the biggest sluts out there. There's hardly a woman left on the West Side he hasn't fucked, to say nothing of Jersey and Westchester."

"I know his reputation," Medora said defensively. "I've known Randall since I was freshman in college. He was the first guy I ever took seriously."

"That's amazing!" Trudy said with a snicker. "Was he a dog back then?"

"No. Not all," Medora said, remembering for a moment the shy, studious Randall that she had been drawn to the moment she saw him. "I was young, eighteen. We were in the same honors classes. We were good friends at first. The only two black kids. You know how that went."

"I had no idea you and Randall went that far back."

Medora shrugged. "For what it's worth," she said.

"For what it's worth," Trudy repeated with a smirk. "Anyway, I had some fantasy that Gregory would leave his barren wife and take up with me if I gave him a kid, and when that didn't happen, it was too damn late to do anything about it. So there I was, twenty-four, with a kid who would remind me every day of her life what an asshole I'd been."

"You made the choice you had to make," Medora said, still thinking about herself and Randall, and wondering if she would someday feel like an asshole, too.

"A lot of people thought I was the bitch from hell for giving her away like I did, even my mother." Trudy's glance told Medora that she was still puzzled by people's reaction, and Medora avoided her eyes. She had been one of those people, stunned and dismayed by her friend's choice, too. How could you name, nurse, hold a child, then give her away? But Trudy was always true to Trudy, and always took the path most folks would never travel.

"Do you ever wonder what happened to her?"

"I gave her my mother's name, Joyce, did I ever tell you that? Like it was some kind of talisman," Trudy said, not answering her.

"Well, do you?" Medora wasn't going to let it slide.

"No," Trudy answered with so little hesitation, Medora wondered if she was telling the truth. But you could never tell with Trudy Douglass.

Trudy Douglass, "with two s's, like Frederick," had always been a rebel, and Medora had always been in awe of her. She did exactly as she pleased—with women as well as men now, she was quick to say. She French-kissed, petted, had sex before any of her other friends when she'd been a girl, and when she talked about doing them, it was never with the sappy innocence that characterized the conversation of other girls her age, but with an irreverent mix of disdain and racy humor that sent Medora into hysterical laughter. Trudy's affair with a respected art professor in college had been indiscreet and passionate, and when she became pregnant she defied everybody—parents, friends, lover alike—by choosing to bear the child. And then to everyone's astonishment, six months later, when everybody had gotten used to the situation, she defied them again by giving her daughter away. Medora hadn't known whether to respect her independence or despise her selfishness. Even now she wasn't sure.

"Would you make the same decision again?" Medora asked.

"Yes, if it was the same situation with the same man," Trudy said without missing a beat. "Except I'd get rid of it early. There would be no reason to go through with it. By the way, how's your work going?" Medora shrugged and sighed. "Do you have any shows coming up?"

"A group show at The New Walls Gallery."

"Isn't that Randall's gallery?"

"He's a partner with Lillian Wingate."

"When's the show?"

"September."

"Here's one thing you should consider before you make your decision," Trudy said with a slight, amused smile. "Can you think of one serious female painter, I mean serious, selling big work, getting big shows, who has a kid? Kids and art don't mix; you choose one or the other, that's the truth of it."

"But every artist has to find her own particular truth, Trudy, or she wouldn't be an artist," Medora said quietly.

Trudy shrugged, giving her the point. "So, you really have no idea what you are going to do about it?"

"About my baby?" Medora said, without realizing she made her decision the moment she uttered those words.

By the time Medora called T.W. and Aunt Tillie, the "it" was firmly her "baby," and she was as sure about her decision as she was about anything in her life. She thought it best to tell them together. If she told them separately, one or the other would be mad that he or she hadn't been first. She also decided to do it over dinner in an environment she could control.

Whenever T.W. and Aunt Tillie were in the same room, Medora ended up being the peacemaker, a role formerly held by her mother. Occasionally, her efforts at creating a cease-fire failed, and the two of them would scream her down. They rarely disagreed with a decision she made once they knew that she had definitely made it, but she wanted them to be as excited about the baby as she was becoming.

She was nervous that Sunday night when the doorbell rang. In the spirit of the evening, which Medora had declared would be a "family discussion," Aunt Tillie had picked up T.W. and chauffeured him to Medora's loft. When they entered the room, Medora could tell that the drive over had not been pleasant.

"Pour me a drink. A strong one!" T.W. quipped as he pulled off his coat and handed it to Medora. "I need some liquor! Wine ain't gonna get it."

Aunt Tillie rolled her eyes. "Maybe you *should* have something strong to improve your spirits and settle your nerves," she muttered.

"Won't be so much to settle my nerves as celebrate still being alive after that drive from hell!" he said.

"Maybe if you'd kept your trap shut and stopped all that backseat driving, it would have been smoother," Tillie snapped. "For someone who can't half see, you've got a heck of a lot of say about the way I drive my car."

"Be quiet, the two of you!" They were both slightly stooped now, but Medora, taller than both, always felt like the grass beneath two warring elephants. They looked at her in surprise as if they'd forgotten she was there; then Aunt Tillie smiled.

"Don't mind us, honey. Me and this old man will be at each other's throat till the end of our days." She pecked a kiss on Medora's forehead, and Medora sighed. For the first time she noticed how thin her aunt's hair had gotten at the crown. Whenever she looked at her aunt Tillie, she could see hints of her mother. Although Minerva had been far prettier than her older sister, they had the same eyes and bone structure, which she herself had inherited. Medora caught a whiff of lily of the valley from the White Shoulders cologne her aunt always wore. White Shoulders, for a strong black woman. The thought made her smile.

"Who you calling an old man?" T.W. said to Aunt Tillie, half joking.

"Who the oldest thing in here?" Aunt Tillie said back.

"Not by much," T.W. replied.

"Let's eat!" Medora announced with a nervous glance at the two of them, deciding in that instant that her news would best be delivered on full stomachs.

"Now, what is this family discussion you pulled the both of us over here to share?" T.W. said after dinner, as he picked his teeth with the ivory toothpick he always carried with him.

"Patience has never been one of your virtues, has it, Thetas? Why don't you let the girl tell us when she gets ready to tell us?"

"If I wanted your advice, Tillie, I would have—"

"First of all, I'm not a girl," Medora said irritably. "I haven't been a girl in twenty years. And I'm sick of the two of you arguing." She was suddenly annoyed with them both. Her tasty dinner, a stir-fry of scallops, udon noodles, and fresh spinach, had been nearly ruined by their sniping and veiled threats.

"Sorry, baby." T.W. looked contrite. Aunt Tillie bit her lip.

"The two of you are the only family I have, and I want there to be peace between you. And not just on my birthday." Medora's voice took on a lecturing tone.

"Duly noted," T.W. said as he emptied his glass.

Aunt Tillie sipped her wine and studied Medora expectantly.

Medora took a deep breath. "Well, in two words: I'm pregnant."

Tillie and T.W. took collective breaths, slamming their glasses down on the pine table at the same moment.

"What did you say?" Aunt Tillie asked, her eyes grown big.

"Did you say you were pregnant?" T.W. said, as if he couldn't believe his ears.

"Yes," Medora said. "I'm going to have a baby, in late October or early in November if my calculations are right, and I wanted to share the news with both of you." She anxiously searched both their faces for a hint of how they were taking it. Both faces were blank. "I don't know why you're both so surprised," she added after a moment, trying to lighten the tension that had suddenly enveloped the room. "I'm not the first middle-aged woman to decide to have and raise a baby by herself."

This last statement brought a gasp and then a scowl from T.W., which made Medora wonder if she should have kept it to herself for the time being. "What do you mean, by yourself? I don't mean to get into your business, sweetheart, but you didn't . . . uh . . . create it by yourself. Why the hell should you take care of it by yourself? Who the hell is the father? Is it somebody I know?"

"First of all, my baby is not an it!" Medora said testily. "Frankly, this is my body and its my decision to raise my baby by myself. I have the means, and I will do it."

"So what does *he* say? There is a he, isn't there? Or did you use some kind of . . . uh . . . artificial insemination or something?" T.W. looked skeptical.

Medora glared at her father, the old anger creeping back as she wondered if he was trying to make some kind of joke at her expense, but then she realized he was serious.

"Yes. There is a he, and he hasn't said anything yet," she said.

"Hasn't said anything?" Aunt Tillie looked incredulous.

"What the hell kind of man is that?" T.W. stood up with righteous paternal anger, his hands tightening into fists. "Who is he? Do I know this son of a bitch?"

"Sit down, Daddy. Who he is is immaterial because I haven't told him yet. And I wouldn't marry him if he asked me," Medora added. "And I am not telling either of you anything more about him than that, so don't ask me," she said, her mouth set in a firm line.

"What? Why haven't you told him? You can't be pregnant and not tell the father." Aunt Tillie's eyes grew large with disbelief. "Is he married?" She lowered her voice in horror.

"No, he's not married."

"Why won't you marry him if he asks you?" T.W. asked.

"I have my reasons," Medora said.

"I don't know what the hell kind of reasons they could be. If the man was good enough to sleep with, he should be good enough to marry!" T.W. stood back up, as if preparing to leave, then turned around and sat back down. "Damn it, girl! A woman having a child should be married! A woman can't do it by herself. She needs to have a man in her life. She—"

"Shut up!" Aunt Tillie screamed suddenly. "I am so sick of the hubris of men. I am so damn sick of it!" It was her turn to stand up now, and she did, a scowl on her face, her back ramrod straight.

"What the hell are you talking about? What does hubris have to do with it?"

"Hubris is arrogance. Pride. The assumption that the world functions at your beck and call! What in God's name do you know about marriage or love or commitment?" Her eyes were brimming with tears as she confronted T.W. "As far as I can see, marriage is *death* for women. Death! A cruel, selfish man can kill a woman as quickly as a knife through her heart! He can maim and cripple her until she has no more reason to live!"

"Oh, Jesus, woman! Give it a rest! Minnie, wherever you are, please tell this woman to leave me alone!" T.W. said, dramatically raising his arms in supplication and casting his eyes to the heavens.

"That's right, you no-good something-or-other, you're looking toward the right place! We know where Minerva is, God rest her soul! She's in heaven, that's where she is. And that's one place you'll never see!" Aunt Tillie's usually modulated voice was a snarl.

Medora began to cry. "Do not call my mother's name. Either of you! Just shut up! I am the only person in this room who has the right to call my mother's name!"

She closed her eyes as she spoke and tried as hard as she could to call up the image of the woman who had caused so much enmity between these two people she loved and to ask for her assistance in healing them both.

It didn't work.

"Why don't you give it a break, woman? Why don't you just let the dead rest in peace?" T.W. said, his voice softening in deference to his daughter's tears.

Aunt Tillie hissed back, "You never let her rest in peace when she was alive, did you?"

"She never let herself rest in peace!" T.W. screamed, now dismissing Aunt Tillie with a wave of his hand. Aunt Tillie began to cry. T.W., shaking his head back and forth as if shaking something out, let it drop wearily into his hands.

"Mama, please help me!" Medora whispered softly, and the image of Minerva Jackson, weeping as she always was, finally came to her. In high school, when she had first seen a photograph of one of Picasso's paintings of Dora Maar, one of his many weeping women, she had thought immediately of her mother, whom she loved with all her heart but who always seemed so sad. One of Medora's earliest memories was of her mother crying. But despite what Aunt Tillie believed, Medora could never bring herself to blame her father for her mother's death. There was no doubt that he had been the husband from hell. His countless liaisons, selfishness, and fiscal irresponsibility had made her life a continual nightmare. He made no secret that art came first in his life. And after that came his daughter. Minerva was tossed the remainder, which was never enough.

So she willed herself to die. Piece by piece, she let her body go, ignoring its messages, rebellions, and failures. She focused all of her energy on T.W., never allowing herself to hear her own voice or even that of her daughter, which was something Medora found hard to forgive. Her mother was consumed by her father's fire, and Medora, caught between the two of them, had to fight her way through the ashes.

Yet the memory of Minerva Jackson's love had contributed as much as anything else to Medora's decision to have her baby. Despite T.W.'s absences, Minerva Jackson had made her daughter's childhood a joyful one, filled with sweet, enchanted memories that still made Medora smile.

Her mother had been the delight of her young life, and this baby would be her mother's continuing piece of immortality; that thought pleased Medora.

Nobody spoke. The three of them sat in their respective poses for the next two minutes, until Medora, her voice harsh from tears, said, "I am bringing a new life into this world. A baby is always the future. This baby will be our future—mine; yours, Dad; Aunt Tillie's. And Mama's." At the mention of the word "mama," both T.W. and Tillie were startled, as if they were hearing her say it for the first time.

Looking his age, T.W. crossed to where his daughter was sitting and hugged her as tightly as he could. Medora let herself be swept into his body, losing herself in his hug that she had craved so as a little girl.

"Are you ready for this, Bunny?" He used his nickname for her. Bunny, short for March Hare because she was born in March. She couldn't remember the last time he had called her that. "If this is what you want, I will help you out any way I can. I'll be the best granddaddy you ever saw," he added, which made Medora cry again because she knew that was his way of saying he'd make up for the father he hadn't been, and that it wasn't too late for him, either.

Warily she glanced at Aunt Tillie, who didn't bother to hide her concern, but who managed to smile despite it.

"If this is what you really want and need to do, Medora, of course, I will support you in any way that I can," she said, and Medora knew that for the time being, that would have to be enough.

Nobody said much after that, but the squabbling had stopped, and Medora was thankful. After they had left, she made herself a pot of tea and sat in the dark, rocking in her chair. She thought about T.W. and Aunt Tillie and then about her mother and the baby she was carrying. And she thought about Randall, who had been on her mind constantly and whose name she had avoided mentioning in most of the conversations she'd had in the past few weeks. He'd called four times since her birthday, and she hadn't bothered to return his calls. She had no intention of calling him now. She had told him then she was through with him, and she meant it.

Later that night, Medora dreamed that her mother sat on the edge of her bed, a half smile on her pretty face, her eyes as mournful as ever. Medora awoke with a start, not sure if her mother's presence had been a dream or a visitation, but whatever it was, it wouldn't let her go back to sleep. When dawn broke, she sat at the window, watching daylight come in streaks of pink and silver creep across the sky, and then went to her long pine table and wrote the letter she needed to write.

Chapter Six

"She wrote me a letter, for Christ's sake! What kind of shit is that, to write me a goddamn letter?" Randall asked Ana, who was sitting across from him at her kitchen counter. They were sipping cinnamon-topped cappuccinos, but what he really needed was a drink. He didn't like to curse around women, but this situation with Medora had gotten the better of him.

"Medora is Medora Jackson, right? You sold me some of her work, right?" There was disapproval in Ana's eyes.

"Yes," he muttered, embarrassed. "I represent her."

With T.W. acting as emissary, he and Medora had decided that he would continue to represent her. At least for the time being.

"So you had a *personal* relationship?" She stumbled over the word as if she had trouble saying it, and her eyes probed his for the truth. He avoided looking at her.

"Not any more. I stopped seeing her a couple of weeks before we started our relationship," he said, implying that it had been his decision to break things off. He took a sip of coffee and stared through the living room window to the pool and garden beyond. It was a beautiful view, cool and serene. The random thought that a dip in freezing water would probably do him good passed through his mind. That was one quick way to wash away his sins.

"What do you feel for her now?"

"Medora?"

"Who else?" she said with annoyance.

"Nothing now," he said too quickly and wondered if she could tell he was lying, but she looked relieved.

"Do you still have the letter? Sometimes it pays to read things like that again, after your emotions have cooled."

"I was so bummed out by it I almost threw it away, but I think I stuck it somewhere in my desk. She says she doesn't want any child support or my involvement in raising it. I feel like she hijacked my sperm and then made a decision that affects me without my permission. I'm really mad about it. But, fine! If she doesn't want anything from me, then that's what she'll get!" He said it more bitterly than he meant to, and the shadow that passed over Ana's face told him that his harshness disturbed her.

"Sometimes letters are more important than spoken conversations, particularly when one is angry," Ana said. "My first husband and I wrote letters to each other when we were too angry to talk. Writing things down can help you figure things out. Maybe that's what she was trying to do."

"Your first husband?"

A shadow crossed Ana's face. "Yes. His name was Daniel, same as my son. Danny was the one good thing that came out of our marriage. You can never tell what a child will bring into your life, what a precious gift he or she will be."

"How can it be precious if you can't stand the person who is giving it to you?"

"But I thought you said you cared about her!"

"I did," he corrected himself, even though he hadn't been talking about Medora. He had been talking about his own parents and what they never meant to each other, and the thought of that made his eyes water. He'd been on the verge of crying from the moment he walked into Ana's house. *What the fuck is wrong with me?* He could tell she wasn't sure what to make of him. He couldn't blame her. What was she supposed to think about some off-the-wall bullshit like this? What would any woman think? First the cop, now this.

But for the life of him, he couldn't think of anyone else he could talk to. In the last few weeks, they had been seeing each other almost daily. If he wasn't busy negotiating with an artist-client or taking a new collector to a studio, they'd meet for lunch or dinner either in the city or in Jersey. Each evening he'd call her, and they would share humdrum bits of information they forgot to mention during the day. When he'd gone out of town the week before to view the work of an up-and-coming artist, he'd called her that night, and they talked until she fell asleep. He had to sort this situation out with Medora, and if he'd learned anything about Ana Reese-Mitchell in these last few weeks, it was that she had good sense and any advice she gave him would be wise. He couldn't ignore the faint lines of disapproval that had popped out around the edges of her mouth, but he had no choice but to talk. It was that or go crazy.

Every time he thought about Medora's letter, written in her beautiful script on the ridiculously expensive linen paper that only an artist would buy, he felt dread liberally mixed with rage. The tone of the letter had been stilted and prim, nothing at all like the woman he'd known for so many years. It began formally, with a colon, no less.

Dear Randall:
There is no easy way to say this so I'll just say it straight and clear.

He smirked when he read that. When in her life had Medora *not* said something "straight and clear"?

I am pregnant. You are the father.

Oddly enough, considering the number of women he'd slept with over the years, he had never been told those words before. He'd always wondered how he would react, and he knew now: He went completely numb.

I must have conceived on Valentine's Day (I hope you remember Valentine's Day!).

Of course he remembered! How could he forget it? It was one of the most erotic afternoons he'd ever shared with a woman. How typical of

Medora to assume that he wouldn't remember their lovemaking that day
as vividly as she did!

*I have decided to continue with my pregnancy and have this baby,
which according to calculations made by my obstetrician, will be born
in late October or early in November.*

"Oh, my God!" he'd screamed out loud when he read those lines. He
felt hot, then cold, then weak in the knees. His stomach turned upside
down, and for a moment he thought he was going to be sick.

*I don't want you to think that my decision requires any particular action on
your part, which I'm sure you will be loath to take. I don't want or expect
money or anything else. I'm aware that this pregnancy is unwanted and
unplanned, but, because this is my body, the choice as to whether someone will
grow inside of me or not is entirely mine. It's my call, and for reasons of my
own, I have decided to have this child.*

Why was she always so unwilling to accept how much she meant to
him? Why the hell did everything, including his own feelings, have to be
on her terms? She was so damned bullheaded. A man had to love Medora
Jackson the way she wanted to be loved or not at all! And to see a doctor
and make a decision like this without so much as a call, ignoring his contribution as if it were worth nothing at all! As if he were worth nothing at
all! He'd balled up her letter and hurled it into the trash, only to retrieve
it to read it again. Then he picked up the phone and called her. He got her
answering machine.

"What the hell are you doing, Medora? How could you write me
something like this? How can you—" The machine cut him off and he
banged down the phone, dialed her number again, and finished his sentence with a scream. "How can you have a child that belongs to me, that
is part of *me*, without *my* permission?"

He banged down the phone. A minute later, she called him back. "I
see you got my note," she said.

"Yes, I got it! How can you make a decision like this without talking to me first? Medora, we've been together nearly all our adult lives! How can you just decide something like this without even the courtesy of—"

"Courtesy has nothing to do with it," she said, calmly cutting him off. "I told you the last time I saw you that things were over between us. As far as I'm concerned, they still are."

"You are being absurd! Absolutely absurd! Why don't you start dealing with reality? How can things be over between us when you've made a decision like this, to have a kid, a fucking baby, for crying out loud!"

" 'Fucking baby'? Hmmm, I can tell from that statement how you feel about it. Well, it's my decision and I've made it."

There was dead silence for a moment or two, and then Randall asked, "Do you want to get married?"

Before he said them, he had no idea that those words would leave his mouth, and he was as surprised to hear them as she was. He certainly didn't want to get married. He had no intention of getting married. But it seemed like the right thing to say, so he said it. His proposal hung in the air for a moment or two, and then, eager for some kind of response, he asked, "Did you hear what I said?"

She burst into what sounded like laughter.

"Did you hear me, and what's so damned funny?"

"Of course I heard you. I'm not deaf! And that marriage proposal is damned funny."

"Well?" His heart was thumping so hard he could count the beats.

"Now who is the one who is being absurd?" Medora snapped.

"What's so absurd about it?" *Where did those words come from? Do I really want to get married, to anyone? he wondered.*

"No! Of course not! I don't want to marry you, and I'll tell you why: Because we can't walk down the street together without you checking out some woman's big behind! You can't walk into a restaurant without some woman catching your eye. You could never be faithful to me because you can never be satisfied with just one woman, and believe me, unless you're an utter fool, that's not the characteristic one chooses in a husband. I learned that from my parents."

"Oh, God, Medora. I'm like every other red-blooded man in the world. I'm not a goddamn saint."

"Well, that's the truth."

"How can you be so damn selfish and unreasonable? How can you—"

She cut him off. "How can I be so selfish and unreasonable! You've always had more than your share of ladies! You know everything there is to know about women! You figure it out!" she said and hung up.

For the next few days, he tried to get in touch with her, but to no avail. Finally, in desperation, he'd driven to her studio in Jersey and slipped into the building behind a cable repairman. Not to be discouraged by the broken elevator, he'd climbed the twelve flights of stairs to her loft.

"Medora! Open up! Let me in! We have to talk!" he screamed, banging on her door like a madman. Her next-door neighbor Barney, a six-foot-five giant of a man whom Randall routinely avoided, cracked his door and eyed him suspiciously. "What the fuck you want?" he growled.

"I'm looking for Ms. Jackson. Do you have any idea where she is?" Randall tried to display a pose of calm dignity.

"Seems to me the lady ain't home, man. Least not to the likes of you," the man grunted, scarcely concealing his contempt. "Seems to me you better be on your way."

Throwing up his hands in frustration at Barney's veiled threat, Randall ran back down the twelve flights of stairs, staggered to the sidewalk, and sat down on the curb.

"If this is the way you want it, Medora Jackson, this is the way it will be," he yelled up at her window and then drove home. The next day he wrote her a letter, as formal and prim as the one he received, informing her that his attorney, Marvin K. Brown, Esq., would be in touch with her about his "legal responsibility and interests" regarding the "matter at hand" and for her to make all inquiries and requests to said attorney.

He hadn't seen or spoken to her since.

If Medora has made up her mind, and she is determined to have this child, there's not a lot you can do about it. She may not want any financial help now, but she may need some later, so you were smart to get your attorney involved," Ana said, bringing his thoughts back to the present. He had avoided her eyes during his confession, and he looked at her now. She looked sympathetic and sounded philosophical. She was being adult about the whole thing, mature and objective. He felt like a woebegone client seeking a social worker's reasoned advice.

"I don't think she needs any money," he said.

"Raising a child alone is a very difficult and very expensive undertaking," she said as if speaking from experience.

"Medora's father is T. W. Jackson, the painter. I'm one of his dealers, and he's been getting about a quarter of a million a pop for his early pieces. She's an only child, and I assume he'll help her out if she needs it."

Ana was silent, as if mulling over this new fact, and then added, "I think you should make sure you secure your parental rights, even if she doesn't want any help financially. A child is a child, wanted or not, so you should establish some kind of understanding with her. At some point, you may want to request visitation rights." Her voice was formal again, as if she were trying to distance herself from his problems. He couldn't blame her.

"I don't have what it takes to be a father," he said. "I can give her money if she needs it, that I can do, but the rest of it? Forget it! No way!" Ana broke into a slight, amused smile, and its appearance made Randall realize how tense her expression had been up until this. "You don't have to worry about that," she said, reaching across the table and taking his hand into hers. Her touch was warm and soft, reassuring, but it was more the touch of a benevolent counselor than a lover. "Good parenting comes naturally to those who were lucky enough to have it. You had a good father, so that's what you'll be. Think about your own father, Randall, how much he loved you, and how much you learned from him before he died. Remember your father and how much he loved you, and that's what you draw from with your own children. Love is really a family legacy. You pass it down. Yours was good, so that is what you will give your child."

Her words stunned him. For an instant, he thought she was trying to hurt him by saying the cruelest thing she could possibly say, and then he remembered the lie he had told her. He snatched his hand from hers, too ashamed to continue holding it.

"I lied to you, Ana," he said quietly. "About everything."

It took his words a moment to register, he could see that. She drew in a breath as disbelief, then apprehension appeared in her eyes. *Maybe I should just get the hell up and leave,* he thought. He'd done that before when things got too uncomfortable. Not physically. He never left a woman's presence. He'd stay where he was, smiling, drinking, making love. But he wouldn't be there emotionally. He'd remind himself that whoever she was, she really didn't matter, that there was always somebody else, somebody smarter, prettier, more interesting just around the corner, and that she was the one who was really important.

But he was sick and tired of doing that. He trusted Ana and that surprised him. He liked her, everything about her. But he knew that maybe the best thing he could do for her would be to get out of her life. Yet he was too selfish for that. Hadn't Medora told him that? And it was too late now, anyway.

"Exactly what lies have you told me?" She tilted her head slightly to the side, the way a child who has just been betrayed does. It startled him and made him remember a lost part of himself.

So many, he thought. *Too many to tell.* But he started with the most obvious. The one that was the easiest. The one that affected everything he did.

"I never knew my father," he said. "He never married Lydia. I don't think he gave a damn about me or her one way or the other. I know I didn't give a damn about him. He's dead now, like I said. But he died a few months after I was born. Some woman's old man put a bullet into him one night when he was coming out of a club. I lied about him, Ana. Maybe I was trying to impress you, maybe I just wanted something to say to get your sympathy."

She gazed at the space beyond his shoulder, then brought her eyes slowly to his mouth, as if tracing the source of the lie, and then to his eyes.

"Why?" She could barely say the word.

"Because that's what I do sometimes," he said.

"But why did you feel the need to lie? A lot of people don't know their parents or don't get along with them." He tried to interpret the expression on her face, and decided it was a combination of things: Sorrow. Anger. Disgust. Pity. He picked up the cappuccino and finished it off. "Hey, listen, Ana. If you want me to leave. If you . . ."

She looked puzzled for a moment, and then asked, "What else?"

"What do you mean?"

"You said *lies*. What else did you lie about?"

She was forgiving him, offering him redemption. He could hardly believe it. He closed his eyes, thanking God, soaking in her love.

"My mother," he said.

"You don't *have* a mother?"

He caught a glint of amusement in her eyes, a spark that let him know that things between them might not be over. Not yet. As long as he told her the truth. And he would tell her the truth.

"Yeah. I actually do. Her name is Lydia. She's dying of lung cancer, like I told you. I love her, but sometimes I hate her guts. I can almost see how my father couldn't stay with her. She would drive any man crazy. Sometimes she drives me crazy. She's like a vampire who sucks somebody's blood so they end up walking the streets at night looking for new victims." He laughed bitterly at this characterization. It was one that he had never shared with anybody else. "Is that honest enough for you?" Her expression told him that perhaps he shouldn't have said it, and he made his voice less harsh, trying to make things lighter. "I lied about my age, too. I'll be thirty-seven, not thirty-nine."

"You actually added two years to your age?"

"Well, you were so put off by my being younger than you, I didn't want to ruin things before they got started. But I did anyway, right?"

Ana didn't say anything. Nothing moved in her face, no light in her eyes, no change in the tight line of her lips.

She thinks I'm a compulsive liar, he thought. *She's through with me*.

"And Medora. How do you *really* feel about Medora and the fact that she is going to have your child?" She was watching him closely. He chose his words carefully.

"I'm closer to her than I like to admit. She told me to get out of her life in March. When I got the letter about the baby, I asked her if she wanted to get married. We've been lovers on and off for years, so I thought it might make sense. I figured that we could go our separate ways after the baby was born if things didn't work out. Basically she told me I was being absurd, and she was probably right.

"She's too smart to marry a man like me, and I guess I knew that when I asked her, but her having this kid, my kid, brings up everything about me that I hate. Everything I want to forget." He spoke quietly, more to himself than to Ana, and he could tell by the look on her face that she was puzzled by his words. But so was he.

"So, how do you feel about Medora?" she asked again.

"I honestly don't know how I feel about Medora. Sometimes I miss her because she's been in my life so long," he said. "But it doesn't matter how I feel about her. She's made up her mind how she feels about me, and she's through with me, even though she's carrying my kid. That should tell you something right there, shouldn't it?"

Ana stood up slowly, took the cups off the table, and rinsed them out in the sink. She made a lot of noise doing it, more than was necessary, which made Randall think that this was her way of telling him to leave. He stood up, preparing to go.

"I know this is a lot to handle, me telling you everything like this. About Medora, the baby, the business with my father, but I . . ." He hesitated, not sure for a moment how to finish it, but then said, "I had to talk about it."

She gave him the hint of a smile with an edge of sarcasm in her response. "I can certainly understand that."

"Does it make a difference?"

"I don't know."

"If you forgive me for this, I promise you that I will never lie to you again."

There was doubt in her eyes.

"Can I see you again?"

"Let me think about it?" Her voice was toneless, which meant she probably didn't believe him, but she had phrased it like a question, as if she were asking his permission.

"Yeah. Sure. Of course."

He paused. "I'm sorry, Ana."

"So am I . . ." She looked as if she were searching for something else to say.

Before she could come up with it, the front door opened, then closed with a slam, and they both turned toward it.

"Ma! You in there?" Danny called out.

Ana's face relaxed and the smile that came to her lips tore through Randall's heart because he knew that not once in his life had Lydia ever smiled like that at the mere sound of his voice.

"I'm in here, son."

As Danny bounded into the room, Randall studied them both. He had her looks, that was for sure, but his height was probably his father's. He had the lanky ease of an athlete and that casual self-assurance. His smile was open and boyish as he offered his hand.

"Danny Mitchell," he said with authority, claiming his space in his mother's home.

"Randall Hollis. It's great to meet you, Danny." Randall returned his firm handshake.

"Nice to meet you, too. Finally," Danny added with quick wink at his mother, and Ana threw him a warning look. "Is that your ride out there? It's nice, man. How fast does it go?"

"Faster than I drive it," Randall said with a grin. "It's German, you know, so it was designed for the autobahn. It doesn't know speed limits, but I'll tell you this, eighty feels like fifty-five, so I got to watch myself on the turnpike." Both men laughed. They were on safe male territory. Cars.

"I keep telling Ma she should get a new car. A beamer at the very least, but she's sold on these American things."

"In honor of your grandfather, who considered it unpatriotic to buy anything else," Ana said with a chuckle, and turned to Randall, the smile still on her lips. "My father drove a Ford truck, but his dream car was a Cadillac, so that's what I bought the minute I could afford it."

"My stepfather had a Porsche. A red one," Danny volunteered, and his eyes shifted to the floor, but Randall caught a glimpse of his poorly concealed pain. "Dude, my late stepdad, *never* let me drive it," he added with a glance at his mother. She didn't conceal a sigh that told him as much about the relationship between Jerrod Mitchell and his stepson as anything that either of them could say. They were together, compatriots and confidantes. She was probably closer to her son than she had been to either of her husbands. Or maybe could be to any man.

"I'd better go." He stood; there was nothing more to say. Not with her son here anyway. Probably not at all. He kissed her forehead gently, with no commitment or presumption. She gave him no hint of her feelings one way or the other. He assumed he would never hear from her again.

So when Taylor Benedict called him on his cell phone inviting him to dinner as he was coming out of the Holland Tunnel, he turned toward Brooklyn, stopping on the way to pick up two bottles of the very dry, very costly French wine she requested.

Chapter Seven

After Randall left, Danny asked, "What's wrong, Ma?"

"What makes you think something is wrong?" Ana said, but knew she couldn't fool her son. He could always tell when she was distressed, even before she admitted it to herself.

"Well, for one thing, you didn't ask *the* question."

"And what is *the* question?"

"'Did you like him, Danny?'" He did a gentle imitation of her voice that made her smile.

"So, did you?"

Danny piled ice chips from the dispenser into a tall glass and then leisurely popped a Coke and poured the soda into the glass. It was a delaying tactic.

"I guess women would say he's good-looking," he said cautiously. "He seemed cool and all that, but he had all the answers. Too smooth, if you know what I mean."

Ana, somewhat surprised by her son's frank assessment, settled on the stool across from him as he continued his commentary. "Maybe it's just because he's handsome. Or because he drives that car. That's a *mean* ride. But it shouldn't matter what I think. I didn't listen to you about Taylor. Why should you listen to me about him?"

"But I was right about Taylor," she said, then wished she hadn't. She poured the remainder of Danny's Coke into a glass, avoiding his eyes. It bothered her that Taylor Benedict kept coming up in their conversations.

"Well, I could be right about Randall."

"So, you think I should stop seeing him?"

"No! As long as he treats you good, as long as he's not being too smooth with you."

Ana shook the ice around in her glass as she thought about her son's take on Randall. "Trouble is, I don't know," she said after a moment. She rarely confided details about her social life to her son. It struck her as inappropriate for a son to know too much about his mother's love life (or lack thereof), so her dates, such as they were, went undiscussed. But since Mali's death, she found herself listening to Danny's opinions. He had good instincts about people (with the glaring exception of Taylor Benedict), and she was pleased to find that his advice was often wise and surprisingly judicious. She only wished he could apply his good sense to his own life.

"Let's have it, Ma. How come you have doubts?" He used the voice she once used when he was a kid, a gently demanding tone with a no-nonsense edge.

"So, you're the adult now?"

"Have been for some time."

If only it were true, she thought. "He told me a few things about himself I found, well, disturbing," she said, choosing her words carefully.

"Disturbing?" Her use of the word alarmed Danny, but he shook it off and broke into a grin. "Here's what I'm going to do. I'm going to ask you a series of question and you can nod your head yes or shake it no according to what you want to answer, okay?" Another tactic pulled from his childhood. How long had it been since she had used that one? Danny began, "So, has he done time in Rahway?"

"Prison? No!"

"Is he married and cheating on his wife? Does he have a gambling problem, like every couple of days he's gaming in Atlantic City? Is he flat broke? Is he bugging you to invest in his uncle's oil wells in Arkansas? Does he have a tragic, incurable social disease?"

Ana, caught up in the spirit of the inquiry, answered each question with a laugh and a definitively negative nod.

"I covered the big stuff. What's left?"

"I'm not sure."

"Do you like him?"

"Yeah."

"Really like him?"

"Yeah, I really do."

"Then take a chance! Not everything is for sure! Enjoy life! Savor the moment! Live a little!" Danny spread his arms wide in a gesture of zest and vigor, and Ana chuckled at her son's antics, despite her misgivings.

"A word of wisdom from my wise son?"

"You think I should take my own advice, don't you?" Danny asked and slumped down on his stool.

Ana waited a beat, then asked as casually as she could, "So, how did the latest interview go?" She watched him closely for a revealing emotion. He was good at hiding his feelings.

"Okay, I guess. He said he'd call me back, one way or the other, but I'm not sure if I want to take that job, even if they offer it. You know, Ma, I just can't see myself sitting around an office all day for that kind of money. It seems like it would be kind of a waste of my time."

Ana took a deep breath before she spoke, but it didn't do any good. She couldn't hide her irritation; she was sick and tired of doing it anyway.

"What wouldn't be a waste of your precious time?" she snapped, and in the next moment thought, *Why in God's name bring this up now?*

"Can we not start?" Danny said. His voice was whiny and irritable.

Ana closed her eyes, counted to twenty until she could control her temper. When she spoke again, her voice was composed. "Why don't you think about going back to school, Danny. You've got to finish something, you've got to—"

"Enough, Ma, please!" He didn't raise his voice, but she could hear the anger in it.

"What are you going to do with your life, son? You've never finished anything. You've always . . ." She stopped midsentence. She could hear the nagging tone that took over her voice whenever they talked about the direction of his life. His face fell the way it always did, and she could plainly see the anguish in his eyes. It didn't do any good to nag him, she knew that. *Why do I always do it?* She softened her voice as much as she could and continued, "I know how essential having a goal in life is. It's important to start each day knowing that something you do will change the world in some small way, that it will make a difference."

"So what do you do?" There was a hint of sarcasm in his voice that annoyed Ana, but she chose not to address it.

"When I was your age, I finished college, got my degree, got a job, and took care of my responsibilities. Now, I raise money for the charities that mean something to me, and I'm trying to establish a collection of African-American art that will someday be important."

"So that's where Randall Hollis comes in?"

Ignoring the question, Ana stayed on track. "It's just that I know how smart you are. I want you to find something to do with your life, not just waste it sitting around here." They were the same words spoken in the same tedious way that came out whenever they discussed what she felt was his failure in life—the inability to finish anything he started.

Danny had dropped out of every college he had ever attended, first Morehouse, then Rutgers, and recently the local community college. He'd never been able to hold down a job for more than five months. There was always something wrong—not enough money, hours too long, no future, too much disrespect. On charitable days, Ana gave him the benefit of the doubt: He was finding himself. He had had more than his share of trauma in his life. Sooner or later he would land on his feet. But at other times she had to face the truth: He was content to float through life with no direction or sense of where he would be in six months, to say nothing of six years. He was content to live off what she gave him. The children of her friends had finished college, gone to graduate or professional school, started businesses, yet Danny always seemed to end up doing nothing.

"You've got to focus, son, get some direction," she said.

"Like what, Ma?" His eyes narrowed with hostility.

"Anything but—"

"But sit around spending my dead stepdaddy's money?" he said, finishing her sentence with a harsh bitterness that made her shudder inside.

"What's next, Ma? Not paying for the car? Cutting the money you give me to live on until I get a job? Isn't that what always comes next?"

There was no point in her saying anything because her threats meant nothing. As long as she had money, he would have it, and both of them knew it.

"When is this going to stop?" Ana said.

"When is *what* going to stop?"

"You know what! The fact that you are not doing anything with your life."

"I'm doing something with my life. I get up. I get dressed. I go to the gym. I—"

"Stop it!" Ana said, her voice loud and out of control. His mocking tone brought back the voice of his father when he was drunk—the slur of his words, the taunting tilt of his head. She could see it in her son, and it scared the hell out of her. "I just don't want you to end up like—" She stopped herself from saying it, but they both knew what was on her lips.

"Like my father?" Danny said. "You're scared I'm going to end up drunk, doing drugs, a no-good nigger like my daddy, aren't you?" Danny continued, and his words reached his mark. He couldn't have hurt her more if he had slapped her across the face.

"No! Of course not. You are not like your father. Never like your father," she said, but neither of them believed it.

She had promised herself years ago that she would never mention Daniel Reese to his son with anything but respect, so she had ended up saying nothing. Danny's questions about his father never ceased at first. Where is he living? What is he doing? Why won't he come to see me? Why can't we call him? The questions had been endless, then grew fewer as the years passed. Maybe he sensed her unwillingness to talk about him. Maybe he could see the anguish in her eyes. The questions had finally stopped altogether, and she hoped he had tucked the memory of his father away with the other forgotten memories from his childhood. She couldn't recall the last time either of them had spoken Daniel's name. Perhaps she was a fool for not realizing the impact of a father's absence from his son's life. She hadn't thought about her conversation with Nate since he'd told her that Daniel wanted to see them, but in the past weeks, after their last few fights about his inability to find his way, she had begun to think that maybe Nate was right. Maybe Danny did need to see his father. Maybe it would do him some good.

"Do you ever wonder about your father, about what's become of him?" she asked. She was cautious in choosing her words, and her voice betrayed her apprehension.

Danny's anger was still written in the tight line of his lips. "Now we're changing it to my father, wherever the hell he is, whatever the hell he's become. I'm probably just like him anyway, right? Is that what you think?"

"No. I don't think that at all. Would you like to see him?" she asked, quickly cutting to the chase. Her words took him by surprise.

He looked startled, then fearful. "What do you mean, do I want to see him?"

"Have you been curious about him over all these years?"

"What do you think?"

Ana said nothing; the truth was obvious. "Your father wants to see you, Danny. He asked Nate a couple of months ago to get in touch with us, and I was supposed to get back to him. I told him I'd check with you, but I . . . well, I . . ." She couldn't finish the sentence because she knew there was no excuse for not mentioning it to him, for forgetting about it. The expression on his face told her she was right; she had made a grave mistake.

"Why didn't you tell me? Why didn't you say something? He could be dead or dying! Didn't it occur to you that after all these years there must be a reason that he wanted to see me!" He wailed the words out, his voice seething with anger. She knew that rage. She had seen it before. It came from the same place his father's had come from, a place where she could never go and that she had never understood. It sent a chill through her, straight to her bones. But she concealed her fear when she confronted her son.

"Don't you dare to speak to me in that tone of voice! What is wrong with you, screaming at me like that? Didn't you hear enough of that from Jerrod? You sound like some violent, sulky kid, not a grown man. Not the kind of man you should be."

Danny didn't lower his voice, not one decibel. "Don't you get it yet? Don't you get it? I will never be the kind of man you think I should be. Never!"

He was right, and she knew it; the truth of it and the fact that he knew it brought tears to her eyes.

"I'm sorry, Ma," Danny said, seeing her tears. "I shouldn't have yelled at you like that. I'm sorry." The expression in his face told her that he remembered Jerrod Mitchell, too, and there were tears in his eyes now. "But you should have told me. You really should have told me!"

Would they ever rid themselves of the pain that Daniel had inflicted? Would they ever fill the hole?

Don't let him see Danny. Don't let him talk to him. Don't let him touch him. Don't let him love him because he will lie to him the way he lied to me. Don't let Daniel hurt my boy the way he hurt me.

Those had been her guiding principles.

"I didn't tell you because I didn't want you to see him. I don't want to see him myself. I don't want him to know anything about us now. I don't think he should have any place in your life," Ana said.

"You didn't have the right to make that decision, Ma. You really didn't have that right." His voice was hushed, the anger of a moment ago gone. In that moment, Ana glimpsed the thing she had loved most about his father—the tenderness and vulnerability that had touched her heart.

He was right, she realized. How could she have kept something like this from him? And once again, as she always did whenever she doubted her judgment, she wondered if she was the cause of Danny's shortcomings. Was *she* the reason he seemed unable to shape his life and grow apart from her? Was her love so overprotective that it crippled him?

"You know what I remember most about him?" Danny's voice dropped into tenderness. "You know when we had the car, the red one with the racing stripe?"

Sure, she remembered it. She remembered how Daniel had sold it for whatever bullshit piece of change he could shake lose to take care of his habit. She forced herself to smile.

"Yeah. You used to love that car, didn't you?"

"It wasn't the car!" Danny's eyes showed his amusement. He had gotten that from his father, too, that quick change of moods, that ease in charming her. "It was riding with him, with Dad. You know we'd go all over the place. A lot of times he'd take me to the Delaware Water Gap. We'd just drive over there and get out, look around, come back home. We went to the city once or twice, to Coney Island. I was too little to ride anything alone, so he held me on all the rides, the big wheel, even the roller coaster. I remember being with him. I remember him being so big, a tough guy, strong."

"Yeah," was all Ana could say. She remembered those trips, too, when he'd take their son without a moment's warning, and she'd be scared he'd wreck that ragged-ass car. Or he'd lose her precious child, misplace him like a coat or sweater in his endless search for drugs. Yeah, she remembered it. All of it. It made her sick, the waiting, when he didn't come home, the prayers and curses muttered aloud, the paralyzing fear that he would kill them both on some bullshit druggie tip.

"Your father was an alcoholic and an addict," she said, sick of Danny's romanticizing the past.

"Tell me something I don't already know, something I haven't known all my life."

Defeat was in his eyes and in the set of his mouth. Was that where his debilitating sense of failure came from, what he sensed about his father? Jerrod Mitchell was always undefeated, she had to give him that. He was the winner Daniel Reese could never be, and he had seemed such a fitting role model for a son who from the beginning was at such loose ends.

"I don't drink, I don't do drugs," Danny said.

"I know," she said as if she knew it was the truth, but she had smelled marijuana at least once when she visited his apartment, and on more than one occasion she'd seen him drink more than he should. She had also noticed the subtle way that alcohol could change his personality. She knew that much about drunks after life with Daniel Reese. Whenever they drank, another soul slipped into their bodies. She had warned Danny from the time he could understand that alcoholism was a disease passed on from parents to children, so the son of a drunk should never touch liquor, never drink at all, and he hadn't through his teen years, but now some-times he did drink, defying her, defying his history, and that worried her.

"I'll call Nate myself. I'll tell him I want to see to see my father. If you don't want to see him, that's your business," Danny said. He finished his Coke, draining the glass quickly.

"I'll see him when you see him," Ana said. "I think we should see him together."

Danny nodded. "Okay." He was still mad, she could see it in the way he avoided her eyes and how stiff his body had become.

"Danny," she called after him as he was leaving the kitchen. But it was too late. He'd left in a hurry, slamming the door behind him.

Ana poured some tonic water into an ice-filled glass, topped it off generously with Tanqueray, scolding herself as she did it. Here she was taking a drink to ease her nerves; who the heck was she to yell at Danny? But it was different, and she knew it. She went out to her garden, settling down in the chaise longue in front of the pool.

It was late May, her favorite time of the month. Not quite summer, with its humidity and warmth, but solidly, undeniably spring. She made herself listen to the sounds of nature—the chirping of the birds, the rush-ing of the wind—and focus on the peacefulness she found in her garden. It was a serene spot, and she closed her eyes, feeling the cool of the evening air as it touched her face. She was trembling from her encounter with her son. She hated to fight with him. It tore her heart to fight with him, even more than it had with his father, much more.

Leave him alone. He'll find his way.

She gazed pass the turquoise water in the pool and the pink and white impatiens at the far side of the yard. If she listened hard, she could hear Mali's voice when she needed it. Sometimes it advised like a mother's. Often it comforted like a sister's. Occasionally it was her own voice, stronger than she expected it to be.

Let him grow up. Let him find his way by himself. Don't you know how blessed you are to have him?

But what did that mean? she wondered. She was so afraid she would lose him to what had taken his father. She feared there was a weakness within him, a tendency toward self-betrayal and a refusal to do what was best for himself. It was there in his preoccupation with Taylor Benedict, in his inability to hold down a job. How much like his father was he? Did her strength create weak men? It was a fear that had haunted her for years after she'd left Daniel. It was what had drawn her to Jerrod. Now that had been a man who was stronger than she. There was no weakness or gentleness in him. He took care of things with no hesitation or self-doubt. A man's man, that was who Jerrod Mitchell had been. And look what that had gotten her.

"Oh, Danny," she said to herself. Sang it softly for a moment. It was a little boy's name, Danny. Not Daniel. Never Daniel. Or even Dan. But Danny. It made her think of her father singing "Oh, Danny Boy," when she'd been a girl. He would have held her boy in his brawny, clumsy arms and whispered that old song to him in a ridiculous Irish brogue. A big black man hamming it up in an Irish brogue. That thought made her laugh. But the gin made her weep, which she did for a moment remembering Danny's accusations. She was so afraid for him. So disappointed in him.

And in Randall Hollis, too.

What would Mali say about all of this? she wondered. About Randall and his news.

He had all the answers. Too smooth, if you know what I mean.

Yes, she knew, and that bothered her. There were other wrinkles, too. There was bitterness in his voice when he spoke of his mother. Would her own son ever describe her in such a way?

What should I do?

Nothing. See how things turn out.

Ana eased back into the chaise longue. The gin offered her a sense of dreamy well-being as her thoughts eased back to the last time she had made love to Randall. Things were better each time. She felt a freedom with him she'd never felt with another man—not even with Daniel and that young, energetic passion that had consumed them both. Making love to Randall was more subtle, more satisfying, and even more loving in its own way. The ease and willingness with which she responded to him continued to surprise her. He seemed to know instinctively what she liked, what aroused her, and when he didn't sense it, she felt free enough to tell him. Maybe that came with age, the freedom to explore yourself sexually. Sex did get better the older you got, she was sure of that now. She had a stronger, deeper sense of who she was sexually, of how to give and receive passionate love. And this was new to her, all of it. Her relationship with Jerrod had ruined the sensual aspect of her, and she had learned to close herself off from it, unwilling to be touched or even touch herself. It frightened her to remember how deadened her sensuality had become. But it also scared her how quickly Randall had reawakened it, how essential he had become to her well-being, to her appreciation of herself as a woman. When she thought about the first time they made love, she wondered if the anniversary of Mali's death had played a part in her decision, and decided that perhaps it had. Some part of her knew that it was time for her to make new attachments, to venture into a neglected place in her life. Her attraction to him was so intense it enabled her to come outside herself and enjoy their engagement for what it was—a measure of sensual and physical pleasure she'd forgotten she was capable of enjoying.

But could she trust him?

After Jerrod, she had developed a cynicism about men. Mali was cynical, too, but her skepticism had a tongue-in-cheek quality to it that even loving Nate for so many years hadn't altered. Mali tempered her pessimism with a belief in the possibility of love and the certainty that growth, no matter how painful, always followed a bad relationship.

Was she exposing herself too much? Was she mistaken yet again?

She had managed to disguise her feelings when he told her about Medora Jackson's pregnancy. She was sure he thought she was being the understanding, compassionate woman that she looked to be, but she'd been shocked. The steadier she looked, the more torn and shaken she was inside. Her marriage to Jerrod had taught her how to keep a poker face, how never to show what she really felt, how to look reasonable and calm when she wanted to pick up the nearest glass and hurl it across the room. It had served her well this afternoon.

She faced those feelings now. Was Medora the kind of woman who would choose to have a child only if she loved the father? Ana had no idea, but if she was that kind of woman, then she had to be getting something back.

On the other hand, maybe she didn't love him.

When she thought about it, Ana realized that she could understand Medora's decision to continue her pregnancy, even as she ended her relationship with her baby's father. Pregnancy could be a joy within itself. Ana could still recall the delight of her pregnancy with Danny. Although Daniel was supportive, he had not been essential to her happiness. Her connection was to her baby; each moment of his developing life had become a secret between them. Each day of her pregnancy seemed imbued with a singular joy, a connection to everything that was meaningful and eternal in life. As young as she had been, she had understood the gift her son would be, and that understanding had very little to do with her relationship with her baby's father.

On impulse, Ana went into the living room and with a dispassionate and critical eye gazed at the painting that hung over her couch. Randall had explained it to her when she bought it as an "early Medora Jackson" whatever that meant. It was oil on linen, and Ana had fallen in love with its lyrical rhythm the moment she laid eyes on it.

But had she actually bought it because she wanted to impress Randall? Had he pushed it? It had been one of three that she had been drawn to, and for investment purposes a painting by an artist whose work had recently been featured in ARTnews seemed a wiser buy. Yet he had recommended Medora Jackson, and she had taken his advice. Studying it now, she tried to get a sense of the woman who had done it. How much could you tell about an artist from her work?

There were no flowers, whimsical designs, or conventional turns of line. The colors were bold and exciting, and her choices in the use of space and design were balanced and well-considered. She took chances where other artists would have gone for the predictable. Her work was distinct and original, and there was an honesty in it that told Ana the woman who painted it was an honorable woman. She had assumed it was the work of an older artist when she saw it, and it had occurred to her that she was the type of woman who could be her friend. Mali reincarnated as an artist instead of a writer.

Mali had dreamed once of having a child with Nate, but had decided not to do it because of the pain she knew it would cause him and Essie. But Randall wasn't married and Medora was a mature woman in her mid-thirties, and women's bodies marched to the unyielding beat of a biological clock. She was an artist whose sensitivity and appreciation of life was essential to who she was. Ana could understand how this woman could make the decision to have her baby on her own and to make the arrangements concerning its care that she had made with him.

It was dark now, and the evening breeze made her shiver. She closed the patio doors, thought about ordering some curry from her favorite Indian restaurant but poured herself another drink instead. Two drinks before dinner. She was drinking too much, edging close to those times with Jerrod when alcohol numbed the pain. That was no good. She had to have more discipline than that. She poured it out, and opened a bottle of Pellegrino instead.

Lying was the one thing she said she would never take from a man again. Even Jerrod had never lied. He'd spit out the truth with a cruelty that had nearly destroyed her, and it had seemed then that the comfort of a lie was better, but now she knew it was the one thing that had saved her. She could trust him to be cruel. She knew he would always be against her, so she could plot her life accordingly. She knew exactly who he was, so she could protect herself. There was safety in that.

But there was no defense against a lie. It caught you unaware. It made you feel a fool because you had not had the good sense to see through it. A man lied to you when he really didn't trust you. Or when he thought you couldn't live with the truth. Or when he couldn't live with it. Or if he was simply too much of a coward to do anything else.

What kind of a liar was Randall Hollis?

What kind of liar was she?

Was she lying to herself about how important he had become? She thought about him constantly. She liked to please him. He'd complimented her once on the shade of a piece of lingerie and she'd gone to Neiman-Marcus the next afternoon and bought three more of the same color. She had started coloring her hair again because it made her feel prettier, younger, and she liked that feeling. Everything about him—the way he spoke, chuckled, sipped his drinks—thrilled her. She feared she was being reckless with her feelings, but it was too late to do anything about it.

But he had lied to her.

But he *admitted* he had lied to her.

Not everything is for sure. Take a chance. Live a little.

She was so damned tired of being alone.

She picked up the phone and called him.

Chapter Eight

Taylor snatched Randall's ringing cell phone from his hand, turned it off, and shoved it under her pillow.

"You can't talk to anybody but me while you're here," she said. Her voice was playful, but she was dead serious.

"Well, there's nobody else in the world I would rather talk to," he said, then ran his lips down, then back up, the space between her chin and belly button, which made her shiver with delight. They had just made love, and the thrill of it came back to her in a quick wave of desire, which she decided to ignore. "Please give it back," he said in a mock, pleading tone.

"No! Maybe when you go home, if you're nice," Taylor said and then added, "It's bad enough you only see me on Thursdays. Never on weekends anymore. Thursday is the day you do things that you don't want to waste a weekend doing. It's the day you put all the stuff that's not important. Is that the way you feel about me, Randall Hollis? That I'm not good enough for the weekends?" She frowned and poked her lip out petulantly, watching him closely for a hint of what he really felt.

"I do business on the weekends, baby," he said convincingly, but it was impossible to tell what Randall really thought. "Okay, I promise, you can have all my weekends from now on. Starting tomorrow. How's that? I had some plans, but I canceled them earlier today," he added, and a shadow, quick and fleeting, passed over his eyes. "Thursday is my free day. Weekends are usually crazy."

"Okay," Taylor said, choosing to believe him because it was too much trouble not to. He had been so distracted during dinner, she'd been tempted to tell him to go home. She still wasn't sure what she really felt about him. Even now, cuddled in his arms after having just made love to him, she felt distant, as if they were both playing roles. She just wasn't quite sure what hers was supposed to be.

She had no idea what Randall felt about her and what part she played in his life. She knew he enjoyed taking her out. He liked giving her things; she could count on him for expensive bouquets, perfume, and anything else that struck her fancy, like the wine he'd picked up for tonight. He stretched out and closed his eyes and she studied him as he fell asleep. She thought he enjoyed making love to her. But she wasn't sure how much she really enjoyed making love to him, too. As much, she supposed, as anybody else.

Taylor had been sixteen the first time she had sex, and after she'd done it, she couldn't figure out what all the excitement was about. Her boyfriend of the moment was a good-looking jock named Leon who had everything going for him except a brain. They made quick, frantic love in the guestroom of his family's summer rental in Sag Harbor. She was sick and tired of being the sole virgin in her junior class and only too ready to take this final leap into womanhood.

She could still vividly recall the prelude to her lackluster first experience. Is this your first time? he'd wheezed into her ear. Of course not, she said, knowing full well that the only foreign object that had ever found its way between her legs was a Tampax. From somewhere, a Trojan appeared and was deftly slipped on, and later she'd wondered if he kept a summer's supply tucked in a secret compartment underneath the bed. She'd felt nothing but irritation when he entered her, and after the first few minutes was completely bored. As her young lover pumped his way to orgasm, she'd gazed at a crack in the ceiling and recalled reading somewhere that British mothers once advised daughters on their wedding night to close their eyes and think of England; she'd thought about the main floor of Bergdorf-Goodman.

Nine years had made a difference in her attitude toward sex, but not much of one. Her friends routinely told her that it was because she hadn't found the right man, and she suspected they were right. Truth was, despite her veneer of sophistication, Taylor hadn't made love to all that many men. In nine years, not counting the jock, she'd had only four lovers, which was small pickings compared to most of her friends. There was James Lawson. A fling with a married professor her first year of graduate school. Danny Mitchell. James again. And now Randall Hollis. So when her friends got to talking about varieties in length, width, and shape, and how each variable could affect her satisfaction, Taylor nodded her head as if she knew what they were talking about, but had no idea.

The person she'd enjoyed having sex with most was James Lawson, which baffled her. In his own awkward way, James was an enthusiastic, generous lover, and he genuinely enjoyed it, which made his ardor contagious. He was the first man with whom she reached a climax, which had surprised her.

Danny Mitchell was a different matter. He thought he loved her, and she was inclined to believe him, but since she felt little for him, she found his outpouring of affection puzzling and a bit scary. For Danny, making love was an exercise in one-upmanship; he seemed hell-bent on showing her every sexual turn he knew. Unfortunately, in his determination to prove he was the best lover she'd ever had, he ended up proving just the opposite. He was the only man with whom she had to fake an orgasm. He worked so damn hard trying to make her come, she felt compelled to give him what he wanted—especially since each stroke had been accompanied with a heartfelt declaration of love.

Randall Hollis was affected by the same performance goals as Danny, except he was more adept at reaching them. God knew, he was far more experienced than poor Danny and knew all the right moves—what to do, when to do it, what to do it with. Problem was, he did it by rote, as if checking off points on a scorecard. Randall was strangely removed when he made love to her, as if watching—then applauding—himself. Afterward, she always felt strangely empty, as if she'd spent the last hour with a vibrator. It was as if he could make love to her without being much of a participant himself, which gave him a power over her she found disturbing.

But she also had power over him.

The year before Taylor lost her virginity, she discovered the difference between boys and men. Thanks to her brother, boys were no mystery. They had always been part of her life—teasing, threatening, throwing basketballs and softballs in her backyard. She knew what motivated them and how to control them. They were guileless and easy to read. When she competed with them, she usually won, and they grudgingly saluted her superior talents with good humor. In their own way, they considered her one of their own. Her brother's friends greeted her coming into woman-hood with a combination of awe and admiration. She was charmed when they treated her differently and annoyed when they tried to date her. She—and they—knew she was out of their league.

Men were a different story. Her father's friends were the first she took note of, not that these lawyers, bankers, and entrepreneurs ever did any-thing inappropriate, with the exception of Mr. Potter, who would let his hand linger a tad too long on her backside during family gatherings. From the others, there was simply a wistfulness in their eyes when they gazed at her, a lingering attentiveness that made her uncomfortable at first, then told her she had gained some kind of an advantage. She began to realize that she was on equal footing with them; she could look them straight in the eye, female to male, with no hint of little-girl diffidence, and she grew comfortable around them, sure of herself because she knew she would always be the unacknowledged center of attention.

There was also a subtle difference in the attitudes of their wives, who now regarded her with a combination of suspicion and contempt. She didn't mind that either because she was on equal footing with them as well. There was no more condescension on their part or deference on hers. She no longer felt the need to pretend that she was anything less than she was, and that empowered her.

Several of these women became overtly hostile; she could feel their eyes following her around the room, listening to her, studying her as if waiting for her to make a mistake. They were competitive, which struck Taylor as pathetic. She pitied these enviers of her youth and hoped when she grew old she would not be like them. She knew that beauty was fleet-ing and the power she gained from it temporary. Even at twenty-five, she understood that her looks would soon fade, which occasionally depressed her. Instinctively, she knew that basing her self-esteem on the passing admiration of men was risky business, and she reminded herself of that simple fact whenever she did it.

But fleeting as it was, she enjoyed the power. She was amazed at the foolishness men put up with to be in her favor and viewed their adoration with a combination of detachment and disdain. It delighted her to be able to call a man on a whim, divert him from wherever he was going, to come to her apartment for a carelessly tossed together dinner toting two bottles of expensive red wine.

She thought about that wine, how much it had cost and how quickly she had gotten it as she watched Randall napping beside her. His breathing was easy now, and even. His eyes were closed, and she wondered what he was dreaming about. She doubted it was her. Maybe it was that show he'd been talking about earlier. Or some sale to some rich collector to whom he was about to make a sale.

He was in reasonably good shape for somebody his age. But he reminded her of someone distasteful; it took her a moment to think of who it was, then she shuddered when she remembered. Professor Hendricks. Anthony Hendricks. Tony. He was older than Randall by a couple of years, but Randall's body was aging in the same way his had: a slight flabbiness here and there, the hint of "love handles," a sprinkling of gray hair where you least expected to see it.

Professor Anthony Hendricks was an experience she didn't like to recall. He taught honors English at a nearby college and was married to the dean of the school of social work. He was good-looking in a professorial way, and he had a quick, sardonic wit. But he was a cheap date—a habitué of Ponderosa Steakhouses and Howard Johnson Motor Inns—and a callous lover more concerned with his own too-quick satisfaction than with hers. But she was flattered he'd chosen her over his older and obviously willing grad assistant, and she was eager to please him. The affair lasted most of the school year and into the summer. Two weeks before he started his sabbatical, he dumped her with a half-assed excuse and a poorly written poem she flushed down the toilet. Yet she cried as if her heart were breaking. She felt utterly rejected. His unceremonious dismissal was humiliating and made her feel like a fool. After a week or two of moping around, however, she admitted to herself that she hadn't really liked him very much, and there had been nothing about the relationship that made her feel good.

That was the difference between Randall Hollis and Anthony Hendricks, even though there were some similarities, which made her uncomfortable. James's words about Randall being an "old-ass dude" who just wanted some "young, fly chick to buy expensive toys for" had the ring of truth, even though there hadn't been any really expensive toys. She knew if she wanted them he would buy them. He'd brought over the wine without a moment's hesitation. Maybe a sugar daddy was what she needed.

Careful, you're turning into Pamela.

Her thoughts turned to her father, as they sooner or later always did. What a fool he was to end up with somebody like Pamela. Couldn't he see through her? Was her father actually as much of a creep as Anthony Hendricks had been, sleeping with a woman as young as his daughter just to prove he still had it? The thought of it made her sick.

She hadn't spoken to her father since he left, and she missed him more than she had ever missed anyone in her life. She longed to hear his humor and to see the way his eyes sparkled whenever he looked at her. She yearned for his unconditional love and unwavering support. When she dreamed of him now, she was always transported to her childhood, when she was once again the center of his universe. She always awoke with a sense of loss as deep as if he had died, leaving her forever.

Thinking about her father and how much she missed him made her weep, her tears coming unexpectedly as they often did when she was alone. She shifted away from Randall, unwilling to expose so much of herself, but her sudden movement awoke him.

"What's wrong?" he asked.

"Nothing."

"Something's wrong or you wouldn't be crying." She could see his concern and she was touched by it. Why did she always feel so awkward sharing the details of her life with him? To avoid talking to him she offered her body to him again, snuggled close, rolled into his arms, grazing him with her breasts. He kissed her, his tongue gently pushing its way into her mouth. She changed her mind, pulling away.

"I don't feel like it," she said.

He gave her a peck on her forehead and moved away from her. "Tell me why you were crying," he said.

"I told you, nothing is wrong." Reaching for a cigarette, she lit it and inhaled in a motion. He let her have a few drags and then grabbed it from her, holding it out of her reach. "You're too young to smoke."

"Not in my own house," she said and snatched it out of his hand. Defiantly, to prove her point, she French-inhaled, pulling smoke up through both nostrils, something she hadn't done since high school.

"Touché." Randall cracked a smile.

"If it really annoys you, why don't you just say so?" She snubbed it out in a nearby ashtray.

"Because I often don't tell people the truth, even people I care about and with whom I've been intimate, which is inexcusable at my age. I hate cigarettes because they're killing my mother," he said.

"So you would probably prefer I not smoke around you?"

"Like you said, you can do what you want to in your own place, but I'd rather you didn't in mine anymore."

"Why didn't you just tell me that in the first place? Every time I see you I smoke at least half a pack."

"I'm telling you now. So, why were you crying?"

Without realizing she was doing it, she glanced toward the cigarettes, and Randall, taking the hint, lit one, and handed it to her. "Your place," he said.

Taylor relaxed as she smoked. "I've got a lot going on in my life. I have a lot of things that are really freaking me out."

Randall raised his eyebrow slightly, which made him look amused and skeptical. "What trials and tribulations could a beautiful, bright, twenty-something lady who has everything in the world going for her possibly have?"

"Don't fucking patronize me! All right?" She hadn't meant to snap at him, but his attitude angered her. When she was with him, she routinely cleaned up her vocabulary and attitude, and the look on his face told her that this was the first time he'd heard her curse.

"Okay. I won't 'fucking patronize' you. Now, what's going on?" The concern in his eyes made her think about her father, and her eyes watered again.

"I really miss my father."

"Oh, I'm sorry. When did he pass away?" His eyes filled with sympathetic concern.

"He's still alive, I just haven't seen him in a long time."

"Then why haven't you seen him?"

"Because I'm very angry at him."

"Why are you so angry?"

"Because he left my mother for another woman, and I'm having a hard time dealing with it."

"But if you really miss him that much, you should reach out to him."

"I'm still too angry at him to do that."

"I've heard that can be rough. So, when did he walk out?"

"About a year and a half ago."

"A year and a half?" *And it's still bothering you?* He didn't say it, but she could read it in his eyes.

He has no idea what I'm talking about and how hurt I am, she thought.

"Yes, but there are other things, too."

"Like what?"

"I don't think I'll go into it," Taylor said quickly, realizing how foolish anything would probably sound after the confession about her parents. If he thought that a year and a half was too long to mourn the loss of a relationship, what would he say about twenty-four years? And what could she say? I had a twin sister, but she died when we were both a year old. Most of the time I don't think about her, but when I'm depressed and unsure of myself, I think that maybe she should have been the one to live and I should have died.

"I'm sorry for whatever it is," he said, but his eyes had no real understanding, and she realized that she should have let the gaps between them stay where they were.

"Do you have any brothers or sisters?" she asked, because the silence made her uncomfortable.

"Not that I know of."

"Are your parents still together?"

"My father died right after I was born, and my mother is very ill with lung cancer, like I said. So do you have any siblings?"

It was such a formal word, "siblings." It threw her off for a moment.

"My brother. That's all. So do you have lots of aunts and uncles and people like that?" Taylor had a large extended family in various parts of country, and she assumed that most people had a similar collection of relatives. The look in Randall's eyes told her she was mistaken.

"No. Nobody except my uncle Reynard," he said.

"Has he been like a father to you?" she asked, feeling awkward and foolish, like a dumb foot-in-mouth teenager. He laughed, a contemptuous guffaw that she knew wasn't aimed at her but at the thought of this uncle Reynard, whoever he was. It made her wish she hadn't asked about him.

"As much a daddy as anybody else," he said. "I gather your father was everything a father should be." There was a note of condescension in his voice, a hint of sarcasm.

"Like I said, I'm very angry at him now, and I don't have much good to say about him. I really don't want him in my life. I don't want to talk about him."

"But you brought him up!"

"I hate him for what he did to our family."

"He loved you. He provided for you. He took care of you. Wasn't that enough?" There was an implied criticism in his words and voice.

"No, I guess not."

"Do you know how lucky you are?" He said it gently, almost kindly, but the words made her wince. Hadn't she heard them all her life?

Do you know how lucky you are to be born into a family that lived in a gorgeous house in a nice neighborhood paid for piano and tennis lessons went out to nice restaurants on weekends vacationed in the islands during winter breaks gave you your very own credit cards and cell phones and on and on and on.

"Yeah, okay. I know how lucky I am," she said in a flat voice, adding a fake smile. She *was* lucky, she knew that, and somebody or other was always trying to jam it down her throat. She *was* lucky to somebody who had grown up poor without a father and nobody but a weary mother, but she hadn't grown up that way, and nobody she knew had grown up that way and her kind of "luck" was its own burden, and she was sick of carrying it. Why the hell should he care about how torn up her insides felt? She was too damn lucky. "Tell me about the show in September," she said, the fake smile still glued on her face. It was an awkward segue, but she didn't give a damn.

"Why?" He looked genuinely puzzled by how quickly she had changed the subject, but Taylor didn't want to talk to him about her life now. She was sorry she'd brought any of it up. She wanted to be on familiar ground.

"I'm sick of talking about myself. I want to know about you and the show you mentioned. I'm really interested." Her tone was little-girl kittenish. She'd learned long ago that most men were more than willing to change the subject of a conversation to themselves if given half an opportunity.

"Well, I'm a partner in a gallery in SoHo, the New Walls Gallery. It's a small place but it's making its mark. The show is featuring recent work by four women of color from different cultures. An African-American, an Asian, a Chicana, and a Nigerian. I might call it Quartet or Four Women, like that song Nina Simone used to sing if I can't come up with something more inspired."

"Who's the African-American?" Taylor had no idea what "Four Women" was because she hadn't heard the Nina Simone song since her father used to play her albums when she was a little girl.

"Medora Jackson."

"You have a lot of her work at your place. I like what she does."

"Yeah, she's really a talent." He shifted his eyes away from hers, picked up the wine, and finished what remained in his glass.

"I don't have time to curate the show myself, so I'm trying to find somebody else to do it. I need somebody to do the research, write the critique, get the artists' statements, do the footwork, organize—"

"Let me do it!"

Randall looked surprised and then doubtful. Taylor pushed off the cover and sat straight up. "Let me do it! I know I can handle it. I know I can do a good job. Please!"

"Taylor, I don't know . . ."

She was nearly shaking with excitement. "Please, Randall, I've really never asked you for anything—"

"Except these ninety-dollar bottles of wine!"

She giggled self-consciously and then turned serious. "But never anything like this! This could be so important for me!"

She didn't like to beg, but she wanted this. It was a chance to do something important, something to focus on before school started again and to make into her own. She didn't want to lose it. Randall looked skeptical, as he ran the pros and cons over in his mind, but then he relented. She could see it in his eyes. Men always did in the end.

"Please," she added for good measure.

He thought for a moment and then smiled. "Why not? Okay. But these are very important artists."

"You can trust me."

"I know I can, but one of them, Medora Jackson, I'd like to deal with directly. I have a long-standing relationship with her, and she's going through a . . . a difficult time." He avoided her eyes. Taylor vaguely wondered what the trouble was, but she was too excited and pleased with his decision to press him.

"Thank you. Thank you. Thank you."

"You sound like a kid."

"I *feel* like a kid," she said as she covered his face with kisses. Like a little girl eager to please her daddy.

As soon as Randall left, Taylor called James to tell him her news. His response was less than enthusiastic.

"So, Mr. Big is an art dealer," he said, crunching on what sounded like potato chips. "I should have known he was something sleazy like that."

"Art dealers aren't sleazy. Have you forgotten that's what I want to be? And don't call him Mr. Big."

"What's his name, then?"

"Randall Hollis."

"Isn't that the guy who lectured at my mother's club?"

"Yeah. Why don't you stop eating whatever you're eating and congratulate me," Taylor said.

"Congratulations, then. But tell me this, Taylor. What's so different about the way you got this job and the way some hoochie fucks some rapper to get in his video?"

The comparison took her breath away. She couldn't find her voice for a moment. "I don't believe you said that to me, James," she finally said.

"Well, believe it." His words had been delivered like a punch, and for a moment Taylor thought she might vomit.

"I called you because I consider you my friend and you're coming at me with something like that? Are you calling me a whore?"

James didn't back down. "I just want to know the difference between what you're doing and what some downtrodden sister with no other options does. Most of them have a lot less going for them than you do, so I can forgive them that shit! I'm just fucking disappointed in you. That's all!"

Taylor slammed down the receiver. For one moment, she thought about calling him back to curse him out. In the next, she thought about calling Randall and telling him to forget the whole thing. Finally she just fell out on the bed and cried, releasing everything she had felt for the last hour and a half.

Was that really what she was doing, sleeping with a man for what he could toss her way?

No. It wasn't that. She was sure of it. She liked the way he made her feel, as if she was worth something. She liked the admiration in his eyes when he looked at her. He was smart, he could be funny, and he treated her like she was the best thing that ever walked into his life. She liked spending time with him. She liked talking about art with him. He generously shared what he knew about artists, galleries, and collections. She found that visiting museums with him was more informative than a graduate seminar in art history. His knowledge of contemporary and historical African-American art was nothing short of phenomenal. Randall had become a mentor, and in some ways their professional bond was stronger than their personal one. James was wrong. He was just jealous and that was a disgusting thing to say to her.

But all the joy she had felt before was gone and the self-doubts came back. Who did she think she was? Why did she think she was special? The special one died.

"No," she said aloud to herself. She wouldn't let the depression come again. She would fight it this time. She would have to. She picked up the phone again. She *should* call Randall back and tell him she had changed her mind. No! To hell with James. She needed to talk to the person whom she could count on to give her unconditional love and absolute support. But calling her father was out of the question. So she called her mother.

After

You've

Gone

Chapter Nine

Each time that Randall visited his mother in the apartment where he grew up he was struck by how dismal the place had become. Even the June sun made no difference. The shrubs and grass, which he remembered as being green and lush when he was a boy, grew pale and stunted. Tulips planted by some ambitious soul the spring before only half opened. As he stepped out of his car, his stomach clenched with anxiety the way it used to with hunger when he was a child.

A TV sitcom blasted through an open window on the first floor. The laughter was canned and ridiculous, and he wondered how anybody could watch something that sounded so asinine. He rarely watched television; he had never developed the habit. Television bored him when he was growing up because it was so clearly based on fantasy, and it still did. The families he saw on television bore no resemblance to reality. Even as a child he felt contempt for them. As he entered the building, he smelled the familiar odors—cheap fried food, yesterday's garbage, rotting wood. He got depressed just walking into this place; it amazed him how often it came back to him in his dreams.

He pushed the button and the elevator creaked down the shaft the way it used to when he lived here. A kid, not more than ten, got out and sized him up, putting a price tag on his linen shirt, pressed gabardine trousers, Gucci loafers. He could see the hunger in the boy's eyes and knew he was wondering what kind of rich dude like this would wander into his territory and what he might be carrying. He gave the kid a nod that told him he knew what was on his mind and that he wasn't a chump; he could kick his skinny little ass with one hand tied behind his back. The kid got out of his way.

It took his eyes a moment to adjust to the elevator's dim light, and he cursed to himself. He paid enough for this firetrap, why couldn't they at least put a decent lightbulb in the elevator? What the hell would it take? Why wouldn't she let him move her out? What in God's name held her here? His anger grew, heightened by everything around him—the dirty walls, the abandoned newspapers, the raucous voices in the hall. He jabbed the fourth-floor button hard and got out quickly when it reached the floor. He walked the ten steps to his mother's door, silently counting them like he used to do when he was a boy. His heart beat fast with each one. His hand shook as he put the key into the lock. *Why does coming here still have this effect on me?* he asked himself. *Why do I let it?* Because this place had been his home, he reminded himself, and he knew he would carry a piece of it within him forever, a stone within his heart.

"Lydia?" he called out as he closed the door and locked it. He panicked when she didn't answer. He called her name again, then went into her bedroom. She was asleep. Her breathing was calm, with none of the wheeziness that usually characterized it. He sat down in the overstuffed chair beside the bed and gazed at her face, struck by how sleep relaxed the lines that so often distorted her face in anger. She had a pretty face, the disease hadn't taken that yet. Anybody who looked at her could tell he was her son—same cheekbones and lips, same dark eyes with lashes grown women envied. But her eyelashes were gone now, taken by the chemotherapy. The red paisley scarf that hid her hair loss was askew. He straightened it, gently kissed her cheek.

"You're still beautiful, Lydia," he whispered to her.

He had been almost as proud of her looks as she had been, and when he'd been a kid he'd always been afraid that men would take advantage of her. He smiled at that thought now. The man hadn't been born yet who could take advantage of Lydia Hollis. She was tougher than any man he knew. She knew it and so did any man who crossed her path, although there hadn't been one in years, decades maybe. She was a loner. Always had been. He couldn't even recall any woman friends she kept for more than a couple of months. Women were untrustworthy. He'd heard that from her often enough. So, what did that make her?

"Lydia?" he said again, and she stirred without waking, her face troubled. He picked up a bottle of tiny pink pills that sat on the night table, studied the label, then put it back where it was. At least she was taking the damned things. Her pain must have gotten worst. It must have become unbearable.

The room had an odor he couldn't identify. *It smells like death*, he thought, then put that thought out of his mind. She kept the windows closed, even in summer when the air conditioners he'd bought her did little to cool down the place. He took a dying fern off the sill and forced open the window. Dust swirled. The place was dirty, he could see that. The windowsill and walls surrounding it had a grimy feel to it. He wondered what had happened to Mrs. Washington, the nurse's aide who lived next door, whom he had hired last month despite Lydia's protestations. She was a kind, good-natured woman, with an easy smile and warm disposition. She'd agreed to clean as well as care for Lydia, and call him if there was anything she needed. Lydia had probably fired her, like she had all the others. She liked to keep this tight, dark place to herself. Anyone who entered it was intruding. Except for him.

He carried the fern out of the bedroom, stopping in the living room to pick up some discarded magazines, and gave the room a once-over. The place looked the same. She had always had pretensions of grandeur. The dainty French provincial couch that took up nearly all the space in the small room was far too grand for the humble space. The expensive wallpaper for which she'd paid a week's wages was now smudged with dirt and peeling and probably the source of the smell of decay. She loved ornate mirrors, and as he walked through the room, his image flew back to him half a dozen times. *It's like a damned funhouse*, he thought.

He took the fern into the kitchen to water it, cursing when he found the sink piled high with dirty dishes. She must have fired Mrs. Washington. Why the hell did she have to be so hard on everybody? Rolling up his sleeves, he filled the sink with water and soap and scrubbed the dishes, piling them high in the cheap plastic rack. Next he turned to the stove, then to the cabinets above the counter. He tore an old sheet in half, sprayed it with Fantastic, and went through the living room and hall, cleaning everything he saw and replacing lightbulbs that had burned out. He cleaned the bathroom, putting out clean towels on the rack and unwrapping two rolls of toilet paper, placing one in the dispenser and the other on the commode.

Thirsting for a beer, he went back into the kitchen and opened the refrigerator looking for a cold one. To his relief, it was clean, although empty of food. At least Mrs. Washington had a chance to clean it out; she must not have shopped before Lydia dismissed her. What the hell was she eating? She needed food now more than ever, and she was still starving herself. She had always been obsessed yet repulsed by food. Cooking was a skill his childhood had taught him; he learned to cook because he didn't have a choice. He gulped down a Budweiser and reached for another, drinking at intervals as he swept the floors, ending up finally in the small corner bedroom where he spent his boyhood.

It was a narrow room, hardly big enough for a twin-size bed. The walls were still the robin's-egg blue he had chosen as a boy. He remembered the day they painted it, the mess they made, how hard they laughed, how proud they were when it was finished. He had loved her that day more than he knew was possible, as much as he knew she loved him.

The bed was shorter than he remembered it and sagged to the floor when he sat down on it. Slipping off his shoes, he laid down on it, his stocking feet hanging off the end. He could remember measuring the length of his body against the bed, eager to finally grow its length because when he did, Lydia promised to buy him a new one, but by the time they could afford it, he was ready to go to college.

Nearly all of the plaques and awards he had won as a child still hung on the walls where he had put them. She must have been proud of him to have kept them up for so long, but for the life of him he couldn't remember her showing much emotion one way or the other when he won them. Her mind was always somewhere else, and the weary look that never left her eyes hid behind every smile. Half the time she was too tired even to talk.

From the beginning he had been a diligent student, sensing that scholarship was the best way out of the life they led. Although he was a natural athlete, Lydia felt that sports were dangerous and forbade him even to try out for any athletic teams. But maybe that had been to his advantage. The classroom was where he excelled, and he greedily lapped up the smallest bit of praise from teachers, principals, or anybody who would throw it his way. That had brought some problems, too. On more than one occasion, his behind had been soundly kicked by less industrious students. He didn't care. The stronger he got, the less he was challenged, and he wasn't that keen on making friends anyway.

He was a loner, too, like his mother, and proud of it. He dressed differently, brought different lunches to school, talked like a white boy, or so they told him. And Lydia was unlike the mothers of his friends, too, and he was proud of that. She was an artist, and that was what she told people if anybody asked. The jobs she did on the side—the temping, the hospital aide work, the receptionist job—were done to support herself while she did her art, which she was always too tired to do. There were times when he envied his classmates' mothers, though, with their indulgent hugs, generous bodies, and spontaneous laughter. They worked as domestics, waitresses, short-order cooks, and came home each night, with or without some man to curl up beside them. They didn't leave their sons alone to fend for themselves at night while pursuing some dream that never became reality. Yet, as a child, he remained fiercely proud of his mother, no matter what. His admiration was all that she had.

Years later, when he had developed a critic's eye and knowledge, she showed him some of the drawings that she had managed to finish, and he'd nearly wept when he saw how good they were. She was clearly talented, and his belief in that talent had been real; neither of them had imagined it. Yet she had never been able to achieve her dream, and they both knew it was because of him. What could she have been if she had had the time and energy to do it? Where would all her talent have taken her?

Her belief in her talent and their loneliness was all that they had, but the loneliness was what he remembered most about his childhood. His return to the empty apartment, dark and scary despite the afternoon sun, the blare of the TV that he kept on for company as he gobbled down a sandwich, soggy from the refrigerator, that was meant to hold him until she returned from either art class or one of the jobs. He was always asleep by then, and she was too tired to talk.

He understood now how hard she must have struggled to keep food on the table and clothe a boy who outgrew clothes faster than he could wear them out. He was all she had. No man. No life. No art. And that was what had destroyed her, not being able to do what she was meant to do. He knew what that loss meant because he knew so many artists now, and what their work meant in their lives. But Lydia had nothing but him, and it had been that way for as long as he could remember. He'd read somewhere that children interpret deprivation as neglect, believing that a parent's unwillingness to care adequately for them is because she doesn't want to rather than because she can't. He had always been resentful of children who had more than he, secretly angry at her because she was not able to give him what he needed. He was ashamed of that now.

He made few friends because he sensed she would resent anyone who took him away from her. She had given up so much that he knew she wanted all of him as well. That was why she hated Reynard, although she would never admit it. In so many ways, his father's younger brother stole him from her, offering the things she could never give him—the casual comfort of another male, the devil-may-care good times, the irreverence and craziness that added such joy to his young life. Even after thirty years, the memory of his first meeting with his uncle made him smile.

He had been fast asleep, facing the walls, hands balled into fists, the way he slept as a kid, and sometimes still did. Reynard had shaken him awake. When he opened his eyes, his first thought was of Lydia's safety, and he was terrified that this big, cocoa-colored man with his wide, gap-toothed grin had committed some unspeakable act against his mother. He jumped out of bed, fifty-five pounds of six-year-old male ready to defend whatever needed defending. Reynard laughed his deep belly laugh that hadn't changed in all these years.

"He sure don't look like him, do he? At least he got his name, though. Randall Oates, Jr., don't he?"

"No, he looks like me, and his name is Randall Hollis. No junior. Just Randall Hollis." Randall could hear the tension in Lydia's voice as she shouted her response from the living room, but she was smiling when she peeked into his room. She took a sip of the drink in her hand and handed one to the stranger. Randall settled down on his bed, taking in the man who sat on the edge beside him.

"Hey, boy, I brought you something from your daddy." His smile was vaguely familiar, and Randall realized that he looked like the picture of his father that his mother kept tucked away in her drawer. He stared at the stranger in silence, and it occurred to him that maybe his father wasn't gone, maybe this was the man who had played a role in his fantasies for as long as he could remember, despite the fact that Lydia insisted his father was dead. Maybe Lydia had been lying to him, playing a joke on him. Maybe his father was still alive and would come back to take care of them both.

"You know who I am?" The smile widened.

"You my daddy?"

The stranger chortled and slapped his knee. "Hell no, boy! I ain't your daddy."

Frowning, Lydia came into the room, which told Randall he had said the wrong thing. "You know better than that, Randy."

"My daddy is dead," he said, not taking his eyes from his mother's disapproving face.

"I'm Reynard. Your daddy's baby brother. And that's almost as good as being your daddy!" Reynard grabbed him in a bear hug, which Randall returned as if he really were his father come back from his grave.

"What did you bring me?" He suddenly remembered what Reynard had said. Reynard pulled out a Bulova watch, pure gold, that sparkled like new. Randall held it for a moment, then slipped it on his tiny wrist. It was the most beautiful thing he'd ever seen.

"That's your daddy's name and the day he got it," Reynard said when Randall looked at the inscription—RANDALL OATES, JULY 12, 1961—stenciled on the case. He said his father's name as he pulled on the watch, as if saying the words were a magical chant.

"You'll grow into it, boy. Don't worry," Reynard told him when it didn't fit, and he finally did almost grow into it; it was always just a bit too loose. He'd worn the watch for a couple of weeks his freshman year in high school, and then, scared it would drop off, put it back in the desk drawer and forgot about it.

He opened the drawer now, only half expecting to find it, but it was there, tucked under a mess of old photographs and report cards. He put it on; it fit perfectly. So, he was the same size now as his old man when he had worn it. He was already older than his father was when he was killed. Thirty. Too young to die and leave a kid who would never know him. He slipped the watch into his pocket. Maybe he'd get it polished and give it to his own kid someday. A gift from his dead granddaddy. The thought, coming randomly as it did, startled him, and he realized that he was thinking more about Medora's baby than he wanted to, more than he should be.

As he shuffled through the photographs, his memories came back. They were mostly pictures of him, grinning and holding academic awards, standing in front of the Museum of Natural History, where Reynard would sometimes take him on weekends, laughing with Reynard. One picture in particular caught his eyes. He sat at a chessboard, waving his king above his head in a gesture of victory. One of Reynard's many women had taken the photograph. This one was exceptionally pretty, Randall had noticed that even then, and Reynard had lost probably because he was distracted, but it had been a sweet victory nevertheless. Reynard had taught him to play the game, and he had finally been able to beat him at it.

Tucked among the photographs he'd taken with Reynard was a sketch Medora had done of him in the early 1980s; he pulled it out to examine it. The drawing bore little resemblance to him as he remembered himself, but rather as she must have seen him then. He was preparing his hair to be dreadlocked, and it stood in a flamboyant bush around his head. The drawing hinted of the artist she would become—the attention to detail coupled with the spontaneity that always marked her work. He recalled the night she drew it, and his eyes watered at the memory.

W ell, here we are," she said, giggling like the girl she was when they entered the room in the small off-campus hotel where they'd decided to spend the night.

"Yeah." He spoke half heartedly, trying to be cool. He was nervous and sure that he showed it. On Reynard's advice, he hadn't mentioned that this would be his first time, too. No woman wants to lose her virginity to another virgin, Reynard had advised. So Randall had kept his secret to himself.

"Well, what do you want to do?" He asked the inane question as they sat down on the bed as cautiously as if it were alive. And for all the noise it made it could have been. The mattress was a virtual whoopee cushion that sagged from the trysts of countless young lovers, and they exploded in fits of nervous laughter at the sound of it. Their bodies touched. They pulled away. They touched again. This is crazy, he thought, remembering how many times they made out to the point of orgasm. Here, finally, was the chance they had been waiting for, and neither of them was sure how to get things started.

So they sat side by side watching TV, Randall trying desperately to remember something—anything—that Reynard, his adviser on seduction, had told him. Not that Medora needed to be seduced; she was as eager as he, but she was also his best friend, closer in spirit to a sister than what Reynard referred to as "his woman." Reynard's advice about sexual entice-ment seemed fake and insulting.

She remembered suddenly that she had to call her mother to tell her she was spending the night with a girlfriend. He lived on campus, but Medora still lived at home. She dropped her eyes guiltily as she lied. He could imagine her mother's face. He'd met Minerva Jackson only once and had been struck by her vulnerability. He put his arm around Medora and kissed her lips to take the sting out of the lie. It was a chaste kiss, a peck on the edge of her mouth. They sat back down on the bed and ordered pizza from room service even though it cost more money than they planned to spend. They knew if they left the room they probably wouldn't come back. The pizza came, they gobbled it down, and Medora began to draw. She was always writing or drawing something: Brief poems to cele-brate a moment or feeling. Quick sketches of anything that caught her fancy. This time it was of him, done on the sly. She finished it and shyly gave it to him.

He studied it critically. "Doesn't look too much like me!" he said. A foolish thing to say to an artist who has graced you with a gift. She snatched the drawing back, grabbed a pillow, threw it at his head, and missed. Randall tossed it back. Medora pitched another as hard as she could. He pulled her toward him, and she came into his arms, the pillow fight ending in passionate kisses, which marked the beginning of the first time they made love.

He smiled slightly and shook his head wearily. Their first time together had begun with a fight. He folded the drawing up and tucked it back where it was, then quickly sorted through the other photographs as he tried to put Medora out of his mind. He stopped at one taken at Reynard's thirtieth birthday party. He was thirteen then, old enough to have his first drink, which Reynard had given him with a flourish, and which had made Randall sick as a dog. To this day, the smell of bourbon made him nauseous.

Reynard at thirty, the age when his big brother got a bullet through his head. He never spoke much about his older brother. Random facts about him would slip out from time to time, and Randall would feel as if he'd unearthed some hidden gems. Much of it came down to the fact that his father had been a "player"—piano player, who formed a band and played from time to time in clubs; card player ("good, too," Reynard would say with a grin) woman player, which finally got his "playing self" shot. *Their* father was the one Reynard talked about with pride. Randall's grandfather had been a good man, and that neither he, Reynard, nor his brother had measured up to him or done much to make him proud pained Reynard even to this day. But Randall, Jr., which was what he insisted upon calling him despite Lydia's protestation, would make up for the both of them. It was up to him, Randall, Jr., to make the family proud.

Yet Randall suspected that he had become his father's son. Going with a young girl he had no business seeing. Messing up a good woman's life. Laying a kid on a woman who hadn't planned to have one. Even though this child was Medora's choice. Like he had been his mother's.

Would Medora end up like Lydia, bitter, with no sweetness left?

No. She could never be Lydia, he was certain of that, and that was what had first attracted him to her; she was the antithesis of his mother. Where Lydia was secretive and critical, Medora was open and expressive. Where Lydia was dependent and manipulative, Medora was independent to a fault. Where Lydia talked about painting, Medora actually did it.

From the first, Medora's talent was the thing that drew him to her, and he had become infatuated with her—the way she could find and capture beauty in the most commonplace things. He admired her ambition and determination to fulfill herself as an artist—her debt to the muse, she called it. There was also her ease and access into a world that he could only dream of entering. That world was her birthright, her legacy from the great T. W. Jackson, and it had made her all the more desirable and intriguing.

There were other things about her, too. She was everything good he loved about his mother, and as strong-willed, as tough in her own way, as his mother, too. That scared the hell out of him. Yet it was one of the reasons he had fallen in love with her, and why he was afraid he might fall out of love with her.

How had things gotten so bad between them?

Despite what she claimed, he knew she held expectations he would never be able to fulfill. Why did she expect more than he was able to give? Why couldn't she just accept him for who he was? But women always held expectations about the men they loved. Lydia had held them about his father. She was nineteen when she met him, closer to Reynard in age than to his older brother, Randall. Reynard had seen her first. But then in stepped his older brother with ten years' more sophistication. Ten more years of charm that could persuade a talented young artist that she was better off with him than pursuing her dream. And then he had left her. Who could she have become if Randall Oates had simply left her alone? Why had he bothered to seduce her and then leave her with a son?

Lydia must have been too young to see his weaknesses, too naïve to see him for who he was, and he was hungry for admiration; she fed his ego. His mother had probably had the same appeal for his father that Taylor

Benedict had for him. So, he was no better than his father was, and if he needed any proof of that, all he had to do was consider the last time he had seen Taylor. His reaction to her troubles had hurt her, but he simply hadn't been able to disguise his true feelings. She didn't know what real trouble was. She was privileged and spoiled with an unerring sense of entitlement. But wasn't that what he found so attractive?

Love is really a family legacy.

Ana had told him that. But so was envy, hatred, neglect, and anger. So was possessiveness and jealousy. What would Ana say to that, with her generous view of the world? he wondered. Maybe he would ask her someday. She was still speaking to him, despite everything that he had told her. He had been sure it was over between them, even though he knew she was a forgiving woman, too kind for her own good.

"I've thought about it. I don't want to give up what we have. Give me a call when you can," she'd told him in her message on his cell phone when he'd finally gotten it away from Taylor. His heart had leaped at the sound of her voice, and he'd called her back the moment he got home. That had been several weeks ago, and they had taken up where they had left off, but with a deeper understanding of each other and a new intensity. It was as if he had transferred his feelings for Medora to Ana. She had become his friend as well as his lover in the same way Medora had once been, and he confided in her in the same manner. She seemed genuinely interested in the minutiae of his life—his comings and goings, new artists he'd discovered, new collectors he'd met—and that endeared her to him. He hoped that their relationship was as good for her as it was for him.

But still there was Taylor. He'd already agreed to work with her on the show in September by the time he spoke to Ana.

And the truth was, he didn't want to give her up either. When he was with Taylor, he saw himself through her eyes. She gave him something that with all her warmth and wisdom Ana simply couldn't give. Taylor gave him a sense of strength, of power. A belief in his own invulnerability. He slammed the desk drawer closed, sick and tired of his memories and the feelings they evoked.

He went back into the kitchen for another beer, gulped it down, and called his answering machine to check for messages. There was one from Lillian Wingate, the director of the New Walls Gallery, where the September show would be held. He called her back and gave her Taylor's name and number so they could meet and begin planning things. There was a call from Ana canceling their lunch date. That was good. By the time he finished here, he wouldn't feel like seeing or talking to anybody anyway. The third call was from Joshua Littleman, whom he had played racquetball with the week before, and their conversation of that day came back to him.

So how pregnant is she?" Josh had asked when he told him about Medora. They had just finished a fast, furious game and were relaxing in the steam room.

"About four months. She conceived on Valentine's Day." Talking to Josh's disembodied voice, Randall felt as if he were having a conversation with himself.

A guffaw from Josh. "Valentine's Day? So you actually know the day and time? Now that's rich!"

"What can I say, man. It was a special day."

Respectful silence from Josh, which allowed Randall to recall again Medora's letter and the assumption that the day couldn't have had the significance for him that it had had for her. He'd searched all week for a florist who would be able to get that particular mix of flowers in time for the fourteenth. Roses, calla lilies, and lilacs weren't the easiest flowers to find in the middle of February, even in New York City. As for the bouquets she assumed he was dropping off with other women, didn't she know by now how little most of those other women meant?

"So, uh, do I hear wedding bells in the next couple of months?" Josh didn't bother to conceal his amusement.

"Naw, she's not interested."

"Not interested? That's Medora for you. What about you?"

"Ever try marrying a woman who doesn't want to get married?"

"Do you love her?"

Randall paused. "Well, to tell the truth, man, things have gotten complicated."

"Complicated meaning there is another party involved?"

"A couple of parties involved."

"Aw, shit, man!" Josh laughed, slapping his thigh for emphasis, and the sound of flesh hitting flesh resounded in the small room. "You're still a player, aren't you, Randy?" Josh laughed again, and Randall realized that Josh was the only one besides his mother who ever called him by that name.

"It's really not that way at all. I've met this woman." He paused for a moment. "I've really gotten involved with her quickly. She's a little older than me. Very wise, very beautiful. I'm really into her."

"Sounds like it. Them older women will do it to you. Does she know about Medora and the baby?"

"Yeah. I feel like I could tell her almost anything about me, and she'd accept it."

"Sounds good. But didn't you say parties?"

Randall didn't answer him.

"So Randall the player has *almost* been transformed. Well, maybe that's good enough for now. Do it in small doses. I know what you mean, though. That running-around shit got old quick for me, too. It reached the point where I just wanted somebody to have a glass of wine with when I came home from work and snuggle up beside at night. To say nothing of my kid. My boy, man, I can't even explain how much I love him. I was happier than Lynn when I found out she was pregnant again."

"But not everybody can wear the same color shirt, man," Randall said.

"You don't know what color will look good until you slip it on, Randy. Hey, it's getting hot as hell in here. Let's get out of here and get a brew somewhere," Josh said as he left the steam room, which put an end to the conversation.

Randall returned his call, and left a short message on his machine, telling him he'd get back to him later.

He searched the refrigerator for something to eat, found some frozen frankfurters, and boiled them. The bread in the bread box was moldy, so he threw it away, annoyed with his mother and then with himself for not checking on her more often. Holding the hot dogs in a napkin, he smeared them with mustard and wolfed down both.

"Randy? Is that you?" Her voice startled him.

"Yeah, Lydia. It's me. Do you want something to eat?" He searched the shelves for something nutritious; there was nothing. He'd have to buy some groceries before he left. He went into her bedroom and sat down in the chair beside the bed. She looked weaker than when she was asleep, more vulnerable. She'd lost another ten pounds, and her face, relaxed in sleep, was gaunt and drawn with tension. He reached for her hand and held it. Her fingers were ice cold and so thin he could feel each fragile bone. He let it go.

"How do I look?" she asked.

"How do you feel?"

"How does it look like I feel?" she said, her voice more sorrowful than sarcastic.

"You want the truth?"

"Isn't that what you always give me?"

"We give each other, Lydia," he said. She could be manipulative and vain, but she had always told him the truth, even when he was a child and it was more than he could bear.

"Rub my neck, Randy. Will you do that for me?" He moved to the edge of the bed, careful not to knock off the pile of pillows surrounding her. She slid next to him, and he massaged her neck and shoulders. Her body felt thin, almost breakable, so he used the tips of his fingers rather than his full hand. A wide patch of light brown skin of her scalp peeked through what was left of her hair. A pang went through him. She had always considered her hair one of her best features. He let his hands rest for a moment on her shoulders.

"Why did you fire Mrs. Washington?" He felt her muscles stiffen.

"Got on my nerves." She pulled away from him.

"She's a nice woman. She took good care of you. She works in a hospital, so she knows—"

Lydia interrupted him. "She's nothing but an aide."

He finished his sentence. "—so she knows what to do if there is an emergency."

"She talks too damn much. I get sick of hearing about her damn kids. They're losers, just like her."

"She's a nice woman. Don't talk about her like that. You can't keep doing this, Lydia. You've got to have somebody in here with you. Somebody to cook and keep this place clean. I can't keep coming over from the city four and five times a week. You've got to have somebody to help you out."

"What do you care?" It was the whiny little girl voice. He was hearing it more often now. He moved away from her to the window to avoid looking at her. He didn't want her to see the anger that he knew might be in his eyes when he answered.

"Don't say that. You know how much I care."

"I'm sorry, Randy," she said. This voice was the confident one, the strong Lydia who had taken care of things when he was a kid. Of the several Lydia voices he knew, this was the one he felt most comfortable with, the one he could call mother.

"You don't need to apologize to me, Lydia."

"Come back over and sit with me, Randy." She held out her arms, and he came back over to the edge of the bed and drew her body into his, feeling the tension leave her thin frame. He moved next to her in the bed, knocking off some of the cushions, and edged himself against the headboard.

"I'm going to call Mrs. Washington back. I'm going to beg her to come back tomorrow morning, and give her a bonus if she asks me. She's the best one you've had. Promise me you won't give her a hard time, okay?"

Lydia, twisting her mouth like a petulant child, agreed. He reached into his wallet, peeled off six twenty-dollar bills, and gave them to her. "This is if I can't get over here and you need extra money for anything. Just keep it somewhere safe. I've taken care of everything else. This is for an emergency." Obediently she tucked it under her radio on the other side of the bed.

"So, what did the doctor say on Monday?"

"He said I'd be dead in a month," she said with a cackle that broke his heart. He reached for her again and hugged her as tightly as he could, the way he used to when he was a boy, but she broke the hold, pulling away like she always did then, and the distant look that appeared in her eyes whenever she felt embarrassed or uncomfortable shaded her gaze. He never knew whether she was afraid that he was becoming too close or was afraid of her own vulnerability. Pull him to her, push him away. It was the rhythm of their life together. He went back to the window. She rolled over on her side facing the wall.

"You're taking the pills like you're supposed to, right. And it helps the pain." They were statements rather than questions that he knew she wouldn't answer.

"How do I look?" She returned to the question she had asked before.

He stopped short, thinking about the truths between them, and then told her what she wanted to hear. "You look like you always do, Lydia. You look good."

"I look like I'm dying, don't I, Randy? Tell me the goddamn truth."

"All right. You look like you're dying," he said, turning away from her, recalling what the doctor had told him two weeks before. His recommendation was that she be placed in hospice care. It was, he explained, what was routinely suggested when there was no possibility of recovery. In a hospice, she would be cared for humanely in pleasant surroundings and her considerable pain could be managed effectively. There would be no more need for a Mrs. Washington, no need for him to worry if she was eating properly or if she was taking her pain medication on time. Agreeing with him, Randall had found a place in New York City, close to where he lived. If she was there, he could see her more often. Her "passage," the awkward word the nurse insisted upon using whenever the subject of her death came up, would be easier for them both.

"Have you thought about what the doctor recommended? I found a—"

"I don't want to hear it," she said before he could get the words out of his mouth. "If I'm going to leave this damn place I want it to be on my own goddamn terms."

"It would be—"

"Shut up!"

He flinched at the words like he used to when he was a boy, when those words would fly out of her mouth with a rage that confused and frightened him, even though he knew she would try to make it up to him later.

"Okay," he tried to say gently. "Stay here then. I'll get Mrs. Washington to come back. You've got to promise me that you won't fire her, Lydia, you've got to promise that."

"I will." He could tell she was angry by the way she flung herself back on the bed. She was tired, too. Even those few words had taken something out of her. She closed her eyes. He looked at his watch, and thought, *If I go now and stop by Mrs. Washington's place, I can get her to come tonight. I can pay her twice what I've been giving her. But if she can't come, I'll have to spend the night.*

He watched her for a while longer, wondering if he should go home and get some clothes and then come back. No, it would be best for Mrs. Washington to be here, he decided. He would go to get her. If he remembered correctly, today was her day off, and he knew she could use the money. He'd pay her three times more for such short notice. He stood up, preparing to go.

"Where are you going?" Her eyes, suddenly bright and attentive, followed him.

"To get Mrs. Washington."

"Why?"

"You need somebody to stay with you tonight."

"Why can't you stay?"

"I can't," he said, avoiding her eyes.

"You give me nothing of you! Nothing! Nothing! I have no part of you, and I never have!" Her eyes grew wide and feverish with rage.

Her words made him think about Medora and the baby because that was something of him. She had a right to know about it, her first grandchild. It would be part of him and part of her, too. He'd read somewhere that anticipation of a happy event could prolong a person's life; it could give her something to believe in, something to look forward to and live for. Maybe his and Medora's baby would do that for Lydia. Maybe that would make her happy at last.

He sat back down beside her. She opened her eyes and smiled at him. It was a peaceful smile of understanding and kindness, one that he hadn't seen in a very long time. It lit up her face and reminded him how much he loved her and how much of her was in him. This baby would be part of her, too.

"Mama, I have something to tell you." The use of the unfamiliar word startled her, and her eyes grew wary. It was always the same reaction. What kind of mother reacted like that at the mention of that word? He made himself smile and returned to the familiar. "Don't worry, Lydia, nothing earthshaking."

Nothing that will take anything away from you.

"What is it?" She eyed him suspiciously. He knew he would have to chose his words carefully. It was no use pretending it wasn't important when it was. He had never been able to hide anything from her; he wouldn't underplay it.

"I'm going to have a kid. I guess I should say Medora is going to have a child, and I'm the father. Some time in October or early in November. We're not together. I mean, we're not really a couple. We didn't plan it, or anything, but it's going to happen, you know, and, well, I don't know how we're going to work it out, but I've decided that it's okay, that I'll find a way to make it work, for the baby's sake, at least.

"It was a surprise, but I'm getting used to the idea. I'm kind of a starting to like it, a little bit anyway, the idea of a kid, my kid. I was mad at first, but now . . . I don't know. I told Reynard about it, and he's really excited about it, like because he doesn't have any kids, except for me, if you can call me his son, he feels like he's going to be a grandfather or something, like a great-uncle, I guess, surprised the hell out of me, Reynard getting excited about a kid, I guess because it's my kid, but maybe it's a way to connect to my own father, to—"

He spoke in fits and starts, avoiding her eyes because he didn't want to see what was in them.

"Shut up!" She said the words in a hushed voice this time, but it made him recoil anyway. It was never the tone of her voice, but the way she said it, each word pronounced so distinctly and carefully.

"Shut up!" she said it again, then made a sound so deep inside her throat that it frightened him. She turned away from him now, facing the wall again. "When?"

"This fall." He thought he had told her, but maybe she hadn't heard him.

"Leave me alone," she said. He tried to pretend she had said something else, some half-formed thought that her illness had given voice to, but he couldn't ignore the wave of her hand, the undeniable gesture of dismissal.

His first impulse was to do what she asked, head straight out the door, let her lie there in her misery, without so much as a backward glance. But he drew closer to her, shyly touching the back of her head as if to wake her.

"Why do you feel this way?" He thought she would be happy for him, but he knew now how foolish that was. Had she ever been happy for him about anything that didn't involve her? He watched her closely, waiting for her to face him and give him some kind of a reaction. "Please, Lydia, please."

"I said to leave me alone." Her voice was pleading, as if asking a favor.

"No. I want to talk about this, Lydia. I don't understand you. I don't understand why you feel about this the way you do." He demanded that she answer him, even though he knew the answer. Because she was jealous of Medora and always had been, even though it had taken him years to face that about his mother, to admit that to himself. Because she was unable to share him with another person. Even with a child who would be part of her as well.

"I'll leave then, if that's what you want." he said, wanting to force an answer, using the last weapon he had against her—himself. She turned back toward him, her eyes begging him to stay, and then she began to cry, softly at first, and then in sobs that shook her thin body. They went through him, too, and his lips began to tremble like they used to when he was a child.

"Why? After all I have done for you, all I gave up for you?" she said.

He felt numb. He felt as if he couldn't move. "You are all I have, please don't leave me!" Her words went through him like a knife.

"Oh, God, Mama, please don't say that."

"Don't leave me, Randy, Please don't leave me."

He sat back down next to her on the bed, took a Kleenex from the box, and wiped the tears from her face.

"I'm not leaving you, Mama. Medora is having a child. Your grandchild. I'm not leaving you."

"She doesn't need you like I do. You don't need a man to bring up a child. I did it without anybody, nobody at all. I did it by myself. All by myself, so she can do that, too. She can do it, too. Leave her. Just leave her! That's all you have to do. Forget it ever happened. It's not yours anyway, probably. Tell her to kill it!"

The brutality of her words stunned him. "It's not my choice," he said almost by rote. "And if it were, I would never tell her that."

"Then leave her!"

He stared at her in disbelief. How could she say that, knowing how difficult it had been for her, for both of them. How could she wish that on his child, knowing how much he had missed his father, how much he had needed him every day of his life?

"Didn't I give you a good life?" she was yelling at him now, her frail body shaking. He didn't respond because he couldn't, and she turned her back and spoke to the wall. "I will be dead in a week, for what you have done to me."

When she said that, he pulled back from her, trembling with anger, then with love. "I will get Mrs. Washington to come back before I leave, and I will come in a few days to check on you. I love you, Mama, you know that. I love you," he said and left the apartment trying not to hear her cries.

Chapter Ten

Lydia Hollis was off by a month about her death; she died on a Saturday in July, not in June, as she told her son she would. A week later, on the morning of her wake, Randall stood over her coffin in Quentin's Funeral Parlor remembering her bitter prediction and her angry words about his unborn child. He tried to recall the good things she'd done—her love for him and the sacrifices she had made—but his feelings toward his mother had always been complicated and remained so. He knew she thought he had failed her, but not to have done so would have been to fail himself, yet knowing that didn't make his grief easier.

She died in her sleep. He was awakened at four in the morning by a weeping Mrs. Washington, who was crying so hard he could barely understand what she was saying. He told her to call the doctor and then the police because Lydia had died at home. He drove to New Jersey in pouring rain. Day was breaking when he parked in front of her apartment building. He couldn't remember the drive over or even getting dressed. He didn't feel the rain as it wet his hair and dampened his coat. His mind was blank until he sat down beside her bed.

He gazed at his mother's face and tried to cry but couldn't find any tears, even although he knew they must be somewhere inside him. Death had smoothed her face, and he tried to memorize the wrinkles on her brow and to recall how her eyes sparkled when she laughed, but he could only remember how her face would freeze in anger. He tried to hear her voice but couldn't. He touched her hand, which was still warm, and kissed her cheek.

"Good-bye, Mama," he whispered, recalling her reaction whenever she heard that word. A wan smile formed on his lips. "Lydia, then," he added. He kissed her again, then left her bedside.

He spoke to the medical examiner, who had arrived by then, and then called Reynard, who suggested he call Quentin's Funeral Home, which was owned by one of Reynard's old girlfriends, and several hours later an ambulance took her body there. Later that day, Randall called Medora, and the next day, which was Sunday, he told Ana. Although a week had passed, he still hadn't been able to cry.

He glanced around the room as he went back to his seat in the front of the room. Reynard, who had just come in, headed to the front row to sit with him. He spotted Mrs. Washington, who had come in when he did, and nodded a greeting. He hadn't recognized her at first. He was used to seeing her in the neat pink nurse's aide uniform that she always wore in the building. Her navy dress and matching coat with ancient foxtails thrown over her shoulder for style looked like something she wore to church. She dabbed at her eyes every now and again with a lace-edged handkerchief, which surprised and saddened him. A stranger had more tears for his mother than he did.

Medora, belly leading the way, was the first of Randall's women to arrive. She was accompanied by her friend Devlin and his daughter, Jasmine. Medora doubted that a funeral parlor was the wisest destination for a five-year-old, but Devlin's sitter had the flu, and despite her protestations, he insisted upon bringing her. Jasmine, he assured her, would sit in the back row with a coloring book and assume she was in church.

"You ready for this?" he whispered to Medora as they approached Randall, who sat in the row of chairs lined up near the coffin.

Medora took a deep breath and let it out slowly, her feelings clearly written on her face. Devlin, knowing her as well as he did, said, "Then maybe you should marry the guy like he asked you to. You've loved him for as long as I've known you."

Medora shrugged. "Randall is not the marrying kind, and neither am I, for that matter."

Devlin smiled. "Marriage is a lot of things, baby, and most of it has nothing to do with a preacher or the law. It's companionship, sharing a life or part of life, personal commitment—"

"You can stop right there, Dev. Randall Hollis has never been able to personally commit himself to anyone outside of himself. And anyway, we've managed to forge a working relationship in terms of the baby. We even talk once a week. Today is really no big deal."

"Good to know you've worked things out." Out of view, Devlin rolled his eyes in disbelief.

Truth was, it was a very big deal. This morning marked the first time Medora had actually seen Randall since the March morning she threw him out of her loft. It had taken her weeks to return Randall's countless calls, and it was only after Aunt Tillie persuaded her that it was folly not to speak to the man whose child she was carrying did she honor him with a reply. Through their mutual attorneys, they worked out what they both considered a reasonable child support arrangement, and that was that.

Since then, he called her every Monday at exactly ten-thirty in the morning to see how she was doing and to offer any assistance he could give. Their conversations never lasted more than five minutes. Since he called the same day of the week at the same time, Medora had ample opportunity either to take his call or to let the phone ring, depending on her mood. Their conversations were always polite, both of them carefully avoiding any reference to Valentine's Day, wildflower honey, or Red Zinger tea. Of all their transactions, having this baby was by far the most businesslike, and had ended up being as close to an immaculate conception as either of them could have imagined.

At her father's insistence, Medora had decided to keep Randall on as the primary dealer of her work, and the decision turned out to be a wise one. He had sold two paintings in the past few months, a virtual windfall for her. He sent the checks to her lawyer, who forwarded them on to her. Pregnancy was a good excuse to get out of social engagements, and she used the "exhaustion of her condition" to avoid running into people she didn't want to see. In truth, her energy level had never been higher.

To her delight, she found that pregnancy agreed with her and enhanced her creativity. She found new inspiration in *Lightning Tree* and discovered subtle nuances daily. She had begun it as a study of mortality—the dying tree, the cruel cut the lightning made through its heart—and it had evolved into a portrait of immortality. The tiny sprouts taking root in the dying limb promised rebirth, snatching it from the jaws of death, and the significance of that brought tears to her eyes. She worked on the painting night and day, realizing when she finished that it had become a metaphor for her situation. Fate—in the person of Randall Hollis dripping wildflower honey, sipping Red Zinger tea—had changed her forever with its gift of life.

Much of her work for the September show was completed and she had forwarded the slides to Randall and Lillian Wingate, the gallery director, who had called the last week in June to get her mailing list and an updated bio for the catalogue. Lillian told her she would pass the information on to the curator, a person with the pretentious name of Taylor Benedict, who Medora assumed was one of the eager young men Randall occasionally mentored. She had hoped she wouldn't have to see Randall until September, but Lydia's death changed that.

When he called her the day of his mother's death, she barely recognized his voice. It had a tonelessness that alarmed her, and her heart broke for him. Her first impulse was to tell him to come to her place so that she could comfort him. In the past, when Randall was upset or troubled, Medora always offered herself. She stopped herself this time.

"Where are you?" The depth of her concern for him surprised her.

"Home."

"Is there somebody there with you?" She wondered if he was with another woman, half hoping for his sake that he was. But only half hoping.

"Yeah, Reynard is here."

Silence again, and then he asked, "Are you okay?" Before she could answer he said, "I wanted her to see the baby, you know what I mean, it's part of her, too, like it's part of me. But she wasn't too, well, you know Lydia."

How well I do, Medora thought, saying nothing.

"But I really wanted her to see it," he began again. "The wake is next Friday if you want to come. Friday morning. Then later she'll be . . ." His voice broke. Medora assumed she would probably be cremated in some kind of a ceremony that would consist of him and his uncle. Lydia had no friends and few acquaintances. Most of the people who would be at the wake would be business associates of Randall. An ex-girlfriend or two and whoever else he was currently stringing along.

Thank God it wasn't her.

"I'll be there," she told him because she had decided she had to go. For the baby's sake.

Medora had felt her baby move (and she knew it was a "her") for the first time two months ago. She was at her easel, working on *Lightning Tree*. She was putting a stroke of vermillion on a mostly finished canvas, trying to decide if she should paint over it or let it be, and she felt a sudden, bubbly motion, like the effervescence of champagne, inside her womb. She stopped midstroke, focusing on the movement, and when it happened again, grabbed herself, fell into her rocking chair, and asked, "Is that you?"

You. It was the first time her baby was "you" and not an abstraction. *You.* Someone intent upon making Medora aware of her existence with a tiny gesture that started in her belly and traveled to her heart.

"It *is* you! You moved! You are actually here!" Medora screamed as if her expanding body had been lying to her for all these months. Her first thought was that she should call someone, and that someone, of course, should be Randall, but she changed her mind. Their conversations had been so mired in formalities it was hard to imagine how they'd once been familiar enough with each other to share a hug, much less a bed. Although she knew her father and Aunt Tillie were interested in the progress of her pregnancy, they both still harbored reservations, although they tried hard not to show them. She considered calling one of her friends, but it seemed too intimate to share even with them. So she sat in her chair, overjoyed with her secret, as she waited for her baby to move again, which she did, fluttering like a delicate moth trapped within her. Medora wrapped her arms tightly around her womb as if they could touch the tiny presence who grew inside.

As the weeks passed, the movements became more pronounced and stronger, until now, at six months, she could count on being awakened with a kick or a shove from inside. She also noticed that the baby responded to certain types of music—Lee Morgan's "Cornbread," James Brown's "Hot Pants," George Gershwin's "Concerto in F."

The baby was a person to Medora now, with likes and dislikes, fears and joys, so when Randall told her his mother had died, her first thought was that her child had lost her grandmother and it was her duty at least to visit the woman and pay her last respects.

"I'll stay here with Jas, you go on up and say what you got to say," Devlin whispered, giving her a shove toward the front of the room. As if he could sense her coming, Randall turned in her direction. His eyes fastened on her belly, and an odd combination of curiosity and delight came into his eyes as he rose to greet her.

Grief had taken little from him, Medora noted with irritation. If anything, the weariness in his face gave him a gravity that added to his attractiveness. He'd lost some weight, but it only enhanced his bone structure. Black became him. She recognized the middle-aged man who sat beside him as Reynard, his uncle. The years hadn't changed him much. He still radiated a certain sleaziness that confirmed everything Medora had ever been told about him. When she approached them, Reynard gave her a gap-toothed grin and to her annoyance tapped her on the belly. Sensing her irritation, Randall eased in front of him and pulled her to him in a comfortable hug. Medora felt the excitement that she always felt whenever he touched her, pregnant or not; the thrill was still there.

"Medora." He whispered her name with a combination of relief, affection, and gratitude. It was as if they had never stopped touching, and it felt good to feel him against her again, against the baby. She let herself relax into his embrace. The baby seemed to sense it, too; she chose that moment to deliver a hearty kick. Randall pulled back.

"Was that the baby?"

"Who else?"

The both laughed, sharing a sudden gaiety that took them both back to better times away from the solemn surroundings.

"When did he start moving?"

"She."

"How do you know?"

"I just do."

Medora pulled away then, remembering where they were and what they had been through. Randall stepped back, too.

"Thank you for coming." He nodded toward the open casket in the front of the room and closed his eyes.

"Did she suffer long?"

"Yeah," Randall said with a sigh that seemed to take everything out of him.

At least now you are free of her, Medora thought, but dared not say it aloud. She followed his glance to the casket, then panicked. Would it be possible for the hateful spirit of Lydia to infect her baby? Should she turn tail and run? But then she thought, *My mother's spirit is here to protect her, to protect us both. Minerva Jones Jackson lived in the world of spirits, too, and would give her the protection she had been unable to offer in life. Lydia Hollis couldn't hurt her now. Or anybody else, for that matter.* Armed with thoughts of her mother, she left Randall and approached his mother's casket.

Gazing down at Lydia's face, Medora recalled the first time she had met her. She had been nervous about the meeting. Randall told her later that she was the first of his girlfriends she'd met. Not that there had been very many. Despite his looks, Randall had been a late bloomer, awkward and surprisingly shy, which attracted Medora to him because she was shy herself. She'd found it easy to trust him enough to share important things with him. First her classroom notes, then her poetry and drawings, and finally a kiss at her cousin's party, when she knew that things between them would last forever. By the time he took her to meet his mother, she knew she loved him, even though she wasn't sure exactly what "love" was or where it would lead.

So they met in a restaurant that Medora to this day couldn't recall the name of without feeling vaguely ill. When Lydia walked in, Medora couldn't believe she was Randall's mother. Lydia was captivating, lovely, and she looked so young. People gazed at her in admiration as she strolled to their table, and Medora, in jeans and a sweater, felt ugly and small. From the beginning, Medora couldn't understand the woman's hostility, and she was so intimidated she hadn't been able to eat. Her stomach was filled with so much tension she was afraid she might vomit. Randall was oblivious to everything his mother said and did. When the meal was barely over, Medora had bolted from the restaurant in defeat. She didn't speak to Randall again for nearly a year. When she did, and as if by mutual pact, Lydia rarely came into their conversation. But Medora knew she hovered in the shadow of their lives, ready to do her harm if given the chance.

"Well, Lydia, we meet again," she whispered to the dead woman, and then felt so weak she was sure the woman's spirit had taken a swipe at her. Unsteady on her feet, she made her way to the back of the room and collapsed in a chair beside Devlin.

"You look like you've seen a ghost," said Devlin.

"I think I felt one."

"Bad vibes, baby. Time for us to get hat." Devlin grabbed her arm and ushered her toward the door. In their hasty retreat, they nearly bumped into an attractive woman in a gray Chanel suit accompanied by a much younger man in jeans and a denim jacket.

Ana stepped aside to let pass the pregnant woman, the good-looking white man, and the young biracial child, who she assumed was their daughter. She gave the couple a sympathetic smile, assuming by the distressed look on the woman's face and the protective way that the man held her arm that she had taken ill. Being pregnant in close quarters did that to you sometimes, she thought, although she had never been sick a day with Danny, who much to her surprise had agreed to accompany her this morning.

It was thoughtful of him. She hadn't been to a funeral or a wake since Mali's, and she dreaded going to this one, but felt she had to go for Randall's sake. He'd called her the day after his mother died, and she promised she would come. Glancing around the church, she was surprised by how few other people were there.

In the last two months, her relationship with Randall had grown more intimate. They spoke once and sometimes twice a day. Although there were still things about him that puzzled her, she was sure she knew the important things in his life, and that made her feel close to him. She now viewed their conversation of two months ago, when she had been so close to ending their relationship, as the beginning of it. Since that day, he had opened up, sharing things about his family, his mother, and his uncle that she was sure he had never told anyone else. He was vulnerable in ways that reminded her of Daniel, and that part of her personality that Mali called "the healer" responded to him. She thought maybe she had fallen in love with him, although she wasn't exactly sure what falling in love meant anymore, except that he was the first person she wanted to speak to in the morning and the last she wanted to speak to at night. She spent nearly every weekend with him, and he had gradually come to replace Danny as her main companion and confidant.

"You okay, Ma?" Danny asked as they headed toward the front of the room to greet him.

"Yeah, I'm fine, son. You know if you want to go, you can. I'll be okay."

"No. I'll stay for a while. I don't mind." She wasn't sure what his insistence on staying meant. His feelings toward Randall were hard to read. He was unfailingly polite, but she sensed he didn't trust him, and on at least one occasion he had said as much. She suspected his dislike was nothing more than a son's possessiveness, and so she chose to dismiss it. It was natural for a son to feel protective toward his mother and to be uncomfortable about the fact that she was involved with a man.

Once or twice, Danny had dropped by unannounced in the early morning and found Randall and her having breakfast together. It had been awkward and embarrassing for all three of them, and Ana had been unsettled the first time it happened. But later she reminded herself that she had a right to her feelings. Danny was a grown man. He had his own apartment, and he should have called before he came to visit her. She had gently suggested that to him later that day, and he had since begun to do so. She was no longer going to be ashamed of the sensual part of herself, and her need to enjoy, even wallow in, her own sexuality. She was thankful to Randall for giving that back to her.

She let out an involuntary sigh as she approached him. He looked exhausted, but his eyes brightened when he saw her.

"Thank you for coming, Ana," he said, embracing her. She understood grief, and the simple physical contact it craved. She held him close to her, allowing his body to find comfort in hers. She drew back after a moment, and Danny stepped forward to give him a slight manly hug,

"I'm very sorry for your loss, man," he said awkwardly,, and Randall nodded appreciatively at Danny. At some point, Ana knew she would have to share with her son how serious she and Randall had become. She didn't see herself marrying again, but with each passing day she felt closer to him, and Danny would have to find a way to deal with that.

"Ana, I'd like you to meet my uncle Reynard. Reynard, this is my friend Ana Reese-Mitchell."

Ana smiled politely and offered her hand, which he grabbed and held a moment longer than she felt was necessary. So this was the famous Reynard of whom Randall so often spoke, she thought as he gleaned her body for attributes and deficiencies. Dressed as he was in a sleek black-silk suit and diamond cuff links, he looked every bit the player Randall had described him as being. How dare he check out his nephew's girlfriend, and in a funeral parlor, of all places? Some men had no decency at all.

"Pleased to meet you, ma'am. Heard a lot about you. I can see he was telling the truth," he said, his tone deferential.

"I've heard quite a bit about you, too," Ana said stiffly, *and very little of it was good*, she thought. But then again, that wasn't true. Reynard had given his nephew love and acceptance in a way his mother had never been able to, and Randall loved him because of that.

"She was quite a woman," Reynard said, his smile just this side of a smirk. Ana glanced at Randall to see if he had picked it up, but read nothing in his face. She knew his feelings toward his mother were mixed: love laced with guilt and resentment. He often told her how much Lydia had sacrificed for him and how her life had been unfulfilled. But Ana knew that sacrifice was part of parenting, that was the truth of it. You did it willingly without thinking twice about it because you loved your child. How terrible to burden a son with the knowledge that you had given up your life for him! What a dreadful price to make a child pay. You did what you had to do to make sure your child survived, and his happiness was your reward. It was all you asked. She had done that with Danny, always trying to overcome the absence of a father who wasn't around.

She had been appalled when Randall told her Lydia's reaction to the news of his unborn child. On more than one occasion, she had watched his body tighten with anxiety when he spoke to his mother on the phone, and he always seemed sorrowful and distant when she finally let him go. He was secretive about their conversations, as if he knew Ana would disapprove, and Ana allowed him to keep his secrets.

But she had known women like Lydia Hollis all her life. They were vain, self-centered creatures who out of jealousy and insecurity crippled anyone who stumbled into their realm. They fed off the weaknesses of those who loved them—like vampires, Randall described her, and he had called it right. She knew that Randall's childhood had been a lonely one. He had shared bits and pieces about it with her, and Ana suspected that Lydia had allowed few outsiders into their life. She had tried to make her son her possession. Thank God she had failed. Or had she?

But in the end, Lydia Hollis reaped what she had sown. The proof was in this room, empty except for a few friends of her son and a mournful caretaker who had been with her when she died. There were no sister-friends to weep and wail or old lovers with joyfully carnal memories. There were no workaday friends offering solace and food, or family members—nobody except a son who couldn't cry and his uncle, who despised her.

Recalling the wakes of her mother and Mali, Ana considered what a marked contrast they were to this one. Her mother's church had been filled to capacity. It was in the middle of winter, but people had come from four states to say a last good-bye. There had been countless friends with childhood memories, church and club members sharing tales of her wisdom and generosity, even an old boyfriend or two, hobbling and half blind, who tenderly recalled her quick laugh and sweet loving ways. And Mali. How different that gathering had been. Her memorial service had lasted for hours, with writers, poets, musicians, and artists of every discipline singing praise songs to her memory.

She found Randall's hand and gently squeezed it, and he squeezed hers back, letting her know how much her presence meant to him. Conscious of Danny shifting away from her, she let Randall's hand go. She still avoided any overt sign of affection toward Randall when Danny was around. But that would soon have to stop, too.

"Are you going home afterward?" Randall bent down and whispered.

"I'll probably take Danny to lunch, but I can come by tonight if you want me to," she told him, and even now, in these surroundings, she felt an almost primal need for him.

The sound of two voices, one of which she immediately recognized, caught her attention, and she glanced to the back of the room, and then, with alarm, at her son.

"So, she's back with *him* now," Danny said, his face betraying the anguish he felt.

W hat the hell is Danny Mitchell doing here?" Taylor whispered to James, who out of simple curiosity and a sense of obligation had agreed to accompany her to Lydia Hollis's wake.

"He probably came with his mother. According to my mom, when her ol' man kicked he left her beaucoup bucks, and I heard she likes art. She must have bought some stuff from Mr. Big."

"Don't call him that!" Taylor slapped his hand like you would that of a child. "Do you see Lillian Wingate? She's the main reason I'm here." From the first, Taylor and Lillian Wingate, the owner of the New Walls Gallery, had hit it off. They'd had several lunches and met for drinks on numerous occasions to discuss the September show that Taylor was curating. In recent weeks, Lillian had begun to hint that the gallery was looking for an assistant director and she might consider hiring Taylor when she graduated the following year.

"Is she that odd-looking white woman with the buzz haircut looking uncomfortable?" James nodded toward a petite gray-haired woman who stood near the back of the room.

"That's her. You stay here." Taylor nodded toward the last row of chairs. Smirking, James sat down and assumed a somber pose. "And behave yourself. Don't talk to anybody. Don't say anything weird to Lillian," she added in a whisper.

"Okay, Mommy. But don't forget: I'm doing *you* a favor by coming here in the first place, so don't boss me around," he said, his grin softening his words. He settled back, legs crossed, arms thrown out on the back of the pew defiantly as Taylor hurried toward Lillian.

"Thanks for coming. I hate going to wakes and funerals by myself," Lillian said to Taylor and gave her a hug. Taylor nodded as if she agreed, but suspected that as the only white person in a totally black setting, she needed a familiar face there for moral support. "The sooner we go and pay our respects, the sooner we can get out of here. Is that your boyfriend sitting in the pew? He's cute." She nodded toward James.

"He's a boy and my friend. Let's put it that way," Taylor said off-handedly, but her mind was somewhere else. She realized that being here made her uncomfortable, too. As a rule, she avoided funerals and she had never seen a dead body. It frightened her to think about death because it filled her with dread and guilt that hurled her into a depression. Suddenly she felt empty, as if something had been knocked out of her.

"What are you doing afterward? Want to go to lunch?" Lillian asked.

"Not today. Said 'boy friend' is taking me out, but he doesn't know it yet," Taylor said, and both woman laughed conspiratorially. The truth was, Taylor didn't want to risk being stuck with Lillian for the afternoon, which was the main reason she'd brought James along.

"Listen, do you think he'd mind walking me to my car? I had to park down the block in front of a bar and a couple of unsavory characters were sitting on the stoop."

"No problem," Taylor said as they walked to the front of the room, and smiling to herself at how right her sense of Lillian's discomfort had been.

Taylor noticed that Randall's face fell when he saw her. She had seen him the Thursday before his mother died and she hadn't heard from him since then. The weekends that he promised her two months ago had never materialized; it was back to Thursdays, and on that one he had taken her out to dinner, and they'd ended up at his place, the way they always did.

He called a car service around midnight to take her home, which infuriated her; it made her feel like a call girl. He'd also seemed distracted and distant again, and hadn't mentioned his mother or her condition one way or the other.

Taylor hadn't said anything to him about her feelings since that night she'd tried to talk to him about her father. Nothing between them had deepened. Even sex had begun to feel mechanical and less intimate. Their relationship had begun to make her uncomfortable, and sometimes she wondered if maybe James was right, that she was continuing things because of what he could do for her, that she really wasn't better than some of those opportunistic "hoochies" James talked about.

Taylor had assumed the place would be filled with well-wishers intent upon offering sympathy, and that she and Lillian would be one of a hundred associates, artists, and others there to offer their support. But there was hardly anybody here, except for Danny Mitchell. Just her damn luck. The look of surprise on Randall's face dismayed her. But maybe she was reading too much into his reaction. Maybe he was just surprised. As far as he knew, she had no idea that his mother had died, and she wouldn't have known except for Lillian, who had called her last night and practically begged her to come with her. She agreed to go because it seemed the mature, responsible, professional thing to do. As far as Lillian knew, Randall Hollis was simply her mentor, and attending the wake of a mentor's mother seemed appropriate.

He stepped forward to greet them.

"Thank you both for coming." His voice was formal and his body stiff. "Ana, this is Taylor Benedict, who will be curating the September show, and I think you've met Lillian Wingate, the director of the New Walls Gallery. Taylor, this is Ana Reese-Mitchell and her son, Danny."

"I've known Taylor for years, Randall. No introductions are necessary, Congratulations, my dear! Now, I'm sure it will be a successful show," Ana said, extending her hand. "It's good to see you. How are your parents?" Taylor, an expert on fake grins, read Ana's for what it was worth. *This woman hates my guts*, she thought, and that made her sad.

Taylor admired and liked Ana Reese-Mitchell. She was the kind of older woman that she wished she could have in her life to offer advice, a wise nonmother who knew about the world and was willing to share what she knew. She had always admired Ana's toughness and her ability to cut through the bullshit to the essence of things. Taylor wished she could emulate it.

She also liked her because, of all her mother's various friends and acquaintances, Ana was the only one who had come to her mother's aid when her father left her. Taylor knew that many women in her mother's circle considered her irrelevant without a husband. But Ana had offered her friendship and support from the very first. She called weekly to make sure her mother was doing all right and had recommended her personal attorney, accountant, and therapist to see Helena through her difficult times. Although Helena Benedict and Ana Reese-Mitchell weren't close friends, Taylor knew that her mother truly liked and respected her. She hoped that someday she and Ana would be able to sit down over a drink and talk about what had happened between her and Danny. Unfortunately, the look on her face this morning told Taylor it wouldn't be anytime soon.

"My mother is fine. It's so nice to see you again, Mrs. Reese-Mitchell. Good to see you, too, Danny," she added without looking at him. Danny grunted an unintelligible reply.

Gushing wildly, Lillian subtly shoved Taylor aside. "Oh, what an absolute pleasure it is to see you again, Mrs. Reese-Mitchell—may I call you Ana? And I'd like so like to thank you again for your generous contribution to the show and the catalogue."

"It's good to see you again, too, Ms., uh, Wingate, is it?" Ana Reese-Mitchell gently but firmly cut her off. She wore a slight amused smile that clearly put Lillian in her place. "We'll talk again soon, under *different* circumstances," she added. Taylor chuckled to herself. Lillian never missed a chance to pump a potential donor for money, even at a wake. She'd gotten what she deserved.

There was a strained silence for a moment or two, and then Taylor blurted out, "How are you doing, Randall? Are you okay?" The look that crossed Lillian's face and that of Ana Reese-Mitchell made her realize that her question sounded too familiar; they probably expected her to call him Mr. Hollis. Randall looked uncomfortable, which made Taylor feel small and foolish. But it also angered her.

I know every wrinkle and mole on your goddamn body, she thought.

A mischievous smile crossed her lips, and she tried to catch Randall's eye, but he stared straight ahead, studiously ignoring her. "If I can help out in any way, don't hesitate to give me a call. I think you know my number," she added, catching his eye with that line.

"Thank you, Taylor. That's very kind of you." His response made her smirk.

"And that goes for both of us, of course," Lillian said, jumping to ease what she sensed had become an awkward moment. "We were both so sorry to hear about the loss of your mother. We just wanted to come by and let you know our concern. If there's anything either of us can do, please let us know."

"Thank you both again," Randall said, formally.

"Taylor." Danny's voice was nearly a whisper, but everyone turned in his direction. "Nice to see you again. How is James doing?"

"He's sitting in the back of the room; why don't you go and ask him yourself?" Taylor nodded toward where James sat. She hadn't meant to sound so nasty, but she was suddenly sick and tired of the whole phony scene.

"Take care of yourself, Randall." Lillian gave him a brief hug.

"Me, too." Taylor hugged him too, subtly but definitely easing her body into his.

Randall quickly drew back from her. "Thank you, Taylor," he said with a hint of a smile on his lips.

"I had no idea you knew Ana Reese-Mitchell so well," Lillian said as soon as they were out of earshot. "How do you know her? She's becoming a really important collector and donor, and she made a very generous contribution to the gallery for the September show."

"Really? I used to date her son." Lillian's method of prying reminded her of her mother.

"Aha, her son! I knew something was going on there. I could smell it.

Lots of interesting vibes!" A triumphant smile appeared on Lillian's face. "Well, I hope you ended it on good terms. It's always wise to know a generous collector like Ana Reese-Mitchell."

"I suspect Danny's still in love with me," said Taylor, amused by how quickly her stature had grown.

"Do you think there's any chance you might get interested in him again?" Taylor could see the dollars signs popping in Lillian's eyes as she contemplated the possibility of an assistant director with a pipeline to a fortune.

"You never know," Taylor said. "But I *do* have James now," she added, barely able to conceal her amusement.

"Did I hear my name?" James asked, joining the women as they headed for the door. He opened it and the three stepped out into the sunlight.

"Lillian was curious about how I knew Ana Reese-Mitchell."

"She's become an important collector," Lillian added, explaining her intent.

"All the rich black folk in the tristate area know each other," James said mischievously. "My mother knows Taylor's mother. Taylor's mother knows Danny's mother. Danny's mother knows my mother. We all date and marry each other. It's disgustingly incestuous."

Puzzled, Lillian tried to figure out this new information. "What about Randall Hollis? Did the two of you know his mother?"

"Randall Hollis is not a member of the club," James said with a pretentious sniff. When Lillian turned her head, Taylor slugged him in the back.

"So, what does it take to belong to the club?" Lillian asked innocently.

"Money," James said with a wink. Taylor rolled her eyes. "And color, once upon a time. Mostly it's money now. They don't care how dark you are anymore. Look at me!" he said, holding up his arm.

"Oh, I see," Lillian said politely, but doubt filled her eyes as she gave Taylor a brief peck on the cheek and climbed into her silver BMW.

As soon as she had driven away, Taylor said, "Why did you say that garbage to Lillian? She might give me a job. I don't want her to think I have weird friends."

"What does talking about the black bourgeoisie have to do with you getting a job? And anyway, as far as I'm concerned, it's the truth. Plus, I just love to remind white folk that not all of us live on welfare and devour Kentucky Fried Chicken. We can be as snobby as some of them."

"First of all, Lillian doesn't think like that, and secondly, there is no such club."

"If there were, you'd be queen of it, Ms. B.A.P."

Taylor turned on him, visibly angry. "And that's another thing. I'm sick of you and that B.A.P. bullshit!"

James, angry now himself, returned her glare with one of his own. "Then maybe it's Ms. S.K.E.E.Z.E.R. Would that suit you better? I'm out of here, Taylor. I'm sick of you and your phony friends and your fucked-up attitude!"

"Stop acting like a kid!"

James, his eyes filled with indignation, said, "You're calling me a kid, after I've just spent my afternoon taking you to this stupid wake? I feel like you're using me, Taylor, and I'm sick of it!" He pulled out his wallet and peeled off two twenty-dollar bills and handed them to her. "Call a cab. Or maybe ask Danny, your rich former boyfriend, or Mr. Big, your rich current boyfriend, for a ride home. That is, if he'll own up to knowing up."

"What do you mean by that?"

"You know what I mean by that," he said as he climbed into his car. "You know how I feel about you, how I've always felt about you, and you basically treat me like shit, which is how Randall whatever-his-name-is treated you today. You're like a toy to him, Taylor. You don't mean anything to him, don't you see that? If you did, you would have been at his side through all this mess. He didn't even call you to tell you his mother died! You had to find out like some kind of an employee from your boss. Where do you think that puts you on his list of important people?"

"He didn't call me because—"

"He didn't call you because he treats you like a whore, and if you're a phony big shot like him, you don't mention your mama to a whore. Here's how I feel, Taylor. This is for real. I can't deal with a woman who lets herself be treated like a whore." James slammed the door and drove away.

Stunned and humiliated, Taylor watched him speed down the street. She was ashamed of the way she had been treated by Randall and more ashamed that James had seen the way Randall treated her. She thought about calling James on his cell phone to try to explain to him how things really were between her and Randall, and then remembered it had been disconnected. She glanced toward the funeral parlor and considered going back to ask for a ride home from either Danny or Randall, but James's words had found their mark and her pride wouldn't let her. The wave of depression she'd felt earlier came over her with its full power now.

Maybe James was right about Randall and his feelings toward her. He probably was right. Yet she wasn't ready to do anything about it. So what did that say about her? Lighting a cigarette, she smoked it down to the filter and she started to walk.

For the next hour, she walked the streets with no idea where she was going. Tears ran down her face, and she greeted the puzzled stares of both men and women with such hostility that people quickly turned away. Finally she got on a bus and rode to a cab station, and from there, used the money James had given her to catch a taxi back to New York City, crying all the way home.

After everyone had gone, and as Taylor cried on the street, Randall stood by his mother's coffin, trying to cry. He knew it was expected of him and would probably do him some good, but he felt nothing, not sorrow or even love.

"I'm sorry, Lydia," he said, not sure what he was apologizing for, then realizing that it was for everything that had happened—and not happened—in her life. "Mama, I'm sorry."

When he got back to his car he called Ana to say that he didn't feel like company after all, and asked if they could meet for breakfast the next day. He left a message for Medora telling her how glad he was that she had come and how good it felt to feel the baby kick. And, finally, he called

Taylor and left a message on her machine that he was sorry about the way he had acted but he had been shaken by grief and if she had some time to see him Thursday evening he wanted to talk to her about it and give her something special he had picked up for her. And then he went home to his empty apartment and stared at the walls.

I Used

to Be Your

Sweet Mama,

Sweet Papa

(But Now

I'm Just As

Sour As

Can Be)

Chapter Eleven

It was warm for September, and when Ana awoke Wednesday morning, she considered taking one last dip in her pool before she closed it for winter, but decided against it. She and Randall had spent a long weekend in Bermuda and had done so much swimming they joked about growing gills. Five days filled with sun, sand, and good times on a beautiful island hotel had been what both of them needed; neither of them had been ready to come home last night. Sunday was Randall's thirty-seventh birthday; the getaway had been one of her gifts. The other had been a gold Rolex she bought on the spur of the moment after a day of shopping in Hamilton. It was the most expensive gift she'd ever given a man, and she felt reckless and giddy when she gave it to Randall.

They had just finished breakfast on the patio of their suite. She'd read about the hotel in *Travel and Leisure*, a luxurious beach resort where each villa had its own plunge pool and oversized Jacuzzi, which she and Randall made use of each night. The waiter had just brought their breakfast of sweet rolls, fresh fruits, and good coffee served with a flourish on Limoges china and Irish linens.

"I haven't been this happy in a long time," Ana said with a careless giggle, which was the truth. Randall glanced at her, at the beach, and then back at her with what looked like sorrow in his eyes. "What's wrong, Randall?"

"I don't deserve you in my life."

Ana shook her head, telling him he was wrong, and took his hand in hers. "Why do you feel that way? You deserve all the happiness you can get." She was used to his occasional melancholy moods, which she attributed to his tortured relationship with his dead mother and the grief he still felt. The connection between mothers and sons was far more difficult to untangle than that between mothers and daughters, she realized, particularly if the bond had been a painful one.

He smiled the charming smile that always grabbed her heart. "I hope you never get tired of me."

"Don't worry about that," Ana said, with a sly glance toward the unmade bed, and they both chuckled at the memory of last night.

"Oh, by the way, I've got something for you." He pulled a small velvet-covered box out of the pocket of his terry cloth robe.

"But it's your birthday!"

"You've already given me my gift. This beautiful vacation, but mostly you. You're all the gift I need. I wanted to show you how much you mean to me," he added sheepishly.

Laughing with delight, she opened the box and found a pair of diamond earrings, two carats at least. "Oh, they're beautiful," she said as she eagerly fastened them into her ears. "And happy birthday back at you." She pulled out her elaborately wrapped gift.

She had been looking for something for Danny in another part of the store when she had spotted Randall trying on the watch. After a moment of admiring it, she had watched him reluctantly take it off his wrist and put back on the gold Bulova he'd recently begun to wear. On the way out of the store, she'd sent him on an errand and went back to the counter to purchase the Rolex.

He was speechless when he unwrapped it.

"Do you like it?" She was worried for a moment.

"Oh, God, Ana. It's too—I can't accept this, it's too—"

"I bought it for you, wear it!" she ordered, half in jest. He pulled her to him across the table and kissed her.

"Thank you, Ana. No one has ever given me anything so beautiful." He slipped off his old watch and gave it to her. "This is my past, and you're my future. I'm going to try very hard not to be trapped by the demons in my past anymore. None of them."

"I'm glad you like it," Ana said, and genuinely was.

She enjoyed buying gifts for Randall. They meant so much to him, and cost her very little. She could buy a thousand Rolex watches and not put a dent in the money Jerrod had left her. Once she'd wondered what madness could bring a man to buy those whimsical baubles from Bulgari or Harry Winston she saw advertised in *The New Yorker* or the *Times*. How could anyone be capricious enough to spend a small fortune on an airplane pin made of diamonds or a rope of Mikimoto pearls? Well, now she knew. A man who loved watching his woman's face light up when she snapped open a black velvet jewel box—a man who adored her. It made her happy to see Randall smile; his obvious pleasure was enough for her.

She glanced at the clock beside her bed. It was nine-thirty, later than she thought. She peeked at the appointment book she kept beside her bed and noted a manicure appointment at ten-thirty and lunch with Helena Benedict at noon. She called to cancel the manicure; there just wasn't time. She'd almost forgotten about the lunch and wasn't looking forward to it. She liked Helena Benedict, even though she had her doubts about Taylor, but she really didn't feel like going out today. What she really wanted to do was to call Randall so that they could spend another day together, but she knew he was busy preparing for tomorrow.

Thursday, September 20.

She'd circled the date in red on her calendar the day Randall gave it to her. He was excited about the show with good reason. It was nearly all he talked about in Bermuda, and his enthusiasm was contagious. Her decision to sponsor it with the tacit agreement that she would sponsor other shows at the New Walls Gallery was a tax write-off for her, and she enjoyed playing a role in his world.

She lay in bed for a few more moments, then went through her morning ritual—the yoga stretches, stomach crunches, and meditation, glancing for a moment at the three photographs on her vanity table. Without realizing it, she had begun to spend less time reflecting on her dead loved ones, which was something else she attributed to her relationship with Randall. She was living in the present again for the first time since falling in love with Daniel. She looked forward to the beginning of each day instead of remembering the ones that had passed.

She often asked herself where their relationship was going. Truth was, she had no idea. After observing Randall and her together at his wife's birthday party, her accountant had tactfully advised her not to make any "life-altering decisions" without consulting him first. She'd chuckled at his caution. If Randall were to propose, her lawyers and accountants would be composing prenuptial agreements before he got the words out good. As far as she could tell, marriage wasn't in either of their plans. She simply wanted to spend more time with him, to get to know him better.

Glancing at the clock, she showered, then dressed and quickly left the house. She didn't want to be late for this lunch with Helena, who had given no hint as to why their meeting was so important. Ana suspected it had something to do with the business of one of the clubs they belonged to. She hoped it didn't have anything to do with their children.

Helena had made reservations at Fruits de Mer, a stuffy French restaurant where Ana had often dined with Jerrod and thus been spoiled forever. She and Randall routinely ate at some of the best French restaurants in the city, and this pretentious, suburban place with its snobby waiters and outrageous prices struck her as hopelessly provincial. But it appeared to be one of Helena Benedict's favorites, so Ana hadn't objected. It hadn't surprised her that Helena would enjoy the place. Although Ana liked Helena, she struck her as incurably bourgeois. Jerrod had once deemed her the "perfect wife," and often held her up as an example for Ana to follow, which of course hadn't increased her affection for the woman, even though her antipathy had disappeared.

Ana had never seen Helena when she had not been impeccably dressed and coifed. Her dinner parties, of which she once gave many, were always beautifully catered, and from the delectable appetizers to the lavish desserts proceeded flawlessly. She was, as one of their less charitable club members observed, a Technicolor combination of Martha Stewart, Audrey Hepburn, and Miss Manners, which inspired unspoken resentment among those less blessed. Recent conversations with mutual acquaintances indicated that Helena had been through some rough times, and Ana knew only too well the profound lessons hard times taught. She was certain that the last year and a half had changed Helena substantially.

When Ana arrived at the restaurant, she was pleased to see just how much Helena had changed. She sat at a corner table patiently sipping a glass of red wine. In the old days, she was always fashionably late and seemed to enjoy forcing people to wait for her leisurely entrance. Anticipating a long wait, Ana had tucked a novel into her purse.

"Thank you so much for joining me." Helena rose to greet her.

"Thanks for inviting me," Ana said, exchanging air kisses. Helena looked different, too. She'd put on some weight, which made her look a bit more matronly but which also became her. She had always seemed dangerously thin to Ana. Her hair was also grayer, which made her face appear softer. Her chic black suit fit her well, and her diamond-and-pearl earrings accented her clear cashew-colored skin. When she was married, Helena was always tightly wound and on alert, as if nervously anticipating some terrible event. She was calmer now. Serene.

"You look fantastic, Ana, and you've gotten some sun! I've never seen you look more relaxed."

"I just got back from Bermuda. I'm sure that has something to do with it," Ana said, sharing bit of the truth. "You look great, too."

"I *feel* great, and that's what important," Helena said with a good-natured chuckle. "Bermuda sounds divine. Maybe I'll try it someday."

Yes, Helena did seem more sure of herself, Ana thought. But her eyes held sorrow in them that hadn't been there before; she seemed more vulnerable. Perhaps the vulnerability had always been there. Maybe she had just never let it show.

Ana ordered a glass of wine, and the women studied the menu with interest. Helena suggested dishes that were good and those that should be avoided. They chatted easily about nothing through their appetizers and entrées. As they sipped their coffee waiting for dessert, Ana, growing restless, wondered why Helena had called. Helena sensed her impatience.

"How is your son, Ana?" she asked as the waiter filled her cup with more coffee.

Ana shifted uncomfortably in her seat. Was Helena about to propose that they arrange some kind of meeting between Taylor and Danny? She took a long sip of coffee, desperately trying to think of some tactful way to dissuade her.

"Is he okay?" Helena asked, alarmed.

"Danny? Oh, yes. He's fine. Still struggling with what he wants to do with his life, but he's healthy, reasonably happy, and as sane as can be expected," Ana said, and they chuckled at that. Out of politeness, Ana asked about Taylor.

Concern crossed Helena's face and she gave her coffee a rapid stir. "Frankly, Ana, Taylor is the reason I've asked you to lunch."

Here it comes, Ana thought.

"Is she okay?"

"Yes, she's fine, too, but I am concerned about a relationship she seems to be involved in."

"A love relationship?"

"I guess you could call it that."

"Helena, sometimes it's best to let young people, particularly when they're the age of our children, decide what's best for themselves," she said gently. "People make their choices and have to live with their mistakes. That's the only way one learns. No matter how wrong their choices may seem, we really should avoid interfering in their lives."

Helena still looked worried. "You're right, of course, but I feel I need to know a bit more information in this case."

"What do you mean?"

"Well, let me get to the point: Remember that art dealer our club invited to make the presentation on collecting African-American art last year?"

"Randall Hollis?" Ana was suddenly apprehensive; she wasn't sure why.

"Yes, that's him. Well, Taylor apparently has gotten involved with this man, and frankly, I'm concerned because he's so much older than she is. I know you've had professional dealings with him. What kind of a person is he?"

Ana gulped down her coffee. It settled uneasily in her stomach. She avoided Helena's eyes as she motioned for the waiter to refresh her cup. "What do you mean by involved?"

"I mean they're having a relationship."

"Do you mean because Taylor is working with him on the show in September? I don't think you have anything to worry about. I'm sure that there's nothing romantic between them. He's a very attractive man, and I suspect she probably has a crush on him, nothing more than that," Ana said, recalling Taylor's odd behavior at Lydia Hollis's wake. "I'm sure that it is nothing more than that."

"I only wish that were the case," Helena said with a sigh. "No. It's not a crush. Their relationship is mutual and a bit more involved than that."

"What do you mean?" Ana felt as if her heart had stopped.

"Well, for the last few months, she's been dating somebody I've been calling her Mystery Man. I didn't know much about him except that he was connected to the world of art. Taylor is so secretive and private, she wouldn't tell me his name, and I didn't push it. But her friend James Lawson mentioned his name to his mother, and you know what a busybody Candy Lawson can be. She chaired the committee that invited the man to the club in the first place. Anyway, she called me two weeks ago to say that she thought it was outrageous that an invited guest would take advantage of a young woman, particularly the daughter of a club member, and she wanted to know if I thought she should say something to him.

"I told her as tactfully as I could that Taylor was *my* daughter and a grown woman, and that we should *all* mind our own business. But, of course, I am concerned."

Ana didn't trust herself to speak. She focused her attention on the plate in front of her and then on her cup until she could control her voice. "How long has she been seeing him?"

"At least eight or nine months, and he's quite extravagant. He recently bought her a case of very good Bordeaux, and you know how much that can run. Over the last few months, she's been taking me to this charming little Greek restaurant on the Upper East Side, quite expensive, and the mâitre d' knows her by name so I assume it must be one of the places they regularly go." She leaned toward Ana as if confiding a secret. "And there's the jewelry. You know, when we were young, you never took jewelry from a man unless you were practically engaged. But Taylor showed up last week sporting a diamond bracelet that must have set him back a thousand dollars! To say nothing of this show, which he is letting her curate, and she's still a graduate student. I don't want her to get in over her head with a man who . . . Ana, are you okay?"

Ana closed her eyes, squeezing them tight, searching for self-control, and when she found it, she opened them again, changing her face into a mask. "I'm fine. Sometimes red peppers disagree with me," she said.

"Are you sure? I thought for a moment you were going to faint."

"No, I'm really okay." Ana pulled back her lips, beared her teeth, made herself smile, but she was numb.

"I have the same trouble with black olives myself," Helena said with a sympathetic smile. "So what kind of man is this Randall Hollis? Can I trust him to do right by my daughter? I'm sure I'm just being overprotective. He'll probably marry her in six months, and the last laugh will be on me when I deliver a weepy toast at their wedding reception!"

Ana took a long swallow of water. Her hand was trembling. She hoped that Helena couldn't see it.

"Actually, Helena, I've bought some art from him, but in reality I think that is probably the extent of our relationship," she said evenly, her voice toneless.

"Oh, well, I had to ask." Helena gave a disappointed sigh. "I hope you don't think I'm as much a busybody as Candy Lawson, but Taylor is my only daughter, and I do worry about her."

Ana nodded because she was afraid to trust her voice; she was afraid to move.

I have to get out of here. I have to get out of here. I have to get out of here and be by myself.

When the waiter came with the check, she excused herself and went to the ladies' room. She locked the door, sat down on the commode, and made herself breathe slowly, focusing on her breaths, counting them until she got hold of her emotions. Then she went to the sink, filled it with cold water, and splashed it on her face. Finally she was calm enough to return to the table. With a minimum of words, she thanked Helena for the lunch and, using the excuse of the troublesome red peppers, made her way out of the restaurant. She kept herself together long enough for the valet to bring her car and to pull it out of the driveway, but halfway home, she began to sob so uncontrollably she had to pull to the side of the road. She wept for fifteen minutes straight, her face cradled in her hands like she used to when she cried as a girl, and then she forced herself to drive home, holding the steering wheel so tightly her hands were cramped when she finally let it go. When she got home, she bolted her front door as if protecting herself from some unseen force, and took the phone off the hook after erasing any messages that were on it. Her chest felt as if it were coming apart. She knew now what people meant when they said their hearts were breaking; she knew that hers must be.

"I will never see you or speak to you again," she screamed, but hearing herself say those words made her cry again because she missed him already; he had woven himself that deeply into her life.

On the one hand, she wanted to confront him, demand to know the truth from his lips. On the other, she knew the truth already; she had heard it from Helena. She knew now where he had been those Thursday nights when he couldn't be found. She understood why they had never returned to the Greek restaurant where they had gone on their first date. She knew whose perfume she had found tucked away on a shelf in his bathroom. The signs were there and she had ignored them. There was no excuse he could give her that would erase what she knew.

This is over. I am finished. I am through with him.

But everywhere she looked she found reminders of him—the living room where the paintings hung, the kitchen where she made espresso and cappuccino, the bar where she'd stocked his favorite wine and beers—and the bedroom most of all.

In a frenzy, she frantically searched through her drawers for any piece of lingerie that he had given her or that reminded her of him. She tried to rip gowns and teddies, weeping as she pulled things apart and finally just balling them up and hurling them into a pile in the middle of the room. Her heart raced as she went through her closets and the shelves in the bathroom looking for any trace of him or their lovemaking and tossing everything she found onto the pile. Exhausted, she fell down on the bed and then stood back up, unable to be still. In despair, she gazed at herself in the full-length mirror across from her bed.

"I am such a fool," she repeated to herself again and again. "How could I have been such a fool?"

She ripped off the suit she had worn to lunch with Helena. Stripped down to her bra and panties she stared at herself in the mirror, feeling as if she were viewing her body for the first time. All the things she despised about herself—her too-wide hips, her too-small breasts—reminded her of how imperfect she was. Someone had told her once you could always tell a woman's age by looking at her hands, and Ana scrutinized hers now. They were an old woman's hands, wrinkled and dimpled.

How could he not *want a pretty young woman instead of me?* she asked herself.

A man she had dated between Daniel and Jerrod had explained to her once with casual cruelty his theory on why older men liked younger women. Younger women, he said, with their firm bodies and unwrinkled skin had spirit and energy, a joie de vivre that older women lacked because they had lost it to bitterness and life's woes. A younger woman, he said, made a man feel like he could do anything in the world he wanted to do. She could give him back his life.

Ana thought of those words now, and wept in shame and humiliation as she compared herself to Taylor Benedict. How could she compete with her? What had ever made her think that Randall could love her as much as she loved him? How could she not see that his attraction to her had been her money—how much she could buy, where she could take him, what she could give him.

How could she have been such a fool?

Insecurities that she'd chased away twenty ears ago attacked her and stabbed her defenseless body like tiny, well-honed knives.

How could she have let this happen?

Again?

Why did she end up trusting men that she had no business trusting, who would leave her with no dignity at all?

Staring at herself in the mirror she was overwhelmed with a sense of inadequacy and sorrow. She thought about calling Randall, picked up the phone and dialed his number, then slammed it down before it could ring. She closed her eyes again, squeezing them shut because she didn't want to see what was in the room; he was everywhere she looked. Finally she forced herself to open them again, forced herself to stare at the chair where he used to sit, the closet where he hung his jackets, his towels that she could see through the open bathroom door. She made herself look at other things in the room, too, trying to remind herself as she did it that she was full before he came into her life; she didn't need him to exist. But she did need him to exist, she thought. Weeping again, she felt as if she were nothing without him, and she fell asleep with that on her mind.

Disoriented, she awoke at dawn. Her first thought was of Randall, and she reached out for him, feeling the empty space beside her. She could remember every part of him, feel his touch on her body; she could smell his scent in her head. She thought about Bermuda, and for a moment she was there with him, and everything was fine. And then she remembered. She closed her eyes, trying to lose herself again in sleep. But it wouldn't come. The scene from yesterday played itself out in her head: Helena's words. Taylor Benedict.

Why had he betrayed her?

She thought about calling him, waking him to demand an answer. But in the next moment, knew it would do no good. She would not believe anything he said; she knew that much about herself. She closed her eyes tight, trying to fall asleep again. She considered taking a pill and then simply lay in bed for the next hour, alternating between weeping and fitful sleep. Finally she sat up, her body sore and tired.

The room was still dark, but the light filtering in through the window foretold the coming of a new day. Her eyes, sore from crying, focused on the objects in her room now visible in the morning light: Mali's gigantic spider plant hanging in the window like some dreadful monster; the Jacob Lawrence lithograph she had bought the year she married Jerrod. Through the open doors of her closet, she could make out her clothes—yesterday's suit flung on the floor; the one she'd had made to wear this afternoon to the show. The drawers she'd hurled on the floor last night lay like traps, and the pile of clothes in the middle of the floor seemed a multicolored heap of rags. Her gaze lingered for an instant on the Bible on the chest of drawers that she had inherited from her grandmother. The silver glint of the photographs on the vanity table caught her eye. Mali. Her father. Her mother at the Christmas tree with Danny.

So Danny had been right about Randall all along; his suspicions had been justified. From the very first, her son had seen through him. Strange, how men could detect the secrets of other men—the weakness, the untrustworthiness that always fooled women, blinded by sensual charms. Her son had seen through Randall Hollis the same way she saw through Taylor Benedict.

Anger surged through her at the thought of Taylor Benedict. It would serve the bastard right to end up with that little slut. The girl was nothing—a slip of a person too shallow to offer him anything of substance. Look how she had treated Danny! She was a shadow of a woman, a frivolous, foolish girl.

She rolled over into her pillow, disgusted by the thought of her.

And that was when it struck her.

Throughout Ana's life, there had been chance moments of clarity that came in the midst of turmoil. One had been when she knew she had to leave Daniel. *This man will destroy me.* The thought seemed to come from nowhere one night as she lay beside him. She had known in that instant that only one of them would survive the marriage, and she knew for the sake of her son it would have to be her.

Another had been when she accepted the fact that her marriage to Jerrod was the mistake of her life. He had said one too many evil, thoughtless things that morning at breakfast, and the thought suddenly occurred to her that she might end up killing him. A knife that she'd used to cut her bagel lay before her on the table. She thought of picking it up and stabbing him through the heart. She knew at that instant that one of them would end up dead, and that she would fight him for her life if it came to that. But it hadn't. His untimely death had given her a reprieve. She swore on the day he died she would never again sell herself cheap, not for security or the promise of love.

Sitting now in the dim light of her bedroom, a new truth came to her:

Randall has chosen a girl as young as my son over me, and that choice makes him a fool.

A smile, close to a smirk, broke out on her face as she considered the irony of it. It was the same smile that came when she beat Jerrod at one of his own games, the one she had learned from her father, who could look defeat in the eyes and come out grinning.

He is not the man I thought he was or he would not have made that choice.

She was strong, certainly stronger than she'd been at twenty-five, at thirty-five, and even two years ago. Every experience she had been through in her life had changed her in some way and showed itself in each wrinkle and gray hair she bore. Was she really going to negate her life for a man who wasn't wise enough to see what she had to offer? If he was one of those men who reduced her—and all women—to their lowest common denominator, then the best he could ever be to her was a good time in bed and a courteous dinner companion, and that simply wasn't enough for her now. She needed more from a man; she deserved more. She had given Randall all she had to give, and this was her reward? Yes, the sex had been good, but it was she herself, not he, who had rekindled her sensuality. A man could never give a woman back her sexuality; she had to claim it for herself.

She went into the bathroom and washed her face, brushed her teeth, staring at herself in the mirror as she did it. She had been looking at herself through his eyes and not her own. Nothing about her had changed. She was still the same woman she had been six months ago, before she fell in love with him. She was still the same woman she was yesterday morning when she had been so happy, and she would be happy again; it was her choice.

She was Ana Thomas, her father's darling and her mother's strength.

She had watched both of her parents die cruel, painful deaths, witnessed a good man go bad, a bad man get worse, suffered the death of her closest friend, and put up with more crap from more people than she cared to remember.

"I will be forty-eight years old two months from now," Ana reminded her image in the mirror. "In two years, I will be the same age as my father was when he died. Randall has hurt me, but he has not mortally wounded me. I am old enough now to know that each day is a gift, and I can't give even one day to a person who won't cherish me."

Daniel Reese had lit the fire within her that told her she had the right to expect love, and Jerrod Mitchell had tried to put that fire out. But she hadn't let him do it, and no man ever would. She stooped over the pile of linen and silk on the floor and picked up one of the silk robes she had considered discarding. It was her favorite color, a deep maroon that brought out the chestnut undertones in her skin. She slipped it on, forcing herself to feel the luxury of it, thinking as she did so that there was nothing like the feel of good silk against your body. She went into her kitchen, made herself a strong cup of coffee, and for an instant thought about Randall—his smile, his deep beautiful eyes, his tenderness, the things that had drawn her to him. Her sadness broke through and she began to weep again, but she made herself stop.

What do I really feel beneath my anger? she asked herself.

"I am profoundly sad," she said. "And I am profoundly disappointed in him for being what he is, for not being the man I thought he was, and in myself for not seeing it."

She went back into her bedroom and sorted through the pile of things on the floor, putting some things back and leaving others where they lay. She took a large plastic garbage bag from the kitchen and began to collect the things that he'd liked or bought for her. She started with the oversize bottle of Joy that he had given her because she'd told him that once it had been her favorite perfume. She took one sniff and threw it away. She took the diamond earrings out of her ears and tossed them into the bag, along with a sterling silver heart and a gold bracelet still in their Tiffany boxes. Three dog-eared books of love poems were next, and several toothbrushes, along with an assortment of shaving articles and after-shave lotions, black briefs, white undershirts, brown socks, and a pair of blue swimming trunks.

She went into the kitchen next and tossed in his imported beers, Costa Rican coffee, and four bottles of Veuve Clicquot Champagne. She added his CDs and art magazines next, and when every bit of Randall Hollis that he'd forgotten or bought was in the bag, she hauled it to the curb outside her house so it could be picked up by the garbage crew later that morning.

It was half past seven by the time she finished housecleaning. She fixed herself some cereal and had another cup of coffee, but her thoughts took away her appetite.

Six months. That was it. Only six months. Not very long at all when she thought about it. *How could I have been such a fool?* she asked herself again. This time the answer came to her.

You took a chance and fell in love.

She had taken a chance. She had let the best of herself come through, and she had expected to get the best of him back. But she hadn't, and that wasn't her fault.

"I have gotten over the agony of Daniel Reese and the humiliation of Jerrod Mitchell, and compared to those two, loving you, Randall Hollis, was spit in a bucket of water," she said aloud.

It was Thursday, the day of the show at the New Walls Gallery. She would see him this afternoon. She wasn't going to run from that, she decided. She had paid for this show and would be damned if she wasn't going to be there.

And that would be the end of it.

Chapter Twelve

The New Walls Gallery was a small nonprofit gallery in an ornate building filled with many such galleries in the middle of Chelsea. With its elegant twelve-foot ceilings, long, narrow windows, and shiny parquet floors, it was not the smallest gallery in the building, nor was it the most impressive, but it had a cutting-edge hipness that attracted chic New Yorkers with time and money to spend. To her credit, the director, Lillian Wingate, had always actively reached out to artists of color to make sure they got the same shot at success as everybody else.

Lillian had met Randall Hollis many years before through Alexandra Brookings, a wealthy patron who had been instrumental in helping her raise money to start New Walls. Lillian had an eye for a good-looking man, and Randall immediately caught her attention. She was fond of Alexandra and knew more than she wanted to know about her domestic situation, so she quickly guessed the true nature of her relationship with Randall and was glad for them both. She was, however, wise enough not to get involved with him herself. Long ago, a wise older friend had advised her never to sleep with a man with less money or more problems, and Randall had less of the first and more of the second, so their relationship was strictly business.

Lillian admired Randall's devotion to art and his impeccable taste. She had watched him grow from a novice dealer to a major player—representing some of the finest artists working in America. When he offered to become a silent partner in her gallery, she took him up on it. He had a strong sense of what was commercial and had never steered her wrong. Although he was usually too busy selling to wealthy collectors to be bothered with organizing shows, when he suggested this one she jumped at the chance. Yet again, his instincts seemed to be paying off.

The work of each artist was sufficiently different to make for an interesting show. Each had her own style dictated in some way by her ethnicity. All of the art was good, but Medora Jackson's work struck her as particularly exciting. Lillian decided that at some point she would approach Randall about doing a father/daughter show with Medora and T. W. Jackson. As far as she knew, Jackson hadn't shown in the city in more than a decade, and a show like that would make her gallery. She spotted T.W. across the room and gave him an enthusiastic wave, which he returned. *Now* that *had been one good-looking black man in his day*, she thought. Word had it that he'd cut a wide swath through the ladies who lunch back in the early sixties. A show with him would bring some seriously big money out of retirement.

She followed T.W.'s gaze to Medora, who was engaged in an animated conversation with a critic from the *New York Times*. Funny, she hadn't heard who the father of her baby was, not that it was her or anyone else's business. Medora kept her own counsel, and she'd kept quiet about this. Lillian had heard a rumor that she and Randall had once been involved, but she had seen him with at least three women since she'd heard that tale, so she didn't put much stock in it. She'd also heard the same thing about Randall and Trudy Douglass. She gave a quick wave to Trudy, who with the rest of Medora's friends surrounded her like bodyguards. After ignoring her for a moment or two, Trudy gave her a condescending nod. *Bitch*, Lillian said to herself. She noticed an affluent-looking black couple studying one of Medora's paintings in tandem with the price list. That was good, she thought. She liked the look of the crowd that was beginning to assemble. She had a nose for money and could smell it no matter what color skin it came with; the scent was definitely in the air tonight. *This is going to be fun*, she thought.

Randall wasn't having any fun at all; he was too anxious about Ana. He had called her twice yesterday and once this morning, and she hadn't returned his calls. When he left her Tuesday night, they had made plans for lunch or dinner after the show, but his messages had gone unanswered. Worried, he called Danny, who was obviously surprised to hear from him. Danny told him he'd seen his mother earlier that day and had gotten off the phone with her an hour before, and she was fine. Their conversation was brief and awkward.

"I guess she'll get around to calling you back when she feels like it," he said with an adolescent insolence that irritated Randall and left him puzzled and worried.

As far as he knew, there was no reason for her to be angry at him. Although she'd never met Medora, she knew about their situation, so she couldn't be angry about that. Could Taylor have possibly said something to somebody that had gotten back to Ana? More than once, he had worried about Taylor's discretion, but he really didn't think she would say anything to Ana; she was smarter than that. He had explained to her that, professionally speaking, it was best for them to keep their private relationship completely private, and it had taken three dinners, five luncheons, and an expensive diamond bracelet to make sure she accepted things between them for what they were. She was, however, immature in many ways that had begun to annoy him. She also had an unpredictable edge. But every woman he knew had an unpredictable edge.

Take Medora, for example. There she was, standing next to her work, chatting it up with that fool from the *Times* as if she didn't have a care in the world. She hadn't said two words to him and barely looked in his direction. At least T.W., who stood near the refreshment table shoveling down crudités and dip like they were his last meal, had the courtesy to wave, but the rest of them—Devlin, Eliza, and even Trudy Douglass, whose work he had been instrumental in getting into *ARTnews*—seemed intent upon ignoring him.

Oh, to hell with them all.

Where was Ana?

He went to the refreshment table for a glass of wine and scooped up some dip on a celery stick.

"How's it going, man?" asked T.W., debonair as always in a black cashmere sweater and dark woolen slacks. But his eyes, magnified behind his glasses, were inscrutable.

"Hey, man, everything is everything." Randall gave him a warm, macho hug.

"You see Medora, over there?" T.W. nodded toward his daughter. Randall cringed, hoping he wouldn't choose this moment to ask him about his intentions; that was the last thing he needed this afternoon. Could he blame him, though? This baby was T.W.'s first grandchild by his only child, the same as it had been for Lydia. The thought of his mother brought on a pang of sorrow and guilt. She'd been dead two months, and he hadn't been able, yet, even to visit her apartment and pack up her things; he simply paid the rent, kept putting it off, and tried not to think about it.

"This is some of Medora's best work, wouldn't you say?" he said to T.W., focusing on the present to get his mind off of his mother.

"No, Hollis, her best work is yet to come," T.W. replied, sternly glaring at him over the top of his glasses with a look that left Randall wondering if he was making an indirect reference to the baby or a comment on her development as an artist. Randall quickly excused himself and made his way over to Lillian Wingate, who stood near the door.

"This is simply marvelous!" Lillian's eyes gleamed as she gave him a hug.

"Looks good." Randall watched the door for Ana.

"Is the food all right? I usually stick with wine and a block of cheddar, but Taylor convinced the caterer to give us a good deal on a selection of cheeses, and he actually threw in the crudités and dip for free. That girl is such a charmer! It's a delicious dip; did you try it? Green peppercorn. So subtle and absolutely perfect with fall vegetables, and the wine is—"

"Everything is fine, Lillian. Don't worry!" He cut her off with a reassuring pat on the arm, hardly listening to her.

"Taylor Benedict is an absolute jewel! She's very talented, and her research has been impeccable. The artists whose studios she visited just loved her. They had nothing but praise for her."

"Good to hear," Randall said absentmindedly.

"How did you find her?"

Avoiding the question, Randall pretended to wave at somebody across the room, excused himself and quickly made his way to the corner, where the four participating artists had gathered for a group photograph.

"Randall!" The women all sang in harmony as he approached them. He gave each a hug, whispering in turn that he was looking forward to an opportunity to chat before the afternoon was over, and all hugged and chattered back. Except Medora, who after the initial greeting turned her back on him to speak to Devlin.

He'd always heard that women were loveliest when they were pregnant, but he'd never found a woman heavy with child particularly appealing. It was different with Medora. The baby was due shortly, and she was stunning. Her hair was longer and thicker, and her skin, which had always been beautiful, was luminous. For the first time in months, he allowed himself to remember in detail the Valentine's Day afternoon of Red Zinger tea and wildflower honey.

"Medora." He whispered her name, and she glanced at him over her shoulder. Her face softened into the old Medora and then hardened into the new one, tough and unforgiving.

"Hi, Randall. Things look good, don't they?" she said too casually. "Everyone is praising your boy, Taylor Benedict. Is he around? He didn't get to my studio, and I'd like to meet him."

Randall, muttering something unintelligible, looked for another escape route. Amused, Medora turned around to face him. "What are you hiding?"

"What do you mean?" Randall's eyes grew wide with innocence.

"I know you too well, Hollis," Medora said, turning her back on him again to continue with Devlin, who gave Randall a knowing smile accented with a wink that irritated the hell out of him.

"Excuse me," Randall said to no one in particular as he made his way back to the exit and stepped outside, trying again to call Ana on his cell phone but still getting no answer. He went to the refreshment table for another glass of wine. Glancing back toward the door, he saw Taylor enter.

She was good at entrances, he thought, pausing momentarily to take in the room, letting everyone know she had come in even though it would be impossible to ignore her. She walked with the grace and confidence of a dancer—fifteen years of ballet lessons had obviously accomplished their goal. She was dressed in an expensive arty style—every stitch of clothing casually thrown together, nothing costing less than an unskilled worker's monthly paycheck. The diamond bracelet bouncing on her wrist gave what seemed a carelessly thrown together ensemble a snap of elegance, and her dangerously high stiletto heels added three inches to her height. Despite himself, he smiled with pleasure as he watched her cross the room. One of the artist pulled her into the group and another photograph was taken. He watched with alarm as Lillian introduced her to Medora, who smiled graciously, then threw him a look of such undisguised contempt he nearly choked on his wine. He focused on the crudités.

"Great food," said T.W., who apparently hadn't left the refreshment table. Randall nodded in agreement and looked for the critic from the *Times*, who seemed to have disappeared. Taylor, obviously eager to meet T.W. Jackson, dashed toward them; it was too late to leave. Her face beamed with excitement, which was strange for Taylor; she tended to hide her emotions in cool, sophisticated indifference. When she reached Randall, she threw her arms around him.

"Thank you, thank you, thank you, for letting me do this!" she squealed as she planted kisses in the general direction of his mouth. He reared back, embarrassed by her effusive display of emotion. "I know, we're not supposed to show anything in public, but I'm *so* excited! Everybody is saying what a good job I did, and it's because you gave me a chance. You believed in me!"

"You did all the the work, not me. You're good, you deserve the congratulations," he said.

She threw her arms around him again, kissing him hard on the lips. He pulled away and gave her a self-conscious peck on the cheek.

Stepping forward, T.W. extended his hand. "T. W. Jackson," he said by way of introduction as he threw Randall an amused, conspiratorial glance.

"Mr. Jackson, it's such an honor to meet you," Taylor gushed, letting go of Randall's hand and grabbing his. "I'm still in grad school, but your work is one of the reasons I decided to major in art and become an art dealer. My parents bought two of your paintings when they got married, and I've seen and admired your work all of my life."

"Smart parents you've got there. I'll bet those paintings are worth a helluva lot more now than they were . . . what, twenty-five years ago?"

"Yep," Taylor agreed with an easy laugh.

"Well, thank you very much, my dear," he said with a big grin, always easily charmed by a pretty girl.

Taylor, easing away from T.W., grabbed Randall's hand again, and held it tightly. "My mom should be here in a few minutes. I can't wait for you to meet her. I know she's eager to meet you. And you too, Mr. Jackson. I had no idea you would be here. She'll be thrilled to meet an artist whose work she has admired for so long."

"I'll be thrilled to meet the mother of such a gorgeous young woman. Have you met my daughter, Medora? The high-pregnant one." T.W. nodded toward the center of the room.

"Oh, yes! I did, just now. I can see how heavily influenced she is by your work. Randall, did you tell me Medora Jackson was T. W. Jackson's daughter?"

"I assumed you knew," Randall snapped, stepping away from her again.

"Have you known her a long time?" Taylor asked.

"Long enough," T.W. grunted in reply.

"Randall is such an expert on the artists he represents. He recommended which of her pieces should be in the show. Her studio was the only one I didn't visit. He didn't want me to disturb her in her condition. He is *so* thoughtful!"

"Like a fox," T.W. said.

T.W.'s response puzzled Taylor, and the questioning glance she gave Randall made him cringe, and he took a gulp of his wine. He didn't see Ana when she walked into the gallery.

Ana, however, saw Randall and Taylor and her heart began to pound. Her emotions had been in a free fall for the last three hours, swinging between the self-confidence she'd felt earlier that morning and a deepening depression as the hour of the show approached. Again and again, she wondered if she should confront him and demand to know the details of his relationship with Taylor. She didn't want to believe that he had lied to her all these months, that she had misjudged him so completely. But she knew that he had, even after he had promised that he wouldn't do it again. If she were a different kind of woman, if she hadn't been through Daniel Reese with his countless deceptions, if she hadn't endured the torture of loving a man who always let her down, maybe she would be able to give him another chance, but she knew she couldn't; that point had been passed in her life. Yet she was surprised by the depth of her emotions, the swirl of anger fused with love when she saw him. Somehow she managed to avert her eyes from Randall and Taylor now to study the work on the walls, chatting enthusiastically about the show with two acquaintances she barely remembered. But all the time she was thinking, *It was a mistake to come here. I should have given myself more time. Ten more minutes. I will stay ten more minutes and then I will get out of here as quickly as I can.*

Before she could make her getaway, Lillian Wingate spotted her and rushed toward her. "Mrs. Reese-Mitchell, thank you so much for coming. You can see what a marvelous show this is. How long have you been here? Have you had a chance to meet the artists?"

"Please call me Ana." Ana said, offering the woman the favor of familiarity denied in July, which seemed a lifetime ago. "I just got here, and I'm afraid I can't stay—"

"You *must* meet the artists. Why, here comes Medora Jackson!" Lillian beckoned her to join them. Ana immediately recognized her as the pregnant woman who had been at the wake. Medora's grin was warm and open; it made Ana think of Mali. Funny, how men like Randall always picked women with the biggest hearts to break. But Medora, she recalled, had been smart enough not to let him break hers, despite the baby. Good for her.

"I thought this might be you," Medora said. "Thank you for being so supportive of my work."

"Thank you for bringing such beautiful work into the world," Ana said, which brought on another appreciative grin. Gazing again at this artist's work, Ana knew she had not made a mistake in purchasing it; every piece here touched her. But from now on, she would buy directly from the artist, minus the middleman, and to that end she asked Medora, "Do you have a card so I will be able to get in touch with you? I'd like to visit your studio."

"You should probably get in touch with Randall Hollis. He is my dealer."

"Do you have a card so that I can contact you directly?" Ana repeated her question with no change of expression, which made her intention clear. Medora reached into her bag and quickly pulled one out. With no comment, Ana dropped it into her chic leather bag and snapped it shut.

"Come, Ana, and let's get some champagne. It's surprisingly good for this kind of thing—at a good price, too," said Lillian. Clearly empowered by Ana's permission to call her by her first name, she grabbed Ana's arm and pulled her toward the refreshment table. Ana had no choice but to follow her, but her heart beat fast as she approached the space where Randall and Taylor stood.

Be calm. Be calm. Be calm, she repeated to herself.

Randall reached out to embrace her when he saw her, but Ana stiffened, pulling away. "When did you come in? I've been waiting for you all afternoon." There was desperation in his voice, and Ana felt a pang in her heart. She focused her attention on Lillian, who was pouring her a glass of champagne.

"Thank you, Lillian," she said.

"It's quite good, you'll see." Lillian, puzzled by Randall's words, took her cues from Ana.

"What happened to lunch? I've been calling you all day. Why haven't you called me back?" Randall lowered his voice to a whisper.

"Yes, it is good champagne," Ana said to Lillian after taking a sip.

"Good cheese, too," Lillian said. Sensing a dangerous undercurrent between her benefactor and her colleague that she didn't want to sweep her away, she quickly added, "Ana, I'm really going to have to go into my office to smooth down a few details, but can I call you for lunch in a week or so?"

"Yes, that will be fine," Ana said. Lillian gave her hand a squeeze, waved at a man in a blue turtleneck, and rapidly headed off in his direction.

Puzzled by her lack of response, Randall stared at Ana, saying nothing.

"Mrs. Reese-Mitchell, how are you doing?" Taylor squealed as she stepped forward and tried to give Ana an enthusiastic hug. Ana, shifting ever so slightly, moved out of her reach.

"How are you, Taylor? I had lunch with your mother yesterday, did she tell you?"

"No, I haven't spoken to her today." Taylor, not sure what to make of the tone of Ana's voice, dropped her arms to her sides. Ana, catching a glimpse of the diamond bracelet bouncing on her wrist, felt a surge of rage so strong she bit her lip to control it.

"Ana, what is wrong?" Randall whispered.

Ana carefully placed her glass of champagne on the table. For one terrible moment, she thought she might toss the content at him, and she allowed herself to imagine how it would look dribbling down his neck. Mali would have done that, she thought. Mali would have tossed it straight into his face, then, without a word of explanation, left the room without looking back. The thought of her old friend made her smile, and that slight, enigmatic smile remained on her face as she confronted them.

"Don't pretend anymore," she said. Her voice was cool and she was glad that she'd put the champagne down because she was trembling. She held her hands in tight fists at her side.

"Ana, what are you talking about?"

She didn't look him in the eye; she didn't dare. She looked over his head at one of Medora's paintings on the far wall.

"Randall, don't make me into any more a fool than I already am. The fact that you are the father of Medora Jackson's child and she wants absolutely nothing to do with you should have told me what I needed to know about you, but I didn't listen to my instincts. I didn't follow my own good sense.

"I know now that you have been seeing Taylor for the past eight months, during all the time that you were with me. You have lied to me and that has hurt me more than you'll ever know. I don't want to see you again. I don't need or want you in my life."

"But, Ana, I . . . Why are you doing this? Can we talk? Please talk to me!" His eyed grew wide with alarm and there was more anguish in his voice than she had ever heard in it before. She looked at him now, gazed into his eyes, and for a moment she thought she would forgive him because of what she saw there. What danger would there be in talking to him about it, in forgiving him? But in that same moment she knew it was impossible. Daniel Reese had taught her that many years ago. You can forgive a man anything except for being himself. Randall was with women like Daniel had been with wine; he had no self-control.

When she spoke again, her voice was softer. "You lied to me with your heart when I told you the truth with mine. I can't stay with you anymore. It's as simple as that."

He stepped back from her, his face a mask of surprise and anguish, as if she had slapped him.

Ana turned to Taylor next, addressing her in the quiet, confidential tone she might use with a daughter. "You have too much going for you to let this man buy you for a diamond bracelet, a case of wine, or the promise of success. A man who uses one woman will use another, no matter what he tells you, and nothing in this world is worth being used."

"Mrs. Reese-Mitchell, I had no idea, I—"

Ignoring her, Ana continued, "Your self-respect is all you have, Taylor, and once that's gone, you have nothing. I know because I lost mine once and it took me years of heartache to get it back. Don't make the same mistake I did."

Then Ana, following Mali's example, left the gallery without looking back.

After Ana had left, Taylor turned to Randall and screamed, "Do you mean to tell me that you were fucking Mrs. Reese-Mitchell the whole time you were fucking me?" A collective gasp swept through those standing nearby at the use of the vulgarity.

"Taylor, you knew that you weren't the only one I was—"

"So you were fucking Mrs. Reese-Mitchell the whole time you were fucking me? She's like my mother, for Christ's sake!"

"That's none of your business, and I made it clear that the relationship I have with you is—"

"And you're the father of Medora Jackson's baby?"

Another gasp went through the crowd. T.W. sucked his teeth. "I guess the shit's hit the fan now!" he said to no one in particular.

"Now listen—" Randall said to Taylor.

"What kind of a man are you?"

"Well, I—"

"You son of a bitch!" Taylor spat the words out, shaking with anger.

"Taylor, don't get so excited, quiet down!" Randall demanded and placed a hand on her arm, suddenly aware of the stares that her words had begun to attract. She shook his hand off in a quick, violent motion.

"Who do you think you are! Using me like this?"

"You know very well that we talked about the extent of our—"

"Liar!" She screamed the word. It was the only thing she could think of to say even thought she knew that Randall was telling the truth. But Ana Reese-Mitchell had also told the truth, and that truth coupled with her memory of James's words were more than she could take. "You're a liar. You're nothing but a filthy liar!" Tears instantly filled her eyes, and she had no idea where they were coming from and why she was suddenly so uncontrollably angry. "What do you think I am, some kind of a whore?"

"Oh, Jesus. For God's sake, don't take it there!"

A hush came over the room, and Randall dropped his voice to a whisper; Taylor didn't lower hers.

"You used me!"

"No. Let's get this straight. You tried to use me," Randall corrected her. His voice was quiet and conversational, which made Taylor angrier still.

So she made a point that she knew he couldn't dispute. "And you used her, too. You used her, too, Mrs. Reese-Mitchell. You used her for her money! You use everybody! She's right about you. You use women. You're not fit to be anybody's father!"

Taylor knew she had touched a nerve; she could see the change in his eyes, and the slight narrowing of them frightened her for an instant. Never push men but so far, her brother always warned her, never in public and certainly never in private. Always give a man a way out. But Taylor didn't care if Randall had a way out or not.

"Where do you get off talking like that to me?" he said. There was a bitter, vicious edge to his strangely calm voice. "You have no idea who I am or how far I have come to get where I am. You are selfish and self-centered, and I'm about as sick of you as I have ever been of any woman I've ever know." He paused for a moment, as if thinking about something else to say, and then shook his head, seemingly speaking more to himself than to Taylor or the twenty-odd people, drinks suspended, who surrounded them.

"I guess the truth is, Taylor, that I deserve exactly what I'm getting from you. I should have known better, I realize that now. You are fundamentally a pampered, overprivileged child who has relied on her exotic looks and rich parents' connections to get by. You have never in your life needed or wanted something that your parents, their friends, or some jerk like me didn't get you. It's time you grow up, kid. You can't be a spoiled little princess forever!"

It may have been the condescending trace of a smile that appeared on Randall's lips as he spoke those words. Or that he remained so cool in the heat of her attack. Or perhaps it was the phrase "spoiled little princess," which reminded her of James calling her a Black American Princess, that tipped the scale. Or maybe it was simply that she was standing next to the refreshment table and the dip in its fancy plastic bowl called her like an evil charm. For the next few moments Taylor had no control over her mind, thoughts, or the right hand that picked up the bowl and threw the contents into Randall's face.

The next thing Taylor remembered was the deafening silence in the room. She looked down and noticed that the plastic bowl bearing the remnants of dip had landed dangerously close to her Manolo Blahnik heels. Then she gazed into the coated eyes of Randall Hollis, who stood before her covered in green peppercorn dip.

"Taylor!" From somewhere a familiar voice called her name, and Taylor, following the voice that belonged to her mother, ran out of the gallery, out of the building, and into the bright afternoon sun.

Medora, stunned into silence like everybody else, watched the scene between Randall and Taylor play out to its messy climax. She was too shocked to feel anything at all, not pity, embarrassment, or anger on Randall's behalf.

"Was that the young curator?" she heard someone ask.

"What's going on?"

"Why would she do something like that?"

"She sure put his business in the street!"

"Well, that's one little chickie who sure came home to roost," said Devlin, who stood next to her.

"He probably deserved it," her friend Trudy Douglass added, "for the way he's treated you, and every other woman he's ever done wrong."

"This is like when that actress dumped that bowl of spaghetti on that critic's head in Sardi's because he bad-mouthed her friend. Sometimes people simply reap what they sow. It's divine justice!" added her best friend, Eliza, with a self-righteous sniff.

"Nobody deserves to be dunked in dip," Medora said, shaking her head sadly.

"Or sunk in soup," Eliza added, half seriously.

"Or plopped in punch," Devlin, caught in the spirit of the moment, threw in, which brought a titter from the group until Medora, glaring at each in turn, made them stop.

"You are laughing at my baby's father!" she said quietly, and the group observed a moment of silence on the baby's behalf, until Devlin, making an attempt to save the afternoon, asked if anybody was hungry, and they all hurried out to a restaurant near the gallery. As they walked, Medora, a lump in her throat, tried to sort through her feelings about what had happened to Randall.

"Well, I wonder if the critic from the *Times* will mention it in his column," Eliza said as she looked over the menu when they got to the restaurant.

"I hope it doesn't hinder his ability to sell our work," said Trudy, who, like the artists presented, was represented by Randall Hollis. "God knows, you don't want to be affiliated with a dealer whose face will forever be associated with onion dip."

"Green peppercorn dip," Devlin corrected her. "Did anybody have a chance to try it before it ended up on Randall's face? It was quite good. Interesting, zesty touch."

Everyone laughed, except Medora. As angry as she was at Randall, as angry as she had been for the last few months, it tore her heart to see him so humiliated. She knew how soft his interior was, and how easily he was hurt by cruel words or a wounding gaze, and he had received a dose of both this afternoon. For years, she had seen the malevolent tracks Lydia had stomped into his heart, and she knew how easy it was to destroy him. Medora knew that she herself would have been devastated by what had happened, and she was far tougher than he was.

But she kept her thoughts to herself. Nothing else that happened this afternoon had really shocked her. She wasn't surprised to learn about Randall's relationship with Ana Reese-Mitchell. She had suspected as much when he'd mentioned her name back in March. She wasn't exactly sure where to place her in the pantheon of Randall's women, several tiers up from Alexandra Brookings, she supposed, but not high enough for her to substantially change him. Obviously she hadn't known him well enough to suspect his relationship with Taylor Benedict.

Medora doubted if Taylor had been much more to Randall than a diversion. She understood enough about the workings of ambitious young women keen on making it in the world of art to know that she had probably used Randall as much as he had used her. Randall had an insatiable hunger for women's attention and admiration, so theirs had been a deadly combination based on mutual exploitation and need. But Randall was an adult capable of making adult choices, and that didn't excuse what he had done. Not to Ana Reese-Mitchell. Nor to her.

But what had he done to her?

They were over, she reminded herself. She had told him as much back in March, and she had meant it. Randall Hollis was a hopeless case. A flawed individual. There was no hope for this man at all!

Yet she couldn't forget their history. The first time they'd made love on that rocky little bed in that off-campus hotel, those Valentine's Days, birthdays, Christmases that in sixteen years he'd never forgotten; their commitment to a "friendship" they both knew was far more than that. The tears she'd cried over that man, the rage, the betrayals. The way they laughed together, the talk that flowed so easily, his unwavering support and belief in her work.

Despite everything, she knew she loved him and that he loved her. In his way. Their love was more complicated than either of them—or anybody else for that matter—could understand.

But wasn't that always the way with love?

The baby kicked and she smiled, a secret smile, just between them. She had taken to making sketches of the baby on a sketchbook she kept on her night table. They varied from day to day, depending on her mood, but there was always some part of Randall in her drawings—in the lift of the baby's eyes, the curve of her mouth. Someday she would show them to her child. And to Randall. Someday. Maybe.

"You okay, Medora?" Devlin asked.

"What are you thinking so hard about?" Eliza added.

"It's not that fool Randall Hollis, is it?" Trudy narrowed her eyes.

"I'm just feeling the baby move," Medora explained, not answering any of them, and they all reached across the table, eager to feel the baby kicking against her womb.

When the entrées came, she excused herself and went to make a call on the bank of telephones outside the rest room. First she called her father, to make sure he'd make arrangements for a car to take him home. Then she called Randall and left a message on his answering machine, certain for once she'd be the only one of "his women" he would hear from today.

t took Randall several long moments to comprehend fully what had befallen him and several more to react to it. He was conscious at first of the coldness of the dip as it slapped against his face; that awareness came simultaneously with the sound of the dish as it hit the floor, and then there was the cheesy, nauseating smell that overwhelmed him as his eyes burned from the peppercorns. When he opened them, he glared for an instant at Taylor, and then he closed them again, swiping wildly at the dip with his hands. The cold gunk attached itself to his eyelashes, lips, and inside his nose; for one terrible minute he couldn't breathe.

He felt as if he had been brutally attacked, and he was wounded and frightened. But then he heard somebody snicker, which was joined by a snort from somewhere behind him. He was fully aware then of the comedy inherent in the situation. He didn't know what to do next. Should he laugh? he wondered. But he sensed that would bring down the house. He vaguely felt like crying, but feared that would have a similar effect. So he simply stood there, the dip dripping down his face like melting makeup on a clown.

"You okay, Hollis?" He recognized T.W.'s voice as he shoved a handkerchief into his hand; he had never been so grateful to hear anybody's voice in his life. He grabbed the handkerchief and began to wipe the dip off of his face. "Good thing it wasn't grits or we'd be calling an ambulance," T.W. said, desperately trying to lighten up the situation. "Had a woman throw a gin and tonic in my face at an opening once. Group show. The Village. People were raving about my work instead of hers. She was mad about that, but claimed it was because I was tipping on her.

"Had another woman throw a bag of chips at me in a picture show one Saturday. This is a first, though, man. I ain't ever heard of a woman throwing a bowl of dip at a man. That's one wild little chick you got there!"

"Where's Medora?" Randall wiped the dip from his chin and neck.

"Left with her friends."

"Did she see what happened?"

T.W. paused before he answered. "Hate to tell you this, man, but there wasn't a person standing in this room who didn't see what happened. You might want to go on to the men's room and wash that shit off your face. Come on."

Taking Randall by the arm, T.W. guided him away from the refreshment table and through the crowded room as solemnly as if he had been mortally wounded. Randall tried not to look in anyone's face as they passed. Lillian Wingate's, however, was impossible to avoid.

"What the hell was that all about? As if I didn't know!" she hissed. "You should know better than that, Randall Hollis, sleeping with the help. What are you trying to do, ruin us? That girl was employed by this gallery, and her father is a big-time lawyer! We could end up with a sexual harassment lawsuit on our hands. You've made this gallery a laughingstock!"

"Oh, pipe down, woman," T.W. said, leading Randall past her and into the hall. "Ain't nobody done nothing to this gallery. You should be thanking the boy. Folks will be talking about this place for the next six months."

"I'm sorry, Lillian," Randall muttered. "I'm so sorry."

"Aw, don't be apologizing to anybody, Hollis. You made these people's day. I'll wait for you out here." T.W. leaned against the wall outside the men's room.

The full damage of what had happened confronted Randall when he looked in the mirror, and his thoughts raced wildly in a storm of self-derision.

Pie in the face. Wasn't what they did when they wanted to humiliate somebody. Throw a pie in his face. The girl hadn't had a pie, but this did the trick. She wanted to humiliate him because she felt he had humiliated her. And he had humiliated her. And Ana, too. There was no way around that.

But Ana was gone now.

He jammed his fist into the wall again and again until he drew blood, and then he jammed it again, enjoying the pain.

"It serves you right, you dumb son of a bitch!" he said.

Why hadn't he just left Taylor alone? Why wasn't Ana enough? Why wasn't Medora enough?

You are such a fuckup, Randy.

There it was! He heard her voice, as he always did.

And she was right about him. Lydia was always right. She was his mother. She knew him better than anybody else.

Just like your father. She knew that about him, too. Hadn't she told him that often enough, etched it into his soul. So, here he stood, in front of a goddamn mirror, because he couldn't keep it in his pants. Just like his goddamn father. He had lost Ana. Like he had lost Medora. And ended up damaging Taylor. For what?

Because she fed him like a drug. But that was what he did, wasn't it? Used women like drugs? Throw-away things with no worth of their own. Like his father treated women. Like his father used Lydia.

He held his hand under the cold water until the bleeding stopped and then took off his shirt and splashed water on his face and hair, following up with soap from the dispenser. He considered going back into the gallery. He owed Lillian another apology. But facing that crowd was more than he could take. He glared at himself in the mirror.

Handsome Randall Hollis, he thought.

How often had he heard that in his life?

Handsome Randall Hollis with shit all over his face.

Handsome Randall Hollis wasn't shit.

T.W. knocked on the door. "You all right in there, man?"

"Yeah, I'm fine." Randall said. What did T.W. think, that he'd hung himself from one of the rafters? Hell, if there were some in here he might have tried it.

He stepped outside, and T.W. clapped him on the shoulder. "Show's breaking up. Your artists made some money. I decided to buy *Lightning Tree,* that piece Medora has been working on since March. Started it on her birthday. She was pretty excited about it. I got the feeling that she's taken off in some new direction. That girl keeps growing, doesn't she? Don't tell her I bought it, though."

Randall didn't answer because he couldn't. For the first time since he'd known her, Medora had "taken off in some new direction" and he had no idea where she was going. The woman was carrying his child and growing more distant each month. What the hell was that?

There wasn't much to say as they left the building. Randall walked T.W. to his town car, and told the driver the quickest way to get to the Holland Tunnel. Although he lived within walking distance of the gallery, he hailed a cab, not willing to risk running into anybody he knew on the way home. When he got to his loft, he took a hot shower, poured himself a double scotch, something he rarely drank, and turned on the television, trying to lose himself in a football game on ESPN, and then the Vietnam war on the History Channel. He fell asleep on the couch, drunk, and awoke at three in the morning with his mouth feeling like it was filled with cotton and a splitting headache. Out of habit and because he half hoped for a message from Ana, he checked his answering machine as he was about to get into bed. He stopped short when he heard Medora's voice.

"Don't bother to call me back. I just wanted to tell you not to let what happened get you down. I know you do that sometimes, but don't you *dare* do it now." It was a order rather than a request, delivered like a threat, which made him smile. She paused, then continued, "The baby is really jumping around today. She must know that something is up with her daddy. But she's on your side. So am I."

Randall laid down, closed his eyes, and played the message until he fell asleep.

One for

My Baby

(and

One More

for the

Road)

Chapter Thirteen

Fifteen minutes after Taylor threw the dip in Randall's face, she and her mother sat in a bistro about ten minutes from the New Walls Gallery. "What in the world possessed you to do such a thing?" asked Helena Benedict. Taylor was sipping chamomile tea, which Helena, who had a glass of red wine, had taken the liberty of ordering for her. The question was the first words she had spoken to her daughter since they left the gallery; they had walked the eight blocks in silence.

Taylor didn't answer. She just drank her tea in neat, tiny sips.

"He could have you arrested for assault. I'm going to call your father and ask him about that possibility. And it is a possibility!"

"Don't tell my father anything about me." Taylor slammed the cup down on the table. "Don't tell him what happened. Promise me you won't. Promise!"

Helena frowned as if a disturbing thought had crossed her mind, then said, "Well, from what I've heard about Randall Hollis, he probably deserved it anyway." She watched her daughter's face for a reaction, which came in a wan smile.

"Remember when we were little and you used to say that the worst thing we could do was make a scene? That was a scene, right?"

"Yes, I would say it was."

"Are you ashamed that I'm your daughter?" The smile was replaced by a look of concern.

"Of course not," Helena said quickly. "There is nothing in this world you could do that would make me ashamed that you were my daughter."

Taylor's eyes filled with tears. "Oh, God, Mommy, I'm so embarrassed. Why did I *do* something like that. I'll never be able to face those people again." She spoke as if she had just realized what had happened, but then her anguish abruptly changed to amusement and she giggled. Helena, caught by surprise, chuckled as well, and both women, torn between tears and laughter, chose the latter, to the delight of the waiter who had come to ask them what they wanted to eat.

"Well, my laughing ladies, would you like a refill on the drinks, or something light? We have some excellent dips. I recommend the guacamole," he said with a grin. Both women, who had momentarily stifled their reaction, exploded in laughter.

"We'll stick with the wine and tea," Helena finally managed to say.

"So, did you witness the main event?" Taylor asked after the waiter had left.

"I ran into Ana Reese-Mitchell as she was leaving the gallery, and she looked completely shaken. When I asked her what was wrong she didn't answer. I asked if she had seen you, and she said that I should look for Randall Hollis. There was something in her tone that told me that the two things—her anguish and you being with Randall Hollis—were connected. Then I remembered our lunch yesterday and how strangely she acted when I told her about the your relationship with him. She blamed her reaction on red peppers, but I sensed she wasn't telling the truth."

"You told her about me and Randall?"

Helena avoided her daughter's eyes. "Well, I—"

"Mother, how many times have I told you to stay out of my business? How many times?"

"Well, I . . ."

Taylor shook her head in exasperation, forgiving her mother with a dramatic roll of her eyes. "How did you find out who he was anyway?"

"Candy Lawson."

"Candy Lawson! Another one who can't keep her mouth shut! I might have known James would tell his mother." She slurped her tea.

Helena waited a beat, then asked, "Have you two made up yet? Candy mentioned James wasn't speaking to you. You and he have been friends for so long, you shouldn't let the friendship go."

"That's old news. I called him a couple of weeks ago to apologize for something that happened. We're tight again. I can't wait to hear his take on today," she added with a hint of sarcasm.

"What happened between you?"

Taylor hesitated, still wary about telling her mother her business, then giving her the benefit of a doubt, said, "Let's call it a casualty of my relationship with Randall Hollis. But you have to learn not to meddle in my life, Mommy. You see what can happen when you get involved?"

Helena gave her daughter a warning look that wasn't completely serious. "Now, don't blame me for what happened this afternoon. That was your own doing. And, anyway, I did you a favor. Your relationship with that man might have gone on for another six months. Think how you'd feel then!"

Taylor shrugged lightly. "I might have gotten a necklace to go with the bracelet."

The look of horror on Helena's face made her daughter laugh. "I'm kidding, Mother. I think I'll pawn the stupid thing anyway and give the money to UNCF." She took the bracelet off her wrist and laid it across the table. The diamonds sparkled in the late afternoon sun pouring in through the window, and both women gazed at it in silence. Taylor, thinking better of her idea, said, "Or maybe I'll just keep it as a reminder not to have a relationship with a man like Randall Hollis."

Helena picked up the bracelet, slipped it on her wrist to admire it, then handed it back to her daughter, who tossed it into her bag.

"Pawn it and give the money to charity," she said. "But I'd like to know why you were attracted to this man in the first place."

Taylor, who had begun to wonder herself, didn't answer. There were days when she actually believed that she had fallen in love with Randall, and others when she feared she had been drawn into some kind of perverse obsession. He fascinated her because he was strong, tough, and a bit arrogant, yet that forcefulness that bordered on conceit was also the thing she disliked most about him.

"You haven't answered my question." Helena sounded like a prosecuting attorney.

"He had juice," Taylor said.

"Juice, meaning power and influence?"

"And he made me feel important."

"He made you feel good about yourself?"

"Basically."

"That was it?"

"Do you *really* want to know the rest?" Taylor said with a devious smile, and Helena, rolling her eyes, shook her head disapprovingly.

"Do you think I should call him and apologize? I've probably blown my chances of getting anywhere in the art world," Taylor said, her tone mournful.

"Randall Hollis is *not* the entire art world."

"But I'll forever be known as the girl who threw a bowl of dip in Randall Hollis's face."

"You'll be known as that whether you apologize to him or not. Consider your motives, Taylor. Would you be apologizing because you want to save your career, or because you really feel sorry for what you did?"

Taylor's smirk indicated her true concern, and Helena, acknowledging it, continued, "Besides that, I suspect that Randall Hollis is one of those men at whom half a dozen women would love to throw a bowl of dip. It could work to your benefit. You never know how life is going to play itself out. Take it from me."

"I hope you're right," Taylor said, surprised at her mother's reaction. Not very long ago, Helena Benedict would have been so ashamed by what she had done she wouldn't have been able to face her. But Helena seemed almost supportive of her actions, as if they were co-conspirators, and that amused but puzzled her. It also pleased her, reminding her again of how much of an ally her mother had become, and how little she really knew about her mother's life prior to her father. Maybe they were more alike than she knew.

"Not that I'm condoning your behavior," Helena added as if she'd read her daughter's thoughts and was willing to go only so far in supporting her behavior. "But you still haven't answered the question I asked when we came in. Why did you do it?"

Taylor lit a cigarette, which brought the waiter scurrying to advise her that smoking was prohibited. She snuffed it out in the remaining tea in her teacup, which made Helena grimace; she hadn't changed that much.

"I was just mad," Taylor said finally. "I was angrier than I've ever been at anybody in my life. I was mad about what he did to Mrs. Reese-Mitchell and to me. He betrayed her, and that really got to me. That's all."

"Why did you feel that you had to defend Ana? I didn't know that you two were that close."

Taylor continued "Have you ever been mad at someone, so mad you didn't know where to put your rage?" Her face contorted with the anger she was feeling, and she answered her own question. "I guess you were that angry at my father."

"Yes, I was. But you pay a price for anger like that, and if you don't heal it, it haunts you. It's impossible to live your life sanely when you feel that much rage toward somebody."

Helena motioned for the waiter to come and ordered another glass of wine. With a sniff, he picked up the cup that contained the smashed cigarette. When he brought the wine, Helena took a gulp, as if fortifying herself for an uncomfortable confession, then continued.

"Your father and I never discussed anything unpleasant," she said quietly. "We made a habit of skipping over things that hurt. We let things go, ignored them. When I think about it now, I realize that that was what destroyed our marriage. His ability to deny things that mattered and my allowing him to get away with it. There was trouble between us for years, starting probably with Helena's death, which we never talked about, never dealt with as a family."

The combination of the excitement of that afternoon, the sudden intimacy with her mother, and the mention of her dead sister made Taylor's throat tighten into a lump. She was afraid she might cry, which she didn't want to do.

"I think sometimes that the best thing that ever happened to me was your father's decision to leave me. It made me face things about myself, the way I was living my life."

"How could you say that?" Despite her efforts, Taylor's voice came out in sob.

"You said you were angrier than you had ever been at anybody in your life. That's not quite true, is it?" Helena continued.

Anger darkened Taylor's face; she was too distressed to answer.

"Have you talked to your father yet?" Helena asked.

Her mother's question didn't surprise her because it wasn't the first time she had asked it. It seemed now that every time they spoke it would come up one way or another. She usually didn't respond to it, but when she did her answer was always the one she gave now. "No, and I don't intend to."

"Don't you think it's time, Taylor? I know you miss him. I know he misses you."

Her mother's words stunned her and her surprise knocked out any semblance of anger. "How do you know that?"

"Because he told me. He talks about you constantly."

"You've talked to him?"

"We've been talking regularly for about three months. We speak by phone or see each other at least once a week. It's been good for both of us."

The expression on Helena's face was so serenely matter-of-fact, it subdued Taylor's anger. "Where?"

"Sometimes we meet for coffee in the morning, occasionally we'll go out for a drink. There will always be part of me that loves your father, and I know he feels the same about me. But he had to find his happiness, and I've begun to find mine."

"How could you forgive him? How could you let him get away with what he did to us?" Taylor didn't try to hide her disgust for what her mother had just said, and the sob turned into a cry of rage.

"Did to me, not you. And I didn't have a choice," Helena gently corrected her. "I had to forgive him to go on living, and he had to forgive me."

"For what? You didn't do anything."

"A bad relationship is always two people, not just one. I could never let go, Taylor. I tried to control him, control our lives in ways that I'm only now becoming aware of. I could never just let anything simply happen. I think it may have started with Helena's death.

"You have no control over someone you love dying, there is nothing you can do about it, and because I had no control over that, I tried to control everything else. So I've had to go back and think much more about that, about my reaction to that time, how I dealt with it, and even how it affected you as a child. Do you remember all the trauma you had surrounding the fact that your twin had died?"

Taylor, dropping her eyes, nodded that she did.

Helena stopped for a moment as if collecting her thoughts and then continued. "Your father told me recently that in some weird way he felt that by staying together we were setting a poor example, putting up with a bad situation simply because it's the easiest thing to do. And nobody should live his life like that.

"The truth is, he could have gone on seeing Pamela on the side and still kept us, his social position, and everything else that came with it. Men have done that since the beginning; it's as old as marriage. But Alan said, and I believe him, that he didn't want to live that kind of a lie. He had to do what was right for all of us, because, in the end, lies catch up with you and you pay for them. Look at Mr. Hollis."

Taylor thought about this and then asked, "How was it right for me?"

"Your father left me, not you. You have to believe that."

"What about Pamela?"

Helena shrugged. "I finally ran into her by accident. She's a nice enough woman. Not as young as I thought she would be, nor as pretty. I suspect your father may already be bored, but I think he'll stay put, at least for a couple of years, and then he'll go in search of another dream, although I doubt it will take the form of a woman. Once you make a decision to live your life honestly, as true to yourself as you can, which I think your father has done, you don't compromise anymore. I suspect he knows now that life with Pamela will be as much a compromise as the life he left her for."

"Is he still working at the firm?"

"No. He left that, too. He works out of a store front and his apartment. Mainly, he's taking care of his daughter. He's become a real house-husband; hard to imagine, huh? But Alan has always been a dreamer, intent upon fighting the good fight, and you can't fight like that when you represent corporate interests. His lifestyle has scaled down considerably."

Taylor grunted with disgust. "But now he's got another kid. So he'll leave it, too?"

"If he does leave, it will be the mother he leaves, not the child. And 'it' has a name, and her name is Francesca."

"After my grandmother!"

"She's her grandmother, too," Helena said quietly.

Taylor felt a strange mix of emotions: anger, sadness, grief. She couldn't bear to look at her mother, so instead she stared at her hands, which were folded in front of her on the table.

"Have you seen this baby?"

"I asked to see a photograph one morning—curiosity more than any-thing else—and when I saw her I couldn't breathe for a moment because she made me remember my babies. You and Helena."

She paused for a moment, the memory and pain of twenty-four years ago clearly visible on her face. "Your father took one look at me and knew what I was thinking, because he'd felt the same thing. You are your father's spitting image, and so would Helena have been. And so is Francesca. So we both sat there and wept like two old fools. It was a break-through for both of us. It was like seeing Helena again, together, like see-ing you."

"How did she die?" Taylor looked at her mother now, her eyes search-ing for an answer, and she could see that her question had caught her mother by surprise.

"But I explained it so many times when you were growing up."

"I know you did when I was four and found out, but I don't think I really understood it even when I was older. I always knew how unhappy it made you to talk about it. Can you tell me again?"

Helena gave a sad-hearted sigh and nodded that she would. "Helena developed a heart condition. They could fix it now, but there was no hope then. We were just lucky that you weren't affected by the same thing. But you were the sturdy one; the one determined to survive. You saved my life that year. You were the *only* reason I continued to live."

Neither woman said anything for a while. Taylor reached across the table and grabbed her mother's folded hands, thinking how much older they seemed, and how much she loved her. "So, my father's baby reminded you of my sister, Helena, and me." It was the first time she had said her dead sister's name aloud in many years, and it felt strange.

Her mother nodded that she did. She motioned for the waiter and ordered the guacamole dip and chips that he had recommended earlier, and both women munched the chips in silence until they were nearly gone. Then Helena took a piece of paper and a pen out of her bag and wrote down a telephone number and address and pushed it across the table.

"Here is your father's number and address. He works at home, so it will be easy for you to reach him. It's been more than a year and a half since you spoke to him. It's time you confronted the man into whose face you really threw that dip."

Taylor thought about what her mother said over the next few days and tried hard to forget it. Her anger toward her father was too deep for her even to imagine a reunion. But then she would remember the things about him that she loved: how his eyes beamed with love when he saw her; his unwavering enthusiasm about even her dumbest ideas; the pride on his face whenever she walked into a room. She remembered his heartsick voice when he told her he was leaving, his insistence that he would love her no matter where he lived. His voice on her answering machine was always filled with so much anguish she would snap the machine off the moment she knew it was him.

And there was the silver bracelet, her father's gift to her on her twelfth birthday. She came across it one night going through a box of things from her childhood. It was still in the blue velvet case it had come in, and when she tried it on, she was struck by its simple elegance; it was still one of the most beautiful pieces of jewelry she possessed. That birthday night had been an evening of firsts for her: the first taste of caviar, the first sip of champagne, the first serenade (the string quartet had started off with her favorite rock song and ended up with a traditional "Happy Birthday").

TO TAYLOR ON HER TWELFTH BIRTHDAY. LOVE FOREVER, DADDY, read the inscription, and those words so beautifully inscribed still brought tears to her eyes. She had loved her father with all her heart then and knew how much he loved her. How could he have done what he did?

She dreamed about him that night. It was the usual dream, beginning as it always did with the two of them talking easily and happily as if nothing between them had changed. She could hear his deep voice, the laugh so much like her own. But the dream was different this time. His eyes were hollow circles. She knew he was in grave danger.

"Daddy?" she screamed, awakened by the sound of her own voice. She trembled with a sense of dread and apprehension, and as she lay in bed, she was sure she would never see him again. She called him the next morning, but when he answered she hung up. She called again the next day.

"Taylor? Is that you?" he asked before she could put down the phone again.

She was alarmed by the panic in his voice. "Daddy?" she yelled into the phone and was overcome with such a forceful rush of feelings she had to sit down.

"Are you okay, kitten?" When was the last time he'd called her that name? That anyone had called her that? She laughed despite herself at the old nickname. His voice was gruff, which she knew was his way of controlling his emotions. He never would let her see or hear him cry, and all the coldness she held in her heart thawed at the sound of it.

They met with Helena the next week, over Sunday brunch in a restaurant near where Taylor lived. She was alarmed at how much he had changed, how much weight he had lost, how gaunt he looked. She was afraid he was ill, but his eyes lit up in the familiar way when he saw her, and when she hugged him she was reassured by his familiar smell—the blend of pipe tobacco, cologne, wool in his tweed jacket. She fell into his arms, holding on to him for dear life, safe and protected.

Two weeks later, Taylor made lunch for her parents in her small apartment. Things were awkward at first, but it was good having her parents together again, saying familiar things, laughing at their shared memories. They called Ghana to speak to her brother, and for a while it was almost like old times. But Taylor knew it was an illusion. All of their lives had changed forever, and that made Taylor sad. At the end of the afternoon, her father suggested that it was time she met her sister, and he agreed to bring her to visit the following weekend.

Her sister.

It was hard for her to say those words until she held the baby, who looked so much like the pictures she had seen of herself as an infant. When she kissed her on her forehead, the baby gave a gurgle that sounded like a laugh, which Alan Benedict swore he'd never heard her make before, and that made Taylor grin.

"You are my little sister," Taylor said in disbelief, and felt a rush of love and tenderness that brought tears to her eyes.

A week later, she tried to explain the feeling to James as they played chess. "It was like she was a part of me. A missing part that I've found. I know it sounds corny, but that's how I felt," she said as she captured his queen.

James stared at the chessboard and then looked up at her with a sardonic grin that made Taylor realize just how much she had missed him. "It's called family, Taylor. She's your sister. The baby *is* part of you, like my pain-in-the-ass little sister is part of me. It's great that you and your old man are speaking again." Tentatively, he pushed his knight into what he thought was an advantageous position. "Check!" he said triumphantly.

Taylor studied the board. "Yeah, we are. I still haven't met Pamela, and I'm not sure I want to, but I do know my little sister and I'm talking to my dad again, so who knows? Pamela is Francesca's mother like Helena is mine. She can't be all bad, right? It's all good, James. All good!" she said with a smile that told him that things were. "I can't wait to see Francesca again. Isn't that a beautiful name? Every time I say it, I remember my grandmother. You sure you want to keep that move?"

"Of course. Who says you can't win without a queen? Strip poker may be your game, Benedict, but chess is mine. I'm in my element."

"God, you never learn, do you? Checkmate!" Taylor moved her bishop into the position that gave her the game.

A look of disgust crossed James's face. "At least I get to keep my pants," he muttered as he set up the board again. "So, it's been a month since the day of the dip. Have you heard from Mr. Big, a.k.a. Randall Hollis, a.k.a. Serious Asshole?"

Taylor covered her hands with her face in embarrassment, and they both broke into laughter. "What do you think?" she said.

"Do you think he's going to try to hurt your career? I mean, despite everything, he is a hotshot art dealer."

Taylor shrugged and moved her bishop's pawn. "I don't think Randall's that petty. But I've decided it doesn't matter one way or the other. I think I might be something else, like maybe a serious curator. Or maybe I'll just stick to research and try to do a book or something in a couple of years. I really loved talking to all those artists about their work and trying to understand what motivates them. I don't think I'm cut out to be an art dealer."

"You're cut out to be anything in this world you want to be, Benedict. Don't you believe that yet?"

Taylor reached across the board and gave James a hug, her beaming smile proof that she finally did.

Chapter Fourteen

Ana found Randall's gold Bulova watch tucked in a drawer the same Friday evening that she and Danny were going to meet Daniel Reese. She was struck by the irony of it. Her thoughts turned to Mali, a firm believer in serendipity, who had often tried to convince her of its validity. According to Mali, books fell open to a certain passage because you needed to read it; old friends called because you needed their wisdom; lost objects were found when you needed to find them. Ana interpreted Randall's watch turning up when it did as a sign that it was truly time to close his chapter in her life. Just as she was about to close the one on Daniel Reese.

At first she considered simply dropping the watch in the mail, but after reading the faded inscription realized that it had belonged to his father. There had always been both unresolved love and deep anger in his voice when he spoke of his father, and even though he would never admit it, Ana knew that the the watch would someday be of value to him. It was something that should be returned in person.

Her anger toward Randall had slowly begun to fade. It was the last week in October. Nearly two months had passed since the New Walls Gallery fiasco and her memories of that painful day had faded. For the first two weeks, Randall called her nearly every day. His calls were less frequent after that, and he hadn't called at all this week. More than once, she had picked up the phone to return his calls, then changed her mind. Slowly her sense of loss had begun to ease; she could get through the day without thinking about him.

Candy Lawson, spreading her particular brand of gossipy good cheer, had called the Saturday after the show to share the news of Taylor throwing the dip in "that art dealer's" face. Hearing of Randall's humiliation had saddened Ana, but not enough to tell him how she felt.

But she knew she would have to see him again. The world of buying and selling African-American art was a small one. Randall was an influential art dealer, and she was determined to acquire an important collection. There were upcoming shows—at the Puck Building in February and later in the Armory—where she knew she would run into him. They were bound to see each other at museum or gallery openings or at auctions. She wanted there to be enough peace between them to be able to function in the same space without discomfort.

She missed the joy of having a man in her life, the comfortable knowledge that he would be there when she needed him. She yearned for that sense of contentment. But she knew that her security had been an illusion. She was determined not to allow herself to fall back into her old habit of living in the past. That was one thing she had learned from her relationship with Randall, to live and savor each moment of the present. She had no time to waste on people who could not bring her joy, no time to grieve over things that could not be. She and Randall had shared good times, and she tried to remember those times without bitterness.

Often in putting Randall in perspective, she would recall Mali's jaded theory about men and infidelity. Men are men, Mali would say, and they could compartmentalize the women in their lives in a way that was impossible for most women to do. They could love one woman dearly, sleep with another, date a third, and actually believe they had been faithful to all three.

"It's one of life's little patriarchal jokes: They sow the seeds, and we have to reap them," Mali would say with a laugh just this side of bitterness. Ana suspected that was how Mali justified her relationship with Nate and her anger about his staying in his marriage, by trivializing men and their ability to commit. But Mali's bitterness didn't belong to her. Ana had known too many men who loved as deeply as women, and who had committed with the same serious intentions. She didn't believe that cheating on a loved one was the nature of men any more than it was the nature of women to accept it. But she did believe that in matters of love, past tended to be prologue.

The more she recalled the things Randall shared about the turmoil of his past, the more she understood why he was the kind of man he was. In the end, Lydia had made it hard for him to trust women. He only felt safe when there was more than one woman in his life because then no woman could dominate or destroy him. He was saddled with his history. As she was saddled with hers.

So, she placed his watch on her dressing table and left a message on his machine saying that she had found it and would like to drop it off at his apartment on Saturday while in the city on business, and unless she heard from him she'd see him the following morning around eleven. Her voice was formal with no hint of the intimacy that had once been between them, yet she felt regret and sorrow.

And then her thoughts turned to Daniel Reese.

It had been almost seven months since that May evening when Ana had told him that Daniel wanted to see them. She had left it up to him to contact Nate Jones and make the arrangements. Times and dates had been set, broken and set again. Finally Daniel had agreed to meet them tonight, and the arrangements were made. The plan was for Nate to bring Daniel to the club, and she and Danny would meet them there. The three of them could talk, either in Nate's office or the luncheonette across the street, and when they were finished Nate would take Daniel home. Ana never asked where "home" was; she didn't want to know.

Three times during the summer Daniel hadn't been at the appointed place at the decided time. It was easy for him to disappear, and Nate was hesitant to look for him. If he didn't want to come, Nate said, he wasn't going to force him. Danny had been devastated each time that it happened, but Ana wasn't surprised. She had her doubts about this time, too, but this would be the last time she would agree to meet with the two of them. Danny would have to seek out his father on his own after this. She simply didn't want to endure her expectations being met, once again, with disappointment; it had happened too many times in the past. That was another result of the end of her relationship with Randall: She was more self-protective; she was looking out for her own interests for a change.

When the phone rang, her heart jumped. For a moment, she thought it might be Randall and she hesitated to answer, then made herself pick it up on the third ring. It was Danny.

"Ma, you're still coming tonight, aren't you?"

"Yes. Did you check with Nate?"

"Yeah. Dad will definitely be there."

"Don't get your hopes up."

"I know he'll be there this time. I know it." He sounded like a hopeful little boy. It was the same voice bright with anticipation, albeit deeper, she had heard so often in the past. "Don't be so negative. You're always so negative about everything and everybody." The tone of those words, however, was a new and recent one with a peevishness that she was hearing more often. Her affair with Randall was over, but it it had subtly changed her relationship with her son. Danny was more dependent on her than ever.

He had stopped looking for a job altogether, seemingly content to live off the allowance she gave him. Each month, she sent a check into his checking account and paid his rent without comment or criticism, and he had gotten used to it. She had wrongfully assumed that sooner or later he would take the initiative to find a job and take care of himself, but nothing had changed. She feared he assumed that this was the way it would be forever and she wasn't sure what to do about it. When she and Randall had been together, she had been so content with her own life she had hardly had time to worry about Danny, but she was concerned again.

She was beginning to resent his financial dependence, although she was at a loss as to how to tell him. She was afraid that she would lose him, and that he wouldn't be able to take care of himself. And she was questioning herself again. What kind of a man had she raised? How much longer was he going to go on like this?

They shared few details about their lives anymore. In the last few months, a palpable tension had developed between them. She assumed he had gotten over Taylor Benedict, because he never mentioned her, and she hadn't told him about her breakup with Randall or how Taylor was involved. He was also drinking more; she had smelled liquor on his breath in the middle of the day more than once, and it sent a chill through her.

"Can you give me a lift, Ma? I didn't get the check yet to get my car out of the shop."

Ana didn't respond.

"Ma?"

"Okay," she muttered. "I'll pick you up at six."

They drove to Nate Jones's club in silence. It was located on a street about five blocks from where Ana had lived when her family left D.C., and as she drove through the familiar streets, her memories of them and those times came back. She was fourteen when they moved; her father had died a few years later. So much had changed. She hardly recognized her old neighborhood; the buildings looked worn and dreary and the people who lived there looked as if the life had been kicked out of them. She remembered when she'd first come here as a girl, how exciting and fresh everything had seemed. She and Daniel had walked these streets together; they had fallen in love exploring them.

"What's wrong?" Danny asked, always sensitive to her moods.

"Just thinking about old times," Ana said, then added, "about your grandma, your grandfather. I wish you'd been able to meet him. He was such a good man." If only Walter Thomas had been alive for his grandson.

"Were you thinking about Daddy, too?" Danny's eyes, filled with accusation, probed hers.

"Yes, I was," she said, feeling defensive.

When they walked into the club, Nate Jones met then at the door. "He's in the office, Danny." He motioned to the closed door with a nod. He turned to Ana and said in a low voice, "Prepare yourself. He looks worst than he did the last time I saw him."

When they entered, Daniel's back was to them. He didn't move. His head was bent as if he were lost in thought or had fallen asleep. He was so thin that Ana could make out the angles of his body—the sharp shoulder blades on which his clothes hung loosely, the neck so fragile she wondered how it could support his falling, balding head. His jacket, which was cleaned and pressed, was far too big for him, and Ana assumed it belonged to Nate, probably loaned or given to him for the occasion. Once they had been almost the same size, Daniel taller by an inch and far sturdier, but he was a shrunken wreck of a man; his old friend towered above him.

"Dad?" The word was spoken more as a question than a greeting. Daniel turned to face them, his face breaking into a smile. Ana was stunned by what had happened to his handsome face. His skin, once as smooth as her own, was pockmarked; years of bad food, drugs, and alcohol had aged him in a way that made him unrecognizable. If she had seen him on the street, she would have walked past him without a glance. He looked like every homeless man she had ever seen—eyes cast down, hands gnarled and wrinkled, the unmistakable look of defeat written all over him.

Danny stiffened, unsure what to do next. He glanced at Ana, as if asking permission for something, and then he moved toward the stranger who sat in the chair.

"Daniel," Ana said, and he turned toward her now, his eyes lighting up as they used to in the old days. They were the same deep eyes that seemed to peer up from his soul; it broke her heart to see them in such a wasted body. "Daniel, it's good to see you." That was a lie, and they both knew it; she would have given anything never to have seen him like this, and if there was any part of the old Daniel still left, she knew he felt the same.

"Anastasia, Danny. Anastasia, Danny," he repeated their names like a chant, his hoarse voice a shadow of the rich baritone it once had been. He stood up and moved toward them. One leg seemed unnaturally bent, and he hobbled on it, an old crippled man. Ana embraced him, and as his thin body came into hers, she willed herself to give him some of her strength, but there was nothing left of him to take it, and she drew away. She watched Danny hug him, holding on to him the way he did when he was a boy. Daniel began to weep, a motion that shook his frame. He finally collapsed back onto the chair, his head in his hand. Danny rushed toward him, kneeling beside him. Ana stepped away from him, toward Nate, who leaned toward her.

"I don't think I can do this," she whispered to Nate. "I can't do this." He hugged her, enfolding her in his arms for an instant, his body as strong and solid as Daniel's was weak. She thought about her father and the way he used to comfort her, letting her know there was nothing strong enough to hurt it.

"You can do it," Nate whispered back. "For the boy's sake, you can do it." She moved away from him and sat down in a chair next to Daniel and her son.

Daniel looked up at her. "You're still beautiful, Anastasia," he said. How formal he sounded, she thought, like someone from a different age. How long had it been since she heard her full name? Her parents were the only ones who called her that, and Daniel, who would never shorten it. He never shortened his own. Daniel. Never Dan. Always Daniel. Always Anastasia.

"Thank you, Daniel." She took his hands and held them. How rough his hands are, she thought, his nails bitten down to the quick.

"I got some business to take care of, man. Let me know when you want to go," Nate said, leaving the three of them alone and closing the door behind him.

"It's been a time, a long time," Daniel said, still holding on to her hand.

"Yes, it has."

"How long, Anastasia, how long has it been?" He sounded like a lost child asking for directions, and she realized that he actually didn't know. It had been time enough for a life to be wasted and thrown away, time enough for her to become a person he would never know.

"About fifteen years," she said. "Danny was ten. You came to his birthday party."

His face changed, loose and haggard, like that of a senile, old man, and her heart ached for him. He had no idea when he had seen them last. It was a wonder that he still remembered her name. What hell must he have been through? What hell had he put himself through?

"Fifteen years?" He repeated it as if he hadn't heard her right.

"Danny was ten." She glanced at Danny, wondering if he remembered that day. But how could he forget?

Daniel puckered his mouth, sucking air like a baby anticipating a bottle, like a drunk in need of a drink. He let her hand go and rubbed his own together. Ana could hear the roughness of his palms when they touched.

"I don't remember." The confusion and shame on his face when he made the confession made her glance away.

"That's okay," Danny said quickly. "It was a long time ago."

Daniel looked past them, toward the door. Like a trapped animal, Ana thought. He wants to go. He is more uncomfortable even than we are.

But Danny didn't want to let him go. "Dad?"

The use of the word struck them all. She could see it in the way Daniel jumped, startled, as if someone had slapped him; she cringed herself. But there was such love in Danny's eyes when he said it, as he acknowledged again this broken stranger as his father. Tears filled Daniel's eyes, and his back straightened as if accepting the responsibility. There was so much good inside him still, Ana could tell; she could sense that along with the anguish.

"Yes, son?"

"Do you remember that old car we used to have, that old red car we used to have?"

Daniel's eyes filled with confusion again. And trepidation. He nodded that he did, but Ana knew he was lying. She expected that Danny did, too. She watched his face drop, felt his sorrow.

"Remember when we used to ride in that car, Dad? The places we used to go?" Danny was grasping for straws, wanting anything he could get from Daniel to take away with him. Ana wept inside, at the thought of how much this man had meant to her son and how much of that need she had ignored.

Daniel's face was blank. There was nothing in his eyes.

"We had some good times back then," Ana lied, and Daniel glanced at her, thanked her for the lie with his eyes. "I remember that car, too. Red with a racing stripe. You and Danny went all over the state of New Jersey in that car. Delaware Water Gap. Cape May. Asbury Park."

Still nothing in Daniel's eyes, but he nodded as if he remembered.

"What are you doing now, son?" he asked Danny, eager to change the subject, focus on the present and not the past. "What kind of life are you making for yourself?" A light flickered in his eyes, a spark of expectation and love that Ana wished Danny could answer with good news that would give this man something to believe in. Danny dropped his eyes, the first time he had done so since they'd been there. She almost wished he would lie.

"Did you go to college, Danny? Did you finish school?"

"Not yet," Danny mumbled, embarrassed, and the light in Daniel's eyes dimmed.

"That's a shame, son," he said, avoiding Danny's eyes. "You got too much going for you to end up . . ." He didn't finish the sentence. He didn't need to; they all knew what the ending was.

"Well." Daniel rose slightly, glancing at Ana lingering longer on Danny. "Well, I guess I better—"

"Dad, do you want to get something to eat?" Danny interrupted him, still not ready to let him go. Daniel was startled, his eyes darting around for a way out.

"Please," Danny begged.

"I don't know, son, I got to—"

"Why don't you go and get something to eat with your son?" Ana said. It was an order rather than a suggestion, in a tone she hadn't heard herself use in fifteen years, words that she hoped could still touch him. How often had she said them in the past—why don't you read a story to your son (instead of drinking yourself into a stupor!)? Why don't you take your son to the park (instead of doping up with your no-account friends!)? Why don't you think of him for a change (instead of your own weak, irresponsible self!)?

Daniel responded to her as he had then, calling back from within him the best part that was left; Ana was thankful that it was still there.

"Okay, son. Where you want to go?"

"There's a place across the street. I could use some coffee, how about you?" Danny's voice was cheerful, fake. A salesman trying to sell a man something he had no use for.

"Okay," Daniel said, managing a smile, as if he believed him. The two of them headed out the door.

Ana sat still, her hands folded in her lap. She didn't hear Nate enter the room. He had to say her name twice before she answered him.

"You feel like a drink for old times, Dutch?" He reached for her hand to help her out of the seat. She couldn't have moved without his help, she realized. "When they get back you can ask the kid what they talked about. I have an idea, though."

Without speaking, Ana followed Nate into the bar and settled down across from him in one of the booths. A waitress brought over a bottle of scotch and two glasses.

"What you drinking these days, Dutch?"

"Not much. Wine, usually," Ana said absentmindedly, hardly hearing him.

Nate cracked a smile. "Don't get many folks asking for wine in here. Bring us some champagne, honey," he said to the waitress. "Cristal. That's what all the young hustlers drink these days. I know we got plenty of that." The waitress came back with a bucket filled with ice and the champagne, which she opened with a pop and poured into two flutes.

Ana stared at her glass. "This feels like we're celebrating, Nate. I don't have much to celebrate," she said, feeling nothing but grief.

"Sure you do, Dutch." Nate raised his glass in a toast. "You got yourself. You got us. Here, this one's for us. Dutch and Nate, for surviving."

Ana picked up her glass, and with a half smile toasted him as well.

"And this is for the ones we love who didn't. To Mali. To Daniel," he added, his face darkening

At the mention of Mali's name, Ana's thoughts turned to her relationship with this man who sat across from her. Nate was still a very attractive man, Mali certainly thought so until the day she died. Ana would have to agree with her now. Daniel had always been the better looking of the two men, the broader shoulders, stronger physique, more charming smile, but Nate still had a handsomeness that had deepened as he aged.

It was funny what age did to people, Ana thought, accentuating whatever characteristics one had in youth. Nasty people grew nastier, kind ones more generous. Look at what had happened to Daniel, how he wore the impact of the drugs and liquor on every part of his body. But Nate was better looking now than he had ever been. But his appeal was more than that. Even as a kid, Nate had been insightful and sensual, wise beyond his years, and he'd grown into that wisdom. He had always been tender-hearted to a fault. Ana had always considered him too softhearted to run a bar, but he also had a tough streak, a street fighter's sense of life. Nate *was* a survivor, in every sense of the word. And he was right; so was she.

"How long do you think they'll be?" she asked, sipping her wine.

Nate shrugged and he poured more champagne into her glass, leveling it off. "Not long."

"Why do you think he was so intent on seeing us? He actually had very little to say."

Nate sipped his drink meditatively before he answered. "How old is Daniel?"

"About two years older than me. He's going on fifty."

"Fifty!" Nate gave a surprised snort. "My daddy was fifty-six when he died. He seemed like an old man then. Now fifty-six seems damned young. It's right around the corner for me. Daniel's father was younger than mine, though. Fifty, if that. Daniel may suspect he's not long for this earth. He probably wanted to see his son while he was able, wanted his son to see him."

"Why?" Ana asked, exasperated. "Why not let Danny live with his memories? Why force your son to see you in this state?"

"Maybe that is the only thing he could give him," Nate said after a while.

"What do you mean?"

"Do you remember how old Daniel was when he started killing himself?"

Nate's choice of words made her shudder, but it was the truth and they both knew it. "Around twenty-five."

"Danny's age, right? All he could give the boy was what he has become. I think he is saying to his son: Look at me, Danny. Don't end up like your old man. You're at a crossroads. Make something of yourself. Sometimes that's all a man can say to his son: Be anything but me."

Ana's remembered the look in Daniel's eyes when he had asked Danny about college. Danny knew he had let down his father almost as much as he had been let down by his father's appearance; they had disappointed each other. She felt tears come into her eyes, so she stared down at the wine bubbling in her glass to avoid looking at Nate.

"So, when did you get too grown to cry around me, Dutch?" Nate said with a chuckle. "I've known you half your life. I ain't too grown to cry around you."

She noticed that his eyes had filled with tears, too, which he clumsily wiped from his face with a napkin. "Too much champagne on an empty stomach." He gruffly offered an excuse so obviously false it made then both laugh. They sipped their champagne in silence, each lost in thought.

"How are things going for you, Nate?" Ana asked after a while.

"I told you when we spoke in March that Essie and I broke up, didn't I?"

Ana nodded that he had. "Why did it take you so long?" She knew she should have phrased her words differently but simply didn't have the strength to be polite. Nate didn't seem to take offense.

"My boys," he said. "That was it. Mali understood, at least she claimed to. That's one of the regrets of my life, though, that I couldn't give Mali the love she deserved. My boys always came first. Always. Even before me."

"That was a mistake."

Nate looked surprised. "What do you mean?"

"If a parent is unhappy, then a child will be. You can't disguise how you feel; children always know and they take in your sadness and make it their own. Believe me, I know from experience. Danny suffered because of a choice that I made."

Nate was puzzled. "Leaving his father? That was the best thing you could have done for both of you."

"No, not that. Jerrod Mitchell," Ana said, then shared an abbreviated version of her marriage and the cruelty of her late husband.

Nate listened sympathetically, and then said, "But Essie wasn't Jerrod, Dutch. She's a good, loving woman, just not *my* kind of woman. But she loves the boys, and she's been a good mother to them, and a good wife to me, and I loved her in my own way because of that.

"But I know now it was unfair to stay with her as long as I did, which is why I left her when the boys were grown. Mali had my heart, always did, and we both knew it. I chose Essie over Mali because I always had somebody else's idea of what a wife should be. Mali always seemed too wild to tame." He nodded sadly at his own mistake, and continued, "I was too young and stupid to know that marrying a woman is never about taming her. The best kind of woman to have in your life is a wild woman who knows who she is and has her own spirit and fire. Any other kind will drain the spirit and fire from you. When Mali died, she took me with her. The worst part was I couldn't let myself grieve, couldn't mourn her properly because of Essie and the boys."

"I know," Ana said, but still unwilling to let Nate off the hook so easily, she added, "Mali could have raised your boys."

"Yeah. She could have done a helluva job raising them, but they were all Essie had. They were and still are her life, and I couldn't take them away from her."

"You could have had a child with Mali."

When Nate answered, Ana's heart went out to him; his face showed that he had had this argument countless times with himself. "I had three sons. Three boys already here. Essie couldn't have handled them by herself. There are lessons that are too hard for a woman to teach a boy that I had a responsibility to teach. A mother can love a son too much for his own good sometimes."

"What do you mean?" Nate picked up the alarm in her voice and chose his words carefully.

"I didn't raise girls, but I helped my mama raise my sisters after my daddy was gone. He'd done a good job raising me, so I stepped into that role easily. My mama didn't take mess from any of us, but my sisters gave her a hard way to go. They had to carve out their own identity from her, draw their own boundaries. That's how they became women. Girls separate themselves from their mamas with an ease boys never have.

"A boy measures himself against his father, and that's how he becomes a man. That's how he carves out his identity. If that daddy isn't there, then it's harder for that to happen."

"So, what makes a boy into a man?" Ana asked.

Nate shrugged self-consciously. "For me, Dutch, a man is a man when he knows what it takes to survive. A man has determination. Self-control. Self-discipline. He knows where he fits, where he stands in the world. He's come to terms with his own father. Don't get me wrong, a strong woman can raise a son as good as any man can, but it's easier for a man to do it because he's been through it himself."

Ana thought about Nate, and about her son and his father. "It's a little late for Daniel to help Danny claim his manhood, isn't it?" There was a touch of sarcasm in her voice.

"Yeah, that it is," Nate said. "But that's part of why he wanted the boy to see him. It's like I said before. It was his way of saying look at me! Make what I am your boundary, measure yourself against me so you don't become me."

Ana thought about this and about the men she had known and loved. Daniel. Nate. Jerrod. Randall. Danny. And her own father. She thought about the kind of man each had become, and where her son fit into the spectrum.

Sensing that this talk of fathers and sons made her uncomfortable, Nate changed the subject. "And what about you, Dutch. What's going on with you?"

Ana was glad he asked. She didn't want to think about Danny and Daniel for a while; it hurt too much. In broad strokes, she painted a picture of her seven-month experience with Randall Hollis—of falling in love, learning of his betrayal, finally getting over him. She told it lightly, as if she were already over it and better for the experience, but she suspected that Nate read between the lines.

He nodded sympathetically and then observed with a snicker colored by disbelief, "So he was two-timing a good-looking woman like you with Danny's ex-girlfriend?"

"That's the way it went down." Ana, struck by the humor of it all, smiled for the first time about it.

"The man was obviously a fool, and you been through too much to suffer through a fool."

"I've come to the same conclusion," Ana said with sigh.

"You won't be alone long. You're a beautiful woman, Dutch, beautiful the way a ruby is beautiful, or a rose. Your beauty runs deep, gets deeper each time I see you."

Ana was amused and touched by Nate's attempt at eloquence. "Can I come over here whenever my ego needs a lift?"she asked.

"I hope it's more often than that."

She wasn't quite sure how to respond, so she she changed the subject again. "Where will you take Daniel tonight? Where does he live?"

Nate looked uncomfortable, as if he didn't want to betray a confidence. "He lives anywhere he can, Dutch. What he really wants from me is money, and I give him as much as I can until I see him again."

"Tell me how much he needs. Let me give it to him. I can give it through you. You shouldn't have to shoulder it by yourself."

"Giving that man money is not a problem for me. He spends it on booze and drugs and whatever else makes him feel good as quick as I give it to him, but that's okay. You take your money and spend it on yourself. From what you just told me about that bastard you were married to, you deserve it." Then he leaned back in his chair, a sly smile on his face as he shared his own fantasy. "You know what I'd do if I had your kind of money, Dutch. I'd travel. There wouldn't be a place in this world that wouldn't see my feet. I'd be sending folks postcards from all over—Paris. Tokyo. Milan. Rio. Then I'd head to places most folks don't go—rain forests anywhere I could find them, the Galápagos, Antarctica. That's what I'd do. And I'd stay in touch only with those folks worth staying in touch with. You'd be one," he added, finishing his drink.

Danny and Daniel came back into the bar then, and Nate stood to greet them. Ana probed their faces for some indication as to what they had talked about but could see nothing. Daniel looked ill at ease; Danny seemed pensive.

"I'll be seeing you, Anastasia," Daniel said. "Take care of our son for me." His voice was so melancholy, she was sure that this might be the last time she saw him alive. She embraced him, self-consciously at first, holding him tightly until he pulled away. She felt a numbing sadness, deeper even than tears. Did Danny feel that, too? she wondered.

They said very little on the way home. Ana assumed that he was thinking about his talk with Daniel; her talk with Nate was on her mind. What he had told her about fathers and sons had the ring of truth. By her own measure, Danny had not become the man she knew he was capable of becoming, and she knew that by protecting him as she had, she was standing in his way. She had crippled him and she felt guilt and then anger at herself. She also knew what she had to do.

Danny stayed for dinner that night; it had been a long time since she had cooked for him, and they joked and laughed as they used to in the old days.

"So, are you and Randall still together?" Danny asked cheerfully as they cleared the table. She concentrated on rinsing off the dishes and stacking them in the dishwasher. "No. We broke up a month ago."

"Any chance you're going to get back together?"

"No."

"Are you depressed about it?"

"I was for a while, but I'm not anymore."

"That's good. I never liked the dude much, but he seemed to make you happy, so he was okay by me. He did make you happy, right?"

Ana glanced at her son and could see the concern in his eyes. "Yes, but that happiness came with a price."

"Does happiness always come with a price?" he asked casually, but she could tell by the way he glanced at her from the corner of his eye that he was probing her for something deeper.

"Not the kind that comes from within yourself," she said.

"How do you find that kind of happiness, the kind that comes from within you?" he asked with a desperation that instantly told Ana he was as unhappy with himself as she was with him. She thought about her answer a long time before she gave it.

"Everyone has to find out for himself," she said. "I can tell you what makes me happy. I'm happy when I feel self-confident and in control of my life, when I remember to cherish the day I'm living and find the lesson it's taught me."

"So, what lessons did you learn today?" There was amusement in Danny's voice, but she didn't return his smile when she answered him.

"First, you tell me the lessons you learned today," she said.

"That I don't want to end up like my father." Danny's manner turned somber, his voice dead serious.

"It's your choice whether you end up like him or not," Ana said.

She suspected he already knew that, that he had probably been thinking about it ever since he left Daniel. She added after a moment, "I have to discuss something with you. Let's sit down for a while and talk, okay?"

Together they built a fire in the fireplace, and when it was burning strong, Ana told him as gently as she could the decision she had made, one that she had been considering for a while. She would, she said, support him for only six more months, no more, and his checks would come directly from her accountant, never again from her. After six months, he would be on his own completely, and be responsible for every aspect of his life—from renting an apartment he could afford to maintaining his car if he chose to keep it. She would recommend that he begin attending sessions of Al-Anon or Alcoholics Anonymous so that he could better understand the disease that was killing his father and that could kill him, too, if he let it overcome him. He would have to sink or swim, and if he let himself sink, he could end up like his father. But she knew he could swim; she was counting on it. It was his choice to make, though, and he would have to make it alone.

"I believe in you, son," she said finally. "And you know how much I love you." He nodded that he understood, but he looked frightened and lost. Ana's heart fluttered with panic. What if he couldn't make it? What if he ended up in the gutter like Daniel? No, she reminded herself. Danny was not his father. This was the way for him to prove that to himself. And to her. Nate was right. Daniel's life would serve as Danny's boundary. He would have to measure himself against his father and grow from that. She made herself continue: "This is the only way I can think of to let you become the man that I—and your father—know you can become."

They sat awhile longer, and Ana took her son's hand in hers and held it like she used to when he was little boy.

"I will always be here for you, son. No matter what," she said.

"I know, Ma," Danny said. "I just don't want to disappoint you."

"That's up to you, but I don't think you will," she said.

By the time he left, the fire had burned down, and Ana stoked it until it was blazing. It was warm and comforting and she thought about the day that had just passed. It brought back other things, too, and she remembered the last fire she had built, in March, when things between her and Randall were just beginning. She allowed herself to relive that memory for a while—how it felt to fall in love and be swept away in happiness for half a year. She thought about their first night together, his vulnerability in the face of the cop, his tenderness when they made love. But then she made herself stop. She considered again what would happen tomorrow when she returned his watch. How would it feel to see him again? What would she say? Would she be tempted to get involved again?

"Of course I will, but I won't," she said aloud, and then thought with some amusement that she was talking to herself again, but this time that notion came without shame or embarrassment. She remembered Nate's words about how deep her beauty was. She had opened herself to one man and she would again to someone else. Maybe her heart would break or she would do the breaking, but she would take that chance. And as for tomorrow, whatever happened would be nothing compared to the evening she had spent with Daniel, her first love. She had grown strong because Daniel had grown weak. In an odd way, she owed her strength to him. And even to Jerrod.

She made herself a cup of chamomile tea and settled back on her couch to gaze at the paintings that brought her so much joy. Three oils by Samella Lewis, Philemona Williamsan, and Lois Mailou Jones had just been returned from a museum in Atlanta and she thought about how good it was to get them back. She studied again the lithographs by Elizabeth Catlett, Janet Taylor Pickett, and Margo Humphrey that hung on the wall near her kitchen. She ran her fingers over the smooth surface of the small Augusta Savage sculpture she'd bought before she met Randall. With anguish, she remembered the last day she had seen Mali alive. They'd gone to a museum in the city that was showing the Great Migration series by Jacob Lawrence. Both of them had been so inspired by what he had captured in each panel, the unrelenting spirit, the fearless determination of people coming north to find a new life. Like her parents had come— taking chances, praying for the best. And that was the truth of life, she thought, you took your chances, hoped for the best, never knowing what lay before you, but believing it would be good, and it usually was in ways you least expected because life could be taken in an instant, as it had been taken from Mali.

Nobody was promised a day. Not one day. And that made her think of all of the art in all the museums around the world that she had yet to see. There was the the Prado in Madrid, the Uffizi Gallery in Florence, the Hermitage in St. Petersburg.

"What the hell am I doing sitting in New Jersey?" she said aloud, with a wild uproarious laugh, the kind Mali laughed when something struck her funny. Nate was right. She would see what she wanted to see and stay in touch with only those people who meant her well.

I will live the life that was snatched from you, Mali, and wasted by you, Daniel, and that is how I will honor the memory of you both, she thought, and that thought warmed her as she sat by her fire sipping her tea until she was sleepy enough to go to bed.

Chapter Fifteen

Randall sat in the living room of his mother's apartment surrounded by packing boxes. Earlier that evening, he had hauled them up from the trunk of his car, finally ready to commit himself to the job he had been putting off for months. It was the one thing he knew would take his mind off Ana and her visit that morning. He'd been in the apartment for the last four hours, and except for unfolding boxes and setting them up in the bedroom and living room, he hadn't made much progress. Mostly he just sat and thought about what had happened earlier that day.

He glanced at his watch. It was close to midnight. He hadn't planned to be here all night, but it looked like he might be. The thought of that possibility propelled him off the couch and into his mother's bedroom, where he opened the top drawer of the chest of drawers. The smell of lavender swept the room, and he slammed the drawer shut. He hadn't been able to touch any of her clothes that still hung in the closet. Not the suits she'd gotten secondhand at the thrift stores for rich ladies, or the silk blouses bought on sale at Bloomingdale's. Certainly not the furs that hung like limp animals next to the suits and dresses. He couldn't remember ever seeing her in even one of the furs, most of which he'd bought her. Her jewelry, most of it quite expensive, was still in the silk pouches tucked in the bottom of a drawer. He'd never seen her in any of that either—not the diamond earrings he'd bought one Thanksgiving or the pearl necklace, not the sapphire brooch or the ruby ring. Maybe he should have taken her more places. Maybe . . . He stopped himself. It was too damned late now.

Everything would end up going to the Salvation Army. Where else could it go? He winced at the thought. Lydia's precious belongings, all those silks and furs, ending up at the Salvation Army. He'd have to think of something else. But he couldn't keep them.

The apartment was chilly. It always froze in the winter and steamed in the summer, ever since he'd been a kid. But it wasn't only the temperature that made him shiver. It was the lavender that lingered in the air, as if her spirit were still in the room and with him. He felt his shoulders tighten the way they used to when she was alive. She was haunting him, that was for sure. But wasn't that what Ana had said this morning, that she would haunt him for the rest of his life if he let her?

God, if there were a way to make this last few months disappear he would do it. If he could go back to the middle of the summer and change everything around. Forget about Taylor. Keep making Ana happy. Make peace with Medora. He snorted at the thought of that. His life was complicated even then. Medora and the baby. Ana was right about that, too. He knew he hadn't resolved his feelings about Medora. She had resolved hers toward him, which still pained him, but there was nothing he could do about it.

He went into the kitchen and got a beer out of the refrigerator. Mrs. Washington had cleaned it out and neatened things up the day after Lydia died. She left the beer, though. Bless her heart. The image of Mrs. Washington dressed up in her Sunday best for Lydia's wake came to mind and made him smile. Good woman, Mrs. Washington. He lifted the can and toasted her honor. He gulped it down, and forgetting about the bedroom, went back into the living room and dropped down on the couch. He recalled the last time he'd been here, the month before she died. Cleaning up after Lydia. Again. He went back into the kitchen and opened another can.

I don't think you have found your center yet, Randall. You soak up the love of women like a sponge sops up water and then when you're full or she's dry you move on to the next one or two. You can't commit to anybody, and that is probably the way you will be for the rest of your life. You can blame Lydia if you want, but Lydia is dead, and her destructive spirit will haunt you forever if you let it. And you will end up just like her, bitter and alone.

What struck with him most was how calmly Ana had delivered those lines, with no trace of malice or anger. He had certainly seen more than his share of angry women, and he knew only too well how to cope with them. He'd learned that early enough from Lydia. When a woman screamed at him, he simply didn't let himself hear her. He didn't respond. He put his mind somewhere else, and her voice was just so much noise to be filtered out. He met her fury with his calm, her heat with his ice. He always won that way, even when she thought she did. That was how he'd always beaten Lydia. Even during that scene with Taylor Benedict at the New Walls Gallery, he hadn't responded as some men might. And that was a good thing.

But Ana had rattled him. He wasn't sure what he expected when she said she would drop off the watch, but it hadn't been that. He was more than ready to deal with her outrage—in fact, he welcomed it. He was sure that when he saw her in person he could convince her to forgive him. He'd always been good at that with women, persuading them to give him another chance.

He nearly shouted for joy when he heard her voice on his machine yesterday evening. It had been nearly two months since he'd seen her, time enough for her to mull things over. He'd been sure his unreturned calls were simply revenge for what he had put her through, her subtle way of getting even. He was certain that the return of his watch was simply a ruse to see him. The truth was, when he'd taken it off in Bermuda and given it to her, saying that it was his past and she was his future, he had meant every word of it. He hadn't cared if he ever saw the damn thing again. Ironic, that his father's watch might bring Ana back into his life.

So, this morning he had risen early, happier than he'd been in weeks. He'd put a bottle of champagne (Perrier Jouet, her favorite) on ice, taken a cab to Balducci's to get smoked salmon, bagels, and other treats she was fond of. He'd made it home by ten, just in time to jump into the shower. He anxiously awaited the buzzer. But the moment she walked in, he could sense a difference in her manner. She was subdued to the point of coldness; this was a closed Ana, so different from the cheerful one he was used to.

"Ana, how have you been?" He tried to embrace her, but her body stiffened, indicating that a handshake would have been more appropriate.

He pulled away. "Can you come in for a while? Is it too early for a glass of champagne?"

The moment he said that he knew he had made a mistake. The way her face froze said that she knew what he was up to and despised him for trying it. At that moment, he despised himself.

"Do you have any coffee?" she asked.

"Sure, anything you want. How about something to eat?"

She nodded her head "no" without smiling. She had a generous, bright smile that lit up her face, and its absence pained him. "That's very kind of you, Randall. But I'm not hungry. I had a late breakfast."

"I have some of those scones you like from Balducci's. Can I tempt you?" The word "tempt" lingered in the air long enough for both of them to know that the scones weren't the only temptation he was offering. He thought, for an instant, that the old spark between them would ignite, and the way her eyes searched his told him that she had felt it, too. But in the next instant, he could see that she had made her choice.

"Not this morning, Randall," she said, her voice grim, and his face fell. Not this morning. Not tomorrow morning. Not any morning.

"Okay." He accepted her answer. "Do you still have time for coffee?"

"Sure." There was tension between them now. She was self-conscious, and so was he.

He made the coffee. There was no use in making small talk from the kitchen. Anything he said had to be to her face. Too many things had gone wrong between them for anything other than that. He pulled out the silver tray he'd bought years ago from Tiffany's and despite what she said, piled it high with the scones, a small dish of butter, and another with the marmalade she liked. He made the coffee, poured it into a china coffeepot with matching cups and linen napkins, and carried the tray into the living room. The tray, with its peaked napkins, sparkling silver, and gleaming china, made her smile, but it was a sorrowful smile that made him sad, too.

"Okay, maybe I will have something," she said as she buttered a scone and took a dainty bite.

"I know you like scones, and I was in Balducci's . . ." He shrugged, without finishing the sentence.

"It was very thoughtful of you. Here, I don't want to forget this." She placed the scone on her saucer and handing him the watch.

"*This* was thoughtful of you," he said, placing the watch on the edge of the table. "You didn't need to do this. You could have just dropped it in the mail."

"It was your father's watch, and I knew that it was important to you. I was going to be in the city anyway."

He glanced at the Rolex she had given him and then back at her. "Would you like me to give you back—"

"No! Don't be silly," she said, not letting him finish. "It was a gift, and I'm not in the habit of asking people to return gifts I've given them."

"But under the circumstances—"

"That's the way it goes." She cut him off with a proud, dismissive shrug.

He paused and then said, "Ana, I just want you to know how sorry I am."

She sighed, a deep weary sigh that said more than he wanted to hear.

"Ana, I'm so—"

She held up her hand to stop him and said, "Don't, please! I'm here because I wanted to return your watch, but I also felt bad about the way things ended between us, so public like they did. You meant too much to me to allow things between us to end so shabbily. I wanted us to make peace."

"You have no idea how much you mean to me." He deliberately chose the present tense.

They sipped their coffee in silence as Randall desperately tried to think of something else to say. He watched Ana take another nibble of the scone, another sip of coffee, then dab her mouth with her napkin in a gesture that said she was preparing to leave. He couldn't let her go yet.

"Well, Randall, I—"

"Ana, please wait!" He half stood to stop her, his voice pleading with her to stay.

"Oh, Randall." Affection, regret, and dismay were all there in the way she said his name.

"I'm sorry," he said again. It was the only thing he could think of.

"So am I." Another sad smile.

"No, you really don't know how I feel." He raised his voice slightly, and he could see that surprised her. He had her attention now, but he wasn't sure what to do with it. He searched for words that would say everything he felt—self-recrimination, guilt, love—but came up with nothing. "Taylor, well, she was . . ." He stopped midsentence. What could he possibly say? That Taylor had meant nothing to him and that Ana had called it right at the gallery? That he used women to make him feel better about himself? Or maybe that he had simply been in love with them both and didn't want to give either of them up? He stammered searching for words that wouldn't make him sound like a fool or a cad. "I got involved with Taylor before I made my promise to you, and I couldn't think of any way to break it off without hurting her. I didn't think things between us—you and me—would grow as deep as quickly as they did."

There was truth in that, he told himself, but he couldn't interpret Ana's expression.

"But you ended up hurting us both," she said quietly.

"Yeah," he agreed. "I did."

"What about Medora Jackson? You're still involved with her, too, aren't you?" Her smirk was slight but edged with contempt. He'd never seen that kind of expression on her face before, and it saddened him to see it. He didn't answer her question because he wasn't sure of the answer, and if there was any chance that Ana could forgive him, he knew that now was not the time to lie. It wasn't the time to bring up his complicated relationship with Medora Jackson, either. He continued to call her every week as he always had, but despite her comforting message after the New Walls Gallery incident, their conversations had reverted back to what had become familiar—short, cordial, distant. He had no idea how Medora felt about him or what was on her mind.

"I just don't know about Medora," he said, which was the closest thing to the truth he could come up with. "I know I loved her once." He chose the past tense, watching her response.

Ana smiled slightly. He wasn't sure what to make of her smile; it was as enigmatic as the one she'd had on her lips when she told him off at the gallery. "The two of you will have to work something out, you know?"

"We already have."

"I think you'll find that there is more between you than either of you wants to admit at this point. Even more than the baby." There was no anger or resentment in her voice, only what he was sure that she knew and felt.

"It's up to her." He sounded sulky, but there was nothing he could do about it.

"A baby can be a second chance, Randall."

"I want a second chance with *you*." It sounded corny and contrived, like dialogue out of some melodramatic soap opera, but he couldn't think of anything else to say.

"There's a limit on the second chances I can offer, and I don't have any more to give," Ana said in the patient tone of an adult explaining an indisputable truth to a willful child. He was stung by her rejection, and for an instant regretted having shared his feelings so freely.

"But I'm not Daniel . . . I really care about you."

"So did he," she said, her tone turned sharp and defensive.

"How could you let things end between us so easily? I made a mistake. God knows I'm paying for that now. I've learned from it. Why can't we try to work things out?"

Ana gazed at him long and hard as if considering what he had just said, and then she shook her head, an odd, quick gesture as if reminding herself of something she was on the verge of forgetting. "No," she said.

"Why not?" he demanded to know like a spoiled child.

"Because I don't think you have found your center yet, Randall," she said. "You soak up the love of women like a sponge sops up water and then when you're full or she's dry you move on to the next one or two. You can't commit to anybody and that is probably the way you will be for the rest of your life. You can blame Lydia if you want, but Lydia is dead, and her destructive spirit will haunt you forever if you let it. And you will end up just like her, bitter and alone."

She said those words and then left, and he had sat around for the next five minutes staring at the closed door. He got up finally, went into his exercise room and lifted some weights, trying not to think of what she had said. She was a woman scorned after all, he reminded himself, and he'd known more scorned women than he cared to remember. He'd gotten through the last thirty-seven years without finding this "center" or whatever the hell she was talking about. Why look for it now?

After working out, he still felt restless. When he heard from her Friday morning, he had cleared his calendar for Saturday, hoping that Ana might spend the day with him, so the rest of the day loomed before him dull and empty. On impulse, he called Medora, who knew him better than anyone else. He felt a sudden urge to hear her voice, to seek assurance that he wasn't the man Ana said he was, that he could be redeemed. Medora wasn't home. Where the hell could she be? She shouldn't be going anywhere. The baby was due soon. She should be home. He kicked himself for not calling her more often. Hell, he should have been calling her every day. Here he was, thinking only of himself again, calling only when he needed her, not when she might need him. Ana was right after all. Maybe he did soak up love like a sponge, leaving nothing worthwhile in its place.

Have you ever really loved anybody but yourself?

Medora had said it, and maybe that was the truth, too.

He had to get out. He went to a nearby moving and storage company, bought some cardboard boxes, and piled them into the trunk and backseat of his car, preparing at last to perform the task he'd been putting off for months. Despondent, he'd driven to Jersey. It was unfair of Ana to bring Lydia into what was between them, he decided. It was a low blow he'd been unable to defend himself against. Even Ana, with all of her understanding, had no real knowledge of the relationship he had with his mother. Nobody knew but the two of them.

Randall and Lydia.

He returned to the kitchen and searched the cabinets for something to eat. The beer on an empty stomach had made him nauseated. He found some stale crackers in a plastic bag and a can of tuna fish, which he spread on the crackers and gobbled down, then boiled some water for tea. He went back into the living room to finish packing up the room.

There was nothing he wanted to save. The couch, the chairs, all these damned mirrors could go. The furs, the jewels, the clothes. It was worthless to him. Maybe he'd ask Mrs. Washington if she wanted some of the jewelry. She deserved it, putting up as she had with Lydia for those last few months.

Why was he still so angry at her?

He packed things by rote, not caring about breakage, hardly looking at the plates, glasses, or mirrors he stacked into the boxes. The sooner he got through with this, the better off he would be.

But the harder he worked, the clearer he could hear Ana's last words to him.

Did he move through the world of women simply looking for conquests? he wondered. Was that what his life had come down to? Was he trying to find within each of them some missing part of Lydia? Was it Lydia's artistic spirit he really worshiped in Medora? In Ana, was it the warmth and generosity that he had never found in Lydia? Were Taylor and the countless other Jennifers, Monicas, and Dianas who for the past fifteen years had danced in and out of his life really some missing part of Lydia he didn't recognize because he didn't want to?

How long would she haunt him?

How long would he let her haunt him?

He went through the books in his small bedroom. Most of these could be donated to a school or library, he decided, and he threw them into the boxes, hardly glancing at the titles. He wanted no memories tonight. No thoughts of his lonely childhood. There were very few books here that belonged to his mother. When he was a kid, she had been a voracious reader, devouring nearly a book a week. But her eyesight had grown bad in later years, and she stopped reading around the same time she stopped drawing; she watched television almost exclusively. The few books on the bookshelf in the living room were covered in dust so thick it made him sneeze. He piled them into the box, not bothering to brush them off.

A slim soft-covered volume jammed between a dictionary and a hard-cover edition copy of *Roots* caught his eye. He dusted it off and opened it. The pages were yellowed with age, but he could still make out the outlines of sketches that had been drawn, erased, than drawn again. They had all been carefully rendered; her skill again, so evident.

"Oh, Lydia." He said her name in a cry of sorrow, love, and regret. These drawings, done without benefit of training or guidance, were exquisite. Mostly they were of him when he was a child, mostly done by memory, he assumed, because he couldn't remember posing for them, but perhaps he had. She'd captured him smiling, frowning, sleeping. When had she done them? he wondered. How late at night had she worked on them? He turned the fragile pages slowly, studying each line and shadow.

He stopped at a series of drawings she had done of his father. Randall Oates. He slipped on his glasses and took them to the light to get a better look at them. He knew so little about this man. What had they told him about his father through the years? That he played piano in a couple of clubs in Newark, had a band that never got off the ground, seduced a woman fifteen years younger, and was shot by an old man for sleeping with his wife. All he knew were other people's stories, their disappointments, their interpretations of his weaknesses. All he had were other people's memories and the watch Ana had returned. That was it.

Who was this man that Lydia had sacrificed so much of her life for? Who was Randall Oates, the man he had loved, hated, and blamed for as long as he could remember, as long as he had been alive? He examined the drawings carefully, studying each one as conscientiously as he would the work of a master. Lydia's drawings, executed in broad and fine lines, had captured his father in a way the photographs she'd kept of him had never been able to; they made him think of the drawing Medora had done of him that had captured him so well. He studied his father's eyes, so restless and deep, with a wildness in them that told of an unsettled spirit. He could see in the set of the jaw the sadness in the fall of his face, his wounded soul. His head rested on his large, beautiful hands, the graceful hands of a surgeon or a pianist.

Funny, he had never thought about that before, his father's hands. A man's hands told you a lot about him. He thought of Reynard's hands, calloused and rough from his years in construction, and of the hands of a sculptor he knew, who he was sure was destined for greatness. His work was written on his hands: the deep gashes, the broken nails. His sculptures, as profound and beautiful as they were, had taken their toll on each of his fingers and thumbs. He looked at his own hands. A lover's hands, Reynard would say, teasing him with amused but mild contempt. Never seen a day of hard labor.

Lydia had captured in the slant and grace of his father's hands, a part of him that Randall sensed he let few people see. In his eyes, she had caught the vulnerability, the fears, the dreams. Randall ran his fingers around the edges of each of the images of his father as if trying to touch some small part of this man whose absence made him who he was.

He looked at his own hands again, seeing as he had never seen them before, studying the length of them, the shape of the nail, the strength in each finger. They were his father's hands, the drawing told him that. He wriggled them, and then dropped them downward as if he were touching a keyboard. How much music had he dreamed of playing and never been able to perform? Lydia Hollis. Randall Oates. Randall Hollis. They were both dead now inside him—all the good, all the bad. He, their son, was the only thing left from either of them. He held the book close to his heart, unable to put it down.

The doorbell rang, followed by five sharp knocks on the door.

Still caught in his thoughts, Randall didn't answer.

"Who is in there?" A man's deep voice shouted through the door. "I said, who is in there? I got the cops on their way over here. Ain't nobody supposed to be in there!"

Randall quickly got up, opened the door, and was confronted by the building's superintendent, dressed in a robe and wielding a baseball bat. Beside him stood Mrs. Washington, who, still in her pink nurse's uniform, had obviously just come from work.

"Oh, Lord, Mr. Hollis, I am so embarrassed!" Mrs. Washington covered her round face with her plump hands. "I was coming in from work—today is my late day at the hospital—and I saw all the lights on in your mother's apartment. I didn't know who was up here. So, I went down and got Mr. Greene, and . . . well . . ."

Visibly relieved, the superintendent let the baseball bat fall to his side.

"No, that's fine. I'm glad to know that somebody is looking out for the place. Would you two like to come in?" Randall stepped to the side to allow them to enter.

The superintendent glanced at his watch. "Naw, I'm going back to bed." He threw Mrs. Washington an annoyed look, which made her grimace.

"I'm so sorry! I should just mind my own business, my son always tells me that."

"No. It's late, and I should have come here earlier. I just haven't had a chance to pack up things, and I decided to do it tonight. Why don't you come in, Mrs. Washington. How about some coffee or tea?" Randall asked, forgetting what time it was and suddenly needing some company.

"Are you sure? I'm not tired, but it's awfully late. It's going on one."

"No, no. Actually I'd enjoy the company," he said, which was the truth.

Mrs. Washington glanced in the room and noticed the boxes. "It's not a happy job you're doing tonight, is it, son?" she asked.

Son.

The use of that word stunned him, and he felt a lump forming in his throat. He didn't trust himself to answer.

"It's okay, honey. It's always hard to clean up what's left over from those we love," she said. "I know when my husband died, Mr. Washington, I let his clothes hang where they were for ten months before I cleaned them out. You're doing good with three months. But I guess they want to rent the apartment."

Randall realized that she had misinterpreted his distress as grief. And maybe she was right; maybe it was.

"If you want me to, I can come in for a minute or two, keep you company for a spell," she said after a moment. "I'm off tomorrow and I always have been a night owl."

"Thank you," Randall said. He put water in the kettle and waited for it to boil. While they waited, Mrs. Washington began to put some of the things from the kitchen into a box, and the two of them worked together in companionable silence. When the tea was ready, they moved into the living room, and while Mrs. Washington drank her tea and chatted, Randall finished packing the books and wrapping the mirrors in newspapers.

"So, what are you going to do with all these things?" she asked.

"Salvation Army, I guess."

Mrs. Washington glanced around and then examined the worn upholstery on the couch. "My church could use some of them," she said.

"You're welcome to anything you want," Randall said. "And I've got something else for you, too, Mrs. Washington," he said, remembering in a flash the jewelry in his mother's drawer. He went into the bedroom and searched through the chest of drawers for the silk pouches, and brought them back into the living room, emptying the contents onto the coffee table in a pile of sparkling gems.

"Oh, Lord!" Mrs. Washington shrieked, and gazed at Randall in surprise. "I know you're not giving me this jewelry, are you, Mr. Hollis?"

"Help yourself. Donate what you don't want to your church. I don't want it. I don't have anyone to give it to," he added.

"Don't you want it to remember your mother by?"

"No."

Mrs. Washington watched him closely. "That's the grief talking, son," she said gently. "You should save these things to remind you of your mother, then you should give them to your wife someday."

"I don't have a wife, and I don't think I'll ever have one. I'm sick of women!" Randall said, then realizing how strange it sounded to be so candid about his love life with a woman he hardly knew, added, "My girlfriend broke up with me."

Mrs. Washington smiled sympathetically. "Now that's a shame, right on top of your mama's death! I'm sure you're going to get back together. You're a good man, Mr. Hollis; no woman in her right mind is going to let you leave her life," she said.

If only she knew, Randall thought. "No. I don't think so."

"That's the grief talking," she said. "You might have a little daughter someday, and you'll want to give some of this jewelry to her. It would be a nice gift from her grandmother."

Randall shrugged and turned back to his packing. "Don't you have a granddaughter?"

"Well, yes, but—"

"Give it to her," he said, and wrapped another mirror in newspaper.

"Mr. Hollis, I don't know. Women pass jewelry like this down for generations."

"Listen, Mrs. Washington. You're a very nice lady, and your kids are lucky to have you. You're the kind of mother I wish I had had."

Mrs. Washington gave him a stern look that softened the longer she stared at him. "That's the grief talking," she said.

"I know how difficult my mother was and you stayed with her in her last days; please take it!" Randall turned back to his work.

She picked up one of the sapphire pins, held it against her pink nurse's outfit and gazed at herself in one of the mirrors that still hung.

"Before I started my nursing duties, I worked for a rich lady in Short Hills, and she used to say that if you know what to look for, you can always tell the real thing. I know what to look for, and this here stuff is very valuable. Your mama should have kept it in a safe-deposit box, not in her house. She's just lucky nobody broke in and stole it. These here are the *real* things."

"*You* are the real thing, Mrs. Washington." Randall took down another mirror and wrapped it in paper and laid it on the floor.

She sighed and picked up a diamond brooch, polishing it with her sleeve. "I'm going to keep it for you. I'm going to get a safe-deposit box and put it in there, and keep it safe until you have somebody to give it to."

"Suit yourself," Randall said, shaking his head in exasperation.

Mrs. Washington picked up the sapphire brooch again and pinned it on her uniform. "I think I will keep this brooch, though, Mr. Hollis."

"Good!" Randall said.

"Mr. Hollis, I have never in all my life had something as beautiful as this," she said, and Randall, glancing at her, noticed that her eyes had watered behind her thick glasses. He stopped packing for a moment to watch her admire herself in the mirror.

"I'm glad you like it," he said, thinking that in all the years that he'd given women jewelry, this was the first time anyone had said anything like that. "Please call me Randall, Mrs. Washington. I think we've been through enough together for you to call me by my first name." He turned back to his packing.

"Iola," Mrs. Washington said. "That's me. You can call me by my given name, too."

"Iola. Nice name," Randall said. He returned to the kitchen to survey what was left to pack. He wondered if he should give her the rest of that, too.

Iola Washington, sipping her tea, continued talking to him from the living room. "You don't hear it much anymore. My name. It's one of those strange old names folks used to give their children. My mother's name was Iona. Another 'I' name, except she took out the 'N' and added the 'L.'"

"Hmmm, makes sense," Randall said absentmindedly, only half listening. It was nice hearing the sound of another voice in the apartment, he realized, especially one as calming as Iola Washington's. He realized he had never thanked her for calling him the night of his mother's death or for showing up at Lydia's wake. Well, the jewelry would do that, show his gratitude. "You don't get too many old-fashioned names today. You can tell a lot about a woman by her name. There's a lot in a name."

"Got that right," Randall said. He opened the microwave and sponged it out. She could have this, too, if she wanted it.

"I was up on the ward today. Maternity ward for a change. I like it up there, birthing is always better than dying. Most of the mamas are young girls with young girls' names. A whole bunch of Tiffanys, Biancas, Britneys, after that singer."

"No Bessies, huh?" Randall said, keeping up his end of the conversation.

"I used to love me some Bessie Smith. You like Bessie Smith?"

"I have a friend who does," he said, as he looked over a cast iron skillet and thought about the pancakes Lydia used to make.

"No Bessies, but right before I went off duty tonight I checked in one baby's mama who had an old-fashioned name. Haven't heard it in forty years. I asked her what it meant, and she said it meant gift, that she was a gift. That's a real nice name for a mother to give her daughter, isn't it? Give her a name that says she's a gift."

"Interesting," Randall mumbled, packing the skillet away with his memories.

And it wasn't until Iola Washington had left and he had stacked the last of the boxes in the middle of the living room that it occurred to him just who the "baby's mama" might be whose mother had given her the name that meant she was a gift.

ollis, you better get your butt down to Central Hospital. Medora is about to have that baby," T.W. growled at him from his answering machine when he checked it on the way to the hospital. That had been at midnight. It was four-thirty in the morning by the time Randall finally convinced the nurses on duty who he was, and stumbled into the maternity ward to stand beside Eliza, who was acting as Medora's Lamaze coach.

Medora's eyes lit up when she saw him, but when he went to embrace her, Eliza pushed him aside. "She's got to focus on her breathing. You weren't at the Lamaze sessions, so get out of the way!" she snapped.

Embarrassed, Randall stepped to the sidelines, not sure what to do or say, until Medora, between controlled breaths, motioned for him to come close, and he approached her and took her hand, grasping it tightly as she breathed through her contractions. He had no idea how he could be of help. Eliza finally gave him a cup of ice chips and allowed him to place them onto Medora's tongue as she needed them. He placed ice chips and watched, helpless and useless, as the contractions grew stronger and more intense.

"She's going into transition," Eliza whispered to him as if he knew what she was talking about; he had no idea. Fifteen minutes later he saw the peak of the baby's head and caught his breath as the tiny body, eyes closed tight, hair plastered down, squeezed out of Medora in a flash of brown. His eyes locked with Medora's in an expression of joy he would remember for the rest of his life.

"Girl!" the doctor announced, called the time she was born, and then held her up for both Medora and him to see. Randall let his breath out and tears came into his eyes. Relief followed by elation surged through him.

While they tended to Medora and the baby, Randall went to the lobby to call T.W., Aunt Tillie, and finally Reynard to tell them the news. When he got back to Medora's room, the early morning sunlight seeping through the the open blinds bathed the room in a soft golden light. He stood for a while at the door, caught in the stillness, and then bent over the crib next to Medora's bed, where the baby slept. He wept when he saw his daughter, now bathed and clean in pink swaddling clothes. She looked so fragile, far too delicate to pick up. He touched her face instead, amazed at how soft her cheeks were. He could get a better look at her now, away from the buzz and excitement of the delivery room. She was plump, unlike so many newborns he had seen, with hair that swirled in silken curls around her head. He wasn't sure how long he stood gazing at her, still caught in the magic of her birth and unable to believe that she was really his.

Minerva.

Medora wanted to name her after her mother. He could understand the sentiment, but he wasn't crazy about the name; it sounded awkward to him, spinsterish. He didn't like the way it rolled off his tongue. He'd have to get used to it, though. Or maybe he'd call her Minnie, like T.W. did her grandmother. If it had been his choice, he would have named her Medora, after her mother. A mother's gift. A father's, too. He sat down in the chair beside Medora's bed.

It had been a long labor, he'd heard Eliza say, and he'd come in only at the end of it. Medora was exhausted, that was clear, and she slept, her hand tucked under her head, the way she'd slept for as long as he'd known her. He brushing her forehead lightly with his lips, trying not to wake her.

The baby stirred and woke up with a quick, high-pitched cry. He went back to the crib, drew in a breath, and picked her up with apprehension. She snuggled next to him, and he let his breath go, holding her next to his chest. She made a sucking noise and dozed off again. Still holding her, he sat down in the chair next to Medora's bed.

Randall had heard once that at one point or another everyone undergoes a life-altering event. He knew several people who had been through near-death experiences, stepping into the nether land of the hereafter and emerging with kinder personalities. Battling cancer had radically transformed one woman he knew, and AIDS had changed one of his artists from a raging, angry spirit to a gentle one. As Randall held his daughter, remembering the sound of her first cry and her body poking its way into the world, he knew that this was his epiphany, and he would never view life in quite the same way again. Indeed, this whole day had been one of serendipitous events: the trip to Lydia's apartment, Mrs. Washington's surprise visit, finding his father's portraits in his mother's sketchbook.

He wondered if his father had experienced the same tender feelings toward him when he was born. He was sure that Lydia had in her own way. He remembered Ana's words and knew that she was wrong about him. He would *not* end up like his mother; she would *not* haunt him for the rest of his life. Her grandchild was the charm he held against her, and he felt an overpowering love and gratitude toward this tiny being who nestled her head against his chest. He kissed her cheek and whispered an oath into her tiny ear: "I promise that I will protect you from anything or anyone who tries to hurt you. I promise I will spend my life making you as happy as I can."

And he thought about the last seven months and what had happened between him and "his women," as Medora called them, and about how little he had really understood any of them. He thought about Lydia's cruel words, and Ana's kind ones, and the ones that Taylor spoke that he didn't want to hear. He'd read somewhere that a man never fully understood women until he'd raised one, and he knew now that was probably true. He thought about Medora, sleeping peacefully beside them, and about wildflower honey and Red Zinger tea.

The baby cried again, and Medora opened her eyes. They lit up when they saw him and her daughter. Without saying anything, he handed her the baby and she began to nurse her. She smiled at him, the way she had so many times before.

"She's so beautiful, isn't she?"

"How could she not be? You're her mother."

Medora kissed the baby's cheek, and closed her eyes again.

"Are you tired?"

"Yeah. A little bit."

"Do you want me to go?"

"It's up to you."

"This is the only place I want to be in the world, here with you and her." He'd never meant anything more in his life.

Medora kissed her baby once again, then gave her back to Randall. "Another one of your women for you," she said with a tired but playful grin. Randall held his daughter gently and rocked her back to sleep.

Chapter Sixteen

It was the second week in November, three weeks since Medora had given birth, and she was still uncomfortable with "Minerva," her baby's name. Medora loved *her* name and always had. She had met plenty of Janes, Bettys, and Lucys, but never another Medora. Because her name was "different," the term everybody used to describe it, she was drawn to strange, interesting names. When she was a girl, her best friend was Mauve, whose name she adored, and every time she used the color, she was reminded of the tea parties in Mauve's pink-and-purple bedroom and the walnut cookies her mother loved to bake. Ladonia and Ianantha were two other names that had caught her fancy through the years, along with Bathsheba, Hermione, and Tabitha.

Names were supposed to have meanings, Medora believed. She never missed a chance to share the meaning of her own name, and how her mother smiled when she said it. She'd read somewhere that Augusta, the first name of a sculptress whose work she admired, meant "exalted." Tillie, her aunt's name, was short for Theodora. Medora never asked why they called her Tillie rather than Teddy, which she felt suited her better, but whatever the nickname, Theodora meant "given by God," and Medora felt her aunt lived up to it. Her own mother, Minerva, was named for the Roman goddess of wisdom, a quality that her mother lacked when it came to T.W. But Medora loved the name and the sentiment behind it.

So, the day after her baby was born, when the nurse came around with the birth certificate, Medora jotted down the name Minerva Jackson-Hollis without a second thought. Yet whenever she whispered or sang to her baby, it seemed too big a name for such a small presence.

"How are you today, Minerva?" she would cheerfully say each morning, but the name never flowed smoothly from her lips. "What is wrong, Minerva?" she would ask. "I love you, Minerva," she would whisper. But her mouth couldn't seem to fit around the word.

Although Randall never openly objected to the name, Medora could tell he didn't particularly like saying it; it stuck in his mouth the way it did in hers. He'd started calling her Minnie for short, which brought to mind Minnie Mouse, whose squeaky, annoying voice Medora heard in her mind whenever he said it. It also made her think of T.W.'s relationship with her mother. When she brought the baby home, both Aunt Tillie and T.W., forming a united front, voiced their objections, too.

"You know how much I adored my sister, but you ought not to burden the child with the name of a woman whose life was made so miserable," Aunt Tillie said with a quick glance in T.W.'s direction.

"But I loved my mother and I want to honor her by giving my baby her name."

"I loved your mother, too." T.W. shot Aunt Tillie a warning look. "But I agree with your aunt. I think you should choose something else."

Medora, realizing then that every time the name was said sorrow would flow between them, decided that maybe it wasn't the best choice. On her first day home, Randall had given her Lydia's book of sketches. She had been awed by how good they were, and for the first time she understood the vital, hidden part of this woman, who shared with her the bond of all artistic souls.

How terrible it must have been, Medora thought, not to do the work you were born to do. What torture to need to create and never be able to do it. How could she *not* have been unhappy and bitter? Art was a jealous mistress, T.W. had taught her that, and a jealous lover as well. It made you suffer when you didn't serve it; your life became small and miserable when you didn't do its bidding. Medora knew she would never have to suffer its vengeance. Her birthright gave her the means to become the artist she was destined to be. But Lydia had not been so blessed. She had a child and, unlike Trudy Douglass, chose to raise him, art be damned.

Perhaps "Lydia" would be a suitable name for her child, Medora decided, a homage to all artistic women who for reasons beyond their control were unable to do their work.

Reynard Oates put an end to that. "Sweetheart, why you going to go and name that pretty little baby after that old bat?" he said the afternoon he came to visit. "I knew that women and, to tell the truth, I wish I hadn't. If you're that hard up for a name, name her after me. Ain't nothing wrong with the name 'Reynard' for a girl. It's got a sophistication to it. Reynard Jackson-Hollis. Name like that gives mystery to a woman!"

Because Reynard was Randall's only living relative, Medora kept her thoughts to herself.

Randall, however, agreed with him that naming the baby after his mother was *not* a good idea.

"Medora, it's a beautiful thing you want to do, honoring the memory of my mother like that, but it doesn't work for me," he said. "I never told you this, but Lydia was very negative about the baby, and now that Minnie is here it's like bad vibes to give the baby her name." He had been staying at her loft since they brought the baby home. Parenting a newborn was a taxing chore, and Medora, exhausted, had desperately needed someone to stay with her. Although willing, Aunt Tillie and T.W. were physically unable to do it, and her friends had parenting duties of their own. Randall had been the logical choice, and he'd eagerly taken on the role. A few days stretched into a week, and a week became two. They both knew he would leave at some point, but they hadn't discussed when.

It was morning and Medora was sitting in the rocking chair in her bedroom nursing their daughter. Randall was folding the dainty baby dresses he had bought the day before. Medora, watching him carefully fold each item, was amazed by the change in his personality. Through all the years she had known him, she'd imagined him as many things, and a doting father was definitely not one of them. She loved to watch him hold the baby and whisper secrets in her tiny brown ears or kiss her delicate fingers. He gazed at the baby with the same adoration that Medora herself did, and she knew that they were the only two people in the world who shared this special love for this tiny person. It was as if Randall was trying to give his daughter everything he had missed, imagining the perfect father and making himself over in that image. She didn't know how long this new Randall would be around but decided she'd enjoy him while he lasted.

In some ways, their relationship had gone back to what it had been when they met as teenagers. They talked eagerly, laughed freely, played jokes on each other. When he came back to the loft each night from the city, he shared his day and listened attentively as she related small tidbits about the baby. Gradually they began to talk about painful things—her anger over his other relationships, his anger over the letter she'd written him, that fateful day at the New Walls Gallery. Medora was surprised how candid he was about his relationship with Taylor Benedict. He said little, however, about Ana Reese-Mitchell.

When Randall returned from work that night, Medora asked him, "So, how serious was your thing with Ana Reese-Mitchell?" He was sipping a glass of Beaujolais nouveau and watching her bathe the baby.

Randall thought for a moment and said, "I felt like I could tell her anything. I enjoyed being with her. We liked a lot of the same things." He paused for a moment as if running something through his mind. "I think she was a surrogate for you."

"Don't blame me for your madness," Medora said.

"No, no, I'm not. But when you threw me out, I think I found some of the comfort I always felt with you, with Ana. But of course she wasn't you."

"Didn't put up with your mess," Medora said with a hint of irritation as she dried the baby.

Randall smiled slightly, then grew pensive. "Ana said she didn't think I had a center."

"So do you think you'll ever get one?"

"A center? I'm not sure exactly what she meant. I just know I don't want to end up like Lydia. Anyway, I feel different these days," he added after a moment.

Medora, smoothing Baby Magic on the baby's behind, gave him a doubtful glance.

"Medora, everything's changed," he added, responding to her glance. "For the good?"

"Two things have happened to me. My mother died. My daughter was born. Two sides of the same coin. I loved my mother, but I'm free of her now, and I'm different because of it."

"I guess that's one reason not to name the baby Lydia," Medora said, returning to the question of the baby's name, which she had broached that morning.

"Why don't we just keep it Minnie?" When it came to the baby, it was often "we" these days.

"Because it's not Minnie. It's Minerva."

"Well, let's keep it Minerva." Randall yawned. Medora nursed the baby and put her in the cradle next to her bed. Together, they stood watching her breathe as they had done since she brought her home. They then went their separate ways, Randall to spend the the night on the living room couch, Medora to sleep in her bed. There was still some distance between them.

The next morning as she was dressing the baby, Randall brought up the matter of the name again, which told Medora he wasn't really comfortable with "Minerva" either. "Why don't you name her after yourself or after your aunt Tillie? She'd be honored by that."

"I don't want to name her after me. It's hard enough for a girl to find her own space and personality without sharing her mother's name," Medora explained. "And Tillie hates her name. She's always said that one Tillie in a family is one too many."

"Well, I guess it's Minnie then," Randall said.

"Minerva," said Medora.

So, Minerva it was for the time being. But when Medora whispered loving words to her daughter, she called her things that she loved: rosebud, chocolate chip, sunshine, pecan pie.

Medora, aware that a "village" had raised her—namely, Aunt Tillie on her mother's side and her father's artist friends—knew she'd need one to raise her child. The "villagers" she invited to what she billed a "Welcome to the World" party two days before Thanksgiving included the regulars, T.W. and Aunt Tillie, as well as Eliza, Devlin, and Trudy. From Randall's side came Reynard and Iola Washington, which struck Medora as odd, until he explained that Iola had played an indirect role in getting him to the hospital.

Although Medora had asked everybody to bring a favorite dish and not bother with a gift, everyone brought a gift anyway, and they were added to the stack of colorfully wrapped presents sent by fellow artists, curators, dealers, and collectors who knew Medora, T.W., or Randall. Medora had asked Eliza to be the baby's godmother, and when Eliza arrived she shared the fact that she had decided not to name the baby after her mother. Life was tough enough without carrying around the weight of your grandmother's name, especially since Minerva Jackson had led such a sorrowful life. Eliza nodded in agreement then suggested three names beginning with "M"—Mara, Mariah, Mirabelle—to continue the Minerva-Medora tradition. Medora whispered each into her baby's ear and sighed; sunshine and rosebud still came more naturally.

As the two sat next to the baby's cradle and began to open gifts, Medora, for no particular reason, thought of "Sleeping Beauty," one of her favorite fairy tales.

"How about Aurora?" she exclaimed.

"Who?"

"Aurora, after the baby princess in 'Sleeping Beauty.'"

Eliza shook her head. "No way! No Prince Charming needed here. If she gets a kiss, she should be the one to give it or be fully awake when she gets it. Not only that, but didn't some evil fairy show up at the party and put a spell on everybody? Randall didn't invite any of his old girlfriends, did he?"

"What old girlfriends?" Medora said, "After that mess at New Walls, I don't think he has any." Both women chuckled. "Actually, we're getting along pretty well these days."

"I can clearly see that." Eliza grinned with approval. "But Aurora is definitely not the name for this one. You'll come up with something else," Eliza said, putting an end to that suggestion. "When you hear it, you'll know it."

Reynard requested that they unwrap his gift first because he couldn't stay long, adding that "it needed to be on ice, and he wanted some before he left." Medora unwrapped the three bottles of Cristal and took them into the kitchen to give to Aunt Tillie, who was laying out the food.

"Figured we needed the best for a toast," he said when Medora thanked him.

"I was going to ask T.W. and Aunt Tillie to say a few words. Would you say something, too?" Medora had had second thoughts about asking Reynard to comment, but decided to give him the benefit of the doubt.

"I'd be honored. Now I got to think of something to say," he said, but Medora was sure he already had something in mind, which was why he had brought the wine in the first place. With a wink at Medora, he turned back to Trudy Douglass, who seemed enthralled by whatever he'd been saying. Trudy had made a gift of a sketch she had done of Medora when she was pregnant. At the bottom she'd written FOR DIOGENES, WHO FOUND HER PARTICULAR TRUTH, which made Medora smile.

When she went back to the bedroom to join Eliza and check on the baby, Devlin and Jasmine were sitting on the bed. Jasmine handed her their gift for the baby and insisted it be unwrapped in her presence. It was a rainbow-colored blanket that had belonged to Jasmine when she'd been a baby. Medora could clearly remember the morning Delta wrapped it around Jasmine.

T.W. brought two gifts for his new granddaughter. One was a pen-and-ink drawing he had done of Minerva and Medora when she was a baby. When she saw it, tears welled in Medora's eyes. It reminded her of how much she looked like her mother, that she was her mother's daughter after all. She could feel her mother's spirit in the room, and she closed her eyes, thanking her for her presence. The second gift was *Lightning Tree*. Medora gasped with delight and gave her father a hug, suddenly aware as she held him how physically weak he had become; he had once seemed so invincible.

"Thank you, Daddy," she said, and the word "Daddy" came easily this time, with no anger.

"The moment I saw it, I knew I had to keep it in the family. You're becoming the artist I knew you could become. Much better than me."

"Never better than you," Medora said, and T.W. cleared his throat, embarrassed by her praise. "Excuse me, Bunny. I got a few words I need to say to Randall," he said, leaving the room.

"I wonder what those few words are?" Eliza asked as soon as he was out of earshot.

"I'm not sure I want to know," Medora said as she unwrapped the pink and white gift given to her by Iola Washington.

When she emptied the jewelry out of the silk pouches enclosed in the wrapping paper, she and Eliza glanced at each other in surprise.

"I can see the earrings, but why would she give a baby costume jewelry?" asked Eliza, fingering one of the pins. She got up to close the door so Iola wouldn't hear them. "So, where does Randall know her from? Is he into senior citizens these days?"

"She came to Lydia's wake. She took care of her before she died. Randall said that she was indirectly responsible for him getting to the hospital in time to see the baby born, but he never explained exactly how." Medora sighed and tilted her head to one side as she often did when puzzled. "I was really surprised by her greeting when she saw me. She gave me a big hug and then went on about how distressed Randall was that we broke up, and that she'd told him we'd get back together and wasn't it nice that it happened just in time for the baby."

"That's *really* strange that he'd confide so much about your relationship to her."

"Yeah, I thought so."

"She seems like a nice woman, but this is weird. All the baby can do with these pearls is choke on them." Eliza giggled and placed the necklace on the bed. A note written in a spidery scrawl, which had been packed between the satin pouches, fluttered to the floor. Medora picked it up and read it aloud.

Dear little baby,

Your daddy gave this precious jewelry to your grandmother Lydia when she was alive. It is very, very valuable. But not nearly as precious or valuable as you would have been to your grandmother.

Sincerely,
Iola Washington

"My God, they're real!" Eliza said, picking up the pearls again and fingering each one with renewed respect.

"I wonder how Iola Washington got them?" said Medora.

"Do you think Lydia could have given them to her before she died?" Eliza asked.

"Naw!" Both women agreed in unison.

Medora picked up a diamond brooch and one of the earrings and brought them to her heart. "Thank you, Lydia," she whispered. "I'll keep them safe for her." She put them back in the silk pouches and placed them in the drawer next to Lydia's sketchbook.

By the time they finished unwrapping the remaining gifts, Aunt Tillie had laid out the food, and it was a feast. Aunt Tillie had roasted a turkey and made greens with sun-dried tomatoes. Eliza baked four loaves of bread. Trudy made two pasta salads, one with feta, asparagus, and ripe olives, which she knew Medora liked. Devlin brought three pecan pies from his favorite bakery. T.W. had had a case of champagne delivered and brought a box of Mrs. Fields chocolate chip cookies, to which he was partial. Iola Washington baked a pan of macaroni and cheese, which Lydia once mentioned was Randall's favorite dish.

The baby was awake by the time the food was laid out. Eliza pulled the bentwood rocker out of the bedroom so that Medora and the baby could comfortably join the celebration. As Medora looked around the room at all the people whom she loved, she couldn't recall when she had been so happy. Her eyes met Randall's, and she remembered how their eyes had met the moment the baby was born. She could tell that he remembered, too. He came across the room to where she was sitting, picked up the baby, held her for a moment, and then stood behind her chair.

Starting off the proceedings, Reynard opened the champagne and poured it into the flute glasses that Aunt Tillie had given out. He cleared his throat. "I ain't been to many celebrations like this and I'd like to thank you all for inviting me this afternoon," he said, nodding in Medora's direction. "It makes me feel like I'm part of a family."

"You are a part of a family," Aunt Tillie said. "You're as much a part of this baby as me." He hesitated for a moment, as if he were taking it all in, and for a moment Medora thought he might cry. He cleared his throat again and raised his glass.

"This here is for the baby, and for you, Medora, and for Randall Oates Hollis, Junior, who has been like a son to me, more than a son to me. All the Oateses, all of them, dead and gone, would be proud of you, boy, and proud of that baby over there sitting in her mama's lap."

All the guests raised their glasses.

Then T.W. stood up. "Guess I'm next. This is the happiest day of my life," he said quietly. "I love you, Medora, and I love this little grandbaby you've given Minnie and me. I'll be the best grandfather I can be. Grandmother and grandfather. That's all I can say."

Medora knew that her father was weeping. She couldn't see his tears behind his glasses, but she could hear them in his voice. Although T.W.'s words had not been a toast as such, everyone raised his or her glass to salute them.

"Thank you, Daddy," she managed to say. A lump had formed in her throat at the mention of her mother's name. Randall gently placed his hands on her shoulders.

Aunt Tillie stood up for her turn. "Everybody, please put down your glass or finish what's in it, because what I've got to say isn't a toast, it's a prayer, and you can't drink and pray at the same time."

"Amen, sister Tillie," Iola Washington said. When she had everyone's attention, Aunt Tillie closed her eyes and begin to pray.

"Dear Lord, I want to thank You for this day and the gift of all these children. Give us the grace to forgive each other for the sorrows we have endured. Give us the grace to cherish all the blessings You have bestowed. Give these two parents the grace to understand how splendid true love is and the wisdom to raise their daughter right. Please Lord, give us Your grace."

Medora looked up at Randall and smiled. "Grace!" she whispered.

After everyone had gone, Medora and Randall stood over Grace's cradle gazing at the baby as they had each night since they had brought her home. Medora could already see Randall's features in her daughter's face. But she could see her own, too, and her mother's, and Lydia's, as well. In celebration of the day, she brewed a pot of Red Zinger tea sweetened with wildflower honey, and they sat down together on the couch to drink it.

"I'm not sure I know what love is," Randall said as he sipped his tea.

"Nobody does," Medora said, surprised by this sudden confession.

His eyes were distant for a moment, and when he spoke, she could hear the depth of his feelings in his voice. "But I know I fell in love with Grace the moment I laid eyes on her. I knew at that instant that, for better or worse, my life had changed forever. Quick, just like that!" he said, and snapped his fingers.

Medora nodded in agreement. "That's how love comes, quick, before you know it."

"And you know what else? Despite the craziness of my life, I've *really* always loved you, too." He grabbed her hand and held it.

"I know I've always loved you," Medora said, and then, just a bit embarrassed by the declarations they'd both made, added, "So exactly what did my father tell you when he left the bedroom?"

"Take care of my daughter. Take care of my granddaughter. Don't mess things up or you'll answer to me."

Medora chuckled, "I don't believe T.W. actually threatened you!"

"No, not a threat. Just the truth. He said what a father is supposed to say. He loves and wants to protect you as much as I love and want to protect Grace. That's what a good father does."

Randall sighed. "I've been thinking a lot about my own father these days, who he would have been if he had lived, how my life would have been different if he'd been around. I want to find out more about him. All I ever heard was Lydia's opinion of him, and I need to know what other people say. I don't think he would have left me if he'd lived. I know I could never leave Grace."

"You can never really know if he would have left you or not," Medora said. "All you really know is that you're not Randall Oates any more than I'm Minerva Jackson. You're not T.W. and I'm certainly not Lydia. We're Medora and Randall. We can never forget who *we* are."

"So where do Medora and Randall go from here?"

Medora shrugged. "Let's wait and see what happens," she said, and they both smiled because they already knew what would.